Wicked Women

Wicked Women

Wicked Women

An Anthology of the
New England Horror Writers

Edited by
Trisha J. Wooldridge
and **Scott T. Goudsward**

Cover Art © 2020 by Lynne Hansen,
www.LynneHansenArt.com
Interior Layout and Design by Daniel G. Keohane
Published in October 2020 by NEHW Press
ISBN 978-0-9981854-4-6
www.newenglandhorror.org
Printed in the United States of America

Other Anthologies of the
New England Horror Writers

Wicked Weird
Edited by Amber Fallon,
Scott T. Goudsward and David Price

Wicked Haunted
Edited by Scott T. Goudsward,
Daniel G. Keohane and David Price

Wicked Witches
Edited by Scott T. Goudsward,
Daniel G. Keohane and David Price

Wicked Tales
Edited by Scott T. Goudsward,
Daniel G. Keohane and David Price

Wicked Seasons
Edited by Stacey Longo

Epitaphs
Edited by Tracy L. Carbone

For Phoebe Wray, Broad Universe founder,
for her efforts in reminding genre publishing,
"It's a Broad Universe; there's room for everyone,"
and for reminding so many women writers of their value.

And the Honorable Ruth Bader Ginsberg, the Notorious R.B.G,
for working so damned hard to eliminate so many real life horrors for women.

Finally all those who keep writing no matter how many times they hear it said
that people like them "don't write horror" or that they "don't understand
horror." Keep writing, keep getting your stories and your beautiful,
horrible truths out there.

We need them more than ever.

Table of Contents

Introduction to *Wicked Women*
by Elaine Cunningham

Every society needs wicked women.

For one thing, they're versatile. Wicked women play a wide range of roles and possess valued skills. They have honed their various crafts throughout recorded history and in the ancient shadowlands of myth. Goddesses, demons, sirens, nymphs, and the rest of the wicked sisterhood set the bar high—and continue to do so in this collection of tales—but mortals manage to do their part.

Wicked women define boundaries, either as an object lesson for what happens when you cross one of society's lines or as monsters to frighten children into good behavior. As you're reminded in these pages, women shouldn't walk alone at night, not even in Paris, the City of Lights, for something Very Bad might happen. Children shouldn't question society's ways, not even in the peaceful town of Grisbury, or the shodden might get them.

Women need not be evil to be wicked; simply being different will suffice. Such women provide cautionary tales about the dangers of "otherness," reminding members of society to stay within their own tribes. If you marry a fey creature, or for that matter a perfectly nice human woman who insists you live on the strange little island where she was born, things are not going to end well for you.

When wicked women are powerless, they serve as scapegoats, which allows the proper members of society to explain away random occurrences and complex problems. When women do have power, they're witches, and witches can be useful to society in ways that go far beyond dispensing healing herbs, love charms, and the occasional curse.

Take parenting, for example. Society has very definite ideas of what that entails. "Good parents" can't admit they don't want their kids, much

1

less take steps to get rid of them. Fortunately, in the woods of folklore live witches who can be counted upon to eat wandering children. So if you acquire a stepchild who overshadows your own daughters, you can let the hearth fire burn out and then send the girl into the forest to ask Baba Yaga for a light. If your kids are eating you out of house and home, take them deep into the forest and tell them to follow you back, privately hoping they'll stumble upon a gingerbread cottage and a hungry witch. If there are no witch-infested forests handy, you can ask the middle school to assign your inconvenient offspring to That Teacher. The one who has taught for decades, but whose name is seldom spoken. The one in charge of the classroom that, oddly enough, no adult in town seems to have attended.

Every society needs outliers—people who have big dreams and take risks to achieve them. These dreamers occasionally succeed in ways that benefit their society. Their stories lift the general populace out of despondency and lend a veneer of meaning to the daily drudge. But not *too* many outliers, because that would be disruptive. Witches help maintain this balance. They have power and sometimes they will share it, but no one knows when or why. Baba Yaga might send you home with the gift of fire in a flaming skull, but more likely, she'll cook and eat you. The sea witch might grant your impossible wish, but at the cost of your voice and the risk of your life.

Of course, not all wicked women are witches. Some of us merely tell stories. Not polite little tales with improbably happy endings, but dark and disturbing stories and poetry that's distilled from nightmares. This collection spans a wide range, from a grim warning about picking up hitchhikers to a lyrical werewolf story that feels like a folktale reborn. In this collection are stories that explore basic human fears, such as the dread we feel when a loved one moves away (Are they safe? Will they return? Will they change?) and the danger of crossing the line that separates friend from lover. Heritage is another source of concern: Am I destined to become like my parents? Will my child become too much like his?

The nature of wicked women is as varied as the roles they play, and this collection offers many flavors of wickedness. In addition to a variety of witches, we hear from vampires, shapeshifters, and evil spirits. There are two tales of thwarted motherhood and several stories that explore what it means to be the child of a wicked woman. You will meet a private investigator who longs to be a film noir detective, a child who wants to know the truth of her world, a teenager in love with her estranged best friend, and an assortment of deadly creatures who are simply following their nature and doing what they must to survive.

Oddly enough, the most chilling protagonist in this book is a human woman with no special abilities. Her defining characteristic is an absolute sense of entitlement to her vision of perfection. If I had to define wickedness as a spectrum, I'd put "Questioning Societal Norms" on one end and "Narcissism" on the other. Empathy, or the lack of it, is what separates the merely wicked from the truly evil.

And that, I think, is one of the main reasons why we read and tell dark stories. We want to see and experience life from vastly different perspectives. The stories in this volume satisfy our need to know and understand, a desire that has been driving—and often defining—wicked women since Eve reached for that apple.

Tree Limbs Block The Road
by Patricia Gomes

These children of Slaughter
wander unsupervised,
over raw and barren landscapes
to plan treasons and red treachery
in icy caverns
that offer no warmth
to calm their evil proclivities.
No guilt, for what do they know but the soundless White?
Hairless demons with whirring brains,
their elongated teeth impale hope,
invite suicide.
Tendrils slither beneath the snow; close your heart, say your prayers.
You'll hear them—do not be fooled by their childlike stature—you'll hear
them
slide around your doorframes, hissing
lewd and nauseating suggestions, licking your fear
from their bloodless lips.
Do not listen. They leave no footprints
and we've nothing:
no tool
no weapon

no remedy
nothing

to protect ourselves
from Winter Madness.

Milk Time
by Elaine Pascale

The Mountain Peak Middle School was eating Walter alive. His seventh-grade education did not allow for terms like *metaphorical,* yet, to Walter, and, perhaps countless others, the feeling was far more literal.

The summer prior to middle school, Walter had happily digested any cartoon his rickety TV antenna had found, along with candy bars, gum, and jaw breakers obtained from the creatively named *Corner Store* and purchased with lawn mowing and dog walking money. He had also perfected any confection that could be concocted from the staples his mother replenished each week.

He had been slightly excited for the promotion from his one-class-per-grade elementary school to the large middle school that had a swimming pool at its center and separate rooms for classes like art and gym. He had been blissfully unaware of the dangers of the upper grades.

He had been unaware until two weeks before school started. That was when he and his friend, Phil, had ridden their bikes to Mountain Peak to see which section of the seventh grade they had been placed into. They knew that middle school students moved in groups through their requirements, and that the school was not shy about labeling the groups in such a way that the students' academic promise, or lack thereof, was painfully apparent.

"Oh my god! I got 'Tech Ninjas'!" Phil called out before Walter even got the chance to scan the paper that was hung on the school doors. This was an appropriate match for Phil, a boy who had built a completely functioning robot before he knew how to tie his shoes.

Walter accurately predicted that he would not be placed in "Awesome Blossoms," as that was for girls only and at the request of parents who believed that boys were the root of all of their daughters' problems. He was also fairly confident that he would not be in "Game Changers" as he had never been much of an athlete. Thus, he'd invested his hopes in "Mountain Movers," the male equivalent of "Awesome Blossoms." He was perplexed when his name failed to appear in typed print on that particular list.

"It's not possible," he said beneath his breath, hoping Phil was not paying too much attention. "It's just not possible…"

"Walter?" Phil was trying to peek at the list but maintain a safe distance in case of fallout. "Don't get mad—"

"I don't…I don't get mad…anymore," Walter mumbled, but he wasn't really paying attention to the stilted conversation as he was trying to come to terms with his school placement.

His name, his identity in Times New Roman font, was on the list marked "Rounded Scissors." "Rounded Scissors" was notorious for the wrong reasons. It typically housed a group of troubled kids—kids who were disruptive or disrespectful, kids who could not seem to learn at an appropriate pace (if at all), kids who were nothing like him.

His eyes ran over the list of his future classmates. The names spanned from slightly underhanded to perpetrator of the first order. The top offender, alphabetically, was Leslie Abbas, and her only transgression was that she refused to speak to anyone except her pet gerbil.

There was also Cameron Dillard. His face, bright red with acne, was like a neon advertisement for the number of grades he had repeated.

One name made Walter gasp: Gracie Morgan. Rumor was that being in proximity with the girl was uncomfortable. Not only did she smell, she had a white film covering one of her eyes that made it difficult to tell if she was looking directly at you. She also had a neurological disorder that caused her foot to shoot out, kicking those near her. The kicks had such perfect timing and aim that her condition was suspect. There were additional rumors of Gracie floating around Walter's elementary school: she stole from the *Corner Store*, she smoked, she said the "F word" in front of her parents. And then there were two points of gossip that he found difficult to believe. One was that she blew up a cat with firecrackers. The other was that she was the cause of her baby brother's drowning death. While unsure of the veracity of said scandals, Walter felt both humbled and dismayed to learn of his impending closeness to this living legend.

"I don't belong there." Walter was trying to speak softly, calmly. He wanted Phil to agree, but his friend was still looking at the list.

"Oh no," Phil inhaled sharply, "Ms. Gnash."

"You know her?" Walter took a double take on the name of the teacher that would lead the Rounded Scissors to academic excellence.

"I don't know her exactly. I can't say that I know anyone who has had her."

Walter scanned his memory for information about this teacher. The adults in town often spoke fondly of their middle school days and of the educators who made an impact. He couldn't recall anyone speaking of a Ms. Gnash.

Phil gulped and looked down at his shoes. "My brother told me," he lowered his voice, "that people don't survive her class."

"Meaning I will have to repeat the grade?"

Phil shook his head solemnly. "Meaning you really might not survive."

* * *

The night before the first day of school, Walter lay awake, wishing he had the type of parents who would call and complain about his placement. It wasn't that his parents didn't care, they just cared about the wrong things. As long as his bed was made and a few vegetables were eaten and he was clean and maintained him temper, they left him alone.

Literally.

Both of his parents worked very long hours. On the weekend, they claimed they "earned" some couples' time. Walter was basically raising himself. He had become adept at domestic chores, preferring a clean and organized house, even if he were often the only one in it. He was something of a cooking prodigy. He had learned to craft a killer chicken Alfredo, a scrumptious scampi, and a divine shepherd's pie. His specialty was desserts—anything chocolate. Brownies, fudge, mousse, and cookies had become his replacement for parental attention, and he came to crave cocoa based products more than quality time.

He had asked his parents if they knew of Ms. Gnash. At first, they had pretended to not hear his question. When he had repeated his inquiry, they had looked at each other strangely before his mother spoke.

"Is that the name of your teacher, Walter?"

"Yes. I told you that before. Whenever I ask anyone about her, they say they have heard of her, but no one ever had her."

"And how do you feel about that, son?" his father had asked in an intentionally soothing voice.

Walter had thought for a moment. "I don't like it. It doesn't make sense. Most of the adults in town grew up here, went to school here, but none of them ever had Ms. Gnash?"

His father had taken a deep breath. "And what do we do when we are feeling frustrated or confused, Walter?"

Walter had sighed. "I am supposed to count to ten and think of pleasant things."

"Like chocolate," his mother had offered, her tone incongruent to the sweet topic of his beloved cocoa.

*   *   *

Reluctantly, Walter rode his bike to school, ignoring the nervous chatter coming from Phil, who was accompanying him as usual. Phil was eager to explore the curious new world of middle school; he wouldn't have to face infamous classmates and a monstrous teacher.

Ms. Grimina Gnash was simultaneously everything and nothing like Walter expected. She seemed grandmotherly in age and appearance, yet her voice was very young, and her eyes glowed with excessive vibrance. Unlike other teachers, she allowed them to select their own seats in the room.

"But choose carefully, as where you sit will define you for the rest of the year."

Ms. Gnash began her lesson. It was on civic responsibility. She lectured to the students about which laws were fair and just and which laws were "collusion with charlatans." After, they were instructed to write five grammatically correct sentences about their personal civic responsibility.

The room became quiet as everyone bent over their papers.

Squeak

A sound came from Gracie's direction. Her foot had shot out but had failed to make contact with the chair in front of her. Instead, her own seat had given a tattling squeal.

Ms. Gnash calmly fixed Gracie with her icy blue eyes. "Did anyone hear anything?" she asked the class. "I certainly hope not, as writing is a *quiet* activity."

Everyone resumed their work and the room settled into a stillness that belied the twenty students it contained.

Gracie's foot shot out again with a startling shriek of the chair. As before, no contact was made with any other person in the room. This time, Ms. Gnash addressed the child in front of the offender, "Jason, is your chair making a noise?" Jason shook his head nervously. There was something in Ms. Gnash's voice that dared anyone to defy her. The students seated around Gracie glanced at her imploringly. She gave a helpless shrug, committing to the story that she had no control over her foot.

The foot kicked again, and Ms. Gnash slammed her hands on her desk, pushing her own chair back—noiselessly, despite the aggressive movement. "I think it is milk time," she announced in a voice that was too rough to match the soothing words.

The students looked up from their papers in shock. A few even dropped their pencils. They hadn't had milk time since second grade.

"Sharon, Harry, help me pass these out." She pulled two trays of white milk cartons from somewhere beneath her desk. No one had been to the front of the room yet, so they weren't sure if she hid a refrigerator under there. She then took a key from her top desk drawer and unlocked the one beneath it.

"Gracie…" She held a brown container aloft. "I believe that you prefer chocolate milk."

"I like chocolate milk, too," said Carolyn Cliff, wiping her nose with her sleeve. Walter wanted chocolate milk, also, but he wouldn't dare to contradict Ms. Gnash.

Ms. Gnash looked at Carolyn with surprise, as if the girl had suddenly apparated into the room. "Of course you do, but I need to make amends to Gracie. In my mind, and in my heart, I accused her of something that she obviously did not do." She stepped toward Carolyn, leaning over her and giving her a smile that showed every single tooth in her mouth. "Someday, I may need to make amends to you, too."

Carolyn nodded weakly and accepted the milk that Sharon offered her.

The class drank in quiet and finished the morning in silence. Even Gracie's spastic foot was hushed.

At lunch, Walter was able to sit with Phil and his new friends from Ninja Tech. While the other boys were chatting, Walter had nothing to say. He was uncomfortable in his new classroom and embarrassed that they had milk time, as if they were babies. Would there be nap time after lunch?

"Which class are you in?" one of the boys tried to engage him, but it was the worst question he could have been asked.

"Uhm, he has Ms. Gnash," Phil answered for him.

"Isn't she—?"

"He said something about students not surviving her class," Walter pointed at Phil who had turned very pale.

"You told him that?" the boy beside Phil tried to whisper, but Walter heard him. "No one is—"

"Can you believe we get to do a Lego challenge?" Phil steered the conversation away from Walter, who was frustrated by this change of course. He wanted to know more about his placement and why he was with the "bad kids." His therapy had been working. He wasn't losing his temper anymore; that was why he no longer had to go.

While the other boys talked, he eavesdropped on some Rounded Scissors girls. He overheard Gracie saying that had been the best chocolate milk ever. It was "to die for." He also heard something that rang a bell with him; the girls were sharing that they would be going home to an empty house.

"My mom works till 10:00," offered Sharon, "I can pretty much do whatever I want." She was responding to Emily, who had asked if it was okay to call her after 9:00. The other girls in the group, all members of Rounded Scissors, chimed in with their own tales of parental absence.

After lunch, Gracie complained of feeling sick. She looked pale. In fact, she appeared almost translucent. Walter had never seen anyone look like she did, as if she were a dandelion seed head, ready to blow away with the wind.

"You must need more milk," Ms. Gnash said, examining Gracie with critical, yet sparkling eyes.

"I don't…" Gracie's words weakened into a moan.

"Nonsense," Ms. Gnash was at her desk quicker than an older woman had the right to move. Quicker than anyone Walter had ever seen, regardless of age. She unlocked the drawer and pulled out another carton of chocolate milk. "This will cure…" She tilted her head and inspected Gracie as one might watch a dying fly twitch its wings one final time. "This will cure *everything* that has been plaguing you." She stood over Gracie, making sure she consumed the entire container. The rest of the class waited in awkward silence, unsure of what they should be doing during this exchange.

When Gracie finished, her head fell to her desk with a large thump. Ms. Gnash turned to the girl seated beside Gracie and instructed, "Gather her things, all of it. I am excusing her. "

"Should I take her to the nurse?"

"No. She will just go home." Ms. Gnash signaled a few of the larger boys. "Help me to bring her outside."

Walter and the others watched as Gracie was carried out back and left by a copse of trees with her things bundled around her.

"Ok, class." Ms. Gnash brushed off her hands as she reentered the room. "Back to *Crime and Punishment*."

Walter could have sworn he saw Ms. Gnash suppress a smile as she lowered the blinds. The class turned their attention to the illustrated, abridged, and annotated version of the classic tale.

When school was over and Walter was unlocking his bike, Harry— the milk distributor—approached.

"Did anyone come to get Gracie? Did you see her?"

Walter shook his head, which did nothing to ease the worry on Harry's face.

"How will anyone know where to find her? Students are picked up in the office here, aren't they?"

Walter duplicated his head shake. Someone must have picked her up. They could ask her about it the next day.

Only, Gracie did not return to school the following day.

But the squeaks in her chair did.

Walter wondered how an empty seat could make noise. The other students seemed to notice it, too, but said nothing.

As Ms. Gnash lectured on accidental deaths, the squeaks grew more aggressive. She used the example of a child drowned in a bathtub: "Sometimes, children are left alone to bathe themselves, which is entirely unsafe. Children need constant supervision. Other times," she fixed her eyes on the empty chair, "the child in question is left in the care of an older sibling, which is unconscionable and deserving of the highest punishment for both sibling and parents."

After a few weeks of no Gracie, the children seemed to forget all about her. They claimed the empty chair had always squeaked, as some chairs are want to do—even though Walter knew of no chair like this.

*   *   *

Phil had little time for Walter anymore, but Walter was able to catch up with his old buddy one day after school. The boys chatted awkwardly while pushing their bikes home.

"You must be doing some pretty cool projects, huh?" Walter honestly had no interest in Phil's exciting academic work, but he wanted to find a way into a sensitive topic.

"Sure. We just finished rockets and now we are working on voice modulators." Phil laughed. "You should hear how funny Ron sounds when he—"

"Have you ever heard anything about the school being haunted?"

Phil stopped walking. "Haunted? Like ghosts?"

"Yeah...I guess...I don't know, I was just wondering what you've heard."

"Nothing really."

"Not even from your brother?"

"Nope."

"Really? Your brother never said anything? Or, are you lying to me?"

"I wouldn't lie to you."

"You lied the other day at lunch, pretending you hadn't made the comment about no one surviving Ms. Gnash's class. What did your brother mean by that? How did he know? And if you know something, why aren't you telling me?"

Phil started to walk quickly, pulling his bike limply along. "Hey, don't get mad at me, Walter. I started this school the same time you did. And I can't help it if you don't like your placement."

"Stop telling me to not get mad. I can be mad all I want, especially when things aren't fair."

Phil sighed. "I just don't want it to be like it was before...when you would have those tantrums."

"You don't get it, Phil!" Walter threw his bike into the street, not caring if he dented it or even destroyed it. He wanted to hurt something. Or someone. "I am in a class with this crazy teacher. And she gives us milk, and it made Gracie sick and then Gracie disappeared. But I still hear her. I hear her chair."

Phil carefully leaned his bike against a tree and went to retrieve Walter's bike. He handed it to him cautiously. "Count to ten. That's what you are supposed to do, right? Maybe if you can prove you don't get mad anymore, they will switch you to another class."

Walter snatched his bike from his friend. "That is not why I am in Rounded Scissors! It was a mistake and you know it." He climbed on his bike and peddled away, pumping his legs quickly. He wondered how far he could get if he could keep pedaling at this pace. He had spent most of his savings on candy, but he could probably last for a few days somewhere else. Somewhere far away from Rounded Scissors. And then his parents would miss him, and they would want him back and they would talk to the school about moving him...

Walter knew that was nothing more than a fantasy.

*   *   *

Around Thanksgiving, the class was working on recidivism, which took the students the better part of twenty minutes to learn to pronounce. Ms. Gnash lectured that humans cannot be reformed, just as a leopard cannot change its spots.

Cameron Dillard certainly could do nothing about the pus-filled spots on his face. Nor, it seemed, could he refrain from bubble gum chewing, which was a felony in the Rounded Scissors classroom. While many students believed that Cameron had been able to sneak the gum past Ms. Gnash, Walter knew that the smell and bubble popping were impossible to ignore. Walter suspected that Grimina Gnash was simply biding her time.

"Despite rehab, parole, and work release programs, some people are just...programmed to be bad. There is nothing society can do with them, nor cull from them—"

Pop. Cameron sloppily wiped some errant gum strands from his blemished cheeks. He shoved the gum back into his mouth, not caring that it had recently touched his infected skin.

Ms. Gnash returned to pontificating and Cameron went back to masticating.

"Tomorrow, we will look at specific crimes and their punishments. In the meantime, I would like for you to take out your math workbooks." She stood on tip toes and engaged the corners of the room. "Holly and Mason, please distribute the milk. It has been a while since we had milk time." She moved to her locked drawer. "Cameron, I think today is the day that I make amends to you. I should have graded your composition with…more generosity. For that, you earned the chocolate milk."

The rest of the class watched with curiosity as Cameron downed his milk in a single gulp, punctuating the act with a large burp.

"You must have been thirsty," Ms. Gnash said as if this were an accomplishment. "A big boy like you should probably have two helpings."

This time, Cameron seemed to choke a bit on his gum as he drank. Within minutes, he was doubled over, rubbing his stomach and groaning. A boy beside him asked if he were ok, to which he replied, "It feels like my gum is chewing on me, on my insides."

"Poor boy." Ms. Gnash shook her head with concern. "Let's help him to go out back for a breath of fresh air. I will check on him later, but for now, I am excusing him."

A few students helped to lift Cameron from his seat and moved him outside. One boy followed the procession in order to sling Cameron's coat over his shoulders, as it was rather cold.

Ms. Gnash lowered the blinds to conceal Cameron from view and continued with the math lesson.

The following day, there was no Cameron. However, when Ms. Gnash focused her lecture on the evils of arson, a sugary scent entered the room and eerie popping sounds could be heard.

At lunch, Walter could find no empty seats around Phil, so he sat with Matt Ferris and a few other boys from Rounded Scissors.

"That was Cameron's ghost," Matt whispered. "*He* was the one who burnt down that work-station and was sent to juvie for a bit. Gnash gave him that milk to punish him."

"That's crazy." Jason rolled his eyes. "How is chocolate milk punishment?"

"Do you see how the kids react when they drink it?" Matt lowered his head sadly. "I am not drinking it, that is all I am saying…"

"Do any of you know anyone who has had Ms. Gnash as a teacher?" Walter asked.

This was encountered by thoughtful silence, followed by shrugged shoulders or head shakes.

"I can't believe no one speaks of her," Walter continued. "There should be complaints or something. At some point, some parents would go to the school board or yell at the principal."

"Think about our class," Matt whispered again. "Whose parents would complain?"

Jason looked wistfully at the Mountain Movers table. "We are all alone. It just seems like no one even sees us anymore. No one talks to us. Brett was my best friend last year, and now he won't even look at me in the hall or anything. It's like we are already ghosts."

* * *

A week later, Paul Vargas tried to escape.

During lunch, he pretended that he had left his glasses in the gym. Instead of retrieving them, he walked to the back door of the building and pressed on the push bar. That was when the new students learned that the doors were not only alarmed, as they had seen Ms. Gnash deactivate hers, but the exits must also contain a slight current. When Paul was ushered back to the lunchroom, he was sucking and blowing on the tips of his reddened fingers.

Ms. Gnash suggested chocolate milk as a remedy.

* * *

Around Christmas, Ms. Gnash had given Carolyn her turn to have amends made. As with the others, Carolyn did not return to school after being excused. Yet the students swore they could still hear her snapping the rubber bands she wore on her wrists, especially when Ms. Gnash bloviated on shoplifting.

Walter knew that there was something to the chocolate milk theory, but who could he tell? His parents were always too busy to listen, and Phil had become deeply involved with his Tech Ninja friends. The other students in Rounded Scissors had no one to talk to either. Furthermore, who would believe them?

* * *

By March, only 12 of the original 20 students remained. They were also the only class with no parent/teacher conferences, no holiday concerts, and no open houses. Not that the parents would have attended, but it left the Rounded Scissors feeling more isolated than ever.

The next day at lunch, Jason Sanchez informed the others that his parents were going away for a weekend. "You are staying alone?" Matt asked with raised eyebrows. "Party!"

"Yeah, I guess." Jason shrugged defeatedly. "You know what is weird though? I was listening to them talking about their plans and…it seemed like it was for longer than a weekend."

The other boys continued eating, not finding this information to be of particular interest.

"Even weirder," Jason leaned forward and lowered his voice. "My mom was saying how happy she was that the school had agreed to put me in Rounded Scissors."

This got the boys' attention.

"Your parents requested this?" Harry was baffled. "They requested Ms. Gnash?"

Jason nodded solemnly. "I don't know why. What did I even do?"

Silence fell over the table and followed them back to the classroom. At the bike rack later, Harry whispered to Walter, "I know what Jason did…to deserve Rounded Scissors."

"Well, I don't want to know," Walter snapped. "There is nothing bad enough to deserve this."

*   *   *

After Jason earned his chocolate milk, was excused, and disappeared, Ms. Gnash sermonized on the ancient art of pilfering. "Any indiscretion with money counts, such as taking from the offering plate at church or withholding funds raised in the Scouts' popcorn sales."

Walter could feel Harry's eyes on him, and he shrugged, as if he could brush them off, along with the implication. He still didn't care what Jason or Gracie or Cameron or Carolyn or Paul or Cindy or anyone had done. One thing he realized was that Ms. Gnash had been prophetic in her statement at the start of the school year as students needed to be careful of where they sat. There was a spiral of empty desks rippling out through the room. Walter prayed he did not get sucked into its undertow, but it was creeping ever closer.

*   *   *

Walter found both of his parents' cars in the driveway when he returned home from school. They were in the kitchen, eating a snack made for two, while his father spoke on his cell phone.

"This is such great news! And when do you think we can move in?"

Walter's hopes soared. He might survive Ms. Gnash's class after all.

"We're moving?"

His mother shot his father a glance and the remainder of the phone call was conducted in muted tones.

"We're moving?" he asked again.

"Nothing is definite yet, Walter," his mother replied, tapping his father on the arm as she carried the snack plates to the sink.

"Walter, my man." His father put a hand on his shoulder. "How would you feel about staying here for a few days on your own?"

"Alone?"

His father nodded enthusiastically. "My company is sending me on a conference, and I would love to take your mother with me—"

"I am thirteen—"

"That's exactly when I started staying alone. Helped me learn to be a man."

Walter did not want to be a man; he wanted someone to care about him. He wanted someone to listen to him and to explain why bad things were happening to his classmates. He wanted someone to assure him that nothing would happen to him.

"For...for how long?"

His father's eyes darted to the hallway where several large suitcases were packed. They were much too large, and too many, for a weekend trip

"We spoke to your principal. He knows we will be gone. He said that Ms. Gnash will be happy to check on you."

"What do you mean 'check on'?"

"She will make sure that you are doing fine at school." His mother smiled. "She is really something, performs such a service for our community." She avoided Walter's stunned stare.

"I can't go back there...to class...to Ms. Gnash."

"Of course you can, Walter," his father said with forced enthusiasm. "And you will. It's the law."

"Besides," his mother continued, "we were so happy when they agreed to place you in Rounded Scissors."

"You asked..." Walter felt his knees buckle. It was worse than he had imagined; his parents had instigated his torment. "Why? Why would you want me in that class?"

His mother finally looked him in the eye. "We thought it would be good for you, that it would be for the best." She played with the dish towel as she spoke. "You would do well with...remediation...because of your temper."

"My temper?"

His father raised a hand, instructing Walter to remain calm, yet Walter's voice had all of the volume of a whisper due to his fear and hurt. "I am not saying that we haven't seen improvement. But there are still times that we come home to broken plates, cracked windows, holes in the wall…"

Walter could not believe his ears. He was sure that none of this were true. If, in fact, he was being destructive and not remembering, there must be a good reason and none that would merit Rounded Scissors.

"We had hoped that Rounded Scissors would end the tantrums." His mother's face was very sad. Sadder than he had ever seen. "We gave it a lot of time. God knows we did."

Walter didn't speak to his parents during dinner, even though it was the first in a long time that they were able to eat together, and probably the last time that they ever would. His parents chattered nervously about their trip, while Walter awaited his fate with the chocolate milk. What if he skipped school tomorrow? What if he skipped for the entire time his parents were away? What if he ran away and never returned? Would his parents search for him? Would they care?

The plans he had crafted during a fitful sleep were dashed when his parents insisted on dropping him off at school on their way to the airport and watching until he was entombed in the building.

The day's lecture topic was the first in a series: the seven deadly sins. They were beginning with wrath, and Walter understood that he would not be around to learn about the other six.

Perhaps they had been right about his temper: Walter felt it rising; he felt that old blinding rage that used to get him into trouble. He could no longer stand the squeaking empty chair, the ghostly gum popping, the phantom rubber band snapping, or any of the spectral reminders of classmates who were no longer with them. He could not bottle up his frustration over the unfairness of his situation any longer. Counting to ten would do nothing. He knew that he did not deserve Rounded Scissors and he certainly did not deserve the chocolate milk.

Walter slammed his hands on his desk and stood.

"Walter," Ms. Gnash said calmly, "you should sit down. You, of all people, need to hear this lesson."

Feeling hot tears in his eyes, Walter told Ms. Gnash, "I am excusing myself," and he ran from the room, not knowing where he should go. He ran and the act of running felt good. He felt as if he were taking back control that had been lost when that first carton of chocolate milk had been opened. He also felt as if Ms. Gnash were behind him, even though that was impossible. She would not leave the class unattended.

A quick glance over his shoulder proved that he was alone in the hallway, yet he felt knobby fingers digging into his shoulder, trying to hold him back.

At the end of the hallway was the principal's office. Walter felt he had no other option. His parents weren't home; there was no one to help him. If nothing else, he could grab for a phone and call the police. He was not exactly sure of what he would say to the police. "My teacher is trying to kill me with chocolate milk" did not exactly establish him as a serious phone call.

He opened the main office door and rushed past the secretary. He slammed the heavy oak door of the principal's office shut behind him, barricading himself from any interference from Ms. Gnash or Rounded Scissors' law.

The principal cleared his throat, reminding Walter that he was not alone.

"I can't go back there," Walter gasped. "I need...I need to use your phone."

The principal nodded and gestured to an empty seat in front of his desk. "I understand. I really do. Please take a seat."

"But, I need a phone..."

"A seat...Walter." The principal raised his eyebrows and pointed to the chair again. "I told you, I understand *everything*."

"Then you know about Ms. Gnash...she's...she's evil!"

The principal frowned. "I can't have you speaking about Mountain Peak educators that way, son. Ms. Gnash is legendary at this institution." He reached beneath his desk as he spoke. "Look, before we go any further, I need you to calm down." He pulled a small brown carton from the drawer and offered it to Walter. "I would like for you to count to ten, and then drink this."

Walter leapt from his chair, knocking over items on the principal's desk and not caring if he broke or ruined anything. He was not safe here. He had to leave.

He ran from the office, dodging the secretary who tried to stop him. Classes were in session, so the hallway was empty. As he ran, he smelled bubblegum and heard a variety of squeaks and pops. He imagined his fallen classmates rooting him on.

A few doors opened behind him. He heard adult voices commanding him to stop but he did not waste the time to turn and look at them. He zigzagged through various hallways, buying time until he heard it: the warning bell for ten minutes left in the period. This meant the outdoor gym classes would be returning to shower and dress.

He saw the shadow of the teacher at the back door, deactivating the alarm as the teacher had not been informed that a fugitive was loose. Walter rushed the door and pushed past the teacher and the astonished students who stepped out of his way. As he ran, he heard one student say, "That is a Rounded Scissors kid. Good for him." This was followed by some fading cheers as the students were steered into the building.

Walter knew that the police would be alerted soon and that it would be his word against the school's. He did not know where to go for help. He continued running, trying to move without any discernible pattern. He considered ringing a doorbell on some random street and asking for help, but how could he know who to trust?

Just as he felt he would not be able to run any longer, he saw an ambulance driving slowly with its lights off. A hospital might help him. They would at least give him a chance to explain before calling the police.

He stepped into the road, waving his arms frantically. As the ambulance stopped, he collapsed, sucking wind and holding his side, which was aching. He had been moving on pure adrenalin and not realized how exhausted he truly was.

"Do you need help?" A woman with curly hair asked as she exited the back of the vehicle and approached Walter.

Walter nodded, trying to find his voice.

Curly-hair took his arm and helped him into the ambulance. Another woman was seated inside and waiting. While the curly-haired woman helped Walter to lie down on the cot, the other woman began asking questions and entering his responses on her tablet.

"Name?"

"Walter Jones," he managed to say. The curly haired-woman put a cool compress on his head and unrolled a blood pressure cuff.

"Date of birth," Tablet-woman asked, entering the date he told her.

"Do you feel pain anywhere?" Curly-hair asked, and he shook his head.

The other woman was typing on her tablet. Walter noticed her tap Curly-hair, who nodded. Curly-hair began to strap Walter to the cot. "We have to get ready to transport you," she said.

"Are you taking me to the hospital?" He knew he should be relieved, but something about the women's change of posture had him on alert.

"Of course."

When he was secured, the woman with the tablet said, "Rounded Scissors. Milk time."

Curly-hair brought out an IV attached to a bag containing dark liquid. "Just something to calm you down," she said, and Walter began to scream.

Does This Bring You Joy?
by Sara Marks

"What the fuck is this mess!" My Darling Husband yelled from the floor below.

I didn't respond. I don't yell or respond to profanity. Also, I was surrounded by our stuff, and I wasn't sure I could get out of the mess with grace. I smoothed out my blouse, cardigan, and skirt while I waited on the wall to wall carpet of our bedroom. I made sure to cross my legs and picked a piece of lint off my tights while I listened to him curse as he navigated the maze I had backed myself into.

"I assume you're upstairs, and this mess continues," he said, probably at the foot of the staircase.

He knew I wouldn't respond until he was standing within my eye line. He exhaled, exasperated, and stomped up the stairs like he was trudging through mud, his steps uneven as he avoided more items.

"What the fuck are you doing?" My Darling Husband asked when he saw me surrounded by our clothes.

He was wearing one of his many tailored suits. I could see the wrinkles in his shirt, and his silk tie was loose around his neck. I was sure he wanted to change his clothes, head down to the basement, and ignore me for the rest of the evening. I doubted he could find the hideous tracksuits he liked to wear down in his man cave. I had already put them in a trash bag and placed the bag in my SUV to take for donation tomorrow.

"I am trying to end our dependence on things," I said, calm and rational, my smile reminding him that it was obvious.

"How do my clothes fit into this category?" He motioned toward the pile of his business suites on our king size bed.

I closed my eyes and took a deep, cleansing breath before responding. "I pulled them out to see if they bring me joy."

The way he pressed his lips together and the flare of his nostrils made his feelings clear. "Why should my clothes be something for you to worry about?" he finally said.

"I pulled out everything," I said, gesturing around the room. "I'm going through everything!"

He lifted his leg and looked for a spot to put his foot, trying to get to the bed. It took him a few seconds, but he got there and snatched the piled expensive suits I had carefully laid down. He kicked down the carefully organized piles of my clothes between him and the closet. When he got to the open closet doors, he slammed his hangers back on the suit rack.

"Do not touch my things," he said when he turned back to me, leaving to search for his track suits.

I looked at his feet and sighed. At least he wasn't wearing his dirty shoes on my perfectly clean carpet.

*   *   *

My home needs to be a perfect reflection of my inner peace. That's the way I wanted to live my life. It shouldn't be difficult since it was just My Darling Husband and myself. No children or pets should make it easy to live the life I want and have my home reflect that. Our kitchen was state of the art, with every modern appliance we could ever need but rarely used. I'd meticulously selected every piece of furniture to make my home look picture perfect in shades of gray. Glass, granite, chrome, and microfiber covered surfaces and fixtures. No knick-knacks sat on surfaces; everything was stored in its place. Books were recovered to match each other. The technology was hidden. It was all the way I wanted it to look.

I hated all of it.

I'd woken up on New Year's Day feeling unhappy. We had gone out for dinner. Neither of us had spoken. I'd watched My Darling Husband get drunk, and then I'd driven us home in his obnoxious, tiny sports car. I'd felt every bump and pothole as I'd struggled to drive the stick-shift. I had put him to bed in our perfect room and realized I was miserable.

Nothing in this house made me happy. It was no longer a reflection of my inner peace because I no longer felt that.

*   *   *

"Pet, how did you manage to get all your clothes cleaned up?" My Darling Husband asked me later that night as we got ready for bed.

Not only I had put all the clothes away, but I had ordered a wonderful dinner.

I took a deep breath and felt my lips curl into a smile. "I realized all my clothes bring me joy."

He was down to his boxers, and I sighed in disappointment. This man was no longer who I had married. Once, he'd wanted to build the perfect life with me. We'd had plans for two perfect children—one boy and one girl. I'd even had names picked out. We would vacation in the Caribbean when they were young, then we would vacation in the Mediterranean when they were in college, but in the end, we would go back to the Caribbean when we had grandchildren. We would have ski trips, cruises, and our lives would be full of joy. He didn't tell me about the vasectomy until after the wedding. He didn't want kids and, even if I had been willing to adopt, he didn't want to raise someone else's kids.

My smile faded as I looked at him with his beer gut. He had the perfect life, and I had to be happy with the perfect house.

"Keep my clothes out of your crusade to middle-class scarcity," he said, getting into his side of the bed.

"How much of this stuff really makes you happy?" I asked him, turning on my bedside light before pulling up the covers.

I wanted him to see how unhappy I had been. I might have just realized it in the last few weeks, but this had been a problem for a long time. I hoped he would realize he felt the same way, and we could build a new life together.

"Everything in my life brings me joy," he said before rolling over onto his side away from me and turning out his light.

I sat in the king-size bed, realizing the chasm between us had become physical. Maybe decluttering our house could remove both the physical and emotional distance between us, and we could find our way back to our perfect plan.

*   *   *

"Where's my iPod?" My Darling Husband asked the next evening when he got home.

"Which one? You had one from every generation!" I said.

Tonight he didn't come into the house complaining, and there was no mess for him to walk over. The frenzy of my first day of decluttering had become structured and methodical. This morning, I'd taken five boxes of unused and out-of-date tech to a local shop that recycled them. This had been in addition to the bags of his ugly tracksuits. Yes, I'd made sure to do it well before My Darling Husband came home.

"The first generation with the spinning wheel," he said.

We were in the office together. I was sitting at our shared desk, putting junk into boxes. He opened the box at the other end of the room and began removing items.

"I took it to be recycled," I said as I got up and moved over to him, returning the items to the box. "Those items don't bring me joy."

"I used the iPods as hard drives for important documents!" he yelled.

I ignored him and finished filling the box. I walked back to the desk and continued sorting through items. I placed everything neatly on shelves above the desktop, wiped down any lingering dust, and put pens in a cup that matched the paper blotter. I had already ripped off the page that had been full of scribbles from someone testing pens. The tech I had kept was tucked away in a draw so it could be easily found when I needed it.

"Pet, did you hear me?" he asked, taking a deep breath and exhaling to relax. "I used them to store our most important documents."

"How did a five-gigabyte iPod get used to store our important documents?" I asked without looking at him. "You're the CIO of a major corporation. You'd be fired if someone found out anything important was on those drives."

I heard him yell with rage, but I refused to give him the attention he wanted.

"Where are they, Pet?" he said, and I heard the box contents clatter as he slammed it on the carpet.

"I took it to be recycled," I said with a shrug.

I continued to work as I listened to him run down the stairs, slam the front door, and start his car. He didn't come back until I was already in bed. I kept my eyes closed, but he knew I was awake. He didn't say anything aside from elongated sighs and groans. When the light went out, he and I were lying on opposite sides, back to back, with the chasm of the empty bed between us.

Why did we have such a big bed? I had hoped it would be full, our children climbing into our bed, late at night, to cuddle before falling asleep, safe from their nightmares. He had denied me that, and now I was left with an emptiness I had filled with things I didn't really need or want.

* * *

"Pet! Where did the television go?" My Darling Husband called down the stairs.

I had spent most of the day in the den, continuing to get rid of the tech abandoned in the house. My instincts told me to get rid of the massive eighty-six-inch television he had mounted over my beautiful fireplace. I had temporarily replaced it with a landscape painting I had purchased years ago—one he hated. I needed to figure out a better way to hide the holes in the wall and cables protruding from them. The painting would be adequate while I found something perfect. It made the room feel serene and peaceful.

I waited for him to come down the basement stairs to talk to me, bracing for a fight since I was close to his man cave.

"I sold it to someone online, and they picked it up this morning," I said when he was in the basement.

"That television was expensive. What the fuck were you thinking?"

"It wasn't bringing me joy, but the kid gave me fifty dollars, and we can use it to go out for dinner," I said.

I felt the stress and anxiety of my life tumble from my shoulders and sat up straighter as My Darling Husband's face turned red with rage. The previous owners had built shelves in the basement to improve storage. My Darling Husband had commandeered half the space for his man cave, putting up temporary walls, like a cheap cubicle, to set his space apart. He had a second, larger television on a wall, a fully stocked bar, and posters of expensive sports cars. I once had fantasies of finishing the basement for a child's play room, working up designs to make it safe and sturdy. Then our plans had changed and, other than the man cave, all that remained was moldy furniture, damp and decaying boxes of old moldy clothes, and things we had inherited from other relatives.

I had managed to put things into crates and on the shelves. I had organized a furniture pickup earlier that day, and all the moldy pieces had been taken to the dump. The empty space made it easier to breathe down here. Now I played with fantasies of a home gym, complete with a brand new stationary bike so I could get back into shape.

"That television was worth two thousand dollars! You got fifty bucks for it!" He yelled as he stomped back up the stairs. "Like I would ever go out for dinner with you after this!"

I felt my shoulders sag as I realized we only went out together when we had to make an appearance. In the five years of our marriage, we had never gone out to simply enjoy each other's company or to have a romantic dinner just because. It was always a show, even when we went out for holidays. We had to make sure people thought we were happy.

*　　*　　*

I pulled up to the house after dropping off the last load of donations. I saw My Darling Husband's expensive sports car already in the driveway. The trunk of the car and front door of the house were both wide open. I got out of my SUV and walked into my perfect home, closing the door behind me.

25

"Petra!" I heard him yell down to me from our bedroom.

I declined to respond. Instead, I went into the den to start a fire in the fireplace. I wanted to sit by the fire, a blanket over my legs, and a cup of tea on a table next to me. I looked around the room and saw the armchair I could move. I would buy a new side table that would fit perfectly between the fireplace and the armchair. I could see it all in my mind, and I wished I could make it happen right now. At least I could start the fire. I always had newspaper to help me start the fire, kindling to make it grow, and logs to look beautiful as it burned. I busied myself, making my vision become a reality as My Darling Husband continued to yell.

I took my time layering all the elements to get the fire going. If My Darling Husband wanted to talk to me, he knew to come downstairs. I wasn't going to rush for him. I was tired of accommodating him. As the fire grew, I went back to the kitchen and made a cup of tea. As it steeped, I went back into the den, took the fire iron, and stoked the fire. I looked around the room, pleased with how much clutter I had gotten rid of. Removing the television and all the computer equipment was the right decision. It was going to become my favorite room in the house.

"Pet, where did you take all my stuff?" My Darling Husband finally came down the stairs.

His face was bright red, and he was sweating. In his hand, he held a full duffle bag. I had left his precious suits in the closet, and now he had rolled them up into the bag. It would be his problem to get rid of the wrinkles.

"It wasn't bringing me joy," I said, reminding him of my purpose for the past few weeks.

"It wasn't yours to consider." He dropped the bag and balling his fists.

"It was in my home," I said and walked back into the kitchen to get my tea.

He followed me, stomping his feet on my perfect hardwood floors. "This is our home. I live here too."

I slowly pulled the teabag out of my mug, squeezing out the excess water. "You can keep your toys at your office."

I turned to face him, so I could go enjoy my tea by my fireplace.

"I work from home as well. You had no right to give away my things!" His face only got redder as he yelled at me.

"I had no right?" My anger and my voice rose. "No right? What about the things you promised me before we got married? All the things you changed your mind about after our wedding day!"

"It's not my fault you live in denial. I told you I had changed my mind about a family. You didn't care because you wanted your hundred-thousand-dollar wedding and your million-dollar home."

"You knew what I wanted. You should have called it off!"

I wasn't thinking as I threw my mug at him. Hot tea splashed on his arm, and the ceramic mug smashing as it hit the wall, just missing his head.

"You bitch!" He screamed, his hands covering his face.

I grabbed the fire iron and swung without thinking. I slammed it over and over across his head and back, not noticing the blood flying around my perfect room, spraying on the white rug. I don't know what made me stop, but I looked around at the gore as I caught my breath. Brain matter sat in chunks on the fireplace mantle. The beautiful landscape painting was now like a piece of modern art, covered in beige and red. The blood splattered the white rug, but where My Darling Husband's body laid, it pooled and spread as the fibers absorbed. I must have driven the poker into this stomach. I could see his intestines peeking out from under his body. Even I was covered with his insides. I recognized the smell of his body defecating. The rug would have to go. I would get online and buy a new one tomorrow. I had already picked out the perfect one!

I thought about that rug and the new decorations I would have to purchase to replace what he had ruined. I walked into the kitchen, trailing blood behind me, and grabbed my largest, sharpest knife. I would also need to wash the walls and mop with bleach.

He had destroyed my dreams and forced me to fill the void with stuff I didn't want or find joy in. He only had himself to blame. This was all I thought about as I cut up his body like it was nothing more than a Thanksgiving turkey.

*　*　*

It was pitch black in the grocery store parking lot when, hours later, I pulled up next to the charity trailer. There were other boxes there, left by people who had come after they'd closed. This was the time of day when people just left the items they knew the charity wouldn't normally take. Tonight, I would just leave this one last load so I could go back to cleaning my perfect home.

I turned off my headlights and popped the trunk. One by one, I pulled out the plastic trash bags and put them next to the staircase. I taped my note to the heaviest bag.

"He didn't bring me joy."

Bad Trip Highway
by Renee S. DeCamillis

My mushroom high tweaks, zigzagging and spinning along with my car.

I hammer the brake pedal to the floor, spin a 360 across the median, and tear up even more grass on my way back into the glistening southbound lane of the midnight highway. The hitchhiking hobo I almost take out with the rear-end of my Oldsmobile Delta 88 during the hydroplane-fishtail is standing stunned and glued to the guardrail.

The drenched dude beside the ditch holds his head high—in smug regard or a cautionary stance, I can't say—as I come to a screeching stop beside him in the breakdown lane. Hanging from the end of his ape-long arm is what looks like a ventriloquist's dummy case. It reminds me of the one my zany Uncle Charlie used to bring over to the house when I was a kid. The center of the hobo's patchwork top hat is caved in from the torrential downpour. A whirlpool of rain is circling around the brim and running like a waterfall off the lopsided edge in the back.

I've always wondered why so many people warn against picking up hitchhikers. Why not help someone stranded and down on their luck? I've never been able to pass by a thumb without stopping to offer a ride. And every single person was grateful. Some had even offered me gifts of gratitude: a journal; a burger; an amethyst; a couple Viagra; a hand-carved walking stick topped with a quartz crystal; a Rune stone necklace—Raido, for safe travel and safe journeys—(which still hangs from my rearview mirror); and one guy offered me the shirt off his back, a vintage Led Zeppelin concert t-shirt from the 70s. I refused the T, of course—it was meaningful music memorabilia—but I thanked *him* by sending him off with a joint of killer green-bud. And every character I've ever met with their thumb out inspired a new psychedelic tune for my band. And that's *exactly* what I need this time.

Another great tune.

"One more track, another hit, and we need it in four days, before the album goes to mastering." That's what the record company has been breathing down my neck over the last few days. But no ideas have come to me. Nothing.

As the primary song writer in the band, and with all the members waiting on me, and the record company suits tap-tap-tapping their fingers, I'm desperate.

I have one day left!

One day to write it, teach it to my boys, polish the performance, and record it.

So, here I am, tripping behind the wheel in the middle of a rain-choked night, picking up another thumb.

"Gotta find inspiration wherever you can," I always say.

I yell out the sliver-sized opening of my window, "Hop on in, you hipster hobo." I fling open the passenger door. The bottom corner slams into his leg and knocks him to his knees. He jumps to his feet so gracefully it looks like a choreographed dance move rather than a fall.

"Shit, dude! That wasn't supposed to happen," I say through shroom-induced laughter as he tosses his dummy-case on the floor and plops his soggy-wet ass into the seat beside me. "Take a toke to ease the pain." I point to the blunt hanging half out of the open ashtray.

The joint is lit and in his mouth before he shuts the door. "Thanks for the smoke." His words sound strained as he tries to speak while holding in his hit.

Three smoke rings puff out of his mouth, one after the other and float up, wavering in the air. "Alaskan Thunder Fuck—nice choice."

"Well...looks like I found me a weed connoisseur walking the moonlit highway."

"Weed connoisseur?" He shrugs, then nods. "Maybe. But moonlit highway?" He looks out the window at the crying, cloud-smothered sky and smirks.

I say, "Use your imagination. I always do."

I laugh. He doesn't.

We pass a streetlight just as I glance over at him, and I notice something white and pasty above his upper lip. "Hey, dude." He turns toward me and I motion to my lip. "You've got something right there." As I'm talking, I'm also thinking, *Man, I hope this guy's not a tweaker.*

He wipes his mouth on the soaked sleeve of his jacket, which only cleans off some of the white cakey substance. The rest of it smears out toward his chin and cheek, clumping in his beard stubble. I don't mention it. Then he snorts so hard I'm waiting for his nose to concave into his face.

"Oh, and make a note—" He says sternly, staring at me sidelong. "I'm no motherfuckin' hipster." He takes another toke, sucking down half the blunt with his wonder lungs. "I'm a carnie."

"A carnie? Cool. Never met a carnie before. Always something new down the road. Gotta love it!"

"Why?"

"Why what?"

He turns toward me, wearing a sharp expression that can slice through glass. He says nothing. He hands me what's left of the blunt. A veil of smoke wafts out of his mouth and up over his face, like the curtain rising at a sideshow—he's the main attraction.

Blunt pinched between my lips, I speed out of the breakdown lane. A rapid-fire of raindrops pelts the windshield with the sound of throwing knives against unbreakable glass. The one working windshield wiper slaps the water away as fast as a one-legged man swimming laps in an Olympic size pool—hell, in any size pool. Ahead of my headlights, the slick-wet highway glistens like diamonds as my powder blue boat sails along.

"Where you headed?" I ask the carnie, whose head is now blowing up like a beach ball as he sucks down the last of the blunt I handed back to him. The more he inhales, the bigger his head grows, like a balloon on a helium pump valve. His top hat, which is smushing into the ceiling, now looks more like a pillbox hat on top of his enormous noggin.

Man, that was a potent batch of shrooms I ate.

"Where *you* headed?" In a helium-filled voice, my question bounces off the beach ball right back at me.

"That's what I asked you."

"And I'm asking you the same." His voice is suddenly calm, inquisitive—like he's digging for something I don't know is buried. One of the smoke rings he blows out circles around his hat like a plastic ring at a ring-toss game.

My head is spinning in time with the slap-swish of the one wiper.

Where *am* I going?

"Nowhere. Just driving." I don't want to tell him I'm using him for inspiration. That would take away the authenticity of the moment, the authenticity of his character. I want the song raw, uninhibited.

Now the inside of the car is one big cloud of smoke. I cough and the smoky air undulates like the waves of an ocean. The water is inside my boat. I feel like I'm sinking, sinking in a sea of confusion. I don't know what to make of this guy.

"'Just driving,' you say?" The carnie stubs out the roach in the ashtray. "Are you fuckin' trippin' or what, *motherfucker*?" He laughs so loud his voice echoes and reverberates off the crushing confines of my car.

The doors, the dash, the roof, the backseat—all of it is moving in on us, creaking as it comes closer and closer. With every threatening inch it all moves, the vise on my chest clamps tighter and tighter. I'm losing my breath but don't know why.

The carnie's energy feels heavy, like the dagger-sharp look in his eyes. He's laughing and smiling. But those eyes—

They're not laughing.

They're not smiling.

Hey, chill out, I tell myself. *He's just down, down on his luck in a downpour. No worries—he's* laughing. *And you're just* tripping-balls.

He hits the play button on the cassette player of my vintage stereo. The Doors' "Break On Through" rings out of the speakers.

How does he know I'm high, high on shrooms? *I'm definitely not high from that one hit of weed he so generously shared with me. My weed.*

The carnie opens the armrest console that separates passenger from operator. He pulls out my bag of herb, what little I have left.

"Do you have any papers?"

"What—you're not high enough off that whole blunt you just smoked...uh...*by yourself?*"

"What?" His voice jumps an octave from its normal range. "I passed it to you. Don't you remember? Or are you too *high?*" His chortle carves crow's feet at the corners of his squinty eyes.

"One, dude, one hit—that's all. So, no, I'm not high. And, no, I don't have any papers." I try to not sound pissed, but that's all the weed I have. And I need my ganga to enhance my trip, boost inspiration for the song, oh, and, uh...

For my bad back.

"Aha...that's the problem; you're not high *enough*. See, if you were *higher*, you'd know where you're headed. You'd be able to *imagine* all sorts of places to go."

"Yeah, well, I'm imagining myself out of weed before I drop you off wherever *you're* headed. *That's* what I'm imagining right now, dude."

I snatch the bag out of the moocher's mitts, stuff it back in the console, and latch the lid shut. The car swerves; tires rumble over the "wake the fuck up" strip next to the breakdown lane. I jump at the sound. After righting the wheel, I rest my arm on the top of the console lid, hand splayed, with my fingers covering the open-latch. "That's all I've got to last until I get paid again. No. More. Smoking. *Please.*"

His head spins toward me with the speed of a reptile, eyes bulging. He says nothing.

He reaches down toward the floor and into his dummy-case and pulls out something shiny. *A mirror, maybe?* That's my best guess. The passing streetlights bounce reflections off from the object he's holding hidden in the shadows. Rays of light are jumping around the car.

When did my car turn into a disco?

I can feel the carnie's stare boring holes into the side of my throbbing head. All I'm thinking at this point is—*He better not expect to snort junk in my car. No fucking way that shit's going down! I like my trips paranoia-free, thank you very much.*

All of a sudden he yells at top volume. "I won't be disrespected, *motherfucker!*" His voice falsettos with rage and sarcasm.

Tweaker! I should know better than to challenge a potential meth-head.

The vise squeezes tighter around my chest. *Holy, tripping-anxiety!* I've heard about it from fellow shroomers, but I've never experienced it before. My trips are always freeing and inspirational.

Next thing I know, the carnie drives the blade of a knife into the back of my hand. It pierces through flesh, scrapes passed bone, and pins me to the console lid.

My trip goes bad.

I scream. A strangled squeal is all that escapes me. The car swerves into the breakdown lane. The side scrapes and grinds against the guardrail. Sparks shoot up and out in all directions. The pain in my hand is overwhelming, all-consuming.

"What the fuck, dude?!" My baritone voice hits a soprano pitch it has never reached before. *Not the type of feel-good song I want to write—Scream-o shock-rock is not my bag-o-jollies.*

I correct the steering wheel—or think that's what I'm doing. The car bounds across the grassy median again. My body jostles around from the bouncing and jerking motion of the Olds. The weight of my body yanks and pulls at my impaled hand. But the hand remains connected to the console by the blade. Blood oozes and drips. My pain multiplies. And my panic follows.

Headlights are speeding straight at us.

I'm driving southbound in the northbound lane.

Luckily it's the middle of the night—only one set of lights is flying at us. I crank the wheel back toward the other side of the highway. Tires squeal. Mine or theirs? I'm not sure. Probably both.

The car's ass-end swerves. Mud and grass fly everywhere, splattering across the windshield, as I speed back over the median. Tires hit pavement again. My speed decreases. I angle for the breakdown lane.

"Get the hell out, you crazy fucker!" My words time out exactly with the screech of the tires.

We come to a dead-stop.

I reach for the knife, but not fast enough. The psycho carnie yanks the blade from my hand.

Blood gushes.

A choked scream shoots out of my cotton-mouth. My throat feels like steel wool.

"Nah, that shit ain't gonna happen." He presses the cold, flat side of the knife against my throat. "Drive, *motherfucker!*" The tip of the blade pokes my skin but doesn't penetrate.

I drive.

The car remains in the breakdown lane. The speedometer barely hits forty.

"Pull back out, and fucking step on it." He leans toward me. He turns the blade onto its sharp edge. "But not *too* fast." His voice is now creepy-calm.

My thoughts swirl.

What do you do when you pick up a hitchhiking carnie who won't get out of your car?

The knife.

Oh yeah—can't forget about the knife to your throat. And the blood gushing from your hand. And the shrooms you ate thirty minutes before the pick-up.

I imagine hitting a passenger seat eject button and seeing the psycho fly out the roof and down over the highway embankment.

If only I had a rocket-car... Maybe I can switch feet on the gas pedal and kick him hard enough to smash him into the window. Where are those Gumby-limbs when you need them?

First sane thought that jumps out of my cluster-fuck mind—*Grab the knife!*

Next thoughts—*With what free hand? The one with the hole in it that's spewing blood? Or the one steering? Dumbass!*

Then my mind screams, *Elbow the fucker in the face!* As much as I want to, that's not an option. His arm—the one with the knife-wielding hand attached—is in my swinging-range.

Every rational idea I'm able to sift out of my mushroom fog ends the same—with my throat slit. But I take a chance.

I ease my left knee up under the steering wheel and let it take over. With my one good hand, I grab the knife.

Yep. I grab the damn *blade* of the knife.

The car swerves.

It helps to be able to see what you're grabbing for.

I immediately pull my hand away. I grab the wheel again and regain control of the car, but not my thoughts and not the pain. I grit my teeth, biting back my groans. Blood trails around the circle in my hand and drips onto my lap.

Both hands?! My head is screaming. *Thank fucking God my voice is my instrument,* my life. *Without that, I might as well be fucking dead.*

"Stupid. Stupid. Stupid, *motherfucker.*" The carnie is now speaking in a voice so calm it seems surreal.

I don't understand how someone can appear so calm in such a volatile situation.

A sharp pinch-like sensation scatters my thinking even more. The carnie has dug the tip of the blade into the flesh of my neck. The sting of the cut makes my jaw clench. I can't make a sound. More blood. The dripping tickles.

I don't laugh.

"Yeah, that's just to let you know who's in charge here. Now, keep the car between the lines. And don't test me again or you'll get more than a little prick." His voice remains as soft as a lullaby—without the calming effect.

I don't know what to do.

I drive.

Ahead, the highway appears to veer to the right, but it curves to the left. The lines of the lanes split and fork, then come together and cross.

Yes, they are fucking crossing. I see it with my own eyes.

Cold blade against my throat, I drive.

The carnie starts rambling on about who knows what. I don't even think he's talking to me. Who is he talking to? Someone I can't see, apparently. I can decipher only small chunks of his sentences, if they even are sentences: "...apprentice...thrower...best...next show...Carmine the Carver...chick assist...wearing barely-there..."

What the hell?!

His dummy-case is in his lap by the time his lips stop flapping. There's no dummy inside.

Twenty or thirty knives glisten with every passing streetlight. Each handle is strapped to the orange velvet lining of the suitcase.

A knife thrower?!

He pulls the blade away from my throat. He straps the knife to the one empty slot in the case. His fingers then brush across every knife. Back and forth.

He looks at me.

Fear-frozen, I can feel that squinty stare, those sociopath-eyes— deep-set, beady, and penetrating—scraping my insides. He's deciding which blade to remove next, which blade to use. On me.

My thoughts are wrestling. The one that wins—*Sociopath equals narcissist. His ego, caress it.* I've seen *Dexter.* After all, he was once "America's favorite serial killer."

"With a set like that, you must be one hell of a knife thrower." My voice quivers.

He doesn't respond.

But my mind responds loud and clear. *He's got one hell of a set all right! Now, where the hell did I lose mine?*

He somehow keeps one eye on me and one eye on the knives, as I somehow keep one eye on him and one eye on the highway. His rough callused fingers continue caressing the blades. The dead skin is getting caught up on the smooth velvet lining. The tearing pops and rips, like static electricity. The sound echoes in my empty head. It echoes so loudly, it almost completely drowns out the music—The Doors, "The End."

I don't know what the hell to do, but I have to make a move.

I quickly reach for a knife with my hand. I barely feel the velvet lining of the dummy case when Carmine the Carver grabs my hand and squeezes.

I squeal like a piglet. Pools of water fill my eyes and blur my vision. The car swerves all over the highway. Tires screech. The carnie and I are thrown side to side, bouncing off each other like ping-pong balls. He doesn't let up on my hand; he squeezes tighter every time his shoulder bumps into me. The bleeding pain is white-hot. The dummy case is thrown to the floor, but not before he somehow manages to withdraw another knife.

By the time I'm able to regain control of the car, a different blade is pressing against my throat.

"One more stupid move, *motherfucker*, and you're dead." He takes in a deep breath, but never lets it out. "Pull off at the next exit. Got it?"

I croak out a weak, "Uh huh." I can barely breathe.

What is he going to do to me once I pull off into the next no-name-town?

I don't want to think about it. I *can't* think about it.

My head pounds; in and out it pulses. My eyes mimic my head. Everything I see—windshield, dash, wiper, road, guardrails—it's all pulsing in and out, in and out.

The light of my high beams lands on the frame of a bridge up ahead. That next exit—it's just on the other side. Light pulses against metal. A metal cage over a catwalk. I'm not ready to strut my stuff.

It's time to kick rationality to the curb.

I speed up.

At the last second, I veer to the right. Metal collides with metal. The frontend of my boat Vs in from the crunching impact. A loud cracking and shattering sound echoes through the thick air, as my face bounces off the steering wheel. Shards of glass fly out, scattering and skittering across the crushed hood. Spider webbing runs past me. There's a hole in the windshield in front of the passenger seat.

The rearview mirror is now in my lap. Raido the Rune stone stares up at me.

There's a dent in the steering wheel. Blood is dripping down my face. I'm crying rubies. I taste copper.

I'm wearing my seatbelt.

Carmine the Carver, apparently, never buckled up.

That crazy carnie broke on through to the other side, where he had a mind-splitting introduction with the metal cage of the catwalk. His long, lanky body hangs like a sock monkey over a metal beam. The top of his head is open to the elements. Rain is washing away his brain matter.

I glance to my right. The patchwork top hat is sitting on the otherwise empty passenger seat. The rain pouring through the hole in my windshield is puddling on the brim. The dummy case is lying open on the passenger-side floor. The streetlights are reflecting off the stainless-steel knife blades.

I look back up, out the window, surveying the damage to my car.

The carnie is no longer there.

The metal beams of the bridge are bare of his body. Carmine the Carver is gone. Vanished. How the fuck could he go anywhere? I saw his skull cracked open. Gray matter washing away like mud and gravel.

I unbuckle.

I pull out a knife with my least hurt hand.

I reach around, lock all four of the doors.

I ease my cell out of my pants pocket.

The battery is dead.

My car is dead.

Carmine the Carver *was* dead. I *know* it.

Wondering what to do, I fumble around with the knife in my hand. Reflections from the streetlights flash around the inside of my car like a rave is going on.

With my shoulder, I wipe blood from my eyes onto my sleeve. Thankful I'm alive, I stare at my bloody face in the sheen of the blade.

A funhouse reflection stares back at me.

I pick up the rearview mirror. Raido sways like a pendulum. As I'm inspecting my wounds, I detect movement behind me.

My breathing freezes.

Slowly, I turn the mirror about an inch.

In the backseat, a madhouse reflection stares back at me. Ominous grin leers. Black eyes swirl, eager. Top of the skull severed—no blood.

A low raspy voice bellows, "And *that's* why you should *never* pick up a hitchhiker...*motherfucker!*"

Child of Reason
by Christine Lajewski

Beylie was not sure how old he was, although he had grown so tall he could nearly look Mother in the eye. But one spring morning, she gifted him a hunting knife and announced, "Today you've reached the Age of Reason." She said he knew enough to take over important tasks, like gathering roots and setting snares in the surrounding forest.

His whole world was Mother and her garden. In his earliest memories, he sat on furrows of warm earth as she fertilized rows of vegetables with slimy green-black mosses, or weeded masses of flowers in colors Beylie would never see duplicated elsewhere.

Visitors were rare. They were usually men, and almost always hopelessly lost. They stayed for dinner and left before Beylie awakened the following morning. The black loam of the flower beds was always reddened after every departure.

Growing seasons were filled with song. Some of it came from Mother herself, chanted in syllables Beylie did not understand. But some songs seemed to float on the air all by themselves. He'd assumed they came from birds hidden in the forest trees. But that day, he would learn the source was something else.

Mother showed him how to work black mosses into the garden rows. Then Beylie tied the thorny canes of the rose bushes to trellises. She praised the work, gave him bread and honey and berries for lunch, and left him to take a nap.

As she slept, Beylie took a long ramble in the woods—something he had never done before. On this special day, he followed game paths deeper than he ever had into the soft darkness of the trees. He realized just how small their farm was compared to the vastness of the forest. The air exploded with color and cacophony of birds he rarely saw. Their whistles and trills soared straight to heaven. The songs that filled the gardens, on the other hand, were shrill and skittered through the air at odd angles—a quality that, he later learned, most people called *off-key*.

When he realized he could no longer hear that familiar music, he panicked, fearing he was lost. Somehow, he remembered where the sun had been as he entered the woods, sighted its slanting rays, and retraced his steps until he once again heard the sideways song.

Back in the garden, Beylie paced in ever shrinking concentric circles, trying to determine once and for all the source of the music. The crooked notes were loudest at the lush beds shared by roses and snaking vines of bell-shaped flowers. When Beylie leaned in to inspect their centers, he saw fleshy tags, dusted with sulfur, wagging in time to the song. He touched his own tongue with his fingers, tried to imitate the movement, and produced an alto counterpoint to the floral chorus.

Each petaled head swiveled on its stem to face the boy and every voice save his fell silent. Beylie fell backward in the dirt and clapped his hands over his mouth. So overwhelming was the silence that Mother came running from the house.

"What have you done?" she cried. She had never raised hand or voice to her son, but her eyes had an ochre cast that suggested a sky before the onset of dangerous weather.

Beylie hung his head and whispered, "I sang to them."

Mother did not erupt as the boy expected. She took a step back and regarded her child with surprise and perhaps a smattering of fear. "You mustn't do that, Beylie," she said. "They don't know your voice. It disturbs them. They won't grow if they're disturbed."

"Will they be all right, Mother?"

Before she could reply, a new song filled the air. It came from the forest and its notes rose straight up to the sky. From out of the trees stepped a young man, beautiful to look at, and heavenly to listen to. Mother beamed at the visitor in a way the boy had never seen before.

"I'm lost," said the wanderer. "Can you help me?"

Mother prepared a feast that night: a platter of small roasted birds served with wine and nasturtiums stuffed with nuts and mushrooms. Beylie was so fascinated by their guest that he barely touched his food. His eyes darted from the man's creamy skin, even white teeth, and golden hair to Mother's face. Everything about her suggested she was of the earth: Her skin was the color of damp sand, her eyes the yellow of a honeycomb. Her hair fell in waves that suggested rippled river clay. When she laughed, her teeth gleamed a light celery green, and they were all pointed canines. But the man seemed unfazed by the differences between them. He leaned forward and gazed at Mother in fascination.

The meal went on and on. The boy eventually fell asleep at the table. When he awoke, he was alone. Crumbs and greasy dishes littered the rough wooden table. A new kind of song drifted through the open door on the night breezes. Beylie followed it to the swaying masses of silent flowers, their colors melding in the silvered light of the waxing moon. Beneath them, Mother's back was lustrous as she sprawled across the young man, who thrust upward from the dusky green. Beylie gaped but backed away. *I must not meet her eye*, he thought.

He curled up in his bed, trying to form just the right questions about the curious behavior he'd witnessed. He fell asleep before he could settle on any.

The next morning, Beylie found bread and tea waiting for him on the clean table. The golden man was gone; Mother was locked in her shed. She emerged hours later with two sacks of pulpy feed for the garden. She extended a reddened hand to her son and guided him to the flower beds, where they both worked the fertilizer into the soil until the brown earth turned rusty.

That night, the flowers raised their voices to the moon. Mother served a generous haunch of roasted meat for dinner.

The next morning, Beylie ran to the flower beds to listen to the blossom song. He kept his hand over his mouth so he would not be tempted to sing along and frighten the flowers into silence again.

They had all doubled in size. Their bright yellow centers were as rounded as crab apples. The flowers caroled in Mother's secret language, mouth-like creases shaping vowels. Beylie inched closer and saw waxy tongues the size of his pinky vibrating behind rows of seed pearls. Tiny eyes, black and shiny as jet, peered back at him. Horrified, he retreated to the house. He found Mother and asked, "Will the flowers be all right?"

Her smile was radiant. "Have you not looked? I'll show you after we eat."

In the bright afternoon sun, they walked hand in hand through the garden. The blossoms had grown even larger: goblets where diminutive trumpets had been, and huge cabbage roses in place of dainty rosettes.

"You helped do this, Beylie. You should feel proud," Mother said. "Now I have new things for you to learn."

She guided him to the table by the fireplace. From a high shelf, she brought down the first of seven leather-bound volumes. These ones, she explained, had been written by her mother, her grandmother, and herself.

Beylie had learned to read and write from Mother's library of husbandry and garden lore. But he was enthralled by the wonderful illustrations in these new books. Nearly every page ended with strange syllables, which, when chanted, promised magical results.

He longed to read all seven volumes, but Mother told him he needed to memorize and practice each one before he could move on to the next.

Every day, he listened to the flowers sing their sideways songs as he weeded and watered them. Throughout the summer and into the fall, the heads grew defined features: ears to listen for Beylie's approach; rolling, onyx eyes. Solemn, unblinking gazes followed every motion. Beylie never turned his back on them.

By late summer, each little head sported a shock of golden hair. When Beylie fingered a few strands, every mouth stretched into a grin of recognition. The little necks strained away from the petals, emitting cries not unlike those the young man made when Mother straddled him in the moonlit garden. Beylie ran for the shed, terrified.

"Mother, they're not flowers. They're real heads," he blurted. "And they look like..."

"Yes, I know. They're coming along nicely," she said. "They'll be fully grown by September. Wait until you see the harvest."

She gave him another reward that day: the second leather-bound book. It contained much more than mere herbal craft. Each beautifully illuminated page told stories of men and women avenging wrongs, feeding desires beyond human reach, or bending flora and fauna to their wills. There were words and lists of herbs, animals, and minerals needed to work the spells.

"Can you do the things written in this book?" he asked Mother at supper.

"I've done most. Some I have not yet tried," Mother replied.

"Why not?"

"One does not do these things just to play at them. It's greedy to conjure more than we need."

"But I will learn to do them," he said.

"You already are, a little at a time—as there is need."

He did not want to wait until he was as old as Mother to try some of these spells. For the first time in his life, Beylie thought Mother was wrong.

The pages in the new book did not explain the singing flowers or how Mother made them grow. But Beylie had reached the Age of Reason, and he could draw a straight line in his mind through the events of the spring and summer: How Mother had glowed when the golden man appeared in the garden, and how they joined together that night, right under the nodding blooms. No sooner had the visitor disappeared than Mother had her plant food and a joint of red meat. And Beylie had worked the crimson pulp into the flower bed, which yielded the golden-haired heads in their colorful frills, greeting him with familiar smiles.

By September, the heads were the size of turnips. Sometimes, when their little necks stretched forward, he could see twenty rounded nubs ringing the necks like collars of stones. Their tunes turned scratchy and needy.

"They're hungry," said Mother when Beylie asked about it. "I haven't fed them since..."

"The peddler comes soon, doesn't he?" asked Beylie.

Mother's eyes widened with surprise. She pondered a moment before replying, "Yes, he does. But I never invite him to stay. We trade with him for things we need. We must wait for someone else to come."

The boy nodded. He knew what Mother meant.

The flowers bent low on their stalks. It took effort for them to raise their faces to the sun. Their mouths ceaselessly nipped at the very air, as if it annoyed them. One September afternoon, a butterfly landed on one of the faces and disappeared into its gaping hole. The boy realized the heads were snatching insects out of the air.

The constant hum of discontent told Beylie they were not sated. He approached the roses and cautiously brushed one of the blossoms with the tip of a finger. Its mouth snapped as he whipped his hand away. Angry shrieks pierced the air. The faces no longer resembled the golden man who never left. Yellow as rotting cabbages, they sagged on one side while the other grimaced with rage. As Beylie gaped, the nubs shot forward, revealing splayed fingers and toes on two arms and two legs. Fully formed little men, folded at the waist, reached for him from the aureoles of the blossoms, limbs flailing, mouths screeching with hunger.

Beylie ran for the shed and grabbed Mother's curved knife. He raced back to the flower bed and slashed at the boughs. Heads and torsos littered the ground. Sticky green blood splattered his face and clothes. A dozen ripened creatures dropped from their stems and sank their teeth into his bare toes and ankles. Beylie screamed in pain and beat the monsters with his fists. They let go and ran for the woods.

The clamor woke Mother from her nap. She gaped, speechless with rage, at her son and the mangled fruit. Without a word, she grabbed him by the arm, dragged him to the shed and threw him to the floor. She locked Beylie inside and left him there.

The boy watched through a crack in the door for some hint that Mother was ready to forgive him. She spent hours sifting through the carnage and sobbing. "Some ran into the forest, Mother," Beylie called. "We could look for them." He wept, frightened and remorseful, but Mother ignored him. Darkness fell, and Mother brought neither food nor water.

As moonlight brightened the cracks, Beylie heard Mother chant a spell. He saw her kneel on the shorn flowers, a book laid open in the soil, as she sang. Out of nowhere, a sharp black shadow fell over her and she leapt to her feet with a delighted cry. She embraced the man who stood there. Limbs entwined as they lowered themselves to the earth and their cries rose to the moon, like wolf mates. Then they lay side by side in silence.

Finally, Mother spoke. "You saw what the boy did. Our homunculi—all murdered. Have you nothing to say about it?"

The man stood and donned his trousers. He stooped and took handfuls of the dismembered creatures, rolling the heads between his fingers as he inspected them. Finally, he said, "They're deformed. I don't think the boy was wrong."

"We planned this together. I did everything you asked of me. How could they not be what we needed?"

He shrugged. "This wasn't our first failure. The boy has good instincts."

Mother rose and went to the shed. Without a word, she released Beylie, gave him some supper, and sent him to bed.

The man was still there in the morning. He stood in the doorway, watching the boy eat his breakfast. His skin resembled a tanned hide dyed the reddish brown of an overripe apple. Dark hair curled over his neck and ears and he had the eyes of a lynx. He was familiar, but Beylie couldn't place where or when he might have met the visitor. His head buzzed with questions, although he was afraid to let on he'd been eavesdropping. But the man's smile was kind, almost fond, so the child asked, "What's homunculi?"

The man burst out laughing. "You don't miss much. A homunculus is a little manikin or womankin. Your mother and I have been trying to grow them for years. Have you noticed how often those singing flowers have wilted and died in seasons past?"

"I remember so much singing, then the quiet as ever so many flowers lay dead on the ground. But I never ever saw them grow the way they did this past summer. You said I was not wrong for what I did to the...to the homunculi. Why was Mother so angry?"

"I don't think they would have done what we needed them to do. Your mother does not agree."

"Some of them ran away. Maybe we could find them. Maybe see what they're doing.'

The man seemed surprised. He thought a moment, then said, "Good idea. Why don't we find out?"

The man sought Mother in the shed. Beylie crept to the doorway, careful to keep himself out of sight. He could just make out the conversation between the two adults.

"The boy says some of the homunculi escaped into the woods," said the man.

"Perhaps they're headed to the village, as they're meant to," Mother replied. Her voice was angry. "Belith, this was our decision to make, not the child's."

Belith. That's my name, the boy thought.

"I'm going to take Beylie into the woods to see if we can pick up their trail. It's something he needs to learn anyway."

"You're rewarding him. He should stay here while I—"

"No, you stay," the man interrupted.

As Belith turned back to the house, Beylie reseated himself at the kitchen table.

The man stuffed bread, dried venison, and apples into a pack and picked up his carved walking stick. "Fill a skin with water and meet me at the edge of the woods," he said.

They plodded through scarlet trees until they came to a cluster of farms Beylie had never seen before. Men and boys worked side by side, scything hay and loading it onto oxcarts. In the distance, women and girls washed linens and tended babies outside clapboard houses. Laughter and song eased their toil. It was a picture of noisy, happy family life. Beylie could have watched it for hours.

But the man scowled. "This is wrong," he whispered, and beckoned to the child to follow. Beylie was tired but trudged along without complaint.

Deeper into the forest, the man located tiny footprints along a muddy path. He got down on all fours and pushed his nose into the earth, inhaling deeply. Beylie did the same, astonished as odors of rotten fruit, goats, and smoked meat filled his nostrils.

"You have it, don't you?" said the man, smiling.

Beylie nodded.

"This is their trail. Let's follow before it goes cold."

They wolfed down their lunch on the run, scanning for tracks, stooping now and then to breathe in the homunculus musk. Soon the trail was littered with new traces: headless toads, gutted squirrels, strings of entrails.

The warm autumn air was rent by an unearthly scream. Man and boy sprinted toward the cries. They came upon a still pond where they spied a dozen tawny creatures crawling over a fisher. They tore its flesh with savage teeth and slashed it with their claws. The fisher had seriously wounded one of his attackers, who hugged its arms around its gashed and bloody torso. Now the marmot snapped uselessly at the air as he tried to drag himself to the water. The monsters pinned it to the ground.

Belith descended on the scene. He crushed the wounded manikin under his boot and pulled a pair off the dying animal. He used one of his finely honed fingernails to slit the twin throats then tossed them aside to bleed out. The remaining creatures squealed and scattered, but not before Belith scooped up three more. A trio ran for the reeds and took cover while the remainder skittered across the surface of the pond. Beylie plunged into the water after them. He caught one creature by the leg, plunged it under the surface and fixed his boot on its face. He snatched up a second before it could set its teeth on his crotch. He strangled it with both hands. Its glittering black eyes turned dull, and Beylie released it into the dark water. A grackle squawk from the third summoned the creatures hiding in the reeds. They ran right over the ripples, howling with rage, and leapt at the boy's arms and back.

One homunculus clawed its way across the boy's chest and lunged for his throat. Beylie throttled the beast, holding fast, even as the other vermin bit through his shirt. He cried out, but it was less a wail of pain than the furious snarl of a wolf cub. From the corner of his eye, he saw Belith wade out a few feet from the shore, then stop and watch. Beylie wondered: *Why does he not help me?*

As if in reply, the man's feline eyes narrowed as he grinned with pride. He strode through the water and plucked the little predators off the boy, crushing them in his fists.

Beylie bent over, panting with exhaustion. The ripples settled and the water, black as Mother's scrying mirror, smoothed. A face peered back at him. It was the first time he had ever seen more than a blurred reflection in the cabin windows. He recognized Mother's eyes—golden irises and round black pupils—and his hair was the color of river clay. But the locks curled like sheep's wool over his neck and ears and his skin was bronzed, like the man who stood next to him. He smiled with delight and noted that his teeth were yellow, not pale green. The front teeth were flat, but the rest were pointed and sharp.

"I think you have the best of your mother and me," the man observed.

Beylie almost wept with joy.

They collected the dead homunculi in a sack. "We'll need to burn them with the rest," the man said. "We'll start over again next spring." He cut the brushy tail off the dead fisher and presented it to the boy. "Here's a trophy for you. You did well."

"When we get home, should we look in Mother's books for what to do next?" Beylie asked.

"What we're trying to grow is new. We're writing it, even as we try and fail."

"Why do you want to grow these things? Can we trade them for anything?"

"There are people who would pay great sums for such as these. But we want them to drive men to despair—so much despair that they must turn to me."

"Can I help?"

"In time."

They burned the remains behind the farm and buried the ashes in the midden reserved for the foulest waste. After Beylie was sent to bed, he rested his chin on the windowsill and listened as the adults' voices drifted on the night air. He could only pick up pieces of conversation, but he knew Belith was telling Mother of what they saw and did that day. The voices grew louder, and Mother shouted, "You mean drive all men to us. To us!"

Belith laughed and retorted, "So say you."

He disagrees with Mother, too.

His father went away the next day. Mother disappeared into the shed while Beylie spent time reading from the leather-bound books. When Mother reappeared, her son could see she had been weeping. Beylie wanted to cry, too, but kept his sorrow to himself.

The days grew darker. Trees cracked and moaned in the icy winds. Mother broadened the scope of Beylie's education to include home crafts, numbers, beautiful lettering, and sketching the world around him. Not only could he read the volumes from the high shelf, he followed steps to prepare teas and tinctures, to call the moon from behind the clouds, and to bring rabbits into his snares. But the last of the volumes he had yet to see.

Mother rested more often and slept longer than she usually did. Beylie often saw her standing in the doorway, her hands caressing a belly which bulged under her skirt. He had seen drawings of women with similar silhouettes in the books, on pages with teas and tonics for birthing babes. He understood she was growing another child inside her body, and that Belith had helped make it.

One winter morning, after mother and son had spent hours splitting and stacking firewood, Mother took to her bed. She slept through lunch and into the afternoon. Beylie would never have a better chance, so he pulled a stool over to the high shelf and pulled down the last two volumes.

Beylie poured over Volume VI until he heard Mother stirring. He stowed both books under the window seat before Mother entered the kitchen. She was pale and moved slowly.

"Shall I make dinner, Mother?" he asked. "You look so tired."

She smiled with gratitude. "Perhaps you could also make me some tea? You'll need..."

"I know what you need. Something for you and the baby." Beylie pulled just the right herbs from Mother's stores.

"You've figured out what I've yet to tell you," she said.

"You're like the women in the fourth book. I'll give you something to make both of you strong."

"Beylie, I'm so proud. Thank you."

Mother never noticed the misplaced manuals. She spent winter afternoons dozing in a chair next to the fireplace, so it was easy for Beylie to move the books to a new hiding place under his featherbed. He could pull them out to read any time Mother napped.

Mother's hand was not the only one filling the pages of Volume VI. On the very first page, the unknown hand had written: "The Homunculus Plague, To Bring All Men to Belith." Underneath, Mother had scratched out a correction: "To Bring All Men to Us."

The volume began with drawings of men and women intertwined, just like what Beylie had witnessed under fleshy roses and moonlight. The faces resembled his parents'. One page held a date and an inscription: "Son, Belith, Beltane, 1683." There was a drawing of an infant with his eyes and curly hair. He was proud to be Belith's son and longed to tell his father so.

One night, as he pored over the grotesque illustrations and unfamiliar chants of book VII, he began to sing the syllables, improvising on the melodies of the flowers. And suddenly, he was not reading the pages. Words and images, solid and substantial, rose before his eyes and danced across the table.

He saw Mother and Belith in their many attempts, stretching decades into the past, to create homunculi that would bring all men to them. First, they slaughtered animals they hoped would feed the appalling harvest: boars, weasels, wolves, and serpents. Then they tried fascinating and gruesome combinations: a turkey vulture stuffed with carrion beetles; a rabbit's head sewn on the body of a rooster; a wolf with a kid's head in its jaws. Each time, malignant and malformed fruit dropped and broke open on the ground, black and useless.

Then Beylie saw Mother with men she enchanted, butchered, and minced to feed the growing homunculi. There was Belith with young women, making them scream with wild delight until he opened their throats so their blood could pour out on the soil. The human compost produced homunculi, but each was deficient in one way or another, or they died before they reached maturity.

Finally, he saw Mother with her scrying mirror, calling forth the image of the child she carried, a girl she called "Beylie's partner and helpmate." He watched the girl reach her Age of Reason. She was the image of Mother, who said to her, "You are the one who will bring in the harvest." The words stung, and Beylie fought back angry tears.

The images faded, and he found himself looking at the book again. He puzzled over how he might prove he was the One Who Would Bring in the Harvest, not some unborn girl-child. He fell asleep, his head on the table, and dreamt. The images were horrifying, jolting him awake. He found himself outside, staring at the dormant flower bed. His dream had told him that Mother was right, but only he understood exactly *how* his sister could reap the terror.

With the thaw, Mother grew heavy and placid as a cow. Beylie took it upon himself to prepare the soil for the roses and the trumpet vines. The ground was blanched from the winter snows. The flowers would need their bloody fertilizer soon.

Beylie cooked and blended teas for Mother. Then, on the day of April's new moon, he added something he'd read about in the latter books. He crushed juniper berries and rue flowers, adding dried blueberries and lemon balm to disguise the flavor. Mother drank several cups that morning. She liked it so much, she asked for more at supper.

Beylie went to bed, unsure how his plans would unfold. He was awakened by Mother's screams. He ran to the kitchen to see her clutching her belly and staggering out the door. She called Belith's name and gasped out a long string of incantations as she lurched to the flower beds. Then she fell to her hands and knees in the dirt.

Black stains spread across Mother's skirt. The boy approached, curious to see what would happen next.

"Beylie," Mother gasped as the boy stood at the flower bed, staring down at her. "Beylie, I need...to stop the bleeding...the baby. I need..."

"Juniper and rue?" said Beylie.

"No, that will expel the baby." Her eyes grew wide and she gasped, "No. Beylie, you didn't."

"You wrote the girl would be the one to bring in the harvest. This is how it will happen."

Mother doubled over again and howled like a beast. When she reared back again, Beylie could see a dark mass, the size of small pumpkin, between her legs. "Beylie, why did you do this?" Mother sobbed.

"I've reached the Age of Reason, and I figured out something. You and Belith tried everything to make the homunculi. Everything but this."

Mother wept. Her sobs grew softer and trailed away. Beylie, stroked the back of her bowed head, hugged her and offered words of comfort. "This will work, Mother. You'll see." A black flood flowed across the soft loam. It slowed and pooled at the rose canes. Mother pitched sideways, eyes wide, mouth slack and silent.

"Mother? Get up, Mother," the boy urged, shaking her shoulder. The warmth of her flesh was fading. Beylie's lower lip trembled as he understood what he had done.

He waited in the darkness, frightened and alone, for some sign that would tell him what to do next. As rose-colored light filled the sky, Beylie saw the remains of his sister, a bloody homunculus herself, and the rigid gray body of his mother. The loose earth was stained a dirty crimson. But there was something else: Fat buds had formed on the vines and thorny shrubs. They swelled and pulsed before his eyes.

Beylie wiped away his tears and went to work. He unlocked the shed and surveyed Mother's many knives and tools. He couldn't bear the thought of treating Mother's or Sister's remains the way the golden man's had been. But the flowers had already greened so swiftly, he reasoned the gruesome process was probably not necessary. He grabbed a shovel instead and buried the bodies in the loose soil.

He drew water and scrubbed himself clean. He returned the shovel and the shed and did a survey of the tools Mother kept there. Hidden in a chest, Beylie found her scrying mirror, two books written in Mother's hand, curiously etched bottles, and a long knife with golden figures adorning hilt and blade. He put these items in a sack and took them to the house.

As he gnawed on a crust of bread, Beylie wrote the previous day's events in Book VII. He hoped Belith would visit soon and would appreciate what he had done. *He said I have good instincts.* He imagined looking into Mother's scrying mirror and seeing a father's pride in his son's accomplishments. But first, Beylie needed rest. He took to his bed and slept until late afternoon.

He took his supper and Mother's private books out to the flower beds. As he read, he stole glances at the vining trumpets and thorny canes. Buds burst into bloom and broadened before his eyes. *Wait until Belith sees.*

Mother's illustrations were a revelation. She'd drawn a terrifying creature who was Belith but not Belith: taller, with feline ears, a long, narrow face and clawed feet. He held seedlings in his cupped hands. They shriveled under the gaze of his golden lynx eyes. She wrote descriptions of the harms and benefices this being could bestow. She professed intense love, her longing during his frequent absences. But she also feared him. It seemed Beylie's father was not a man at all, and his displeasure was something to dread.

The second book was catalog of implements and spells Mother created to protect herself and her son from Beylie's demon sire. The volume ended with her final words: "Belith does not value my wisdom, handed down from my mother's mother. He is arrogant and ignorant and is teaching Beylie to be the same."

He wished Mother could see *he* was doing the teaching now. He pulled the scrying mirror out of his pack and examined his reflection in the polished black surface. A year had passed since he'd reached the Age of Reason, but it was not a child who met his gaze. The face was longer, narrower, and the eyes had lost their innocence. The mirror showed him standing before Belith, and the son in the image reached his father's chin.

He closed his eyes and whispered a question, as he had seen Mother do. Beylie opened his eyes and, horrified by what he saw, dropped the mirror to the ground. At the boy's feet, the images in the mirror swirled, playing out a drama in which the terrifying Belith of Mother's book loomed tall as a tree and seized Beylie with huge clawed hands. The fingers wrapped around the boy's neck and pulled him toward a mouth full of savage fangs, as if Belith meant to tear his own child in two.

Beylie scooped everything back into the bag and stowed it in the shed. He returned to the flowers, which had sprouted heads. Suddenly, he was seized by his hair, hoisted off the ground. and thrown face first to the ground. Belith's heavy black boot prodded the child's ribs until Beylie turned on his side and gazed up into his father's eyes.

The demon's face darkened to the color of mahogany. He spoke through clenched teeth. "What did you do? Your mother...your sister... Why?"

Beylie shrank from his father's wrath and pointed to what he could see happening behind them. Even as the demon raged, the budding heads, as if given a cue, began to harmonize. Belith turned at the sound and his jaw dropped in astonishment.

Fuzzy yellow faces popped out of the center of each blossom. Clay-colored hair cascaded, lush and loose, around shiny black eyes that beamed at Beylie with loving recognition. Slender arms with lovely, tapering fingers reached for the boy. Tears streamed down his face. He did not know how to put what he felt into words, but he believed Mother understood what he had done, and every smiling womenkin was her blessing on his efforts.

Belith was speechless. He would not look at his son, even as they stood side-by-side and watched the homunculi grow. Within the hour, the entire upper half of their little bodies protruded from the blossoms. Clay-colored hair fell in waves over their rosy breasts. By late afternoon, lithe and sinuous bodies curled and twisted on yellowing sepals. Then they dropped, soft and plump as ripe peaches, onto the tilled earth. The tiny creatures babbled happily as they surged forward.

"See?" said Beylie. "They're waiting for you to tell them what you want."

But the homunculi paid no attention to Belith. They crowded around the boy's legs, raising their arms to him.

"It seems they are your daughters," Father said. His face was unreadable, but Beylie could feel anger radiating from the demon.

"Tell them what they should do," said Beylie.

Belith took one step forward, planting his heavy black boot in front of the homunculi. The womenkin backed away, baring sharp green teeth and hissing like angry cats. His eyes were rimmed with tears as he gazed at the diminutive faces, all in the colors of spring but otherwise so familiar. He swallowed and said hoarsely, "No, they are waiting for you to instruct them."

"Then let's lead them to the village, and they will bring all men to you."

Belith's eyebrows arched. He took a breath, hooded the anger in his eyes, and showed the way into the woods. The creatures followed, screeching in agitation, and grabbing at Beylie's breeches.

"Newborns are always hungry," Belith said.

Beylie nodded, thought a moment, then rolled over a rotten log. His little brood gathered around, black eyes glittering as the boy scooped up pill bugs, earthworms and grubs, then tossed them to the homunculi. They squealed and fought each other, stuffing their toothsome mouths with crawling things. Two of the homunculi, scratched and bleeding profusely, were torn to pieces and devoured. The motherkins turned their faces to Beylie and screamed for more.

He found two snared rabbits, carved them into bits, then tossed them to the creatures. Finally sated, the dwarflings flopped to earth, and curled up to nap. Beylie clapped his hands and shouted, "No sleep yet. Up! Up!"

The creatures snarled, but they obeyed. Beylie pointed to his father. "You must bring all men to him. You must make them hurt and make them cry until they turn away from all but Belith. You can take whatever you wish while you do so. And when you are done, you can rest."

The creatures grinned, displaying more honed teeth than Beylie thought any mouth should hold. They squealed like sows and streaked through the great mossy trees.

"Are they going the right way?" asked Beylie.

"That way is Salem Village," Belith replied.

Father and son followed. The horrified cries of the villagers reached them before the neat fields and houses came into view. The light was failing, but the sky was bright as one house burned, its wailing inhabitants barricaded inside. A field of early grain blazed and quickly blackened. A woman cried, "Where's the babe? Where is my child?" while an infant floated magically above the darkened road. As it passed, Beylie spied sixteen little legs working in unison under the body, bearing the squalling prize into the cover of the forest.

Terror and suffering were everywhere, yet no one called on Belith. They invoked every name they had for their god. Beylie looked to his father for an answer.

"Such things require patience," Belith explained. "First they will call on their god. When he does not answer, they will curse him and turn on each other. Then they will curse themselves when they realize what they have done. That is when they will look to me."

The words were scarcely out of his mouth, when several womenkin ran back to the pair. They gathered in front of Beylie, holding up prizes for his inspection and praise: tufts of hair, bloody lumps of flesh, a human tooth.

It seemed too much for Belith. His eyes blazed with fury. Beylie bolted for the dark woods and ran for home with a speed he did not know he possessed. He locked himself in the shed, lit a candle with flint and blade, and prepared to face his father's wrath.

The demon was not far behind. He tore the locked door off its hinges. His head broke through the roof as he closed a great clawed hand around his son's throat and lifted him off the ground.

Beylie gasped as black clouds scudded across his eyes. He fumbled in his trousers for Mother's incised blade and thrust it into one great glowing cat's eye.

The inky haze cleared as Beylie fell to the floor. Impaled up to the hilt of the knife he gripped was a struggling shadow with his father's twisted, shrunken face.

The boy retrieved Mother's Book of Belith and found the marked page with the spell for snaring demons. The wounded spirit writhed and shrieked with each chanted syllable, shrinking in on itself until Beylie could fold it into a small square and stuff it in a bottle etched with runes. The vessel rattled as Beylie clamped it shut and sealed the clasp with candle wax.

He dug a pit in the foul midden behind the farm and buried what was left of his father. He made a tonic for his raspy throat and a salve for his wounds. Then he slept for days.

*　　*　　*

Beylie spent weeks alone in a fog of sickness and grief, ignoring all but the most necessary tasks. He wanted his parents back. He missed his motherkins, too, and decided at last to search for them. He returned to the village where blight lay on all the fields. It was June, but there were no calves, no kids, no lambs. New graves clustered behind the houses. He overheard talk of matriarchs hauled away in chains, condemned for doing the devil's work. As he surveyed the damage, there arose a din of clattering pots and breaking crockery. Villagers fled their homes, screaming, as growling sprites latched on to their fingers and ears.

The people beat their own bodies until the homunculi dropped into the road. Beylie's eyes blurred with tears as he watched the villagers crush his offspring with staves and stones. The survivors ran for the woods on oddly stilted legs. They smelled Beylie and, with desperate little croaks, made their way to him.

His creatures were grotesquely withered, with filthy gray hair and sagging breasts. They stretched their arms to him, then collapsed at his feet and died. It never occurred to him that his precious fruit would fade and perish like everything else in the garden. He was now all alone in the world.

The villagers raised anew their laments and supplications, calling out of series of ungodly names. Last of all, they implored, "Belith! Belith, come."

Beylie felt a glorious surge of hope. They were calling *his* name. He was forsaken no longer.

His demon fruit had brought all men to him.

Sunsets
by Victoria Dalpe

There was something wrong with her.

Something was wrong on the inside, small and strange enough that even the doctors couldn't find it. Therapists couldn't find it. Priests and shamans couldn't find it. It was so small acupuncturists couldn't spear it with their needles. Hot baths. Long walks. Deep breaths. Mantras. Good diet, exercise, eight hours of sleep. Vitamins. All of it, every fad, every discipline... She travelled, made friends, tried new things, had lots of sex, had no sex, had a little sex. She'd been in love. So many times. She'd sampled as many cultures as she could—the people, the food, the art.

She learned languages, learned trades, learned to coax seeds into plants, coax wood into buildings. She made art, drank from all the sacred springs, stared at many, many sunrises and even more sunsets. She watched celestial dances paint the sky, aurora borealis, meteor showers, eclipses, and comets. Harvests moons, wolf moons, blue moons, super moons. Blood Moons.

Still the wrongness persisted. No amount of washing lepers, holding sick babies, or working triage in war-torn regions helped. The answers weren't in the eyes of the desperate and needy, of the grateful, of the dying. No answer came in the gleaming fresh eyes of new babies.

She ruminated on all this, as she had countless times, countless lifetimes, working it over like a hard candy in her mouth. Sucking it down to nothing and coming away with as much of an answer as always. She was doing this ruminating one late afternoon in the fall, sitting at a corner café, in a smallish New England city with a glass of wine and a sliver of biscotti. The sky was a hot frenzy of apricot and pink, and the bare branches were scraggy black outlines against the backdrop of color. Crisp air smelt of wood smoke, of things dying and drying out.

She was comfortable in a sweater and scarf. The scarf was fine cashmere one that she'd picked up in her travels. Probably Scotland. The sweater, a chunky knit cardigan, had suede elbow patches and wrapped leather buttons. The kind of sweater for professors and retired grandfathers to wear. She sipped her wine, she watched the sunset, and she tried to ignore the persistent wrongness just under her skin.

"Excuse me?"

She turned to see who was speaking. "Yes?"

The man stood beside her. He was tall but slouched, as if shy and trying to make himself smaller. Handsome in a bland way: short brown hair, square jaw, blue eyes. "I wondered if it would be all right if I sat here? It's the only empty seat, and it's so lovely out."

She glanced around at the few other metal bistro sets that hugged the café's sidewalk. The man was right; the others were all full, though she hadn't the faintest idea when any of the people had sat down or if they'd always been there. She'd thought she was alone.

She shrugged and moved her wine and cookie closer, gesturing "all yours" at the spindly chair opposite. He smiled, and his smile was nice. It brightened his whole face, making him look young, boyish even, and oh so hopeful.

He sat and pulled out a notebook and pen. The old Moleskin journal was ratty and well used. He looked up at the sky, smiling. "What a pretty sky. A lot of people complain about fall, on account of it being so close to winter. But I like it. It's so dramatic, don't you think?" He turned that dreamy smile on her, but it disappeared when he took in her blank face. "I'm sorry. Just realized how rude I was being, sitting at your table, bothering you—"

She shook her head. "You aren't bothering me."

"You're sure? You can tell me to clear out anytime you change your mind then."

"Thank you, though I doubt I will need to. You seem harmless enough. Happy, even. Genuinely so."

He scoffed and looked away. He was so wholesome; she was charmed, despite herself. He was like a freshly buffed apple, plucked right off the branch. "I don't know about all that. I guess I'm a happy guy."

"Got everything you want and need?" she asked, not mocking, but just on this side of it.

"As much as you can I suppose. Nice sunset, nice cup of coffee. Someone to share it with... That's always good. And one of my short stories is getting published."

"So, are you a writer then?" She drank some of her wine and wiped at the smudge of lipstick left on the glass.

"An *aspiring* writer. I work as a clerk at a small law office by day, but I'd love to be an author. I know everyone harbors that fantasy, so it's really awesome that my story got picked up."

She raised her glass. "Well then, this is a celebration. Congrats."

He raised his mug; they clinked. "I'm Billy, by the way."

"Billy?"

He rolled his eyes at her. "William Thomas Blythe, the fourth. My dad is Will; my grandad is Bill. And I am Billy. Blame Waspy families with no imagination."

"I'm Fell."

"Fell? That's an interesting name."

"Short for Felicia. But no one calls me that. I never took to it."

"Well, Fell, it's nice to meet you."

"Likewise."

They sat in silence, drinking their drinks, watching the sky darken and the street lights flicker on. As the sun dipped down, the temperature dropped fast. Fell wrapped her arms around herself. She fought the wrongness, but only half-heartedly. "What is your plan for the evening Billy?"

"Not much, go home, clean up the apartment...watch TV. Why?"

"Want to come over my place? I live just down the way. A few blocks. We could continue having a nice conversation. Order in a pizza or something."

"I'd like that a lot." His smile was ear to ear.

*　　*　　*

He was panting beside her, body slick with sweat, one long arm thrown up over his head. "Wow, I mean, Wow. That was something else."

She smiled and curled up into his armpit, kittenish, wrapping an arm around his trunk. She liked the way he smelled, the fading deodorant mixing with his natural musk. She liked the thump of his heart and the sound of his breathing with her ear to his ribs. "Yeah, that was nice. You still want a pizza?"

"That would be awesome. This day is just getting better and better."

Naked, she left the bed and the room to use the phone. Her house wasn't large, but it was fine. Fine furnishings, fine fixtures, everything meticulous, well crafted, tasteful. Curated. The entire world could be found in her small bungalow. Drums and sound makers, vases and traditional blankets. Bowls for ritual perched on shelves next to priceless artifacts. Always looking, always searching.

She caught her reflection in the sliding door to the enclosed back garden and didn't immediately recognize herself. Ten-foot walls surrounded her little house. The ivy covered them a foot deep, creating a soft, sound-proofed fortress in the middle of the little city.

She ordered the pizza, poured wine into two glasses, and slid on a kimono.

"You have so many interesting things," Billy said. He was standing in boxers holding a small wooden figurine.

"I've travelled extensively."

"For work?"

She shrugged, handed him a glass, and eased back on the large leather sectional sofa which took up a large portion of the open room. "Sort of."

He raised an eyebrow. "You are very mysterious, Fell. You've told me so little about yourself."

"I'm hard to know."

He rolled his eyes.

"Fine, I *choose* to be hard to know."

"Why?"

She looked up at the ceiling, at the skylight that reflected them. Billy sat beside her on the couch. Not close enough to crowd. "I don't like people to get too close. They never like what they find."

He crossed his arms, face a little more serious.

"Forget I said that. Really. Let's take a step back and talk more about this story you're having published. Tell me about it and your writing process."

He put his hand up. "C'mon, Fell. You can't say something like that and leave it after bringing me back to your place. You live in this house that looks like a museum; you tell me nothing about yourself. Come on, I want to get to know you better. Please."

She looked at his Boy Scout face, lacking an ounce of malice, and it chipped away at her resolve. Which was never particularly strong. "Fine. Fine you win. But you don't get to be mad at me for what happens next. It's on you." She pointed at him, only half smiling. "I told you I am hard to know for a reason. Get the bottle and bring it here. You'll need more wine."

Billy shook his head ruefully but did as he was told and returned with the wine bottle. He topped off both their glasses, waiting for her to go on.

"I will preface by saying you will not believe anything I am going to tell you. Until you do. And when you do, there is no going back. See there is something wrong with me, inside. I'm not crazy and I'm not sick, not in the traditional ways. I'm something else entirely. See, I have no childhood; I may have never been a child. Nor am I the person you see before you. Fell is someone that I inhabit, that I have become. But she isn't me.

"I can see how you are looking at me, so let me try to elaborate further. The thing wrong is that I am not like you, not like any of you that I have found. I have no memory of ever being a child. Or having parents.

I have no first memory that I can recall. It's not amnesia, though, because I do have a very good memory going back hundreds of years.

"Yes, I said hundreds. Because I have been alive for centuries. In a body of some sort, for I have been all types. I've been murdered. Been burned at the stake even. Been trampled by horses... And I have drowned. I remember every vivid detail. But then I wake, in another body, and have to start a new life. When the body runs out, I move on. With time, I have learned how to do this by choice, so I don't have to stay in someone until they die of old age. It's hard to jump bodies, because I grow comfortable in the skin I'm in. It's like moving to a new place. It takes time to adjust.

"I've been Fell for five years now, maybe more. I like her. She's healthy, has a nice body. I want to stay in her for a while longer.

"But it's lonely, Billy. There must be others like me, others that can move bodies, but I haven't found one yet. Another immortal like myself, because I am growing quite lonely in my old age. I hate how confused I become not only by what day it is but by what *year* and by *who* I am. I don't want to die, and I am not depressed, but I am so detached. I can feel what little humanity I've ever had slipping away. I want to blame time, but I think it's more a wrongness in me.

"Because there is something else, something stranger than the body jumping and the immortality, which I can't prove to you except by showing off an extensive knowledge of history and geography that could easily be pulled up by the internet. If I have you murder me so I come back as someone else, well, that just seems an elaborate and inconvenient situation for all of us. You would be stuck with a dead body. I would have to orient to my new body and get back to you. And if it wasn't planned right, hell, I could be in Pakistan or Argentina. Or a remote region of Russia. It's happened before. Very disorienting. It's why I have learned so many languages to be honest. For fear of that happening.

"Still that's not the upsetting part; that's not the issue. The body jumping, you can take or leave that. You know, I don't even know if I was originally male or female. My internal identity has moved away from either. I am just me, in whatever body I am in. That's not it either. The thing about being me, the wrongness as I call it, is that this longevity has a price. It was never told to me. Or explained. I've never found it in a book or a cave painting. But it's why I think there must be others like me. There is a cultural ripple, all over the world.

"I need flesh and blood. During the full moon. I do realize how crazy that sounds. But I need to kill and eat a human being every month. I have no choice. It's a compulsion and an appetite...something like a werewolf, something like a vampire, something like a ghoul. There is a hunger, and I know there is something to it and my longevity. It takes me the whole day

57

and night, but I drink all the blood and I eat most of the body. Just about anything you can eat gets eaten. I then burn and bury the bones. Then I sleep for a day or two. Like a bear going to hibernate, I am puffed up and fat as a tick. I go to sleep, and I wake refreshed. A battery recharged.

"So, Billy, and thank you for being so quiet while I got this off my chest. I know it's a lot, really, I do. I know your mind is racing because you just fucked me and then I told you I am a bodiless immortal ritual cannibal. That's a lot. I get that. I want to give you the space to respond to all of this. I'd love to have a discussion and not just monologue y'know."

Billy was pale and remote. His wine glass empty. "That's, well... That's the weirdest thing I've ever heard, Fell. You want me to believe you are, like...a vampire thing."

Fell leaned forward and refilled her glass, "Yes, see, that's what I've always thought. Do you think creatures like me are what inspired vampire mythology? Though the garlic, sun, grave stuff wouldn't make sense."

She went to top off Billy's glass, but he put his hand over it. "No! No, we aren't doing this, it's too weird. No, I do not believe you Fell. I'm sorry. Ordinarily, I'm a pretty open minded out-there kind of guy. Was a big X-files fan, even, but this?" Billy stood.

Fell shrugged. "I told you, you don't need to believe me. Proving it to you would be too complicated. I just want to have the discussion. You were the one who wanted to get to know me, by the way. I was content to talk about you and your writing and all of that. We could have had a pleasant—"

The buzzer rang. "Oh, the pizza! One second." She went to the door and out the pathway to the large gate—the only way in or out of the bungalow. Once she paid, she returned with hot pizza and a smile. Billy had pulled his undershirt and pants on in that time, but his feet were bare, which she took to be a good sign.

"Be a shame for you to leave without at least letting me feed you dinner." Fell said, "Please."

They ate at the dinner table, which she set with cloth napkins and fine china. She opened more wine, knowing that Billy would need it.

"Okay, so let's say everything you told me is true..." he said after a hearty swig of his wine and a few bites of pizza.

"It is."

"Fine, let's say it's true, why are you telling me?"

Fell waved her hand, nearly sloshing her wine. "Because I'm bored and lonely! Because I would love some fresh ideas on what I am and why I am. Because after hundreds of years and killing a person a month, racking up thousands of dead bodies—at my last count it was like four thousand and eleven or something—I have never encountered anyone, *anything* like me. I don't want to be the only one."

"You think I'm like you?"

"Are you?" she asked, more hopeful then she wanted to sound.

"No. I'm sorry, I was born to Will and Harmony. I have two little brothers and don't eat anyone on the full moon."

Fell shrugged. "Yeah, I figured, but it never hurts to ask. You have any other observations?"

"I think you are really delusional and should absolutely talk to someone about all this."

"Delusional? Look at my house! Look at all my priceless things! I'm a twenty-three-year-old girl; how would I have acquired such things in that time?"

"This could be your parents' house." Billy liked that idea—it was clear—that she was just some weird girl playing a role in her parent's fancy house.

"Bah. Would you like to see the incinerator? Where I burn them once I have had my fill?" Fell smiled wide over her drink, feeling bold and a little drunk.

"Sure, why not." Bill said resolutely, likely hoping to end what he perceived as silliness once and for all.

She took him down a flight of stairs and opened a door that led to the basement. The floor sloped down into the center where there was a drainage grate. The walls were plastic lined. The air smelled of must and bleach. She watched his face shift as he looked at the space, her fantasy "delusion" becoming more dangerous, more real.

"This is the room where I kill and eat," she said matter-of-factly. "It's easy to hose down and clean after. And this..." She crossed the room and opened a door, turning the light on inside. "...is where they get incinerated. It's hospital grade, for medical waste. It was neither cheap or easy to get this installed discreetly in a private residence, let me tell you. But worth the hassle. It has made my life so much easier."

Billy followed her into the small room. It barely fit the two of them, and the massive incinerator oven with shining steel door. The air smelled of old fires. She opened it and he peered inside; the interior was heavy with char.

"They aren't completely ashes of course, but I gather what's left, pulverize it, and then bury the remains in my garden. The bone meal does wonders for my plants. Things like fillings and bone pins I dispose of in the bay, easy enough to drop them right in. Or a trash can frankly." She pointed to the old dustpan and brush hanging, and below it an old dented metal pail.

"Why tell me all this? Why put yourself in danger?"

She smiled, knowing that she was a beautiful young woman with hair the color of flax and soft eyes. She knew her smile was disarming and her small frame and dewy skin conveyed youthfulness and a human woman ideal. She knew he wanted to believe she was just over imaginative or messing with him. She knew he doubted a woman could be a killer so depraved.

"You know what tonight is?" she asked sweetly.

He swallowed, looking past her at the exit, clearly wanting to get out of the cramped room that smelled like a campfire pit the day after. "Full moon?"

She nodded, face suddenly grave.

He nodded as well, and with no warning, he pushed her backward. He was tall and strong, and the push caught her off guard. She fell back into the main room, hitting the cement hard. He leapt over her and ran to the door that opened to the stairs. He was inches from reaching the knob when she slammed her shoulder into his side, bowling him over. He stumbled but didn't fall, and she ran at him again. She was fast, faster than him. She'd been fighting a long time.

He tried to push her away, tried to use his reach to slap out. But his bigness was no match for her speed. She ducked and darted, getting in a punch to his kidney. He cried out, swung at her again. From her stomp on his instep, he fell. She scrambled onto his chest. Her open kimono revealed her body, naked and straddling him. Knees pushing into his shoulders, she pressed her elbow to his throat, She rode his thrashing body, watching the blood vessels burst in his eyes as his complexion darkened to that of an eggplant.

"I am really happy about your short story Billy, and it was really nice to have someone to talk to about this. I meant it when I said I was lonely. But I'm also starving, and I must do this. I will tell you what I have told all of my victims: If you come back to yourself in another body, please come and find me. Remember my address, 45 Starling Lane. Come find me. I really liked you Billy. I think in another life we could've had something."

When he was dead, she began the long process of devouring him. First, she stripped off her robe—it was hundred-year-old Japanese silk after all—and hung it out of harm's way. She chewed Billy open in vital areas, drinking as much blood as she could coax without a heart to push it around. She then proceeded to eat, starting like all big predators do with the soft belly and the organs. Liver and kidneys, strings of entrails. Once the major organs were devoured, she ate the meat of the buttocks, the bicep and calves. She ate the nose and eyes, the lips and tongue. The act was reminiscent of their earlier lovemaking. She remembered kissing those lips, watching that mouth smile.

When that night and day had passed, what remained of Billy was little more than hair, bones and tendon, with patches of skin at boney areas like ankles and elbows, knees and shoulders. She lifted what little was left—it was very light with the skull scooped out and the rib cage hollow—and placed him on the sheet in the incinerator.

It took several hours in the incinerator to reduce his body to mostly white and bone. A few silvery fillings. She separated the metal and scraped the rest into a bucket, which she crushed down with a sledgehammer kept in the corner for that purpose.

She carried Billy up in the sooty pail and buried him by sunset in her garden. He would help nurture all the bulbs sleeping soundly until spring. Circle of life.

That night, she bleached the basement and destroyed all of his things, smashing his cell phone and burning his clothes. She debated keeping the Moleskin notebook as a memento, as a someday artifact. Then she read through a few pages and into the flames it went.

She was sorry to say it, but he probably would have been better off staying a clerk at that law firm. Billy had had no talent—but he had tasted pretty good.

She curled up in bed and slept, the wrongness quiet for another month.

Silver Heart
by Morgan Sylvia

I first realized that I was different the day my uncle shot me.

It was September and the last of the summer heat hung thick in the air, along with the scents of fresh-cut grass and cow manure. Grandpa and Uncle Joe had come over to help with the harvest. Across the street, my brother Jimmy was navigating our old John Deere tractor through the hayfield. I was sitting on the front lawn, playing with my doll, when they called for me.

They took me behind the old red barn, shooed the cows away, and stood me on a stack of hay bales. Grandpa leaned nonchalantly against the fence and lit his pipe. The sharp tang of tobacco filled my nose.

Papa pulled one side of my skirt up to my hip. "Hold it there," he told me. "And look away."

They should have positioned me better. I looked at the barn's red wall, saw my uncle's shadow raising the gun, and immediately started screaming. A moment later, I felt two sharp stings in my right buttock. I raised my pitch, making the three of them wince.

"There," Uncle Joe said, lowering the gun. "That should do it."

My grandfather puffed on his pipe. "One more," he said. "There should be three."

"Aren't the earrings enough?" My father sounded irritated. "She's only five."

"One more," Grandpa said. "Doesn't matter if she's five or fifteen. You should know that, after Peter."

We never spoke about my oldest brother, Peter. I only knew that he had died in infancy. My father's face tightened, but he didn't argue. No one argued with Grandpa, really. Something in his eyes just stopped you. There was something feral to him.

They had to hold me in place for the next pellet, as I was fighting tooth and nail by then. I actually bit Uncle Joe, hard enough to draw blood. But it was over quickly. One more *ping*, and again, the sharp bite.

My screams rang out against a pale blue sky. The chickens fled for their coop, clucking and fussing. Even the cat ran for cover.

Grandpa spit on the ground, then turned to go back inside. "That's enough for now."

"Don't cry, Katerina." Papa straightened my dress out, mussed my hair up, and kissed the top of my head. "It's all over. That wasn't so bad, was it?" But as I watched his face, I saw his eyes fixate on something beyond me. Following his gaze, I turned and saw a white form at the tree line at the edge of the pasture.

Joe and Grandpa saw the wolf too. They stiffened, but neither of them moved. They looked at the wolf, and the wolf looked at them. Their gazes locked, as though in silent communication. Then, it turned and slipped back into the emerald shadows beyond the wood line.

Papa opened his arms for me to jump into. "Come on," he said. Tears glistened in his eyes. "How about a treat? We have a surprise for you."

He carried me into the kitchen, where Mama and Grandma sat at our old, scarred table, drinking coffee. The smell of fresh-baked bread hung in the air. I saw my parents' eyes meet, but they didn't speak. They often communicated that way, as though they didn't need words.

Mama got up wordlessly and gave me homemade cinnamon toast and ice cream with blueberries on top. I also got a silver bracelet and a new doll. Like me, mom, and Grandma, the doll had silver earrings.

After supper, they locked us in the cellar for the night, as they had once a month for as long as I could remember.

*   *   *

I passed the time dressing my new doll, reading Nancy Drew books, and playing jacks. My parents, Jimmy, and I all had our own bedrooms upstairs, but we also had tiny rooms in the basement. There were two more rooms beneath the barn, for Uncle Joe and/or Grandma and Grandpa, when they visited for what Mama called the *dreamtime*.

I understood the name. My dreams were always vivid on those nights. I slipped through moonlit ancient forests on four paws, my nose filled with the scents of moss and loam, chasing the nectar scent of prey. In those early dreams, the rest of the family ran beside me, Grandpa at the head. The white wolf was often there as well, loping along with us.

That night, I heard muffled voices coming from Jimmy's room, which was next to mine. Realizing what it was, I immediately knocked on the wall.

A moment later, I heard his whisper. "What?"

"You have a radio in there!"

"So?"

"Turn it up! I want to hear, too."

"What's it worth to you?"

I thought hard. "Fifty cents?"

Silence.

"Okay, okay. Fifty cents and a pack of gum."

That was apparently sufficient. He put the radio against the wall between our rooms and turned it up. I fell asleep listening to Elvis singing about hound dogs.

That night, I had the fire dream. I was lashed to a pyre before an ancient cathedral. Searing flames turned my blood and bone to ash. My screams turned to howls and rose to the sky on greasy black smoke.

I woke screaming with the scent of charred flesh in my nose.

In the morning, Mama made us a huge breakfast, as she did after every dreamtime. Our table was piled with food: flapjacks, bacon, ham, sausage, toast, muffins, fruit, and cheese from our own cows. Papa, Joe, and Grandpa talked farm business over coffee, while Jimmy listened silently. The sound of church bells carried to us from town, but we didn't join the silent throngs passing through the old doors.

That place isn't for us, Papa always said. *The forest is our church.*

I grew up silent and shy, with silver in my flesh.

*   *   *

The thing about *normal* is that it isn't the same for everyone. The *normal* in our tiny mill town was hard work, hard seasons, and, for some, hard liquor. Mama always said that we were dirt poor but land rich. She wasn't wrong. Our farmhouse and barn may have been old and crumbling, but they sat tucked into a beautiful fertile valley, surrounded by blue-grey mountains and streams that tasted of ice even in August.

My *normal,* as I grew taller and the lines in the kitchen where Mama marked my height climbed up the wall, was sledding and ice skating in winter, and gathering apples in fall. It was going to the lake with Jimmy and our friends in summer, and grilling sizzling burgers in the backyard. We went to town for sock hops, Bingo, baked bean suppers, and to buy whatever the farm didn't provide. *Normal* also consisted of endless chores. These changed, depending on the time of year, from sowing to weeding to harvest to canning. Even in winter, there was always work to be done.

But it was the moon that ruled us, more than the seasons.

Our laughter waxed and waned along with the cold pearl in the sky. When the moon was dark or waning, life was ... ordinary. Boring, even. Jimmy and I were able to have friends over, to join after-school clubs, to attend dances and parties. On summer nights, we'd gather in front of huge bonfires as fireflies danced through the night fields. Sometimes Papa played his violin, while Mama sang and I played a rattle.

Things altered as the moon waxed. Our eyes changed color, becoming more yellow than green. Our body hair thickened. Our nails grew long and sharp. Our teeth even grew a bit. The colors bled from the world, and I saw things in black and white. My sense of smell grew sharper. I could pick out even the faintest traces of scents. Clover. Soured milk. The musk of deer in rut. And I could hear things much more clearly, even from a distance.

I sort of understood by then why we didn't like to see the sun go down on full moons. Why we sometimes found dead rabbits on our porch and massive paw prints in the snow.

But I thought it was normal.

Until Jimmy started to change.

* * *

There is a crack in my life, a moment that divides my memories into *before* and *after*. That moment came one sunny August morning, when I found a severed cow head in the pasture. I ran home screaming, my bare feet pounding the grass, the scents of blood and death heavy in my lungs. I remember Papa running out of the house with his shotgun. He thought something was chasing me.

"Go on in," he said, after I'd told him what I'd found. His eyes were fixed on the field, and I could see the tension in him. His scent changed, as it did when he was angry or upset. I wanted to ask questions, but I knew better than to push him when he had that intense look on his face. So I dutifully went inside and told Mama. She sat me down with paper dolls and a plate of cucumbers and sour cream.

Sometime later, the door creaked open, and Papa stepped in. "Wasn't ours," he said darkly. "Probably one of the Jones' steers." He put the rifle back on its rack. "Where's Jimmy?"

Mama frowned. "I thought he was with you."

I saw the look pass between them. I knew what they were thinking. There was something going on with Jimmy. Over the last few months, he had withdrawn, becoming sullen and angry. He isolated himself, spending most of his free time in the hayloft. He still played sports with his friends, still did his chores, still ate supper with us. But his temper grew short and his eyes darkened. He raged at me for spilling grain. One time, he almost slapped me for accidentally dropping a bowl of potato soup into his lap.

Maybe that one was normal. The soup was pretty hot.

Jimmy's smell changed, becoming more musky. His eyes grew pale and wild, and began to reflect light. Dogs slunk away from him, and the cows, sheep, and horses grew unsettled when he was around. He quit school and went to work in the mill.

I heard Mama and Papa arguing about him one night.

"Something's not right," Mama said. I heard the tension in her voice.

"Puberty," Papa said. 'He's just sowing his oats. He's too young for the change."

"No," Mama insisted. "He slipped out again last night."

Papa sighed. "He was probably visiting Linda Ferris again. He's sweet on her."

I was in the other room, but I could hear them clear as day. I went to the door and stood there quietly until they looked at me.

"What change?" I asked.

"Go to your room," Papa snapped.

Soon after that, Jimmy and Papa had a terrible fight. When it was over, Jimmy retreated to the hayloft. Papa put his jacket on and went into town. He came back reeking of smoke and pretzels and whiskey.

The legends that hang around us are pieces of a puzzle. They say there's a grain of truth behind every myth, and that certainly applies to us. I cannot tell you our irrefutable truths: I do not know them. But I know more than I did.

Back then, I really only knew the dreams.

*   *   *

Grandpa and Uncle Joe showed up the next day, and we all went to see *The Werewolf* in the theater. After the movie, we had spaghetti and meatballs at Franco's Italian Restaurant. Anger radiated off Jimmy like heat from a fireplace. We all felt it. We barely spoke a word at supper. The smell of garlic was overpowering. I only picked at my food.

"It isn't only the moon," Papa said on the way home, breaking a thick silence. Our old Cadillac easily fit all of us. "It gets stronger at that time, just like the tides. They don't have things right. But that's okay."

"Better that way," Grandpa said. "Still trying to start rumors that we can't bear to drink free whiskey."

The joke fell flat. We were silent for the rest of the ride.

Jimmy fought when they put him in the cellar that month. Later, I heard the lock rattling. I guess they hadn't counted on him picking it. I heard his footsteps change as he walked down the hall. Something on four paws passed my door.

In my dreams, I ran beside him. We took a moose down as the first snow fell through the sky. As its star-filled eyes went still and the soft bleats faded away, the white wolf approached. Steaming organs popped between my teeth, and the sweet wine of blood filled my throat. Bones cracked in my jaws with a satisfying crunch. Ravens watched from the trees, awaiting their turn.

At the edge of the glade, an old woman with yellow eyes and long, ratty hair watched us. My hackles raised when I saw her. She held something out to me: a wolfskin. Its color matched my own fur.

The sound of a scream woke me. I looked out the tiny window, and saw a silhouette on the hill. It was Jimmy, wailing at the moon.

*   *   *

The next morning, Farmer Jones from down the road knocked on our door. This wasn't exactly normal, but it wasn't abnormal, either. Although we kept apart from the townsfolk, we didn't isolate ourselves enough to draw suspicion. We helped with his harvest, and he helped with ours. That was just what people did back then.

Papa popped open a few bottles of Schlitz, and they sat down at the table.

"Wolf got a few of my sheep last night," Jones said. "Tore their throats out. I shot the damn thing, but just got it in the shoulder. We need to finish it off. Wanted to see if you can get your dad and Joe down here."

Jimmy. I knew immediately. My blood ran cold.

"The woods filled with howls," Jones said. "It was on every side of me. Never heard nothing like it. We got ourselves a wolf problem."

Papa swallowed. His voice was tight, his face drawn and harsh. "Maybe not. Might have only been him and his mate. They change their voices to confuse their prey. Make the sound go all around, so whatever they hunt feels surrounded."

I silently turned away and went upstairs. Jimmy's door was closed, but he moaned when I knocked.

He was curled up in the corner, his eyes glassy, his skin sheened with sweat. Blood soaked the left side of his shirt, from the shoulder down.

He looked up at me, and I knew from his face and his voice that his soul was broken. "I can't control it," he whispered. "Help me."

"I can't," I told him. "I'm sorry, I don't know how."

He looked away, tears spilling down his face.

As soon as Farmer Jones left, I ran back downstairs. Mama's face went white when I told her.

We always healed quick. Jimmy was up and about by the end of the week. But they started locking him in every night. He wasn't happy about it. I heard him pacing, restless.

It took him a few days to pick the new locks. When he did, he knocked softly on my door. "You can come along," he said, when I opened it.

I shook my head, terrified.

He looked at me for a moment. Then he was gone, slipping into the night.

A few minutes later, the howling began.

But the moon isn't full, I thought.

I shut the door and turned the radio up.

*   *   *

I woke in the middle of the night to a clamor. There was commotion where there should have been silence. Headlights in the yard. Pounding on the door. Angry voices.

I dressed and slipped downstairs. A few of our neighbors were leaving. Mama sat at the table, her eyes red and rimmed.

"What happened?"

"They found Linda Ferris in the woods," Mama said quietly. "Her body was mutilated."

Papa came down the stairs, buttoning his plaid shirt. "His room is empty."

He started pulling their wedding silver from the hutch.

Mama started weeping. "No." She grabbed his arm. "No. I can't bear it. My baby boy!"

Papa shook her off. "I have until sunrise. Keep the lights on."

Then he picked up the shotgun and walked out. Later, I found out that he had woken up the blacksmith and had him melt their silver spoon down.

I sat at the table with Mama, drinking coffee. The ticking of the clock seemed impossibly loud. Neither of us spoke.

We both jumped when we heard the shot.

I looked up at her. "Papa found him," I said quietly.

Then Papa's anguished scream cut through the night.

Mama smiled, showing sharp white teeth. Her laugh was quiet. Bone-chilling. "Maybe not."

But it was Papa, not Jimmy, who walked in the door.

We never buried our dead. Grandpa always said it had to be fire, for us. We burned Jimmy on a pyre of spruce and rowan, with their silver spoon still in his heart. Mama planted wolfsbane there under the new moon.

After that, we never spoke his name again.

*   *   *

Our house was silent after that. All of my parents' laughter had drained from their eyes. I don't think either of them ever smiled again. Chores were left to me. Papa grew sullen and retreated into a world of whiskey and poker. We sold the livestock off. Crops withered in our fields.

Grandma passed away not long after that. She spent the dark months of her last winter under a thick down comforter in Jimmy's old room. She gave me her earrings and bracelets just before she died, holding them out to me with pale, veiny hands. "You wear these now," she said weakly. "I don't need them anymore. Never take them off."

Her watery eyes fixated on something above her. She muttered something about the sky, and never spoke again. She was gone by morning. We burned her, too, and planted poison in her ashes.

That summer, six children went missing from the town Grandpa lived in. But when we went to check on him, we found his cabin empty, his furniture covered in dust. Six silver pellets and a book sat on his table, along with a locked chest.

We never saw him again.

*   *   *

As I grew, the dreams changed. I often dreamt of being hunted, being burned, being dragged into dark cells where cold black shadows absorbed my screams.

I was changing, too. My growing flesh seemed to shift at times, and I felt the pull of something inside me. It wasn't exactly painful, but it was uncomfortable, like when your clothes are too tight or you're too full or you're stiff from sitting in the same position too long.

My parents ignored my questions, so I sought answers in books. At least, until the day Mama found them and burned them. She faced me with fury in her eyes as she tossed them all into the fireplace. "This is trash," she said. "You're filling your head with lies."

"Then tell me! Why did Uncle Joe shoot me? *Why do I have to wear these earrings and bracelets?*"

I'd never shouted at her before. She froze. And then she, for once, gave me an honest answer. "Silver stops the change. Sometimes."

"You don't change," I said. "But Jimmy did."

She stood up, and lifted her gown. Her thighs were covered in small red scars. I can't imagine how much silver she must have had in her.

"The doctors are always confused about my weight," she said, with a smile that never reached her haunted eyes. "There wasn't enough silver in me when your brother, Peter, grew in my womb. After he was born, when I had shifted back, I had your father shoot me every time I bled."

I knew that Peter's birth had been really hard on her, but this was horrifying. Tears stung my eyes. My rage flickered and died.

"Who are we?" I asked quietly. "*What* are we?"

But she would say no more.

*   *   *

By sixteen, I'd had enough of being locked in the cellar every month. I'd had enough of the silent anger, the isolation. I thought about breaking out or making a copy of the key, but in the end, I chose an easier option. When the moon rose, I just didn't go home. My friend Anne and I went to the carnival with some friends. I stayed over at her place. I knew I'd be in trouble, but I didn't care.

The carnival was overwhelming, a whirlwind of colors and sounds. The scents overpowered me, and the lights and streams of people flowing through pathways hung with colored lights made my head hurt. But I loved it. At one point, I looked up at the sky, and found myself mesmerized.

"What?" Danny asked.

"The moon," I said. "It's so big and yellow!"

He gave me a strange look, then laughed. "You do say the oddest things. You'd think you've never seen the moon before. That's what they call a blue moon."

I was completely confused. "But it's yellow."

"Blue moons aren't blue: it's what happens when you get two full ones in a month. Come on. Let's get some cotton candy and then ride the Ferris wheel again."

Danny won me a stuffed penguin. After that, we went into the house of mirrors. It smelled of popcorn and stale perfume. I stared at my reflection, wondering what I was truly looking at. Wondering if the blue/yellow moon would rip my flesh apart.

But the teenager staring back at me never changed.

The night was a blur of music, food, and laughter. My senses were overloaded, but I didn't care. I'd planned to go home early, but the next morning, a bunch of us decided to go to the lake instead. Danny gave me my first kiss that day.

When I got home that night, every light in the house was on, even the barn lights. Mama was sitting at the table, holding the shotgun, her face smeared with blood. Papa was lying in a pool of blood on the kitchen floor, his lifeless eyes staring up at the ceiling. There was a hole in his chest where his heart used to beat. His silver jewelry sat on the scarred table, beside a half-eaten piece of steak.

The rest of that night is a blur. I remember screaming and sobbing, and shaking Mama, asking her the same question over and over. *Why, Mama, why?* She never answered. She didn't even acknowledge me, but just sat there, murmuring about blood and silver. But I knew even then what had happened. The call of moon and forest had got too strong for Papa.

My voice and my sorrow floated over the pines, toward the silver orb that had stolen the sunlight from my life. My song was not the cheerful song Papa played on his violin. It was not the beautiful shining notes the white wolf sometimes wove through wind and moonlight. It was the keening of something wild, something cursed.

Dawn cast gold and silver pools onto the blood and gore. It was sheer chance that one of the neighbors stopped in, wanting to borrow one of Papa's tools. Then came the howling, shrieking sirens; the men with questions; the pale-faced neighbors huddled at the gate, their eyes a mixture of horror and pity. Danny stood among them. I refused to talk to him.

Mama didn't resist when they put her in the wagon and drove her off. I remember calling Uncle Joe, hysterical, and insisting that Papa's body be burned. He said he was on his way, but I didn't wait. As soon as the police left, I packed a bag, and then walked into town and joined the carnival.

*   *   *

Years and seasons passed in a blur. Like my ancestors, I released the idea of home. My world became the caravan, and the ever-changing scenery outside the windows of the little trailer I shared with three other girls. I loaded myself with silver and played the roles of the fortuneteller, the magician's assistant, the contortionist. My life was the midway, with its bustle of people, its vivid colors, upbeat music, and overpowering scents. I enjoyed the noise, the chaos, even the food. It was the silent times that I hated. That was when the memories crept in.

Every night, I dreamt of a white wolf.

*   *   *

I swore I would never go home. And I didn't, at least until the carnival brought me there. The old scents awakened half-forgotten memories. Not the last ones, the blood and flames and screams, but earlier ones, gentler ones, of holiday meals and camping trips and days spent by silver mountain lakes.

The town had grown. My old schoolmates were raising children of their own now. I felt a lump in my throat when they spoke of their families.

I decided to see if Uncle Joe was still alive. I rented a car and drove up the winding road that led to his mountain cabin. But all I found was a burnt ruin. I drove back with tears stinging my eyes.

It all happened in seconds. I thought I saw something white in the trees and glanced over. I only took my eyes off the road for a moment.

When I looked ahead again, the old lady with yellow eyes was standing in middle of the road.

I swerved to avoid her, and the car spun out of control. There was a sudden, pounding impact, and then the stomach-churning feeling of flying through the air. The ground and sky switched places. Then everything went black.

I woke on the side of the road, my head heavy, my thoughts sluggish and muffled. The reek of blood and gasoline filled my lungs. I heard the howling of wolves. I groggily pushed myself up onto my side, and saw the old lady with yellow eyes standing over me, silhouetted in the moonlight. A pack of wolves stood around her.

The world went dark again.

*   *   *

I came to in the hospital, my leg in a cast.

"Oh," the doctor said. "The x-rays showed that you had some pellets lodged in your right buttock. Did you get shot by a pellet gun as a kid?"

I nodded, unable to speak past the lump in my throat.

He handed me three silver pellets. "A keepsake," he said, flashing a yellow smile. Beneath his slicked-back hair, his glasses flashed with reflected florescent light. "Maybe you can melt them down into a ring for your children."

I knew better, by then, than to have children.

By the time I healed, the carnival had moved on.

A week later, I stood in the empty field where I'd laughed and danced as a child. The paint on the house was peeling, the fields were overgrown, and the barn roof was caving in. I could almost hear the low bleating of our milk cows, feel their silky noses as they nudged for treats. But only ghosts and memories filled the dusty shadows.

Someone—Uncle Joe, I suppose—had planted wolfsbane around the stump where Papa used to sit and play his violin, marking the spot where his ashes lay.

I felt it before I saw it. My skin shivered into goosebumps. I turned quietly and found the white wolf at the edge of the forest.

*   *   *

With the pellets gone, the earrings were not enough by themselves to entirely prevent the change. As the moon swelled, I felt the shift in my flesh, the hot tides rising in my blood. The world turned greyer by the moment. My senses sharpened. My body hair grew thicker.

I dreamt of running through thick winter forests, chasing a shepherd's daughter. I woke with the taste of her blood in my mouth. The blood was more than juice. I read the codes in her cells, absorbed her energy. In turn, it changed me.

I remember staring at the moon and cursing it. I didn't understand the laws that governed me.

But there was one person who did.

*   *   *

The asylum was something of castle and something of nightmare, a fortress of grey stone and iron bars. Tight-faced women in white dresses guided me into a sitting area. They offered tea, but nothing else. This was not a place for niceties. Madness and despair hung in the air, along with the smells of sweat and bleach and human waste.

I timed my visit for the new moon, when Mother would be most lucid. The doctors told me that she was prone to random acts of violence. She had bitten several inmates, clearly trying to eat them. But when I insisted on speaking to her privately, they relented.

We met in a cold, sterile room with brick walls and barred windows.

Her eyes were dead. I could smell the drugs in her blood, even across the table. She ignored me when I greeted her.

We sat in silence until I slowly, deliberately, removed the earrings.

Something flickered in her. Horror rose in her eyes. "No," she said. "No, you should never do that."

"Why?"

Her voice twisted through the air like a snake. "Silver rules the psyche, the emotions, and healing. It is sunlight, transformed, as a reflection in a mirror. As above, so below."

"Tell me," I growled. "Who are we? What are we?"

She took a long time answering. "Herodotus called us Neuri," she said finally. "There are others like us. Others not like us. We have many names. Kveldulft. Lycanthrope. Volkodlak. Skinwalker. Doctors say our blood type is so rare they call it Golden. The medieval peasants said we were the Devil's children."

"Which is true?"

"All of them." Her eyes shone mad and bright. "But we aren't so different from humans. They have beasts within themselves, too. They just can't reach them."

I saw, for a moment, the ghost of the beauty she once was. *She doesn't belong here,* I thought. *She's a wild thing trapped in a cage.*

"I keep seeing an old lady with yellow eyes. Do you know who she is?"

"She was attached to your father's side. His side crossed a line of witches. There was a pact made, some centuries ago. A matter of souls and service."

I sat back, contemplating this. "What happened to Peter?"

Her voice was dry bones and dead leaves. "The last time I saw him, he was standing on the edge of our field, a rabbit in his jaws."

It was only then that I truly understood. The truth slithered over me, cold and nauseating. Mama watched my reaction impassively, her eyes dead again.

Down the hall, one of the madmen raged and screamed.

"They took the pellets out of me," I said finally.

She stared at me, her face unreadable. And then she rushed at me. Her hands wrapped around my neck. Sharp nails dug into me, drawing blood. She was remarkably strong for her size. The air was sucked from my lungs, and the world turned red and black at the edges. Orderlies rushed in to subdue her. When they pulled her back, her wild eyes had turned yellow with rage.

The asylum called a week later to tell me she was gone. She bled to death digging silver pellets out of her flesh with a stolen butter knife she'd sharpened on a cement wall.

*   *   *

Mother hadn't given me much, but it was a start. I went to the Boston library and spent days holed up in a dusty corner. I found a copy of *The Histories Of Herodotus*, from 440 BC. Herodotus did write of the Neuri, who transformed into wolves once a year. But there was nothing useful in the text. I took a stack of books back to my hotel.

By chance, I glanced at the cards in the back of the books. They'd all been checked out by the same person. Someone named Aleks Lupo.

In Italian, the word *Lupo* means Wolf.

*   *   *

Finding Aleks' address in the phone book was ridiculously easy. The hard part was getting up the nerve to walk up his steps. I sat on a park bench down the street for hours, taking in the scents and sounds of his

Cambridge neighborhood: lilac, lavender, car exhaust, the urine of tiny yapper dogs that snarled as they passed me. TVs and radios blared from open windows.

Finally, I knocked on his door, noting the wolf-shaped knocker. When he opened it, the first thing I noticed was that, like the men in our family, he had thick brows and green-gold eyes.

I held the books out. "My name is Katerina," I said. "I think you may be able to answer some questions."

He looked at the books and stiffened. His nostrils flared slightly. I breathed in his scent. Musk. Leather. Soap. His cologne contained a bit too much labdanum.

"Katerina," he said, as though tasting the word. "Katerina, Katerina."

I knew why he said my names three times. It was mentioned in several of the books I was holding.

"That doesn't work," I said. "Nor did wolfsbane, spilling three drops of my blood, voodoo spells, hiring a witch doctor, or converting to Christianity."

He lifted an eyebrow, amused. "It wouldn't," he told me. "You cannot cure genetics. It's in your blood. The only variables are when and how it awakens, and how much you can control it. Those books are incomplete, at best." He stepped back, waving me in. Silver flashed at his neck. "Come in."

He led me to a room filled with books. A stuffed owl sat atop an elaborately carved buffet. The room smelled of wood smoke, ferns (of which he had several), and old books. The scent of bacon and grilled onions wafted in from the kitchen. Paintings adorned his wall. One in particular caught my eye.

"Do you know who that is?" Aleks asked.

"King Lycaon of Arcadia." My voice was quiet. "He served human flesh to Zeus at a feast. Zeus punished him by changing him into a wolf."

His eyes changed color, ever so slightly. "Sit," he said, motioning to a Victorian loveseat. "It seems we do have things to discuss."

We talked for hours that day over coffee and pierogis. As it turned out, Aleks knew little more than I did. Like me, he had searched for answers. His parents had died in the war. But the orphanage had traced his lineage back to Bedburg, where in 1589 Peter Stump had, under torture, confessed to killing and eating dozens of people while wearing the form of a werewolf. He was executed, but some of his children escaped.

"Science says that nothing can be created or destroyed," Aleks said. "It can only change shape. Our people are able to do so, to some extent. Cells are always changing, growing and dying at once. Ours are...different. We can set our spirits free. We can inhabit animals. Our souls, slipped of the flesh, can gather mass, reflect light. We can also shift the light around ourselves. Moonlight, anyway. The sun does not shine in the spirit realm."

I hung on his every word. And then I spoke, too. Bloody memories rose through my thoughts, and truth spilled out of me. Jimmy, his wild eyes, blood on his side. The old lady with yellow eyes. Grandad's feral stare. The missing children. The devoured cattle. Linda Ferris, her pale eyes staring at the clouds. I even told him about the white wolf in the forest, the one we'd never called by his true name.

But when I tried to tell him about the night Papa died, the words stuck in my throat.

We were married that winter, as the wolf moon rose in the sky.

* * *

We honeymooned in Europe, tracing the route of our legends. Whenever we reached a new town, our hopes rose. Someone would find us, take us under their wing, bring us to our kind. We visited the festival of Lycaea, but found nothing like the secret occult ritual we'd expected. We followed myths and folk tales through thick black forests and into quiet Alpine glades. My dreams interposed themselves over these landscapes like a movie, layers lost in time.

I am dragged from my bed, the wound in my thigh as proof, and brought in chains to the dungeon, where my blood and pain ran into damp stone floors.

I am running, running, beneath the cold moon, my lungs filled with scent and song. But that time, I am the prey. Villagers spill over the field behind me, torches and screams raised to the sky. I drop the child's arm and race away. But I cannot outrun bullets.

I am a noble lady, caught in transformation. Burned at the stake.

I am dancing around a Sabbath fire, rubbing an ointment on my flesh, melting into something else.

Aleks said they were ancestral memories. He had them too, though his were different.

In the end, all we found were stories.

We came home with an unspoken question hanging between us. We never said it, but as we stared silently into our woods, I knew we were both wondering if we were the last.

* * *

We almost made it.

We were happy, for a time. Like my parents, we often communicated more by body language than words. Renovating the old farmhouse took years, but we didn't mind. The world beyond was changing fast, becoming louder, colder, and more crowded. In the summer, there was the soft feel of emerald clover beneath our feet, the ever-changing colors of the cold crystal streams. In winter, we spent long nights entwined before the fireplace as the wind screamed. In the dreamtime, our spirits traveled the forest together.

And then Aleks became restless. He had the same short temper, the same wild-eyed look that Jimmy'd had in those last days. His eyes changed from forest green to the yellow of the wheat in our fields. I knew what was happening, though I tried to deny the parallels.

He shifted just after his thirtieth birthday.

He didn't come home one night. The next morning, I found him in the forest, covered in blood, with bits of gristle between his teeth and the remains of a young deer scattered around him. Nearby, I saw old moose antlers sticking up through the leaves. I recalled the taste of its blood filling my mouth, and I had to fight the shift down.

My eyes, when I looked in the mirror after, were yellow. My teeth had sharpened into fangs. I felt the bloodlust rising inside me.

We stared into the fire that night, saying nothing.

Two months later, Carl Bowers' son went missing.

Aleks' kisses smelled of blood and gore. His belly was hard and distended. I knew whose remains he was digesting.

In the morning, I took our silver dinner bell to the smithy.

His heart was silver in the moonlight. My tears mingled with his blood as I ate it.

I burned him on a pyre of spruce and rowan, under a harvest moon.

On the next full moon, I followed the white wolf to a moonlight glade. He stopped beside an old, hollow log. Inside, I found Grandpa's chest. It contained a wolfskin, a jar of ointment, and a grimoire. The old lady stood in the shadows, her yellow eyes glittering.

When I threw my silver jewelry into the water, it shattered the moon's reflection. My brother, who had never been human, cast his head back and howled.

This time, I sang with him.

The Fetch
by E.A. Black

Julie Henderson leaned against the dining room wall at her best friend's house and stared at her scuffed sneakers. She felt so out of place she wanted to disappear into the walls. On the one hand, she didn't want to be anywhere near Linda Kelly since their falling out on Halloween, but on the other hand, she longed for Linda's companionship. Today was Linda's birthday, and Julie wanted to talk to her—to set things straight.

A pair of feet dressed in designer sneakers filled Julie's vision.

"Julie Henderson. I never thought I'd see you here," Jake Cooper said. He was the captain of the football team and Linda's boyfriend. He also hated Julie's guts.

"Linda invited me." Julie spoke in a whisper so quiet she barely heard her own voice. She wondered why Linda had bothered. They had barely spoken in months. Maybe Linda'd invited her out of pity, which made her dejection all the more profound.

"I have no idea why she would do that. She doesn't like you anymore." Jake took a step into Julie's personal space. The intimidation tactic worked.

She cowered beside him, unable to get away. "Yes, she does. You're just being mean. Now go away." She couldn't even look him in the eye.

He towered over her, clear in his intention to mock and bully her. "Why don't you go home? No one here wants to talk to you," Jake said. "Linda told me what you did to her. Stay away from her."

"Leave me alone." She stuck her index finger in her mouth and chewed at the nail until she drew blood. Tears welled in her eyes.

"You still chew your nails. You have ugly hands. You're ugly. Now go away. Linda doesn't want to see you, and neither do I," Jake said.

He was right. No one wanted her here. Her hand-me-down clothes hung loosely on her body, and they were a year or more out of date. She had no friends. The kids said she smelled, and they refused to sit with her at lunch. If she approached a table, everyone got up and left. Jake called her "trailer trash" so often the other kids took up the nickname. Linda even took to calling her a loser now that she was one of the cool kids. Julie couldn't understand why everyone picked on her. She hadn't done anything except exist. The longer she thought about it, the more she wanted to rid herself of her misery once and for all.

If only Linda would be her friend once again... But she knew those days were finished. Gone were the days of braiding hair and talking Disney movies. Definitely gone were the embraces and kisses that walked the line of friendship...

Linda had turned on her shortly after that one kiss, the one Julie had been wanting to give Linda for over a year. She'd revealed far too much of herself, and instead of welcoming Julie's affection and love, Linda had recoiled in revulsion.

"You have cuts on your arms. What's that all about?" Jake asked.

Horrified, Julie pulled her sleeves over her wrists. She had taken to cutting herself a month ago, when the ridicule became especially bad. She'd been nominated for Winter Ball Princess as a joke. Her face burned with shame as all the kids in class laughed at her. Cutting released all the rancid emotions welling up inside her.

"It's nothing. I cut myself chopping onions," she said. Last night, she'd cut herself so deeply she'd nearly needed stitches. Her parents didn't understand why she abused herself, and the therapist she saw feared she'd cut so deeply there would be no coming back. Julie wasn't sure that was a bad thing. She wanted relief from her misery. If only the pain would stop.

"The hell you did," Jake said. "You trying to kill yourself? You can't even do that right."

Julie didn't answer. She couldn't do anything right, even suicide.

"Jake, I'm thirsty. Could you get me a soda?" Linda called from the living room. Jake walked away, much to Julie's relief.

Julie's heart lurched at the sweet sound of her best friend's voice. She remembered how they'd paint each other's toenails and sing along with David Cassidy. They'd shared malted milkshakes at the mall. Linda once had bought her a pretty blue barrette for her hair. Julie cherished it the way other girls cherished an engagement ring. She wore it in her hair today, but now that Linda used pom poms and dated Jake the Football Captain, she was afraid Linda wouldn't even notice. Julie couldn't compete. He was tall, handsome, and very popular. She, on the other hand, could barely string two sentences together whenever anyone attempted to talk to her, and her face had broken out again.

Linda was so busy draping herself all over Jake that Julie feared she'd never get a chance to be alone with her. This was her last chance. What could she do to bring Linda back to her? She ran her fingers through her frizzy hair and found some knots. She headed upstairs to Linda's bedroom. She'd use the bathroom just outside Linda's room to tidy up.

Gone were the David Cassidy posters and the velvet horoscope Linda had once had pinned over her bed. When did Linda stop liking *The Partridge Family*? They had watched every show together. The Tarot cards and Ouija board were nowhere to be seen, and a varsity jacket that was a size too big for Linda draped across her bed.

Linda didn't even watch sports before she started seeing Jake. Julie hated his sneer whenever he looked at her. He stank of weed he smoked in between classes. He took all of Linda's time and energy. There was none left for Julie. At least she was smarter than he was, not that it mattered since the school let his grades slide as the football team captain. She, on the other hand, had collected a string of Fs after years of being a straight A student. She didn't care about her grades anymore. She didn't care much about anything except for Linda.

Instead of Madam Alexander dolls displayed on her bed and board games in the corner, Julie saw ticket stubs for high school football games, gold and green cheerleader pom poms, and a skimpy cheerleader's outfit hanging from the bathroom door.

Who is *this girl?* Julie felt like she was looking at the bedroom of a stranger.

Photos of Linda and Jake filled frames that had once housed their friendship. Julie didn't even see any pictures of her and Linda at the Abba concert they went to only a year ago. Julie's middle school ring on a chain hung from Linda's mirror—a forgotten relic of the past. Linda *wore* Jake's ring.

Tears rolled down Julie's cheeks. *Why am I even here?* she asked herself, then answered, *Because I'm not giving up yet. Not without a fight.*

"What are you doing in here?" Jake walked into Linda's bedroom and tried to grab Julie's sleeve.

Julie moved out of his reach. "Linda's my best friend. I can do whatever I want."

"No, you can't. Not anymore. She doesn't like you." While Jake wanted her out of the room, he blocked her way. She'd have to push past him to get out the door. Instead, she trembled in front of him like a mouse in front of a snake.

"You lie." Her heart ached with grief. Did Linda really hate her?

"I saw what Linda's room was like," Jake said. "Stupid stuff like that Ouija board, incense, and boy band posters. I know you two used to hold séances. How dumb is that? She grew up. You need to grow up, too."

"I'm growing up just fine, and I don't think she'd like that you called her interests stupid." *He's saying my interests are stupid. Maybe they are. I don't care much about them anymore.* She cocked her head and looked Jake in the eye. "If Linda doesn't want me in her room, why doesn't she tell me herself?"

Jake stared her down and jabbed a finger at her face. "You get out of here before I tell her."

"I'm her best friend. She won't mind me being here."

"We'll see about that." Jake turned and walked out before Julie could respond.

Unable to resist, Julie opened a dresser drawer and peered inside. Lacy silk panties and sports bras sat in a neat pile. Linda used to wear cotton panties with the days of the week printed on them. Julie supposed Linda could have outgrown them, but why all the fancy clothing? A second drawer revealed short skirts. Pencil-thin jeans filled another. At one time, she would have shared her clothes with Julie; Julie couldn't imagine wearing a pair of tight jeans.

Did she have anything in common with Linda anymore? How could they have drifted so far apart?

Julie knew why.

*　*　*

Four months earlier, on Halloween, Julie sat with Linda in Linda's basement. Midnight would strike soon. Who could they call forth on this special night?

Julie lit the black pillar candle in the center of the table. It cast a soft glow around the room.

"Why are we using a black candle?" Linda asked.

"It's for protection. Banishing any evil spirits that might try to interfere with our séance," Julie said. "I've also lit white candles on the end tables for cleansing and purifying. Those candles drive away any negative energy."

"I'm not sure I like this," Linda said.

"It'll be fine. Those kinds of candles are standard. They're a 'just in case' measure." Julie took Linda by the hand. Her heart fluttered at the feel of Linda's soft skin. She would welcome any excuse to touch Linda. "There's nothing to be afraid of. We might not even reach anyone."

"I don't know…" Linda said.

"How about we start with the Ouija board? You like to play with that," Julie said.

The girls sat across from each other with the Ouija board on their knees. Julie was about to close her eyes and ask a question when the overhead light came on.

"Hey, turn that off!" Linda yelled.

"No shouting, young lady," Linda's grandmother walked down the steps. "Where do you keep the sodas?"

"In a box by the bathroom door," Linda said. "Let me get it."

"No bother. You keep playing," Her grandmother frowned when she saw the Ouija board and lit candles. "What are you girls doing?"

"We're just playing, Gran," Linda said.

"Those things are dangerous," Gran said.

"Ouija boards? They're only a toy," Linda said.

Julie knew better, but she kept her mouth shut.

"We're going to have a séance, too," Linda said.

"I can't stop you from doing what you want. Just be careful, " Gran said. "You have no control over what you call from the other side. There are all sorts of evil spirits you could attract even if you don't mean to. A fetch. An elemental. A demon."

Linda's Gran had long been interested in the occult. Julie listened to her when she gave advice.

"I know what demons and elementals are," Julie said. "What's a fetch?"

"Have you ever heard of a doppelgänger?" Gran asked.

"Yes. It takes the form of another person, and it's a sign of impending misfortune," Julie said.

"Really?" Linda asked. "You sure know your stuff."

Julie smiled. She was proud of her vast knowledge of creepy things.

"A fetch is similar, and much more dangerous," Gran said. "We're Irish, and a fetch is an Irish spirit. It will appear to you as someone you trust or love, and it will destroy you. They sometimes attach themselves to families. Our family has a fetch. Be careful you don't call it. Wait here one moment." Gran walked to the dresser and pulled out a stick of what looked like dried herbs, a feather, and a box of matches. "This is a sage stick. Burn it and waft the smoke around you before you begin. Use the feather to move the smoke. This is very powerful protection. Who are you planning on calling?"

"Jimi Hendrix, Janis Joplin, or Jim Morrison. Maybe Cass Elliot. We haven't decided who yet," Julie said. She wondered why Linda's gran kept a sage stick in the dresser, but she didn't want to ask. She had often smelled sage incense in the house, but didn't realize it was from a bundle of dried herbs.

"They're probably safe enough, but be careful," Gran said. She grabbed a case of cola and headed up the stairs. "Light the sage stick. It's very powerful."

Once Gran had turned off the overhead light and closed the door, Julie got back to work. She picked up the sage stick and a match. Once she lit the sage, she wandered about the room, with Linda on her heels. She felt powerful and confident as she waved the feather to spread the smoke around the basement. The pleasant smell filled the room.

"I call the spirits listening to us," Julie said. "Please make yourself known. Do us no harm and treat us with respect."

She tamped out the sage onto an abalone shell, and then sat down in a chair across from Linda. Both girls held the board on their knees.

"I have some questions," Linda said. "May I start?"

"Sure," Julie said. Her heart raced. Would she get answers she liked? Who would they call back?

"Will I find true love this year?" Linda said in a loud voice.

Julie's spirits fell. She didn't want Linda to find a boyfriend. She'd already had a steady boyfriend she'd broken up with over the summer. When Linda had a boy on her mind, she neglected Julie, which made Julie miserable. Fridays and Saturdays were no fun when Linda would ditch her to go to the movies or to the fast food joint with Len, the boy from homeroom she had liked. Julie had no other friends, so lonely weekends stretched into the summer months. Then, they'd broken up, and Linda was back in her life again. Julie wanted Linda to love her the way she doted on Len, but she couldn't see that happening anytime soon. Maybe the spirits knew something different. She hoped they had.

The planchette sat still between the girl's fingers.

"It's not working," Linda said.

"Give it a minute," Julie said.

The planchette jerked and then moved to the word "yes," much to Julie's great disappointment.

"Yay! I wonder who he is? Is he cute?" Linda asked.

The planchette circled around to "yes".

"Do I already know him?" Linda asked.

"Yes," the board indicated.

"Who is he?" Linda asked.

The planchette sat still for a moment, and then slid to the letter "J".

"J who?" Linda asked. "I hope it's Jake. I have such a crush on him."

Julie could have leapt up with joy. She had hoped the letter "J" stood for her, not Jake. Linda asked if she'd find true love, not a boyfriend. "J" could easily mean she and Julie could wind up together. With hope growing in her breast, Julie closed her eyes and smiled. *Please, please, please, let her true love be me. I need her so much. She's more to me than my best friend.*

"You can do better than him," Julie said. She brushed her fingers against the back of Linda's hand. Linda in turn squeezed Julie's hand, sending shock waves of excitement up and down Julie's arm. Could Linda ever accept her as a lover?

"I think Jake is totally cool," Linda said. "He gets more touchdowns for the team than any other player."

To Hell with Jake. "Let me try," Julie said. She opened her eyes and stared at the board. *Ask something safe first.*

"Will I get an "A" in math?" Julie asked.

The planchette moved to "no".

"Figures," Julie laughed. "How about this – will *I* find true love?"

At first the planchette did not move. Then, it slowly slid between the words "Yes" and "No."

It sat directly in front of Linda, pointing at her. The meaning couldn't have been more obvious to Julie, but it was lost to Linda. Julie had hoped the board was telling the truth and not toying with her feelings.

"I don't get it. Is that a yes or no?" Linda asked.

"I'm not sure." Julie lied. "Let me try again." She called in a loud voice. "Will I find true love?" Julie often wondered why mediums who conducted séances and used Ouija boards in the movies shouted so much. Were the spirits deaf?

Once again, the planchette circled around to point directly at Linda. Julie stared into Linda's face. The girl had no clue what the planchette was trying to say, and Julie was too chicken-hearted to explain her strong feelings to Linda.

"This is boring," Linda said. "Let's try the séance. Maybe we'll have better luck with that."

Within moments, both girls faced each other in front of the table. They held hands. She held onto Linda tightly as if never wanting to let her go.

"Ouch, you're hurting me," Linda said.

"Sorry," Julie said. Embarrassed, she loosened her grip. What would Linda say if she simply blurted out her love? Would she embrace or reject her? Julie so feared rejection she didn't respond more than saying she was sorry.

"Who do you want to call?" Julie asked.

"How about that fetch?" Linda asked. "Gran made it sound interesting. It's a family spirit, too."

"Are you sure? Those things sound dangerous," Julie said. "How about Janis Joplin instead? At least we know who she is."

"Okay." Linda sounded disappointed. "Let's try Janis Joplin." She grinned. "Then the fetch?"

Julie ignored Linda's last request. Instead, she stood up, walked to the record player, grabbed an album, and played "Piece Of My Heart." The perfect song although it was about a man and woman. Every time Joplin sang, "Break another little bit of my heart now, darling," Julie wanted to cry since it reminded her so much of the way Linda had treated her while dating Len.

"I'm calling on the spirit of Janis Joplin," Julie said. "Let the sound of your music guide you to us. If you are here, please give us a sign."

Did the temperature drop a few degrees or was Julie only nervous? Between calling a spirit and being so close to Linda, Julie couldn't have been any more thrilled.

"Janis Joplin, if you are here, give us a sign," Julie said. "Don't be afraid. We won't hurt you. We just want to talk."

Julie shivered in the cold. She could see her breath. What was going on?

"Why is it so cold in here?" Linda asked. She shifted in her seat, ready to stand up.

"Don't break the circle. Whatever is here will be trapped with us if you do that," Julie said.

"I'm getting scared. It's cold and dark down here," Linda said.

Like a grave. "Let's try a little longer. Maybe she'll show up." Julie took a deep breath. "Give us a sign. I command you."

The table jumped. Linda shrieked. Three loud bangs as if metal pounded on metal sounded from the back of the basement near where the water heater was.

No one else was in the basement except for Julie and Linda.

"Don't break the circle!" Julie said, but Linda let go of her hand anyway.

"What's that?" Linda asked.

Julie squinted to get a better look. A shadow hovered near the water heater, squatting down as if ready to charge at them.

"What is that thing?" Linda cried.

The candles blew out.

Linda screamed.

*   *   *

Why was she here at Linda's birthday party? As the school outcast, the other kids shunned her. She was always chosen last in gym class. Most of the kids ignored her, but a few caught her eye long enough to laugh at her.

She had to pee. She retreated to the bathroom and did her business. After washing and drying her hands and face, she opened the door and turned to the bathroom mirror to brush her hair. It looked like she had stuck her finger in an electrical socket. She brushed until her hair crackled with static electricity. Thunder boomed outside. Hail pounded on the roof.

Lightning streaked past the bathroom and bedroom windows. Julie continued to brush her hair. As she looked in the mirror, Linda appeared behind her.

"Sorry I came to your room. I needed to use the bathroom," Julie talked to Linda through her reflection in the mirror. She couldn't bear to look directly at her.

"Jake told me, but it's okay," Linda said.

"Remember all the fun we used to have? What happened?" Julie asked. She was so nervous asking that question her mouth dried. She craved a glass of water.

"I don't know."

"The last time we were alone together, we had a séance..." Julie let the sentence hang to see how Linda responded.

"I remember," Linda said, face hard to read. "We called back a fetch."

"We were trying for Janis," Julie said. "But you were thinking about what your gran had said. I'm still not quite sure what happened..."

Linda gave Julie a strange smile. "We called the fetch. It's an Irish spirit. Something like a doppelgänger but not quite."

Thunder boomed outside. "That's quite a storm. This would be the perfect time for a séance."

"I know," Linda said.

"Want to have one downstairs? We can get the other kids to join in." If Linda would agree to a séance with the other kids and Julie actually reached someone, maybe that would be enough to impress her classmates. With Linda's help, she could be somewhat popular. Anything was better than being the number one class dork. If she impressed Linda, they could go back to being close friends...and possibly more.

"Maybe."

"Well, let's go downstairs," Julie said.

Julie had turned, but Linda had already left the room. *How did she leave the room without me seeing her? Why didn't she wait for me?* She walked downstairs and headed to the refreshments table. Cake and ice cream had already been served, but Julie was beyond even the normal levels of nervous and depressed that had become her life. She piled cake and chips on her plate, and then shoved a chocolate covered shortbread cookie into her mouth. Sweets always soothed her depression.

* * *

Julie had never before held a séance where the candles had blown out. She ran to a table, turned on a lamp, and rushed back to Linda. Terrified, she reached for the whimpering Linda, who cowered in her chair, too afraid to flee.

"I want to stop. Let's go upstairs. What the hell was that thing?" Linda said, weeping so hard her breath came out in spurts. "I'm scared. I don't like this. It's cold, and what's that awful smell?"

"It's okay; it's okay. We're fine." The stink of sewage had floated about her, but then dissipated in the bright light of the table lamp. Was that the smell Linda was talking about? "Nothing bad is going to happen to us. Here. Let me hold you..." Julie took Linda in her arms. She rubbed Linda's back, trying to calm the girl she loved.

Linda rested her head against Julie's shoulder.

Julie could smell her herbal shampoo. She buried her face in Linda's hair as she ran her hands through the girl's tresses. She then took her big chance. This was it. It was time to make her feelings known. She kissed Linda's tears away. Then, she kissed her forehead and cheeks, and then her chin, and then finally, her lips.

"What the hell are you doing?" Linda recoiled, pulling away from Julie. "You freak. Get away from me."

"I'm sorry. Please forgive me. I thought..." Julie said.

"You thought what? That I'm gay? I'm not a freak of nature like you. I always wondered about you, but I thought it was my imagination. Get away from me. Get out. Get out of my house," Linda said. Her angry tone stabbed Julie in the heart.

Julie walked out of the basement without saying another word. Tears burned her eyes. She had taken a chance and lost. Again. She always lost. Linda was right. She was a freak and a loser. She'd lost the best friend she ever had, all thanks to an ill-timed kiss.

*　　*　　*

"Hi."

Julie turned to see Linda standing in front of her. Julie, mouth full of junk food, wished she could sink beneath the plush carpet and vanish.

"You have chipmunk cheeks," Linda said with a smile.

"Mmmm-mmm-mmm," Julie said as she chewed. She swallowed and then spoke. "It's good to see you. I miss you."

"I know."

"Do you still want to have that séance? It would be fun."

Linda shook her head. "I changed my mind."

Julie saw her chance at popularity disintegrate. Linda wouldn't want to hold a séance. Only dorks hold séances. What was she thinking? Why did her life have to change for the worse since Halloween?

"Why can't we go back to the way things were?"

"I want to talk to you about that. Want to meet me in the living room after I open my gifts? I feel really bad about the way I've treated you."

Julie's hopes raised. Was Linda returning to her? "You treat me like dirt now. I don't understand what happened between us." She couldn't even look Linda in the eye. Embarrassed and humiliated, she picked at her gnawed cuticles. There was nothing left to chew.

Linda placed a hand on Julie's shoulder. "I think you know. I'm seeing Jake now."

"But what about what we had?" Julie stared into Linda's eyes, trying to read her mind, but she knew that was a talent she did not possess. She could not figure out what Linda was thinking. Confused, she lowered her head and sniffed, tears threatening to fall.

"Things change." When Linda took her by the hand, she let out a gasp.

"We used to have so much fun. Seances and ghost stories. Playing games all weekend." Julie paused. "And other things."

"I've outgrown all that. I'm sorry. I know how much you liked all of it."

Julie's voice fought with her sadness. "What about when I kissed you? I thought you felt the same way about me. I'm so sorry I took you by surprise."

"Linda! Everyone's waiting." Her mother called from the living room.

Linda placed her fingers on Julie's lips. Julie hitched in her breath. "Let's talk alone later. I do miss you. We can fix this," Linda said.

The gift exchange felt like hours despite only taking about twenty minutes. When Linda got to Julie's gift, her heart sank. Julie couldn't afford as much as the richer kids who were now a part of Linda's life. Jake gave her a brand new set of skis. Her parents gave her a new stereo set. Julie was relieved to see it contained a cassette player. One of the cheerleaders gave her Chanel perfume. Julie wondered if Linda had tossed the Avon perfume she had given her and would now use Chanel instead. Linda opened the box, moved aside tissue paper, and smiled. She held up two cassette tapes of the Bee Gees and Abba.

"Thanks, Julie. I love them," she said. Julie couldn't help but smile in return.

"Abba?" Jake said. "You hate Abba."

"Shut up, Jake," Linda said.

"What are you getting mad at me for? You don't like them."

When did Linda begin hating Abba? Abba was her favorite! Julie had never felt so alone although she was in a room full of people. She returned to studying her sneakers.

Hail pelted the windows so loudly it was hard to hear anyone speak.

"Wow, get a load of this storm!" Linda said. "I haven't seen hail in years."

Freakish storms revealed the rift between this world and the Netherworld, which was what Julie and Linda had preferred to call the spirit realm. All manner of bogies entered the human world when a storm such as this one raged. If they hosted a séance and called something, the other kids would have to admit Julie wasn't a loser after all if she summoned the spirit of Jim Morrison or Jimi Hendrix.

Imagine hearing disembodied guitar riffs coming from the record player when the machine was turned off. The fantasy brought Julie brief reprieve of hopeful joy. *If something that impressive happened, no one would dare ignore me.* She might still be rejected, but she'd be viewed with awe.

Sadly, Linda had nixed the séance. There went Julie's chance to impress her fellow classmates.

After the gift-giving ended, Linda disappeared into the crowd of teenagers in the kitchen. Julie was too afraid to join the crowd. After waiting fifteen minutes with Linda showing no interest in associating with her, Julie walked to the living room closet to get her coat.

But before she left, she needed to say goodbye to Linda. To give her one last chance to talk.

She walked into the somewhat-emptier kitchen, but Linda was nowhere to be seen.

"Where's Linda?" Julie asked.

"The last time I saw her she was in the basement," Mrs. Kelly said.

With desperate determination, Julie strode to the basement door, turned on the light switch, and headed downstairs. While there was a sofa, chairs, and a TV in the front of the basement, the rest of the room was a scary place with shadows in every corner. Old board games, furniture, and boxes filled the back of the basement. It smelled of mold and wet earth. Julie wanted to find Linda and talk her into coming upstairs.

When she reached the basement floor, the light turned off and the door shut. Childish giggles erupted from the top of the stairs.

Those kids knew Julie hated being the brunt of endless pranks, yet they taunted her anyway. She hated Jake who probably instigated the whole thing with the help of cheerleaders Lisa and Tina. Cheerleaders Linda considered her new friends. Did Linda have a new best friend Julie didn't know about? Heart lurching in terror, she turned to race back upstairs, but she tripped and banged her shin against an end table. She bit her lip to ward off the pain and rubbed her shin until she felt a goose egg beneath her fingertips.

"I'm here," Linda said from the back of the room.

"I can't see anything," Julie said.

"I'll light a candle." Dim light shimmered in the corner of the vast room. Julie followed candle light until she stood next to Linda.

"Do you want to take some games upstairs?" Julie asked.

"I wanted to talk to you. Alone." When Linda rested her palm against Julie's left cheek, Julie's heart skipped a beat.

"What do you want?"

Julie barely saw Linda's smile in the dimness. "You."

"I don't understand. What about Jake?" Her breath came out in short bursts as she felt a blush creep up her neck to warm her face. She stared at Linda so intensely her friend's features seemed to shift and melt before her eyes. A trick of the light.

"Yes, you do. And never mind him," Linda said. "I've always cared for you." Linda's voice deepened to almost an unnatural tone, but Julie put that to nervousness and being trapped in the dark basement.

Julie's mouth parched as Linda stroked her hair and then ran her fingers across her cheek to brush against her lips. She barely managed to ask, "Why don't you want to be my friend anymore? Why do you like Jake better than me?"

"He doesn't hold a candle to you," Linda placed her hands on Julie's shoulders. "Come here. Let me hold you."

As Linda wrapped her arms around her, Julie rested her head on Linda's shoulder. Her heart pounded so hard she feared Linda could hear it. The last time they'd held each other so closely...

This embrace felt different. Linda's fingers drew curliques between Julie's shoulder blades. The familiar caress from months ago took on an entirely new meaning.

Julie shivered. Linda had known her feeling since Halloween. Had she lacked the courage to acknowledge them in a positive manner until now? Julie's fear of rejection and abandonment immobilized her. She couldn't move. She couldn't breathe. *Take a chance. Tell her what's on your mind.* Finally, Julie found words. "You feel good." She cringed. Was that the best she could do?

"So do you." Linda tightened her grip around Julie's back. "I never want to let you go. We're best friends forever, right?"

The air around Julie stopped moving. Her throat seized up as she choked back tears. Heat rose with a blush on her face. Julie needed to take the chance. She blurted out, "Are we *only* best friends?"

"The best that best could be." Linda stroked Julie's hair.

"You're confusing me," Julie said. "What do you want?"

"I want you." Linda gripped Julie's chin between her thumb and forefinger and raised her head until she stared into Linda's eyes. The flickering candle light reflected in Linda's brown eyes that didn't blink. Without saying another word, Linda lowered her face to Julie's and pressed her soft lips against Julie's chapped ones. Julie closed her eyes, allowing herself to be lost in Linda's kiss. Lips parted as tongues flicked at each other, dancing a minuet that kept to the beat of Julie's heart. She hitched in her breath as she fought tears of relief and happiness.

Finally! Why hadn't she told Linda how she felt about her after all this time?

Julie raised her arms and hugged Linda as Linda stroked her hair. Her kiss tasted of moss and dirt. Why didn't she taste birthday cake and mint chocolate chip ice cream? *Maybe it was an effect of the scent of rain from the storm*, she argued to herself. In the moment, she didn't care. She only wanted to lose herself in Linda's embrace.

"Promise me you'll never leave me," Linda said.

"I promise," Julie responded.

The door at the top of the stairs opened.

"Julie? Are you down there? Linda is looking for you," Mrs. Kelly called.

The overhead light turned on. Julie stood alone in the basement, her arms wrapped around air. The ghost of the phantom's kiss lingered on her mouth. Julie screamed, slapped her hands all over her body in terror as if to rid herself of any sensation of the phantom's touch, and raced up the stairs.

"Where are you going? What's wrong?" Linda asked as Julie ran past her and out the front door, the last of her sanity collapsing as she ran home.

It was the fetch. It had to be. It knew all along what I wanted to do. I've never been so scared in my life, but I live on my own terms. The fetch won't dictate my behavior, but it does acknowledge my intent. I've made my decision. It's time to follow through, for once in my life.

Julie raced home and ran through her front door.

"Mom?"

No answer.

"Mom? Dad? You here?"

Silence. *Good. I need to be alone.*

She locked the front door and then walked upstairs. Once in her bedroom, she grabbed three big pillar candles and a stick of amber incense. The painful memory of Linda giving her a box of this incense flashed into her mind. She'd burn it in honor of Linda and what they once had together.

Once in the bathroom, she sat the candles at the corners of the bathtub. Then, she turned on the water until it ran warm. She lit the candles. Soft light flickered around the dark room. From beneath the bathroom cabinet, she picked up a bottle of amber romance bath bubbles, which were another gift from Linda. Julie's eyes teared up. She'd thought she and Linda had a future together. She couldn't have been more wrong. She had no one. Even her parents didn't care. Julie poured three caps' full of bath bubbles into the bath. Bubbles burst forth from the warm water, and the pleasant smell filled the air.

She slipped out of her clothing and left it on a pile on the floor. Angry slashes on her wrists shown red against her pale skin. She fingered a cut and imagined the fetch's kiss. If only Linda had kissed her like that.

Naked, she dipped a toe into the water. Perfect. Never again would Jake call her a snot-nosed twit. Linda wouldn't need to avoid her anymore when she hung out with the popular girls. Julie would never need to worry about kids shunning her at the lunch table or girls laughing at her scrawny body in the girl's locker room after gym class. She'd show them all. Relaxed for the first time in months, she walked to the medicine cabinet and grasped the one thing she knew could end her misery once and for all.

Her father's straight razor.

The Tale of Annette
by Tracy L. Carbone

I was barren and my husband didn't want children, so on the surface it was a perfect match. Except that his lack of progeny was by choice and mine was bad plumbing. I didn't discover my condition until I tried to get pregnant with donor sperm in my late thirties, having given up on ever finding a suitable husband. Years later, when I did meet my suitable husband, Charles, not Charlie or Chuck, but always Charles, he was relieved. He'd gotten a vasectomy but liked the extra insurance my ruined ovaries provided.

Charles was so steadfast in his commitment not to procreate that he'd divorced his first wife when she'd secretly gone off the pill and gotten pregnant. Walked out and never talked to her again except through lawyers. Turned out, he needn't have left her because she lost the baby. That close call, he told me, led him to get "fixed." It's a shame on many levels but superficially because he's so good looking. He'd have sired beautiful children. He's fifty-two but looks forty. Thick, dark hair. Piercing dark eyes. Straight, white teeth.

"Isn't it great, just us?" he was always saying. "We can do whatever we want, whenever we want."

The first few years, I was restless for a child, begged him to let us adopt or even foster. Charles and I had argued a lot in those years. It never got violent, but it got loud. I even called his bluff once. The next day, he handed me a card from a law firm. He said he didn't want a divorce, but he wasn't backing down. And so here we were, settled, childless, but generally okay.

I think Charles and I would have grown old together just fine, because we'd learned to compromise. I focused on all the good he did, and I didn't go digging or looking for reasons to be upset, like my friends did or like the women on TV. He tolerated my OCD, in its many forms, and my fixation of mystery novels and programs. And I tolerated, well, the stuff I chose not to focus on.

It was good and we were happy. Until that family moved in next door.

We lived in a townhouse, on the end unit. It was a place we'd bought eight years before, when it was new, paid in full with an inheritance Charles had received after the death of his father. Suicide, but we didn't talk about it.

The woman who used to live next door, Ella Oldfield, had died of cardiac arrest six months ago. In the house. Her parrot, Victor Lazlo, had eaten half her face before anyone had noticed she'd gone, so the story goes, though I didn't believe it. I refused to believe it in keeping with my Bing Crosby philosophy of accentuating the positive and eliminating the negative. Ella's tragedy only came to light when the mailman knocked on my door with a package that needed a signature, and he'd added that her mailbox was crammed full. "Is she on an extended vacation?" he'd asked.

I thought about the TV that hadn't been on in a week. Ella's living room and ours shared a wall, and like clockwork, her TV with the volume perpetually too loud went off promptly at ten each night. We could set our clock by the "Goodnight, Ella!" that Victor would call out when, we imagined, Ella would say a quieter goodnight to her companion as she covered his cage. Charles and I would listen to her creak her way up the stairs. We'd hear the rushing of water as we imagined she brushed her teeth, or took them out, or both. Then we'd hear her snoring. When the mailman had held out the package, it'd hit me. When did we stop hearing the TV, the snoring? I'd run from him and called 9-1-1.

Ella had been a character actor who'd done well for herself. Her adult children took everything she had, except the house and Victor the parrot. When she'd passed, we took Victor briefly, and then donated him to a zoo. I couldn't get past the remote possibility that Victor had eaten human flesh even if Charles defended him and explained creatures do what they need to survive. Because of the circumstances and the greediness of her children, the house sold quickly and well below market value.

Charles met the new neighbors first. I'd made my weekly trip to the grocery store because it was Wednesday and that was my shopping day. Tuesday evenings I'd collect all the weekly flyers and make my list, sorted by store, to get the best bargains. Charles argued that any money I saved store hopping was lost driving across town, wasting gas. "You can just go to Market Basket and get everything." Charles didn't grasp that if I went to just the one store and bought everything I needed, what the hell else was I supposed to do with the rest of my Wednesday night? We shared a car, and each morning he dropped me at the train station. Wednesday was the only time I took the car and had alone time. I'd stop at Starbucks and the craft store too. It was a four-hour block, and it was all mine. Charles had his weekly poker night, and all is fair in love and war.

On that particular Wednesday, Charles said he heard a knock on the door and opened it to find a harried woman in her thirties. "I'm Molly, your new neighbor."

Charles relayed to me that she'd just moved in and wondered if we had any spare light bulbs.

"Does she have any kids?" I asked as I put away groceries.

"She didn't say." Charles isn't curious. His stance is "It's not my business" whenever I try to get information.

"Seems like a big place for a woman to buy to live in all alone, don't you think?" I countered.

He didn't answer.

I made a batch of peanut butter cookies to bring over, but Charles said not to bother her. He cautioned maybe she had a peanut allergy. Charles had a lot of food allergies, so this was always on his mind. I dumped the lot because I watch my weight, and made sugar cookies. "What about gluten allergies?" Charles said, when the cookies were plated and ready to deliver. "You should leave her alone on her first night." I ignored him and stepped out my door and walked the thirteen steps to Molly's.

A girl about ten years old, in a wheel chair, opened the door and smiled. Her large eyes looked like an anime drawing. She had luxurious brown hair, not mousy and thinning like mine. "I'm Fiona, your neighbor. I brought you and your mom over some cookies, as a welcome."

"You're so nice. Come on in," the girl said as she wheeled down the hall away from me, toward the open kitchen, which had been renovated in the last couple of months. It didn't smell like Mrs. Oldfield or Victor anymore, and the carpets had been replaced with wood laminate. The place was bare so far, boxes lined up along the walls. It was the mirror image of our place, high ceilings and a gas fireplace. Mine was decorated with country; Mrs. Oldfield had done mid-Century. I was curious to see what Molly would do.

"Molly isn't home right now."

"Molly, your mother?"

She shook her held, curled her lip. "She's *not* my mother. Anyway, she took the others to the park. They're rambunctious, and she wanted them worn out so they didn't disturb you and Charles."

"Others? How many are there?"

"Two more. Twin boys. They're seven. I'm ten. Just turned a few weeks ago."

Three children! Right next door! I was elated, and visions of crafts, Halloween costumes, and birthday parties flooded my imagination. The children I could never have were my new neighbors. I smiled so hard I'm sure I looked demented. "I'm sorry. I didn't even ask your name."

"I'm Annette." She put her hand out to shake mine, and I gasped. I didn't mean to but...there was only one finger and half her hand was gone.

"It's okay. I get that a lot. You don't have to shake it."

Mortified, I reached out, took her hand, and shook it the best I could. "I'm sorry; I was just surprised."

Annette shrugged. She held her other hand out. It was severed off at the wrist joint.

"Were you born this way or was there an accident?" Once it was out of my mouth, I pictured Charles telling me it was none of my business.

"Um, kind of born this way? My body, um, well, Molly says I have a rare disease, and I shouldn't feel bad about it."

"Of course you shouldn't. You poor dear."

"It's why I'm in a chair. My legs, one of my legs right now..." I don't know what else she said but I saw her begin to lift the blanket that draped over her lap.

"No need to show me. You're a brave little girl."

Her smile lit up the plain room.

"Can't the doctors do anything to help?"

The door opened from down the hall then. "Molly doesn't believe in doctors," Annette whispered. "I've never been to one."

Two boys ran down the hall. The park play hadn't subdued them much. Twins but not identical. One had freckles and one didn't, and their hair was parted on different sides.

I met Molly then. She was short and spunky with blonde hair in a bob. She had a pretty face and figure and tiny feet, unlike my size tens. "Who are you?" she asked, startled. She stood in front of Annette like a mother lion, even if she wasn't her mother.

"She's from next door. Charles' wife, Fiona," Annette said, peeking from behind Molly. She gestured to the plate on the counter. "She brought cookies. That's all. She's just being friendly."

Molly fake smiled then. "So nice to meet you. I didn't mean to be rude, I just, well I left Annette home alone, and you just never know."

"Nothing wrong with being cautious. We were close to the woman who lived here before, so I wanted to come and welcome you and your family. Is your husband coming home soon? We'd love to meet him and have you all over for dinner when you're settled in." Charles would *not* love this. He hated company and certainly had no interest in two little boys and this poor unfortunate girl. No doubt he'd flip out when I told him. He'd lecture me about opening *that door* and how we'd be stuck and *next thing they'd be over all the time…* But it was my house too, and I didn't want to be rude.

"No husband, no," Molly said.

"I'm sorry. I shouldn't have assumed. Your wife? I'm from another generation and not always politically correct."

Molly laughed awkwardly but didn't add any clarity. "It's just us. We're a modern family, right kids?"

I struggled through small talk, and then left. Try as I might, all I could think about were Annette's hands and what her feet may look like. If she even had any. Even if Molly didn't believe in doctors, wouldn't someone have forced the issue by now? Surely there were surgeries that could have helped correct the issue.

*　　*　　*

"I don't think they have a TV," I said to Charles that night when we went to bed. "You can't hear a peep over there. I was worried about the noise level, a woman and three kids moving in, but they're so quiet. No running around, no TV. They're even quieter than Mrs. Oldfield."

"Maybe they're just on their best behavior, trying to make a good impression." Charles smiled at me.

*　　*　　*

The first week was silent. I worried they were all dead, a Mrs. Oldfield situation all over again. At my urging, Charles finally knocked on their door a week later. He came back home. "No answer. They're probably just out."

Despite Charles and his, "It's not our business" take, I needed answers. "You think they changed the locks? Do you still have Mrs. Oldfield's key?"

"We can't just go in their house," he said.

"I don't want to invade their privacy either, but what if it's a carbon monoxide leak?"

In the end, Charles agreed to try the key but insisted that calling the police was premature. For all we knew, they were on a trip. But after Mrs. Oldfield and Victor Lazlo, I couldn't chance it.

We went over together this time, knocked again. Still no answer and silence from within. Charles used the key and the door opened. "Can't believe they didn't change the locks. That's not smart."

There was a small kitchen table with a vase of fresh daisies and two chairs. "Hello?" I called out. "Sorry to bother you! It's Fiona and Charles from next door." Nothing. "Where are they?" I demanded of Charles, not that he knew.

I opened the fridge. Empty except for cases of water. I tried the cabinets. Bare.

"What are you doing?" he said.

"Why don't they have any food?"

"Maybe they eat out. We should get out of here. No one's dead; that's all we were here to check on."

We left, retreating back to the safety of our world just on the other side of the shared walls.

*　　*　　*

The next day, as Charles and I were backing out of our garage, we heard the hum of Molly's garage. "Stop the car." He slammed on the brakes, and I held my breath as I listened. She pulled beside us and stopped her car. She waved and rolled her window down. I did the same. "Hey strangers, haven't seen you in a while," she said, as if *we* were the ones who disappeared.

"We've been here the whole time," I said.

She looked past me to Charles. Then he shot me "the look," to reprimand me for not having boundaries.

"Hi Molly, good to see you again," Charles yelled across me, from the driver's seat, like I didn't exist at all. "We're just heading out to work, but maybe we can catch up later if you're around."

"Sure, that'd be nice," she replied. She rolled her window up and entered her garage, closing it while we watched, disappearing behind the door.

I fired my own look back at Charles. "Why did you let her go like that? Without explaining anything?"

His eyes were on the road now, not on me. "Let her go? Besides the fact we haven't seen her since she moved in, what crime has she actually committed? Did you expect me to make her account for where she's been, where the kids have been?" It was rhetorical.

"What about Annette's hands and how she said Molly doesn't believe in doctors? And that Molly isn't even her mother?"

"Maybe Annette does have a rare disease. Maybe she has been to doctors, dozens of them, and is lying to get sympathy. Kids say all kinds of things."

"Fine. But there's something weird going on over there, I'm telling you."

"Noted," he said, shutting me and my hysteria down. "Let's just leave them alone until there's something to be concerned about, okay?"

And so we did. Their house remained silent. I saw their lights go on and off, from where I watched across the street, behind the big oak. I showed Charles my log; the timing of the lights was exact and clearly on a timer. "I don't think they're in there."

He pointed out that we were gone from 7:30 in the morning to 5:00 at night and they could certainly come and go all that time. "Maybe during the day she home schools the kids and at night they go to, I don't know, Molly's sick mother's house and sleep there."

One day I missed my train from the city and didn't get home until six-thirty. Charles said he saw Molly and Annette and the boys. They were coming out of the house when he got home at five. "I noticed that Annette had a Bible on her lap. Maybe they're religious and do Bible study at night. A lot of people don't have TVs."

I was gutted that I'd missed them. "Did you ask where they'd been?"

"Of course not. I assume they've been in their house. I don't understand why you're so obsessed with them. You said the situation was creepy, but you're the one being creepy, Fiona."

He was right. But there was something about that little girl that was off. I had a feeling she was being abused. I couldn't put my finger on it, and maybe it was all my imagination. But I wanted to talk to her again, see with my own eyes that she was okay.

Another week went by. Once Charles ran out to get me a salad, and he told me he saw Molly at the restaurant, getting pizza for the kids. He told her I was worried and she confided that she had a boyfriend they'd been spending a lot of time with. I was relieved. That made perfect sense.

The next night was Charles' weekly poker game. He went out every Saturday about eight and got home sometime in the middle of the night. Sometimes his shirts smelled like perfume. Sometimes, I had to admit, like men's cologne. We hadn't been "together" in a couple of years because I worried about catching something. Part of my heart was broken because of these affairs, so I closed myself off. I'd confronted him, but he never admitted anything. With my aging hormones, I didn't care about a physical relationship anymore. He was otherwise a good man. If he got physical with a stranger once a week, what did it really matter? I got all the good parts of him: the affection, the companionship.

It was almost midnight when I finished the book I was reading and shut the side lamp off. It was then I heard a noise from next door. Crying? I sat on the floor and pushed my ear to the wall. It was where Mrs. Oldfield's headboard used to be. It was crying all right. Maybe Molly broke up with her boyfriend.

Early in the morning, I rang Molly's doorbell. Then again. And again. I came back to the house and roused Charles from his deep sleep that had started at three in the morning when he'd come home. "What do you want? I'm tired."

"I heard something next door."

"Not possible," he mumbled as he fell back asleep.

I shook him. "Wake up!"

His eyes cleared. "What?"

"I heard crying next door. I heard crying right there." I pointed to the part of the wall where I'd pressed my ear, where the face print of my Oil of Olay profile had left a stain.

He sat up then. "You were listening? You actually put your ear to the wall?"

"I went over there just now, but no one answered. They couldn't have left. I would have heard the garage door."

He got out of bed, put his robe on over his almost perfect body. He wasn't muscular but his skin was flawless. "You're out of control. All you talk about anymore is that little girl. You met her once. Once! What is it with you? If you don't lay off, they're going to file a complaint." He left the room and I followed.

"For what? Caring?"

He sighed. "When I saw Molly at the pizza place, she said she thought someone had been in her house. I covered for you, of course, but she told me she was installing an alarm system and cameras."

"But—"

"I don't know their situation, but unless you saw anything reportable then you need to let it go. You're obsessed."

Was he right? Was I just a busy body with nothing else to occupy my mind?

That night I heard the crying again. I didn't say anything to Charles, just listened.

I called in sick to work Monday. If Charles was suspicious, he didn't let on. I waited for Bart, the mailman, for two hours. "My neighbor Molly in number five, is she picking up her mail?"

"I can't really discuss that."

"But before. Mrs. Oldfield. She never picked hers up, and she was dead in the house. Remember?"

He sighed. "Of course I do. But," he said as he opened the main door, where he could access the backside of everyone's boxes. Number five was empty. "There's no one registered to this box. The resident never got any mail, not since she moved in. I don't bother putting junk mail there. Maybe she's got a P.O. Box."

Another dead end, but I'd watched too many crime shows and read too many mystery novels in my time to know when things didn't add up.

I went inside. Dismayed but not defeated. I bit the bullet and called Elliot, Mrs. Oldfield's son, for whom I had nothing but disdain. "I know this will sound strange," I began, "but our new neighbor, the one who bought your house—I don't know her last name and I need it to—" I had nothing. "Just...can you tell me what her last name is?"

"Didn't sell it to a woman," he said. "It was a Trust. I remember that because the agent said it could muddy the waters. But it went through fine."

"Do you know the name of the Trust? The woman I met, her name was Molly."

He grunted a bit, shuffled through some papers. "Not Molly. Hold on. Here it is. It's the Living Trust of Annette Grundy. Never met Annette or the Trustee. We did it all through lawyers."

I thanked him and called the real estate firm. That didn't help as the agent said the party who bought the house, the Trust, had never actually viewed the property. "A representative of the Trust bought the property. We really weren't involved except to send them the docs to sign."

In the afternoon, I tried Molly's house again. No answer. And then I crouched in the corner of my bedroom and listened. Nothing. I banged on the wall with my fist. There was a quiet thud from the other side. I banged again and so did the person on the other side. *I'm not crazy!* I heard a voice cry out but it was so faint I couldn't make it out. We used to hear Mrs. Oldfield snore at night on the other side of the wall, but now everything was muffled, far away. Was Annette bound and gagged?

Take it easy, Fiona. Talk it though with Charles. Don't let your imagination rule you. My hands were shaking, so I took a tranquilizer left over from two years ago when I'd had a mini-breakdown.

* * *

I was in the shower, listening to my meditation app, when the bathroom door swung open. "It's me," Charles said. "I was worried about you so came home a little early. Are you feeling better?"

I shut off the water. I remembered then I was supposed to be sick. "Yes, much better. I'll be out in a minute."

When I toweled off and got dressed, I found him in our shared office. He was looking at my notes, scribbled on a legal pad. "What's all this?" he asked.

I told him everything. The research I'd done, the continued crying, the pounding on the wall. "There's something sick going on over there. I think Annette is being held in that room, in that house. Maybe Molly leaves her behind when she goes to her boyfriend's house."

I waited for the "mind your own business," or his condescending, "Are you okay? Do you need to go back to therapy?" But it didn't come. He said nothing for a few minutes, just looked through my notes. "Give me a little while to process this okay?"

What a relief. Maybe he believed me. "I'll go make myself something to eat. Come down when you're ready."

Charles and I never ate together. He had a bad stomach, so he never ate dinner. Every morning I packed him a gluten free muffin, and he ate a big lunch in the office. In the beginning he'd eat dinner with me in restaurants, but he had so many allergies and digestive issues that it wasn't worth making him sick. It was disheartening at first, but I'd gotten used to compromising. He'd have broth with me, sometimes, and water, but mostly he stuck to his nighttime fasting.

When I checked on him after an hour, I found him napping on the bed. Finally, at six o'clock he came down.

"Okay," he said. "Let's do this."

"What? Call the police?"

"Let's go into the house, check it. We'll call the police if we find anything. Is Mrs. Oldfield's key still in the key tray?"

"I tried it already. She must have changed the lock."

He went down the hall, called to me in the kitchen. "Maybe it was just stuck when you tried. I'll try it, if not we'll call the police."

"What about the alarm you said she installed?"

He had already walked out. I threw on a sweater and shoes and ran over. "You got the lock open?"

"Probably just stuck like I said. I don't see an alarm system."

I opened the door to the garage. No car.

"I'll go upstairs. You stay here."

I snooped around for more clues, keeping a careful eye on the door should Molly or the police show up. There was a couch now and a small coffee table. There were photos on the mantle. A pretty woman and a younger Annette. I had to bring it closer to believe what I was seeing. Annette was in bare feet. Normal feet. And her five-fingered hands were above her head catching a ball. The woman was laughing. Next to it was another picture of the woman with an even younger Annette. It was from a mall picture studio. Annette's left arm was missing from the elbow down and her right hand was gone. How could she be missing them at that early age, then be intact in the more recent picture, then be missing them again? None of this made sense. "Charles! Something's not right here!"

I ran up the stairs, carrying both pictures with me. I smelled what was in the room before I made it there. When I was a teenager, I'd found a half decayed homeless man in the woods behind my house. It was a smell you never forget. I knew what I was going to find. The whole family, murdered, decaying. But my curiosity and my concern for Charles pulled me forward. From the doorway, I saw a pole in the middle of the room. A stripper pole? Was this a sex thing? At first, I thought the walls were quilted. White quilt. But no. Soundproofing. *Oh my God!*

Charles sat numbly on a pink bed, surrounded by ruffled pillows and stuffed toys. He stared into a corner, tears streaming from his eyes. I looked and saw Annette, gnawing on a small bone. There wasn't much meat on it. A pile of other bones sat on a blue plastic tarp. Big bones, not pork or beef ribs from barbeque. The bones were bright white and eaten clean. Annette had blood smeared around her face; her hair was matted with it. A half empty case of water bottles rested a few feet away. There was a bookcase filled with children's books and an iPad plugged into a charger.

Annette's hands were normal; her feet were normal. She had two arms, one of which was chained to the metal pole. She set down the bone and smiled at us.

I wanted to run to her but was so confused. I handed Charles the pictures. "This doesn't add up. What does this all mean?"

"Did you come to save me?" Annette's smile was so bright and sincere, even with the meat sinews in her jagged teeth. She didn't seem frightened or upset, just happy to see me.

I moved toward her, took the bone from her and set it down. I curled up next to her, put my arm around her. "You poor thing. Yes, we're here to save you. Can you tell us who left you here? Who did this to you?" Charles didn't react. He simply looked at the pictures, and to Annette, and to me. "Charles do something. Call 9-1-1!" I tried to loosen her chain and set her free.

"Look at her cleft chin," he said. "Look at her eyes."

I did. "What about them?"

"She looks like me, don't you think?"

"What are you saying?" My attention went back to Annette. "Are you okay?" I hugged her hard, my latent maternal instinct kicking in. "Are you cold?" She shook her head. Her chain was long enough that she could reach the bed and probably the bathroom.

I looked to Charles. His face, and her face. "Why aren't you calling the police?"

"Molly was my sister-in-law," he said, flatly. "She brought Annette here because she couldn't handle her anymore."

"Is Annette your niece? Where's Molly? Where are the boys?"

Annette answered for him. "Molly handed me over to my dad and said, 'You deal with her.' Right, Daddy?"

"She's *your* child? You've known she was here the whole time and kept her chained up like an animal? Did Molly sneak in and feed you?"

"She's chained up for her own good," he said.

I held her tighter, protectively.

"Molly never came back after the day in the driveway," Charles explained. "You go shopping on Wednesdays. Always the same time. I bring Annette food then and visit with her. I take her chains off, she takes a shower, comes downstairs. I read to her. And she has a phone. She texts me if she needs anything, and she could have called the police anytime. She knows this is how it has to be."

"How could you do this? To your own child? Lock her up like a monster?" I hugged her to me, patted her head. "She's just a little girl. How can you be so cavalier about it? 'I bring her food on Wednesdays.' What the hell is wrong with you? Give me the key and let her out."

He sighed. "I told you I didn't want kids. It's not because I don't love them. It's because…because she *is* a monster. I'm a monster. We have to—we have to eat human flesh or we disappear."

"That's ridiculous! Unlock this. We can discuss this later." By "discuss this later," I meant I'd take her to our place, get my phone and car keys, and take her straight to the hospital. And I'd call 9-1-1 on the way to have Charles arrested. He was a monster, all right, but only in his sick cruelty.

"You saw the pictures," he explained. "You saw her when she arrived. She's whole only because she's been eating. Molly couldn't stomach it anymore. I didn't know Annette had been born. Natalia told me she'd lost the baby after we divorced. I told you that. Molly called me out of the blue a few months ago. She told me Natalia died in a car accident, and Molly had taken Annette in, but she couldn't do it anymore. I didn't need her to explain. Honestly, I can't believe Natalia took care of her, kept her alive as long as she did. Ten years. Jesus. Natalia was a vegan for god's sake. That's irony huh?"

"I don't know what you're talking about. Kept her alive? What does that mean?"

"When Molly took her in, a few months ago, June I guess, well, Natalia hadn't filled her in on her special needs so to speak. Molly didn't feed her what she needed. Annette's limbs started disappearing It's what happens if she, or I, don't eat human flesh. Our bodies eat themselves."

It was incredible, a terrible, crazy story.

He continued, seemingly relieved to stop lying. "So I went to meet her. My daughter." He looked to Annette and they shared a smile. It was impossibly sweet to watch. "I loved her right away, of course, and had to take care of her. Had to get her fed. And I couldn't leave you because I love you too. I was going to tell you eventually, but I had to act quickly, get her home, with me where she belongs. With us." He paused, seemed relieved that I didn't run out screaming. "I bought the house with a trust I set up. Molly came by to drop her off, establish a back story until I could tell you. She stayed with her a few days until she got settled. I didn't expect you to go visit Molly or force your way in with cookies. I thought if Molly didn't answer the door, you'd assume they wanted to keep to themselves."

"But you saw her...at the pizza place!" I insisted. "She told you about the alarm system...and the cameras. You told they'd all been staying with her boyfriend."

He shook his head.

Of course. He'd made all that up. "*You* changed the locks. *You* had the new key." He nodded. "But—" I looked at Annette's blood-smeared face. "You're not like this. You eat regular food. I've seen you. And you've got all your parts."

He got off the bed and joined me, sat on the other side of Annette who cuddled up to him, as natural as a wolf cub to its mother. "My poker nights. I feed then. My food allergies, my nighttime fasting, just excuses so I don't have to explain that I don't eat what you do."

The perfume and men's cologne smell on his clothes, coming home in the middle of the night, the times I found specks of blood on his cuffs and he told me it was ketchup. He'd never had affairs; it was something far worse. "You kill people? You're telling me I've been worried about you sleeping round, and you've been killing?"

"Not always. I've got a storage space with electric, at Lock-It-Up by the industrial park. I've got a freezer in there. A body takes a long time to eat, and now I share it with my daughter." Like that somehow made him a great parent. "And sometimes I get bodies from the morgue. Bodies that are going to be cremated, I buy them. I know a guy."

I was furious, sickened. "You're a horrible man who chained an innocent little girl away for God knows what sick—give me the key."

He pulled it from his pocket and unlocked the cuff. And I, God forgive me, picked up a copy of Dr. Seuss' *Oh The Places You'll Go* and smashed the binding into his windpipe. He grabbed for his throat. I put the cuff on his wrist and pulled Annette to her feet. We closed the door of the soundproof room behind us.

*   *   *

I'd watched enough mysteries to know how to start a new life, but I needed to decompress. First I took Annette home and had a good cry. It was too much for me to deal with, too much to absorb, so for a couple of days I stayed home from work, gave my aromatherapy machine a run for its money, and planned. Annette and I gave each other manicures. She baked cookies with me, even if she didn't eat them.

On day three Charles came home. He was missing the lower half of his arm so the cuff had slid off. His throat was bruised, but he was fine. I have to admit I was relieved. So much for the life on the run I'd envisioned, in a remote town with forged papers. "I'm sorry, Fiona. Really I am. Can I come home?" Damn Charles and that charming grin of his.

Annette, with her matching charming grin, pleaded, "Can't we be a family?"

*   *   *

Our daughter is not a monster. She's an honor student in high school now and has been sterilized, for her own good, as much as I'd love a grandchild. We'd thought of adopting more children, or getting foster kids, but with Annette, bless her heart, we have to be careful.

On Wednesdays I go shopping, and I don't ask what she or her father do in that four-hour block, or what he does on his "poker nights." Like any family, we've got our secrets, but we make it work.

Souls of the Wicked Like Crumbs In Her Hand
by Suzanne Reynolds-Alpert

The woman in the corner made an incongruous figure. Hunched over the small table, she rocked a bit in the wooden chair with a leg slightly shorter than the rest. The bony index finger of her right hand hovered over the cupped palm of the left, dipping in and making small stirring motions.

No one else in the café seemed to notice her. People worked on their laptops; others stared glassy-eyed at their phones. A few chatted with friends, their laughter tinkling through the cinnamon-scented air. Some, like Megan herself, had a child in a stroller. Some had two or more young charges. A mother or nanny sat gulping coffee from a to-go cup, eyes darting between three boisterous children who all looked to be under six years.

Everyone else was too busy to notice that one strange woman, sitting against a wall at the back of the shop.

Megan shifted her attention back to her son. Sami was a good baby, not colicky or cranky. At seven months, he already slept for hours at a time, and a wide, toothy grin often split his cherubic face. His eyes were changing from post-birth dark blue to hazel, and he'd inherited his warm, tan skin from his father—a welcome departure from her own pale complexion.

Megan's phone on her own small table—twin to the table where the strange woman sat about ten feet away—vibrated. She picked it up, glad she'd remembered to turn off the sound. It was Faizan, checking up on her. His text read: *Had a few minutes in between meetings. How are you and Sami?* What he really meant was, *How are you? Did you manage to leave the house? Did you feed the baby? Is today a good day?* But he knew enough not to text that outright. She was still climbing out from the brutal depths of post-partum depression, and any insinuation that she was not functioning, not able to *mother*, reduced her to tears.

Both she and Faizan had desperately wanted Sami. She'd become pregnant while they'd been dating, and they'd hastily married to appease his conservative family. That pregnancy had ended in an inexplicable miscarriage just before her eighth month. Megan had held that precious, impossibly small, still, baby girl in her arms for only a few minutes before her body had been whisked away. A chasm of despair had opened within her, an emptiness she didn't know was possible. She'd wanted...*needed* another child.

Sami was her treasure.

It was tragic that she couldn't enjoy him the way she'd envisioned. She was still haunted by the utter lack of emotion she'd had, holding her crying, badly-wanted child in her arms, stroking his soft, downy head, inhaling the milky newness of him and feeling *nothing*.

But she'd carried on. She pretended. She had slowly learned what others expected her to be, went through the motions of being a mother. Slowly, things were getting better.

Most days.

Today was not one of those days. The entire week had been overshadowed by a text she'd seen on her husband's phone. It was from Liz, one of his younger, female coworkers, and it had struck her as entirely too friendly and familiar. Although it might mean nothing. It might mean nothing at all...

Still, the unbidden thoughts that she was a failure as a wife and lover and failing as a mother sent her spiraling around that dark place, staring into the mouth of that hopeless pit she hadn't been sure she could escape from the first time.

Motion caught her attention. Two young women approached the table where the odd woman sat. They appraised it as if looking to sit down, then one said, "It's empty, but I don't like the *feeling* back here..." The other mentioned outside, and they walked past Megan's table, out the door, and sat at one of the two-seater, cast-iron tables under the café's colorful blue awning.

It's empty.

Why did those women act like no one was sitting at that table? How could they not see her? Megan saw the woman as plainly as she could see her own son.

Her heart beat faster and her breath hitched as she picked up the thick ceramic mug that held her coffee. She told herself that maybe they'd given her full-caf instead of the decaf she'd asked for. Her hand shook slightly as she raised the mug to her lips, staring at the strange woman over the brim. The woman wore a calf-length skirt emblazoned with white, grey, and black geometric shapes. Peeking out from below the hem were legs covered in opaque black stockings. Sandals that looked like

Birkenstocks were tossed under the table, and one stocking-clad foot was propped up on a chair—a posture she'd seen teenagers assume.

Putting down her mug, Megan pretended to fish something from the diaper bag hanging on her chair as she took another furtive look at the peculiar woman. Above the waist she wore a thin, cream-colored sweater that was well-tailored and looked expensive. Several strands of colorful necklaces—none of which matched—adorned her neck. Honey-colored hair was caught up at the base of her neck in a messy bun. A long pin of some kind held it in place.

Her face was an enigma: a few wrinkles; smooth and luminous cheeks; dark eyes framed by long and curling eyelashes; and a wide, thin-lipped mouth. She looked both old and young.

The plastic ring of teething toys Megan had been pretending to fuss with fell on the floor. She cursed under her breath at her clumsiness, still spying on the woman as she bent to pick them up.

The woman lifted her cupped left hand, depositing what looked like crumbs into a small, disposable, paper coffee cup. She murmured something inaudible then ripped the top of the cup vertically four times, folding down the tabs she'd created so that they closed over the open top. She stowed the cup in a large denim tote bag hanging from the second chair. Then she pulled the remains of a pastry closer, picking at it with the thumb and forefinger of her right hand, extracting several large crumbs. She placed the new crumbs in the palm of her left hand.

She replicated the same gestures she'd done minutes before, stirring at the crumbs with her forefinger.

And then she spoke: "So. It appears you can see me." Her voice somehow carried across the ten or so feet that separated them. Her accent was strange. She was still looking down, slowly doing whatever it was she was doing with her finger and her palm and the crumbs.

Megan's heart began to beat even faster. *She can't be talking to me.*

"You are probably wondering if I'm talking to you. I am," the woman said, still not looking up.

Megan's eyes darted around the café, rising panic clutching at her throat. She sucked in a lungful of air, willing the familiar scents of ground coffee beans and cinnamon to calm her.

"The question is: How *is it* that you can see me?" the woman murmured to her palm. "Interesting," she said after several seconds.

There were times during those horrible, worst depths of the post-partum depression that Megan had questioned her sanity. That same feeling crept up her spine now, and those familiar, dark thoughts swam through her head. *Just because I think it, doesn't make it real,* she thought to herself, a tool she'd learned in therapy. The woman couldn't be talking to her—or could she? There was only one way to be sure… *Just ask.*

Megan glanced at the nearby tables of happy, normal-looking people, afraid of looking strange, herself, if she were about to talk to a woman no one else appeared to see. She swallowed down a bitterness that rose into her throat, coffee churning in her stomach. As if sensing her distress, Sami moaned and fussed in his stroller. He would soon be awake, wanting his bottle.

She looked in the woman's direction. "Are you talking to me?" she asked, very softly. Too softly, really, for the woman to hear.

The woman stopped whatever she was doing with her hands and caught Megan's tentative gaze. "Of course I am talking to you, silly! Who else would I be talking to? The question is, why? Why you? Why now?" As she said this, a bone-chilling, cocky smirk crossed her face, making her look not quite sane. "There is...something here, though," she finished. Her dark eyes were shiny with an inhuman luminescence, and Megan had the sensation of being undressed.

"I'm... I'm sorry! Sorry I was staring at you. I didn't mean to be rude. I—I was staring off into space, really. Thinking of something, and I realize it *looked like* I was looking at you. But I wasn't." Megan realized she was contradicting herself and sounding like an idiot.

But the woman made a motion with her right hand, as though she were flicking away a fly. "No problem. It is no problem at all. In fact, I'll come join you as you finish your drink. And who is that with you? A baby boy or girl? Is it yours?" She stood up and jammed stocking feet into her sandals, reaching for her tote bag and pulling it over her left shoulder. The pastry crumbs were still clutched in the woman's left palm; with her right she grabbed paper cups from her table and a small paper bag. Smiling, she stalked over to Megan's table.

Every instinct Megan had was screaming: *Get away! Get away now!* But she remained frozen to her seat, unable to move.

Sami fussed again as the woman approached. His mouth turned down, and a small mewing escaped his cupid-bow lips. Pulling out the empty chair at Megan's table, the woman tossed the cups and bag on the table. She sank into the seat with the grace of dancer. Up close, Megan could see small wrinkles creasing the corners of her eyes and lips. Otherwise, her skin was a smooth, polished shade of warm tan and her eyes were so black that the irises were indistinct.

The woman sat to her right; Sami on her left. A suffocating sense of claustrophobia struck Megan, and she fought down a rising gorge.

"So," the woman began, as if they'd already mutually agreed to the terms of this strange engagement. "As I suspect you now know, no one else here can see me. I am not so much invisible to them as I am a place of negation. They *see* me; but they cannot *process* me." She smiled very widely as she said this. "Plus, I cloak myself in shadows and liminality. It is, almost always, quite effective.

"But there are cases, some cases…when a person can see through my illusions. There is always a reason why. 'Fate', some might say." She paused to unclench her left hand and peer at it. Still looking down at her hand she said, "Take a look."

Too scared to do anything other than obey, Megan craned her neck and looked at the woman's hand.

A spattering of crumbs dusted her palm. They appeared to be from a muffin or scone of some kind; something with mixed berries. A smear of dark blue colored the spot under the woman's long, tapered middle finger and two bright, red splotches of strawberry or raspberry dotted the soft part beneath her thumb. *Blood*, Megan thought. *It looks like blood.*

The woman began to move the crumbs with her right index finger. "I need to be invisible, to do what I do. To be who I am. I have lived a very, very long time. I no longer even remember my childhood; I don't know if I *had* a childhood. As far as I know, there is no other creature like me in all the world."

Megan fought a frightening sense of vertigo as the woman speared her with a gaze. She shook; her mind went blank as she tried to form a coherent plan for escape.

"You poor thing," the woman crooned. "You are petrified! I truly mean you no harm. It is not you that I hunt, nor is it the babe you birthed…"

"H-hunt?" Megan choked out.

The woman inexplicably became distracted, mumbling something to herself and peering intently at her palm once again. For two agonizing minutes she continued to mumble, occasionally closing her eyes and stirring at the crumbs in her palm.

Megan thought she might be able to just push the stroller away quietly, slip from behind the table, and go home…

"See here," the woman said, her attention suddenly back on Megan. She pursed her lips and inclined her head toward the palm holding the crumbs. "The large morsel, right there in the center? That is a businessman flying out of Tokyo. He is of half Japanese descent but has made his fortune in his 'sacred' halls of Wall Street. He would be well-known to you." As Megan watched, the woman closed up her palm, making a tight, pale fist. She blinked rapidly and said, "It is done." She then pulled one of the paper cups she'd brought to the table toward her, made four vertical tears as she'd done before, and brushed the crumb remains inside. "For one such as me," she continued, "the souls of the wicked are like crumbs in my hand. I know not why I am this way or who made me. I know that I have this need to snuff out souls. They sustain me somehow—it feels right that I do this. And the wicked souls are the tastiest, the best." Her eyes met Megan's once again, the deep blackness of them shining with a fierce light. She slowly and lasciviously licked her lips.

Megan trembled all over even as she realized she was safe. *She* was not wicked, nor was her innocent baby. But what was this creature? What was this monster that ate souls like they were food, licked its lips like it was tasting a delicacy? Another thought tore its way through Megan's brain—what if none of this was true? What if the woman was simply crazy? An insane person could do anything, so maybe she and Sami *were* in danger. On impulse, Megan decided to confront her. "Who are you? How do I know anything you say is true?"

"The evidence is your own eyes, girl. You have observed me since you sat down. You have witnessed that no one here—no one save you— can see me.

"And the soul I just spoke of? The plane has landed. You will soon see news that Takashi Mori, aged 62, formerly of New York by way of Tokyo, is deceased. Died of a sudden, massive heart attack despite his excellent health. The efforts of a physician on board his private charter could not save him. And before I came to sit with you? There was this man down in Miami—'Street Rat,' he was called. A homeless, hopelessly insane young man who derived pleasure from killing. Men, women, children… He didn't discriminate. I'd been following him for some time. He began torturing animals when he was four years of age."

"How do I know any of this is true!"

"The young man's death won't make the news. He lived on the streets, after all. But the businessman? The news should be…breaking. Check your phone."

Megan fumbled for her phone, her shaky hands clumsily dropping it into the stroller and startling Sami, whose eyes shot open. He began to cry softly. "You could have known that before I even walked in," she said desperately, "it could have happened an hour ago."

"But it didn't," the woman smiled. "Check. I'll bet people on the plane even posted photos of it."

Thumbing her phone with one hand and soothing Sami with the other, Megan saw a headline: *British Supermodel Live Tweets from International Flight the Sudden Death of Takashi "Ted" Mori, Billionaire.*

"Honestly—and I don't know why this matters, I think it is simply such a novelty having someone see me without revealing myself to them first—it's been decades since that happened—but if you still don't believe me, I'm sure I can find someone around here…" The woman's voice trailed off and her eyes clouded over with dark grey swirls.

Megan sucked in a shocked breath; Sami began to cry more earnestly. Should she grab him and leave while this monster was distracted? She had to do something: hearing Sami cry was intolerable, throwing her back to the worst of the depression when she couldn't bring herself to do anything with the baby. Indecision tore at her. *What should she do?*

"There..." Her unwelcome companion inclined her head toward a sharply dressed woman waiting to pay for a coffee, her left foot clicking impatiently in her Louis Vuitton pumps. The obviously wealthy woman stared daggers at the portly, middle-aged cashier bidding a young man good-bye. "Oh! She is a tainted one! She is solely responsible for the decisions causing that food-borne illness that ran up and down the east coast last summer." With the woman—the monster's—attention back on her, Megan was again frozen to her seat. Sami's cries had quieted a bit, but he whimpered in his stroller as Megan unconsciously rocked it.

"H-how can you know that?" Megan's voice quivered.

"It is simply something I know—just as you know you love your child." She paused, cocking her head at Megan, her eyes once again black and unfathomable. "Or how you know your...husband...loves you. You do know these things, yes?"

As the woman said this, she tilted her head, peering at Megan, who felt nauseatingly as though she was tipping into a void. The woman smiled too widely, and Megan sensed the woman could see her heart and soul laid bare.

"Ah... Yes, *that's* it." The woman laughed. "Now look, poor little chick, and see what happens to the truly evil once I become hungry and have taken notice of them." She gestured to the well-dressed woman, now arguing with the harried cashier. "This one will be tasty! Not only has she knowingly caused numerous deaths because of decisions made at her job, she regularly gives money to known white supremacist groups. She is cheating on her second husband, having thrown away the first after he put her through business school. And, oh! She is even cheating on her lover!" The woman clapped her hands gleefully. "And—this is the best part—she previously seduced her 18-year old stepson. And his best friend!"

Sami's cries increased. Others in the café who had been ignoring her began to look in Megan's direction. Some looked slightly confused, as though they could hear something but couldn't quite tell from where it was coming.

Megan's companion murmured something, snatched a large crumb from the bits of pastry she'd brought to the table, and withdrew the pin that held her hair in place. Curling tendrils of dark blonde fell across her face as she said something incomprehensible and stabbed at the crumb with the pin.

The woman in the Louis Vuittons cried out in terror and grabbed at her head with both hands. Megan had the sensation of watching a gruesome movie in slow motion: The woman's coffee cup smashed against her forehead as both hands clutched her skull; brown liquid ran down her face leaving scalding red trails. She tripped over her computer bag in her shuffling blindness. One expensive pump sailed through the air as her body fell and convulsed. She screamed—inhuman, terrified wails— as one eye burst out of her skull, a pulsing rush of blood following it...

Then time appeared to run normally again. The café was in chaos. Megan looked around the shambles of her morning, eyes brimming with tears. Someone screamed into her phone for 911. A man near the center of the café threw up over his table. The woman with three children hurried them out the door as they all cried. The cashier was pale and stricken-looking as she approached the dead woman and gently placed a soiled tea towel over the bloodied, inanimate face, frozen in a stricken rictus.

"Sorry that was so inelegant."

Megan looked back at the human-looking monster sitting at her table, blinking tears away.

"Normally, I have time to use more finesse," she said. "But I was trying to prove a point. This is your fault, really." The woman shrugged. She brushed the crumbs from her palm into her second paper cup, tore down the sides as she'd done twice before, then stashed both cups in her tote bag. She then twisted her long hair back into a messy bun and placed the pin in it.

A combination of deep anger and shame blossomed in Megan's chest. In that moment, she did not fear the woman, the monster—a creature of a fairy tale too dark to fully tell. A nightmare that stalked the living to feed her own perverse needs. So what if the people she killed were immoral? Who was she to judge? She was not God!

"I'm leaving," Megan said through gritted teeth. "I will tell no one I ever saw you—not that anyone would believe me—and I expect I'll never see you again. I am not evil; my child is not evil." She stood and shouldered her diaper bag, and then gripped the stroller's handles. As she looked the woman in the face, her bravery began to falter. Not because the woman looked angry, not because Megan had the sense she or Sami were in danger, but because the woman now looked so inhuman— perhaps she was allowing more of her true essence to show.

Her black eyes glowed with that inhuman luminescence, and a satiated smile twisted her lips. She regarded Megan lazily. "So go. I did not seek you out; you *made* me appear to you. Go back to your pointless, unsatisfying life. Run back to your faithless husband and fickle friends. Call your unhelpful mother."

Megan began moving the stroller through the crying, terrified people still in the café and toward the door before the creature's words really penetrated. "Faithless husband?" she asked dumbly, turning around.

The woman flicked a hand at her. "It's no big matter. It's not as if you could do anything about it anyway. Who wants a fat, worthless, unemployed nobody who's too depressed to have sex?"

"But...do you mean...has he..." Tears spilled down Megan's cheeks as Sami cried and sirens wailed in the distance. With everything else that had happened in the café, no one paid her any attention. A dark greyness pressed in around the corners of her vision.

"Don't you already know the answer to that?" the woman asked, smiling crookedly.

"How...how could he?" Megan whispered into the chaos. Her son's hungry cries went unheard.

"Eh. You'll figure something out. Something to ease your pain and make things better for everyone," the woman said, her voice somehow quiet next to Megan's ear even though she remained sitting several feet away.

Numbly, Megan pushed the stroller with her crying child through the café's door, narrowly missing the paramedics rushing in. She didn't notice that the stroller's wheels had trailed through the small pool of blood, leaving thin, fading red trails on the sidewalk leading home.

*   *   *

Faizan sat at his kitchen table, a double shot of good Scotch untouched before him.

"Did you have any idea that your wife was planning to kill herself?" the police officer asked. He was an older man who looked every bit the stereotypical cop. He had been very kind as he questioned Faizan, probing gently and compassionately. The cop's partner stood next the table, her back turned as she spoke to Pamela, Megan's mother. Pamela had allowed the younger cop to hold Sami, and she was happily rocking the baby in her arms as she questioned Pam about Megan's therapy and how she'd interacted with her child.

"No," Faizan answered after a pause. "She'd been depressed since the birth—may have been depressed since she lost the first baby. But she'd been in therapy, was taking her meds. We didn't even leave her alone for two months after the baby was born. After that, her therapist agreed that she wasn't a danger to herself or anyone else, and that it would be good for her to begin to do things that...a new mother should do. 'Build her competency', she'd said. And Megs was getting better. Or at least, not getting any worse."

The cop nodded sympathetically. "My wife had a nasty case of the baby blues after our daughter was born. It was tough on all of us," he said.

Faizan nodded back and wrapped his hands around the glass in front of him. He blinked back tears, but one slid down his cheek and splashed in his Scotch.

The authorities finished asking questions in the kitchen as the coroner's office brought Megan's body down from the bedroom. Faizan glanced their way through eyes fuzzy with tears. Thankfully, her body was in a large, zippered bag. *Body bag*, he thought, trying not to choke on a sob. He would not have been able to look at his beautiful wife's pale, lifeless body again. Except for his stillborn daughter who had looked like a doll rather than a baby, he'd never seen a dead body before coming home from work—immediately alarmed at Sami's screams—and rushing upstairs to find Megan still and otherworldly-looking in death. An empty bottle of sleeping pills had sat on the bedside table; the room had been redolent of piss and death.

"Again, we are very sorry for your loss," the cop was saying.

Faizan managed to murmur some thanks as his phone buzzed. He pulled it out of his pocket. A text from his coworker, Liz: *I handled the client for you. Both Shoshanna and I are so sorry. Let us know what we can do. Shosh is already making some meals that you can freeze.* He texted back a simple "thanks." He was grateful to have Liz on his team. She was very sharp and great with clients—better than he was—a real "people person." She'd recently told him that she'd been living with her girlfriend for over a year and that they planned to marry this summer. Finance was still a conservative field, and Faizan was glad Liz had felt she could come out to him.

He felt something brush his shoulder: His mother-in-law, her own eyes red and puffy from crying. She'd taken Sami back from the police officer and was now holding him out to Faizan. He stood and took the sleeping bundle, warm and soft and angelic in his sleep.

* * *

The woman in the café—the woman who was no woman at all—had slipped unseen from the café. An absent, satisfied grin decorated her face. She had not told Megan the complete truth.

She'd lived a long, long time—that part was true.

Also true: She did choose to snuff out the souls of those humans who were the worst of their kind. Not because she cared about human morality; that was inconsequential. The vilest of humans were tasty, but actually quite tiresome. They were completely motivated by their own selfish needs and desires. That made them predictable, and predictable was boring. The "good" humans, the ones who were less corruptible, were more interesting. They could be surprising, which was rather delightful to observe for a long-lived creature such as herself.

And although the evil *were* her preferred prey, her palate sometimes craved something different. The taste of a human who'd given up all hope was a nice treat. Even if they needed a small nudge to get there.

The Hungry Man
by Lindsay Moore

The first time I ever saw the Hungry Man was just after my tenth birthday. Dusk had fallen, and I was about to go upstairs to get ready for bed when Mama put her hand on my arm and told me to sit with her awhile. I was excited at the prospect of staying up past my bedtime. I remember sitting at the kitchen table, swinging my bare feet while Mama made tea for us. I was excited for the tea as well. To me, it was a grownup drink, but it was far fancier than Uncle Jim's beer. Mama said that the Queen of England drank tea, and the idea of drinking the exact same thing as royalty made me downright giddy.

Mama set cups and saucers down in front of us, and I drank the tea even though I thought that it was bitter. Later on, I'd learn to add milk and honey to sweeten it, but at the time, I just sipped the sour stuff and pretended that I loved it.

I was about to ask Mama just how late she'd let me stay up when there was a knock on the front door. Mama got up, motioning for me to come with her.

"Mama, who is it?" I asked.

"It's the Hungry Man," she told me. "Come on. I need to show you what to do."

The man standing on our front porch was tall, just about the tallest man I'd ever seen. His shoulders were so big and broad I wondered if he'd be able to fit through the doorway. Strangest of all, he was covered in flour. It was caked over his head, neck, and shoulders, as if someone had upended a gigantic bag of it all over him. He stared at Mama, his eyes wide and glazed. I was grateful for the screen door between us and the Hungry Man, but it looked like he could rip it off its hinges if he chose to.

I stood beside Mama, trying my hardest to be brave. After all, I was ten years old. I was old enough to stay up past my bedtime and drink tea; surely I was old enough to meet the Hungry Man and not be afraid of him. I wished that Mama would just slam the door in his floury face, though, no matter how impolite such a thing would be. I didn't want him

118

on the doorstep, and I certainly didn't want him in the house. I glanced back over my shoulder. The stairs were right behind me. I could easily turn and run up to my room and hide under the bed. I immediately felt awful for thinking about leaving Mama alone with the Hungry Man. I glared at the Hungry Man, refusing to show him just how scared I really was.

"Can I borrow a cup of sugar?" he asked in a deep, throaty voice that raised the hairs on the back of my neck. "I'm trying to bake a cake, and I'm afraid I'm plum out."

I looked up at Mama. She stood stock-still, her shoulders squared, looking ten feet tall and like she was made out of steel. All my life, Mama had been a small, plump woman with quick, nimble fingers and a soft voice. She hadn't undone the braids piled up on her head, and they reminded me of a crown. All of a sudden, Mama was a noble queen telling a dirty bandit to get off her land. Seeing her looking so brave made my heart swell up.

Mama narrowed her eyes at him and put her hands on her hips. "Why, you were baking a cake last night, weren't you?" she asked. "And you were 'plum out' of flour."

I had never heard her talk to anyone like that before. Her voice was firm, never wavering, and she sounded a little bit rude, as if she was angry at the Hungry Man for interrupting our evening and she was about to give him a piece of her mind. The only time I'd ever seen her give someone a piece of her mind was when Mrs. Wilkins' grandson, Terrence, came to visit and trampled her rose bushes.

Mrs. Wilkins had tried to say that he didn't mean any harm. Mama had said that the next time she saw Terrence, she'd call the police. Mrs. Wilkins had gotten all hot and bothered, and even though she'd never said that she was sorry, she'd been unable to look Mama in the eye on account of how bad she felt about the whole thing.

It was no secret how much Mama loved her roses. Every morning, she'd sing a little song to them while we pruned them. I think if there had ever been a rose contest, she would have won every prize.

Seeing her speak to the Hungry Man the way she'd spoken to Mrs. Wilkins made me feel better, braver even. I squared my shoulders and gave the Hungry Man my sternest look.

He continued to stare at Mama, never even noticing me beside her. "I bake a lot of cakes," he said finally.

"Mmhmm." Mama reached up and flipped the latch the screen door, locking it from the inside. It made a loud, reassuring click as it slid into place. "Well, I guess you'll have to go without sugar. I haven't any to spare."

The Hungry Man nodded, bobbing his head low and slumping his shoulders. "Thank you anyway, ma'am," he said as he turned and ambled down off the porch. I almost felt sorry for him, because of how sad he looked and because I knew that the sugar jar in our pantry was full to the brim. I kept my mouth shut, though, watching quietly as he loped off into the darkness.

Once he was out of sight, Mama closed the front door and locked it. "That's the Hungry Man," she told me. "He comes around just about every night, asking for something to bake a cake with. You never give it to him, and you never, ever let him in the house. You hear me?"

I nodded. "But Mama, who is he? Why does he come by looking for food?"

Mama only shrugged. "He's the Hungry Man," she said patiently, taking me by the hand and leading me back to the kitchen. "And you must never give him food or let him in the house. You hear me?"

"Yes, Mama."

Mama stared at me, her brown eyes boring into mine, searching for something besides a simple *yes*. "This is important, Tonia," she said. "You can never feed the Hungry Man, and you can never, ever, ever let him in the house. I need to know that you understand."

"I do, Mama. I'll never feed the Hungry Man, and I'll never let him in the house."

"Good girl." Mama patted my head before nodding at the stairs. "Now off to bed with you."

I went up to bed, but it was a long time before I fell asleep. Every time I closed my eyes, I saw the Hungry Man standing on our porch, his eyes glassy like someone looking at a TV set without actually watching the program.

Every night after, Mama let me sit up with her in the kitchen. We would drink tea until the Hungry Man arrived. Then we'd both go to the door, and Mama would tell him to leave. He asked for different things every night, usually flour, sugar, or eggs—the kind of things you'd use to bake a cake.

I asked Mama about him when we sat in the kitchen together. I asked her every question I could think of: Who was he? Where was he from? Why couldn't we give him any food?

Mama never had any answers, though. Not real ones. "I don't rightly know who he is or why he keeps coming around," she told me, sipping her tea.

"But if we gave him some flour, wouldn't he go away?" I asked.

Mama shook her head. "Lord, no," she said. "The Hungry Man's like a wild animal. Feed him once, and he'll keep coming back for more."

"Is that why he keeps coming around? Because someone fed him by mistake?"

Mama shrugged. "Could be," she said. "I've never fed him."

"Why don't we call the police? Like we almost did when Terrence was stomping on the roses."

Mama shook her head. "Ain't no law against asking someone for a cup of flour so you can bake a cake." She sighed. "You know, when your daddy was still with us, he'd answer the door with his shotgun to chase the Hungry Man off."

"Why don't we use the shotgun?" I asked. "We could tell the Hungry Man to leave us alone forever or else we'd shoot him."

Mama arched an eyebrow and looked at me over the rim of her teacup. "Do you really think the Hungry Man is afraid of a shotgun?"

I looked down at my own teacup before spooning another helping of honey into it. Mama was right. He wouldn't be afraid of a shotgun, and we both knew it. I could picture Mama standing behind the screen door, pointing the shotgun right at the Hungry Man's heart. He wouldn't even blink. He'd just ask her for sugar or flour or eggs or milk or whatever his cake recipe was missing.

I think that somewhere in the back of my mind, I knew that the Hungry Man wasn't quite human. He looked and sounded the same, night after night. His clothes and his hair never changed. Even the floury powder he was always covered in stayed exactly the same. I'd never seen him around in the daylight, either. He only came after sunset.

Every night, Mama and I drank our tea and waited for the Hungry Man. Weeks melted into months, and I got used to him. I wasn't afraid of him anymore. If anything, he was starting to get annoying.

"What if we put a sign on the door telling him to go away?" I asked Mama. "Or what if we set a trap in the yard for him?"

Mama just nodded at the empty porch. The Hungry Man had just left, wandering back into the darkness. "A trap won't do much good." She leaned forward, pointing at the porch without opening the screen door. "What do you see out there on the porch?"

I squinted in the darkness, studying the weather-beaten wood. "Nothing."

Mama nodded again. "No footprints." She glanced at me. "You'd think a man covered in flour would leave some of it behind, wouldn't you?"

I looked out at the porch again. There was the usual layer of brownish-gray dust from the road and a few errant blades of grass that were probably tracked up by my sneakers, but no flour. Our porch should have been coated in the stuff from the Hungry Man.

"No," said Mama, "a trap won't stop a creature like the Hungry Man. The best we can do is tell him to leave. I'm just glad he listens."

Even though I wasn't exactly afraid of the Hungry Man, I was still too shy to really be confident around him. I was glad Mama was there beside me, that she was the one who spoke to the Hungry Man and told him to leave. I liked the way she would puff up, like a bird ruffling its feathers to look bigger and tougher than it really was.

Every day, Mama was her usual self, tending her garden, baking, sewing, and occasionally complaining about her back or her knees. She always said, "when you get to be my age, your body starts to get old a whole lot quicker," but whenever I asked her how old she was, she'd just laugh. At night, though, when the Hungry Man came around, Mama turned into someone big and brave. Sometimes, I would practice puffing up in the mirror, squaring my shoulders and putting my hands on my hips like Mama always did. I always hoped to see a miniature version of her, but instead I just saw my small, awkward self.

"What does everyone else tell the Hungry Man?" I asked. Surely we weren't the only house he came to. There were four other houses on our street. Mrs. Wilkins lived across the street, next to Mr. Kemper. Mama always called him an *odd duck*, but I think he was just lonely on account of his wife died.

Mr. and Mrs. Clarke lived next door. Mr. Clarke's mother lived with them, although I almost never saw her. Sometimes she would come outside and wander around, like she was looking for something that she'd lost. I'd tried to help her once, but she'd gotten upset and began to cry. Mr. Clarke had come running out of the house and brought her home.

The night after, when I was supposed to be asleep, I'd heard muffled shouting coming from Mr. and Mrs. Clarke's house. The next day, Mama had driven Mrs. Clarke and her suitcase to the bus station. Mama had told me that Mr. Clarke's mother sometimes didn't know where she was, and that made her angry and scared. Mama had said that having Mr. Clarke's mother around made things too hard for Mrs. Clarke and that she needed to rest a little.

There were other houses on our street, but they were all empty. They poked up out of the ground like decaying teeth. Their lawns were overgrown and weedy, and I always thought that it would be fun to play in them and pretend that I was in the jungle or on a safari. Mama wouldn't let me, on account of the long grass being full of ticks. Instead, I just watched as the unkempt lawns slowly ate up the crumbling houses. Mama once told me that all the houses had once been full, but when the factory where Daddy used to work closed down, people started moving out.

Mama shook her head. "He doesn't go to their houses."

I was glad that the Hungry Man never bothered Mr. Clarke and his old mother, but it also felt unfair. How come the Hungry Man only ever came to our house? How come he never asked Mrs. Wilkins or Mr. Kemper or Mr. Clarke for whatever he wanted to bake with?

"I don't know why," said Mama. "He only ever comes here. When I asked Mrs. Wilkins about it, she looked at me like I was crazy. Said I must've imagined it."

I thought about when Terrance had stomped all over Mama's roses and how she'd marched straight over to Mrs. Wilkins about it. I tried to imagine her doing it every time someone was unkind, but I couldn't. It made me sad and angry that Mama would protect her rose bushes like that, but she wouldn't protect herself.

"Tonia, someday I'll be gone," said Mama one night. "And you'll have to tell the Hungry Man to leave."

The thought made me choke on my tea. Mama rubbed my back while I coughed and sputtered. The gesture was a kind one, but I wasn't comforted. I knew deep down that Mama wouldn't live forever, that one day she'd grow old and die. I knew that she was teaching me how to get rid of the Hungry Man because someday, I'd be alone here and I'd have to do it myself. But at ten, that was a harsh truth that I didn't want to acknowledge.

That night, for the first time in months, I was afraid of the Hungry Man. When he came to the door asking for eggs, I stood behind Mama, grateful that she was there to protect me. After he was gone, I lay in bed, staring at my window and scanning the darkness for him. As frightened as I was, I desperately wanted to see him out there. Seeing him would mean knowing where he was, and if I knew where he was, I could keep myself and my mother safe.

The phone rang sometime just before dawn. At that point, I'd stopped searching for the Hungry Man, but I was still half-awake, caught in a dreamy sort of limbo beneath my covers. I padded to Mama's room. She was sitting up in bed with the phone pressed to her ear. She glanced up and shooed me out of the room. I went back to bed and fell into a thick, dreamless sleep. I think something about seeing Mama still awake made me forget about the Hungry Man, at least for a little while.

Mama woke me up a few hours later. I sat up, rubbing the sleep from my eyes and squinting at the bright sunshine that was streaming in through the window. It was nearly ten o'clock. Mama never let me sleep that late. We always got up with the sun.

"Tonia," she said hoarsely, "your granny's down sick. I have to go away for a few days to look after her." She wiped at her eyes, which were red-rimmed and bloodshot. Before this, I'd only ever seen Mama cry once, when Daddy passed. It had scared me then, and it scared me now.

"You'll stay here," continued Mama, patting my shoulder. "Mrs. Wilkins is going to come and stay with you."

I shook my head. "Why can't I come with you, Mama?"

Mama sighed. "Your granny's real sick, dear, and I don't want you catching what she has."

The idea of Granny being sick was upsetting, but the thought that Mama might catch whatever she had made my eyes well up with tears. I threw myself into Mama's arms, holding her as tight as I could. If I just held on tight enough, she wouldn't be able to leave me behind.

"I know, baby. I know it's hard." Mama stroked my hair while I cried. "But I need you to stay here for me. I need you to stay here and keep the Hungry Man away."

Hearing the Hungry Man's name only made me cry harder. I didn't want Mama to leave me alone, not when the Hungry Man was still out there. Would I be able to keep him away? Would he listen to me when I told him to leave? He always listened to Mama, but she was a grownup. I was only ten, and I suddenly felt much smaller and younger. You're always taught to mind your elders, but no one ever listens to children.

Mama rubbed my back. "You'll do just fine," she said. "You remember what I taught you. He'll go away if you tell him to."

An hour later, she had packed her bag and Mrs. Wilkins stood in the living room, holding an overnight bag and a loaf of fresh bread. Mrs. Wilkins was tall and skinny. She reminded me of a bird with long, spindly legs and a thin, pointy beak that I'd seen in a book once. Her white hair was piled up on her head in a bun. I always thought that she should have had a pair of glasses perched at the end of her nose. She wore a small gold cross on a chain around her neck, and Mama always said that her first love was Jesus and her second was cleanliness. I never knew Mr. Wilkins on account of he'd died long before I was born, but I always wondered how he'd felt about coming in third place in his wife's heart.

"For your mother." She pushed the bread into Mama's hands. "I baked it yesterday morning," she said proudly. She took a small, red jar out of her apron pocket. "And some of my famous raspberry jam."

"Thank you," said Mama. "That's very kind." She put the bread and jam into a paper bag. Mrs. Wilkins gave us a jar of her raspberry jam every year for Christmas. It was too tart for me, but Mama liked having it on her toast. I wondered if all the raspberry seeds would get stuck in Granny's false teeth.

Mrs. Wilkins nodded while Mama told her about things like my bedtime and how much TV I was allowed to watch. I liked playing with the rabbit ears more than I liked watching TV. It was more fun to try and unscramble the fuzzy channels than it was to actually watch. Mama called it one of her *pet peeves*, along with when I used to play with the circular dial on the telephone, poking my fingers through the little holes and watching as it spun.

"Do give your mother my best," said Mrs. Wilkins.

"And keep the Hungry Man out," said Mama as she dug through her purse one last time, checking to make sure she had her keys and wallet.

Mrs. Wilkins raised an eyebrow. "The Hungry Man?"

Mama nodded. "He comes around every night about an hour after sunset and asks for food. Never give him anything and never let him in." She gestured at me. "Tonia knows what to do."

Mrs. Wilkins frowned. "Alright then," she said, her voice unsure. She glanced over at me, as if to silently ask whether or not the Hungry Man was real.

I nodded eagerly. "You never ever let him in," I said quickly, "and you never give him any food either."

Mrs. Wilkins smiled, but it didn't quite touch her eyes. Instead, she just nodded again and turned back to Mama. "I'll keep the Hungry Man out," she said the same way you'd talk to a child telling a fib. It was a voice that said, *I don't really believe you, but I'll humor you because I think you're stupid.* Mama didn't seem to notice.

"Thank you." Keys in hand, Mama looked over at me. "I'll call you when I get there, and I'll call again tomorrow morning. Mind your manners, and keep the Hungry Man out."

"I will, Mama." I decided then and there that Mrs. Wilkins probably wouldn't do a thing about the Hungry Man. It would be my job to keep him out of the house and away from our food. I squared my shoulders and fought the urge to beg Mama to stay again. It wouldn't be right to cry in front of Mrs. Wilkins like that.

As soon as Mama left, Mrs. Wilkins sat down on the couch. She wiped it with her hands first, as if clearing away a layer of dirt. This made me even madder at her, because Mama always made sure our house was spotless.

"Why don't you play for a bit before lunch?" Mrs. Wilkins pulled a book out of her purse and pointed at the door as she spoke to me. I hesitated, wondering if I should tell her more about the Hungry Man. I could tell her after dinner. That way, she'd have it all fresh in her mind when he came to the door.

I went to the shed and got my gardening gloves and spade. This would be the first time I'd tended the roses without Mama. It wasn't hard. After all, I was old enough to know what weeds looked like and how to dig them up without hurting the roses. I missed Mama though. We would always sing to the roses. She taught me about all the bugs in the garden and what they did, how some of them hurt the roses and how others helped them.

"Always wear your gloves when you're tending the roses," Mama would say. "That way, you're safe from the thorns. The thorns are a rose's way of protecting itself."

The rest of the day passed uneventfully. I weeded the garden and watered the roses. I sang Mama's songs to them, even though my heart wasn't really in it. When it was time to come in, I wiped the dust and dirt from my shoes. Mrs. Wilkins made me take them off anyway. She wrinkled her nose at my old worn sneakers, but I thought it was kind of her to be so concerned about the sweeping Mama would have to do when she got home. That evening, as the sun began to sink low in the sky, I tried to help Mrs. Wilkins make dinner, but she shooed me out of the kitchen.

"The last thing I need is you getting underfoot and making a mess," she said. I tried telling her that I helped Mama make dinner every night and that I wouldn't make a mess.

"Why don't you tidy up the living room instead?" she asked.

I went into the living room, but it was exactly as I'd left it earlier. The only difference was Mrs. Wilkins' book on the end table by the armchair. I rearranged Mama's knickknacks until Mrs. Wilkins called me for dinner.

"Mrs. Wilkins," I said, watching as she piled mashed potatoes neatly onto a plate, "my Mama's right about the Hungry Man."

"Don't talk with your mouth full. Besides, there's no such thing as a Hungry Man."

"No, ma'am, there is. I promise. He comes around every night after sunset. He always says that he's baking a cake and he needs ingredients, but—"

Mrs. Wilkins glared at me. "Tonia, stop it."

I took a deep breath. I was trying to be polite, even though Mrs. Wilkins wasn't listening to me. After all, she had made me dinner and had agreed to look after me while Mama was away. I owed it to her to be respectful. I don't think Mama and Mrs. Wilkins were friends, at least, not like I was friends with some of the girls at school. Sometimes Mama went to the sewing circle that Mrs. Wilkins had at her house, and she'd give her rose cuttings every now and then. I sat up straight and tall in my chair and set my fork down.

"Please, listen to me. I'm not lying, I swear. The Hungry Man always comes by, and Mama says—"

Mrs. Wilkins slapped the tabletop, making the plates and silverware rattle. "That's enough! You stop this foolishness right now or I'll send you straight to bed."

"I didn't mean—"

Mrs. Wilkins pointed angrily at the stairs as she scolded me. "Get upstairs now!"

She looked so angry I thought she might throw her plate at me. I'd never been afraid of an adult before, besides the Hungry Man, of course, but I wasn't sure if he really counted on account he wasn't human. I pushed my chair back and ran up the stairs, taking them two at a time.

I ran into my bedroom, shut the door tight, and paced back and forth in front of the window. The sun was edging closer and closer to the treeline. Soon, it would dip beneath them, and it would be dark enough for the Hungry Man to come. I stopped, staring out the window, begging the sun not to set, desperately wishing that it would stay up until Mama got home.

I heard Mrs. Wilkins moving around in the kitchen, heard the clatter of dishes in the sink as she washed them. The little bit of food I'd eaten knotted in my stomach as the sun began to sink, painting the sky in bright reds and pinks that seemed to mock me with their beauty. How could the sunset be so lovely when it signaled the Hungry Man's arrival?

I was still standing by the window when dusk settled. In the falling darkness, a shambling figure ambled toward our house. I recognized the Hungry Man's gait and ran downstairs, nearly tripping over my own two feet.

I ran past Mrs. Wilkins in the living room to the front door and locked it. "Mrs. Wilkins, the Hungry Man's outside! We have to keep him out—"

She rolled her eyes at me and got up off the couch, tossing her book onto the seat. "I am tired of this Hungry Man nonsense! There's no one out there. Now get back up to bed right now—"

She was interrupted by a knock on the front door. We both froze. I think Mrs. Wilkins was stunned that there really was someone at the door. I'd never met an adult who had ever admitted to being wrong before. For a moment, I thought that Mrs. Wilkins would believe me and send the Hungry Man away. Instead, she shook her head as if clearing her mind, and then marched over to the door. I stood in front of it, pressing my back against it and holding my arms out, as if my small body could keep anyone from opening it.

"Tonia, move out of the way right now." Mrs. Wilkins put her hands on her hips and narrowed her eyes. Normally, I would have obeyed her, but the Hungry Man was outside and I couldn't risk her letting him in. I'd rather be scolded or even spanked than have the Hungry Man come in.

Mrs. Wilkins reached out and grabbed my arm, yanking me sideways. I wasn't surprised by her anger, but by her sudden strength. I stumbled, tripping, and landed hard on my rear end at the foot of the stairs. I watched in horror as Mrs. Wilkins unlocked the door and opened it. The Hungry Man stood on the other side of the screen door, staring vacantly.

"Yes? Can I help you?" Mrs. Wilkins asked him, her voice cold and polite.

"You can't come in!" I shouted, staggering to my feet. "You can't come in and you can't have any food either! Go away!"

Mrs. Wilkins turned to me, her eyes wide and her face the color of the ripe tomatoes in Mama's garden. "Tonia!" she hissed. "That isn't very Christian. Get upstairs now!"

"Can I borrow some eggs?" asked the Hungry Man. He stared emptily at Mrs. Wilkins, as if he hadn't heard me at all. "I'm trying to bake a cake, and I'm afraid I'm plum out."

"No!" I shouted. "No eggs! Now go away!"

Mrs. Wilkins whirled around. Her hand reached out and I felt her palm hit my cheek hard. I staggered back, nearly falling over again. My vision began to blur as tears filled my eyes, but I remained focused on the Hungry Man. No matter what, I wouldn't let Mrs. Wilkins give him any food, and I certainly wouldn't let her let him in the house.

"You can't come in, and you can't have any eggs," I continued.

"Tonia, stop it!" Mrs. Wilkins reached up and unlocked the screen door. She smiled apologetically at the Hungry Man. "I'm so sorry. She's upset because her grandmother is ill. Won't you come in while I get you those eggs?"

I lunged for the door, grabbing at the lock and trying desperately to push it back into place. "No!" I yelled. "No, he can't come in! He can't!"

Mrs. Wilkins pointed angrily at the top of the stairs. "You're being very unChristian right now," she scolded. "Now get upstairs and stay there."

Behind her, the Hungry Man opened the screen door. It creaked, as if the hinges were upset at being forced to open for him. For the first time since I'd seen him, the Hungry Man's eyes were sharp and focused, like those of a hawk. I felt my insides twist, and I suddenly wanted to be far, far away from the house. Once the screen door creaked open, it stopped being a proper home. The whole house felt unclean and alien, as if it wanted to spit me out. I scrambled up the stairs, too frightened to think straight.

I ran up to my bedroom and slammed the door. My door didn't have a lock, so I began pushing my furniture in front of it to barricade myself in. To this day, I'm not sure how my scrawny ten-year-old body managed to push my heavy wooden dresser in front of the door. I crawled under my bed, the only place I could think to hide from the Hungry Man. I lay on my belly, not noticing the dust bunnies and spiderwebs, weeping.

I heard the Hungry Man and Mrs. Wilkins moving around in the kitchen. Pots and pans clanking over muffled conversation and laughter. I wanted to tell myself that maybe the Hungry Man wasn't so bad. Maybe he just wanted to bake a cake. Maybe he'd bake a cake and then leave and everything would be fine. I knew deep down that none of this was true. By letting the Hungry Man into the house, Mrs. Wilkins had unleashed something horrible.

I lay under the bed, listening to the incessant bustling from the kitchen until the sun began to rise. I heard the sound of pots and pans clattering together, accompanied by the rhythmic squeak of the handle on the egg beaters. I heard cupboards opening and closing. I didn't hear any voices. Every time Mama and I baked, we filled the kitchen with laughter and songs. The thought of two people baking without talking to each other felt unreal, like the feeling of flowers made out of paper or cloth. As my room grew lighter, the noises ceased. The silence engulfed the house, making me more frightened than all the noises had the night before. Was the Hungry Man still here? Had he left? Had I heard the door open and close? Surely he wouldn't still be here. He couldn't just stay in the house, could he? Plus, it was daytime, and he never came out in the daylight.

I had been able to ignore my cramped arms and legs, but I couldn't overlook my full bladder any longer. I crawled out from under my bed. Aside from the furniture stacked in front of the door, my room looked exactly the same as it always had. I carefully pushed the furniture away from the door, wincing as my muscles protested. I opened the door slowly and peeked out into the hall.

The hall was empty and quiet, looking like it always did. I tiptoed out, avoiding the squeaky floorboards. I hung back in the shadows, trying desperately to ignore my bladder and think of a way to relieve myself without crossing in front of the stairs to get to the toilet. In the end, I cautiously stepped in front of the stairs because I had no other choice.

There was nothing at the bottom of the stairs. I paused, waiting with bated breath, sure that the Hungry Man would step out any minute. The seconds passed in silence, but I didn't feel relief when the stairwell remained empty. Not seeing the Hungry Man was worse than seeing him. Seeing him would mean at least knowing where he was. I tiptoed to the bathroom and relieved myself, and then slowly descended the stairs, pausing to listen on each step. The house remained quiet as a grave and just as unsettling.

I locked the screen door, then closed and locked the front door. I looked around. From where I stood, I couldn't see into the kitchen, just the living room. The living room was pristine and untouched, just the way it had been last night before the Hungry Man had arrived.

I walked into the kitchen, dreading what I might find. I stood in the doorway and stared. The kitchen looked the same as it always did, except for the cake sitting on the table. It was enormous, taking up nearly the entire tabletop. The cake was topped with roses made of red frosting, the kind I'd only ever seen in pictures of fancy cakes for weddings. It was so beautiful, it didn't even look real.

My stomach rumbled. I was dimly aware that I was walking toward the cake, although it felt more like I was floating, and I don't remember the floorboards creaking under my feet like they usually did. The house felt so still and quiet, like I was moving through a photograph. I walked around the table, taking in the enormous cake from all sides. The frosting was perfectly smooth, almost slick-looking. It didn't have any of the little ridges and swirls I'd always seen on Mama's cakes.

I had to stand on my tip-toes to get a good look at the roses. They covered the entire cake top like a huge garden. They were as red and vibrant as the roses in Mama's garden. I reached out and touched one as gently as I would one from the garden. The frosting had developed a sort-of crust, and my fingers came away clean when I pulled my hand back. I looked down at my hand, surprised not to see frosting smeared across my fingers. I pressed my finger against the red frosting petal and slid it down, toward the bottom of the flower.

Something sharp pierced my finger, and I yanked my hand back. A red bead of blood had formed on my fingertip. I'd been so entranced by the red roses on the cake, I hadn't noticed the green vines circling each one. I leaned in, squinting at the vines. Each one was studded with several little green thorns.

In spite of the hunger gnawing at my stomach, I suddenly felt sick, like I was about to throw up. I pressed the tip of my bloodied finger against my pajama top, watching as the crimson stain spread out against the pale yellow fabric.

I looked back at the cake, noticing for the first time just how close I was to it. The tip of my nose was less than an inch away from the shiny white frosting. I stumbled backward. A rancid, meaty scent had invaded my nostrils. It reminded me of the dead rabbit that had laid on the side of the road for the better part of last summer. After a week of calling animal control to come and get it, Mama had buried it in the yard.

I pressed both hands over my mouth and nose as I gagged. It smelled like someone had taken that dead rabbit and shoved it right up in my face. I could almost feel its stiff, blood-caked fur against my nose and cheeks. I turned and ran out of the kitchen, nearly blinded by the tears that were welling up in my eyes.

I ran out to Mama's rose bushes. I was looking for her, even though I knew she wouldn't be there. At least I could hide in her roses until she came home for me. I crawled under the bushes, ignoring the thorns that scraped at my arms and legs. I curled myself up into a ball and hugged my knees, breathing in the sweet, cloying scent of fresh flowers. I lay there for a few minutes, breathing deeply and trying to calm my racing thoughts.

I couldn't stay under the rose bushes for very long. It was too small and cramped. The thorns wouldn't protect me from the Hungry Man. If a shotgun couldn't keep him away, neither could thorns, no matter how sharp they were. I wondered if I could go to Mr. Kemper's or Mr. Clarke's houses. Would they believe me about the Hungry Man? Or would they just shake their heads like Mrs. Wilkins and tell me that I was being childish and silly?

I'm not sure how long I lay under the rose bush. I crawled out when my arms and legs began to cramp again. As soon as I emerged, I was struck by the stench of rot and decay. I pressed my hands over my nose and mouth, gagging and trying not to throw up. I plucked one of the roses and held it under my nose as I circled the house.

I stood on the porch, pacing back and forth as I waited for Mama. The sun was high in the sky when I saw Mama's car turn down the street. She pulled over when she saw me and got out. She swept me up in her arms and kissed my head while I cried. I felt awful for failing her, for letting the Hungry Man come into the house, for whatever fate had befallen Mrs. Wilkins. Mama held me while I cried. I didn't fully register it, but she was crying too as she held me.

"Baby, I'm just glad you're safe," she said. "It's gonna be OK, I promise."

She put me in the car and drove the rest of the way to the house. She made me stay in the front seat while she went in. I expected to hear her scream when she saw what was in the kitchen. Instead, she came out a few minutes later, her face ashen yet stoic, as if she was trying her hardest not to cry.

She reached through the open window of the car and patted my shoulder. "Stay here, baby," she said. "Everything's gonna be OK. Just stay here until I come get you."

I don't know how long I sat there in the car, watching the front of the house. Every now and again, I'd see Mama moving around through the windows. Once or twice she came out holding a bulging trash bag. The sun was just starting to slip down toward the horizon when she told me that I could come inside. The lemony smell of disinfectant invaded my nostrils the moment I stepped over the threshold, but I didn't care. I went upstairs and took a hot bath, and then Mama made me a sandwich and let me sit in the living room to eat it.

Even though the kitchen had been scrubbed, I couldn't bear to go in. After I ate, Mama sent me up to bed.

"What about the Hungry Man?" I asked. Even though I was tired and scared, I didn't think it would be right to leave Mama by herself. She had included me in the Hungry Man ritual because she needed me there with her. No matter how scared I was, things wouldn't be so bad as long as Mama and I were together.

Mama just shook her head. "Go to bed, baby," she told me. "I'll be fine."

The next day, I noticed the giant mound of dirt in the backyard where Mama had buried the Hungry Man's cake. Mama had buried it as far away from the rose bushes as she could, but that was the last time I ever saw them bloom.

Mama and I had our evening tea in the living room. I think we both knew that I'd never go into the kitchen again—at least, not if I could help it. I was adding another spoonful of honey to my tea when the knocking started. Mama got up and went to the door. I followed her, frightened and curious.

Mrs. Wilkins stood on the other side of the screen door. She wore the same clothes she'd had on the last time I'd seen her. She was covered in flour and sticky, half-congealed egg. She stared vacantly at Mama.

"Can I borrow a cup of sugar?" she asked, her voice flat and lifeless as the Hungry Man's had been. "I'm trying to bake a cake, and I'm afraid I'm plum out."

Ristra
by Mary Robles

Telescope
to the horror
of the world.
Pinned down
body,
the torturing
shifts.
you live
by the gun,
a man with
his hammer
at the temple
Iron and calf
at the stone table.
The ristra you made
some summer
day/ Don't say
you're not the one
who showed me
how to thread
the dead chile heads
into the ristra,
tattered and devilish
dried intestines, dark laugh
at their bells?
Go into hell,
Go into the darkness again.
Say you don't

remember the ristra
its broken smell
say you won't stand/
say you can't
but don't tell me
You can / see the brushfire
and don't care / if you're lit
You mourn on
the snow but can't
shovel it like
drunks You know
your daughter's hand
but can't see it/
for smoke.

Three Sisters Island
by Hillary Monahan

I knew it was bad when Ali stopped answering my calls.

There's a notion twins have preternatural connection—an ESP granted by womb cohabitation. It's more like from the time you're spurted into the world, you're relegated to spending every hour of every day in close confines with another human who looks like you but isn't you. Who's dressed the same as you by doting parents who sometimes switch your names, *oopsie*. Who gets the same birthday and Christmas gifts so no one gets jealous. Who is, it's agreed by the world at large, your other half.

We were SAMANDALISON, never Samantha and Ali. Sisters. Twins. Paired forever. Christ, we even got our periods within a week of one another because Mother Nature seemed to buy into the twinsie bullshit too.

To say I knew my sister was an understatement. I knew her better than anyone ought to know another human, so when Ali took off with a guy she'd met on Spring Break last year, I got it. My parents didn't, but I did. She needed a life beyond me, an identity that didn't have me attached to it. It wasn't *smart*—running off to live with a guy she barely knew was reckless at best—but I understood it. Aidan was her way out of our forced dual proximity, and Aidan lived on Three Sisters Island.

He didn't seem like a bad guy. A professional fisherman, his father owned a boat, and the two of them followed in the footsteps of three generations of Shallows' men hauling cod off the shores of Cape Cod. He met Ali when he'd come to the mainland for a supplies run, and they'd hit it off. *Really* hit it off, she'd overshared; he had her down to her skivvies and below the deck of the *SS Jodie-Ray* in an hour. He was a good looking guy in all the pictures, tall and lean with angular features. The shadow of scruff around his jaw and his black flat cap made him look like the product of another era—a fresh-off-the-boat Irish immigrant in the nineteenth century maybe.

Ali adored everything about him. I could hear it in her voice when she talked about him on our daily calls, which became every other day in

January, then twice a week in February, and then maybe once a week in March. April came, and I'd gone three whole weeks without hearing from her at all. It wasn't right; we were twins, joined at the hip forever by the invisible rules of twinning. It broke the silent pact, which is why I stood on the big dock in Woods Hole at five-thirty in the morning, suffering the spring cold. My snot was frozen inside my nose, and my glasses fogged up with every exhale of breath. The wind ripped through my wool pea coat like it wasn't even there. I'd considered the giant pink ski parka Mom had given me at Christmas—the exact same one she'd given Ali, only in purple—then decided it was too ugly to wear in public.

Mistakes had been made.

I overpaid for coffee at the snack hut and waited to board, milling around with a half-dozen other cold, tired travelers. The coffee was too burnt to drink, but it served another purpose: keeping the feeling in my fingertips. At quarter to six, we were called on. Most people bee-lined for the inside seats, but I couldn't. I needed fresh air or the vessel's rocking motion would see me puking my brains out, a lesson whale watch field trips had painfully taught.

And the reason I'd put off seeing my sister for the year she'd lived on Three Sisters. I kept telling her I'd make it out, but...

Shit.

Shit, shit, shit.

I settled onto the bench closest to the swinging double doors of the cabin. The passengers venturing outside to take selfies leant me interior heat with every passing. I fumbled inside my coat pocket for my phone, my thumb swiping over to my texts. Dozens to Ali with no reply, and as of the last week, a dozen to Aidan, equally ignored. Last night's all-caps message stared me in the face. "AIDAN IF YOU DON'T REPLY I'M COMING OUT THERE" hung so very loudly in unanswered silence.

I pocketed the phone and stifled a yawn against my shoulder. It was early, yes, but I was rundown beyond the hour; my upset over my sister's absence had destroyed the last few weeks of sleep. When the lights went down, the scenarios started like films in my head: Aidan had done something awful to her and she was chum in his boat or something had been done *to* both of them... It scared me, but...

It's strange. As much as I insisted—insist—twins don't have ESP, my gut told me if my sister was dead, I'd *know*. And I didn't know anything other than she wasn't talking to me for the first time in my life and I hated it. I was going out there as much to sooth my fear of abandonment as I was to check on her welfare if I was being honest with myself.

Maybe they went on vacation. She has a life beyond me now.

I sipped the stale coffee, forgetting how terrible it was. The lukewarm temperature did nothing to improve the flavor.

Three hours of travel. My stomach slopped with every wave crest, but I managed to stagger off not covered by my own vomit.

A gull heralded my arrival with a screech, a flap of wings, and a dive into an overflowing trash bin. No one had changed the bag since the previous day, and the wet, salt air had wilted all the contents. The smell persisted despite the cool temperature. By noon, it'd be a real travesty. I skated my way across the condensation-slick dock to escape it, grateful to find footing on one of the strewn-about rubber safety mats.

When Ali described Three Sisters to me, she told me to imagine a neglected Nantucket.

"It's the same architecture, only no one kept it up," she'd said. "Everything's rusty. Can a place be rusty? Three Sisters is rusty. And foggy. So much fog. I swear it's where the sun goes to die, but at least I like the smell of the ocean, and the beaches are quiet."

It was an apt, albeit unflattering, picture. The island looked like a fifties-era beach town postcard left in the sun too long. The colors were bleached, shades of gray intersecting other shades of gray, with hints of an old color palette. Sometimes, under an eave or on a shutter, I'd spy the vestiges of blue or green, but everything else was New England's stark, Puritanical white and black combination, and even those had gone gray thanks to sea salt and grit.

Between damp boards and copious amounts of gull detritus, getting off of the dock was a feat of athleticism, and perhaps the only thing to go right since I'd rolled out of bed. When I'd crossed over from sodden wood to parking lot pavement by the ferry booth, I looked behind me. I'd always considered the Atlantic an angry ocean, roiling and spitting with frigid fury, but it was soft and somber then, the charcoal depths and gentle waves alien to me. I knew these waters, had lived by them my whole life. The strong tides and rocky beaches were tenets of my childhood. That too-still shore, that cold, balmy serenity was wrong—as wrong as everything else in my world since my sister's disappearance.

"Where are you, Ali?"

The dull, distant clang of a fisherman's bell was my only answer.

I faced the town. The cobblestone streets were thirsty for repair, the potholes deep enough to devour car shocks for breakfast. Ali had warned—and I knew from our innumerable dropped calls—cell signal here was precious. Five bars in Woods Hole plummeted to two on the island, which would make calling for an Uber challenging if not impossible.

… if this place even offered rideshare. There were few people and fewer cars despite the nine-thirty timestamp. The streets were peppered with rusted-out pickups, each parked curbside in front of small businesses either boarded up with plywood or so dimly lit they looked like black holes. A handful of drivers passed—old, grizzled men in plaid flannel shirts, their eyes fixed on the road before them. None of them smiled. No waves. No curious stares. I was an unacknowledged ghost to the point I had to sidestep a truck that got within inches of me on a crosswalk and gave no quarter.

"Hey! Watch it!"

The driver said nothing. He *did* nothing. My voice was insignificant beyond flustering the gulls. They flapped their wings irritably at me before returning to their garbage breakfast.

I walked. I had no clue where I was going, no forwarding address for my sister, but it wasn't a big island—five miles at its widest point and only twelve hundred year-round residents. Someone would know the Shallows, and as they were fishermen, the dock was as good a place as any to start looking. I passed shop after shop, looking through dusty, dark windows, searching for a local to talk to, but to no avail. If there was staff, they were hiding, and I wasn't so brave as to enter strange, unlit buildings in this strange, unlit place.

Hal's Garage on the corner provided my first real opportunity to make my inquiry. It was small: two gas pumps, a truck occupying the right lane, an SUV the left. The building behind was half garage, half convenience store. A half-dozen neon signs promised everything from an ATM machine to KENO to a selection of American beers. I approached. A few people milled around inside and convened at the register, and by the casualness of their postures, I'd hit local gold. It was, by appearances, a friendly, neighborhood hangout, like something from a Norman Rockwell cover.

Except when I walked into the store, everything *stopped*. Three men at the counter, the front-most one sporting an unlit cigarette on his bottom lip, seized. They'd been laughing seconds before, but my presence siphoned the joy from the room. Smiles withered to frowns as they stared at me, expectant. Even the little kid filling a plastic bag with penny candies—"Stuff a bag for a dollar!"—stopped perusing his bounty to eyeball me.

"Thought you took off with them," Cigarette man said. "That's what Ian said."

Them? And who was Ian?

"I'm Sam Mathers. Ali's my sister. We look just alike. Other than this. Heh." I gestured at my dark, chin-length bob. The severity of the cut was the only way most people could tell me and Ali apart. She wore hers almost to her hips, whereas I'd been shearing myself to various degrees since puberty.

The man glanced at his companions, first the clerk behind the register in his navy blue work shirt, Hal stitched above the pocket, then to the other customer whose grimace was etched into his leathery, sun-beaten skin. They exchanged no words, but a whole conversation played out between their stiffening postures and the narrowness of their eyes.

It wasn't for me, but it was definitely about me.

"Ah. That'd explain it," Cigarette man said on a grunt.

He offered nothing else.

I stepped all the way inside the building. The glass door with the stenciled lettering closed behind me with a clatter of tin bells hung from the push bar.

"I was hoping to find Aidan Shallows. To ask him—wait, who did she leave with? When did she leave?" My voice was high, almost birdlike. I winced hearing myself, feeling ridiculous I'd lost my cool less than twenty minutes after arrival. But, as much as I hated it, that slip of vulnerability actually helped me. Cigarette's expression softened, his mouth working to roll the cigarette over to the corner of his lips so he could speak.

"Sick, Ian said. That's his father. Aidan took sick a couple weeks back." He cleared his throat before looking over at the kid. "Finish filling that, Jack, or we're leaving as is."

Jack stopped gawking at me to go back to throwing candies into his bag.

"Two streets up on the left," Hal offered. "Mockingbird Way. Number thirty-seven. Aidan's there. He can prolly tell you what happened. Not sure how he's feeling though."

"*Poorly,*" the third man offered, almost too quiet for me to hear. "Fucking women."

He shook his head, sliding his wallet into his jeans' pocket, and made his way back to the gas pumps. His ride was yet another rusted-out pickup truck, this one white where the paint still clutched the Ford frame, and he drove off with a squeal of tires, leaving black tracks on the sun-faded pavement.

"Don't mind Charlie. He's a salty old bastard," Cigarette said. "Just a lot going on lately. Aidan grew up here. He should have known better than to bring a mainlander back with him. We're all on edge."

"A mainlander? What does that mean?"

"It means exactly what it sounds like. It's no good for you here, and that makes it no good for us." He turned his back to me, gesturing at his kid and making for the door. I sputtered at him, demanding he wait, but he went outside to light his cigarette and climbed into his battered SUV. Jack crammed three more candies into his too-full bag and chased his father. Outside, he paused to look back at me through the glass storefront, and for a moment, I could have sworn that six year old felt sorry for me.

*　　*　　*

Hal escaped.

I was so busy watching Cigarette leave, by the time I turned around, Hal was gone, too, disappeared into his back room. I called for him, even rang the bell on his counter for service, but he'd ghosted. All that shit about mainlanders being bad for the island. What did that mean? And where did Ali take off to? And with whom? And was no one going to give me answers?

Agoraphobic assholes.

I'd have gloried in a good tantrum, maybe ripping the bells off the door and throwing them to the floor with a scream, but it wasn't worth it. None of it was worth it. *They* weren't worth it, but Ali was. I had to find Mockingbird Way. GPS would have been nice, but the cell phone signal wasn't having it, and I suspected it'd get worse before it got better: Fog was rolling in. I couldn't recall too many instances of day fog, not even in Plymouth. My parents' house was nestled among ponds, marshes, and ocean. Even then, fog was a nighttime phenomenon. Here, it played out in broad daylight, boldly creeping up and wisping over the old cobblestone to swirl around my feet like ghost cats.

I walked along, squinting to read the street signs against the gray-white skies, trying not to notice how cumbersome my wool coat had become. The frosty early morning had given way to a moist mid-morning with scattered spots of drizzle. It was the kind of weather where, when you were driving, it was too dry to put your windshield wipers on the lowest setting, but too wet to not manually run them twice a minute.

At least the street wasn't too far away from Hal's—maybe half a mile. It was on an incline, and I trudged to the hilltop, sweating despite the barely-sixty temperature. Each cottage was a near replica of the last save for variations on what exact type of rust-covered vehicle lurked in the waist-high grass of the front lawns. Cracked windows, cracked paint, cracked driveways. It was a place of better yesterdays, and I craned my neck at each wilting mailbox to see exactly where my sister had lived over this past year.

Thirty-seven was one of the better kept properties in the line. The shutters had new paint, for one—an olive green I knew Ali must have picked. She loved her earth tones. There was a garden, though it was looking overgrown and wilted, like no one had been at it for a few weeks. If she'd disappeared at the time our calls stopped…

Don't borrow problems. Yet.

I navigated a brick walkway leading to a side porch with a screen door to knock on the wood frame. Inside, a male groan, deep and low.

140

"Aidan? It's Sam. Ali's sister. I texted last night."

Another groan.

And quiet.

He'd heard me, that much was certain, but what condition was he in to receive me remained to be seen. I knocked again, louder this time, and reached for the handle, just in case. The trepidation and exhilaration when it allowed me entry—was it good or bad? I didn't know, but the promise of answers drove me onward. I walked into a small kitchen, ten by ten, with a table for two under the window to my right, where a wilted flower was going to dust in a slender glass vase. Dishes were stacked on the counter and in the sink, old food dried to cracked paste on the surfaces.

"Aidan?"

This answer wasn't a groan so much as a mumble. I followed the noise to a living room sparse of furniture. The walls were bare, dusty shadows of rectangles marking where pictures used to belong. The rug and rug pad were rolled up and leaning against the bookcase, which had also been pushed into the corner. For that matter, *everything* was in the corner, including the absent wall art, including the man slowly and deliberately stacking his earthly belongings into a quarter of the space the room offered.

It took me far too long to recognize him from Ali's pictures. That man had been handsome and strong. His sinewy frame spoke of his hard labors hauling fish and of a running hobby he'd had since high school. But this person was…not fat, precisely. Puffy? Puffy and *wrong*. He was tall but stooped, his head hanging low, his shoulders slumping. Dark hair, oily and thick, clung in greasy lines to his scalp, the ends curling behind his ears like he hadn't seen a haircut in months. His clothes were dirty, straining against swollen flesh, and his skin was a translucent white, like skim milk. Dark veins, more blue than black, stretched out in spidery tendrils along his cheeks and neck, or at least the parts of his cheeks and neck I could see thanks to a wiry, untrimmed beard.

He was also drenched all over. Rivulets ran down his neck and dripped from his sodden clothes. Beneath bare feet with long, talon-like, black toenails, a small pool had settled into the grooves between the wide boards of hardwood. It ran in my direction, the speed of it telegraphing the old house's not-so-subtle listing.

I glanced at the windows. Still misty outside, more fog rolling in. It was nowhere near rainy enough to do *this*. To be so wet, he'd have had to have taken a swim or gotten into the shower, but in his clothes, which made no sense.

Fever, maybe. They said he was sick, I thought. "Aidan, hi. Sorry to barge in. I'm looking for Ali?"

He'd been shoving at his corner stack, cramming a lamp into a gap between an upholstered chair and an end table, but finally, he registered my presence. He turned to me, his movements exaggerated and jerky, more marionette than man. His face was a moon, pale and full and round, with dots of moisture collecting at the hairline. The beads grew before my eyes, then burst, each raining water over the sickly, plumped skin.

"Madddddddy?" he rasped, a question, not a statement. "Ali! You're back again." The smile bisecting his face was genuine, beatific even, despite his haggard appearance. He shambled my way, throwing the lamp behind him into his furniture pile, not even flinching at the sound of shattered glass. As he neared me, mumbling "Ali" over and over again, I could see the silvery gray film that had formed over his eyes. I could see the thick, oily discharge that had formed around his nostrils and at the corners of his mouth.

Aidan Shallows was a very, very sick man.

"Not Ali, Aidan. Sam. Samantha. I'm looking for Ali, but you're really sick so why don't I call you an ambulance, okay? I'll get you help—" I fumbled in my pocket for my phone, scared, unsure of what to do. Why would they leave him like this? Why would his own father not check on his son if he'd had the wherewithal to tell the locals about Aidan's illness in the first place?

"Ali!"

Aidan swiped for me again. I reared from his lunging grasp, but his fingers fisted in the collar of my pea coat. I'd had it buttoned to protect me from the elements outside, and so I was trapped inside a heavy, woolen straightjacket that he easily hauled back, toward him, so my back collided with his front. His arms, heavy and thick and wet, encircled me. My shrill yelp stabbed the pervasive quiet, but Aidan either didn't care or he didn't notice. He squeezed me like a lover.

"I didn't think I'd see you until tonight, but the fog brought you back early," he whispered, his cold, rubbery lips brushing against the shell of my ear. Unwanted, uninvited intimacy was as infuriating as it was terrifying; I kicked out with my legs, struggling against him with all the fury my hundred and fifty pounds could muster, but then I felt the scuttling and I *froze*. Legs, too many legs, tickly and light as a feather yet unmistakably present, scurried over my ear, then up, into my hair, and danced across my scalp.

I shrieked again, saying over and over "It's Sam. Not Ali. I'm her sister!" but Aidan wouldn't free me, and so I suffered the terror of that which goes unseen. Of something pushing through the heavy threads of my hair and traversing my skull and then going still, like it had found a proper landscape in which to nest, and it never wanted to leave.

Again Aidan mumbled, nuzzling at my neck and ear, a wet, cold wall behind me. He crooned; he held me in his embrace; he rocked on the balls of his feet and cooed like a sea-sodden teddy bear. Declarations of love—most of them incoherent—poured from his lips, but after a long, ragged slurp of air, he said almost too clearly, "I'm ready. I've been preparing."

For what? Did I want to know? I wondered. *Oh, Ali. Where are you?*

I closed my eyes, hot, unshed tears sealing my lids to my face. It reeked in the kitchen—not just of old food and trash, but of him. Salty. Sour. Sweat and piss and low tide all in one. None of it made sense. What was happening made no sense. He made no sense. He wouldn't believe I wasn't my sister, which—okay, fine, he was clearly sick so differentiating between us would be even harder than usual. But why would my sister have anything to do with the fog? Why did she only come at night? What was he preparing for?

I have to get out of here. Out of this. I have to find Ali. I tried to think of something. *What do I...*

"Show me," I said.

If he wouldn't believe that I wasn't my sister, I'd be her if for no other reason than to make the least heroic escape in history. It was the right tactic; he dropped his clutching hold and shuffled back toward the living room, each step laborious. When foot met floor, he sloshed, leaving puddles of water in his wake. It couldn't all be from his clothes, not with how it poured down his face and neck and pearled on his brow. His hair couldn't possibly hold that much water, so *where the hell was it coming from?*

The question plagued me as I tore away, scrabbling for the door. My lizard brain, the place deep in my mind where instinct was borne, demanded I run, but then what? Who else would know about my sister, or at least, who else would be willing to tell me what happened to her? And the fog—it had risen. What was knee height was up past my face, thick and dense like a cloud had dropped from the sky to sit upon the earth awhile. I had nowhere to go, no clear way to get there, and not a single person to help me.

An itch reminded me of my invader. I shredded at my scalp, searching the dense, damp mass for the mystery *thing* claiming the crest of my head. My fingers pinched around something hard and pointy. I yanked, freeing it along with a few of my own hairs. The hermit crab was a tiny thing—a few millimeters at most—but oh, the pincher claws and legs. I threw it across the room with a shriek, dispassionately watching it collide with the wall and slide across the tile floor to come to rest beneath the fridge.

"Come see, Ali. It's good, like you said. Is it good?" Aidan slurred from the other room.

No, no, it's not good. Nothing is good.

Go or stay, go or stay? Aidan had indicated Ali came with the fog, but that was madness, wasn't it? So why did I keep looking outside hoping she'd step out of it to explain everything? Hoping she'd hug me and tell me her boyfriend was having a fever dream that he'd somehow dragged me into, but everything would be fine soon; I just needed to wake up.

I sucked in a breath, steeling myself to make a losing choice no matter how I spun it. Cowardice trumped curiosity in the end, though, the fear too consuming to overcome. I turned on my heel, reaching for the door handle to cast myself off into the unknown.

Only to come face to face with my sister, her smile as serene and placid as the morning Atlantic.

* * *

My sister was beautiful in ways that defied the reality of us.

We were never ugly—conventionally pretty was a fair thing to say in our dark haired, dark eyed, Mediterranean way—but in that moment, she was so much more than her usual self, or at least, so much more than usual me. Her face, her skin, her eyes were all mine, but she had a celestial radiance to her, too, like all the color missing from the island had somehow congregated to saturate her and only her.

Maybe it was the framing of the fog. Maybe it was her palpable joy. Maybe it was something terrible and fucked up and indefinable. Aidan's condition certainly fit into the latter category, despite me never even recognizing the category's existence before.

Weird.

Other.

Eldritch.

Ali's arms opened, offering the hug I'd wanted so badly the minute before. Her head tilted to the side, sending that long hair cascading around the swishy summer dress flirting by her hips. I should have crushed her to me, drowning in relief that she was here and safe and alive, but I couldn't move. She was twin, but she was not, and I had to grapple with the odious reality that a part of me was terrified of my own mirror.

"I've missed you," she said. "I hope you'll stay."

No, "why are you here?" No, "sorry I haven't called." No reason for the thing that had been her boyfriend sloughing ocean water onto the living room floor. Just like every other islander in that godforsaken place, she offered no explanations, only generated more questions with her colloquial riddles.

She just got here, give her time…

But to my overtaxed mind and patience, she was one more ugly mystery, and I'd had enough of it.

"What is *wrong* with you? With him? What the fuck is going on? I've been calling for three weeks—"

"I'm sorry. You'll understand when you meet them," Ali said. "Let's go see Aidan. He's ready."

"Who are 'them'? And what is ready?" My gut told me to run, not just from Aidan, but from this deviant version of my sister. But because it was Ali, when she reached for my hand and guided me from the kitchen, I followed despite the trillion sensible reasons to do otherwise pummeling my brain.

I don't understand, myself or her. I'm lost.

In my brief absence, Aidan had resumed his stacking in the living room. There wasn't anything left there to add to the corner, so he'd begun bringing in things from the bathroom: towels, a bathrobe, the upright TP holder. He shoved them into the mess, fussing with them until they met some condition that only made sense to him.

"Aidan, I'm here," Ali said.

I tried jerking my hand away from her, recoiling from the whole scene, but she wouldn't relinquish me. Her grip was indecently strong. Aidan spun to peer at us, and his brows lifted, sending a torrent of water raining down his neck and shoulders.

"Two of you. Two, two, two," he chanted with a rictus grin. His hair parted in the front; another hermit crab made an uninvited appearance to tap dance across his brow and disappear behind his ear. He never acknowledged it, never dashed at it to sweep it away. To him, this was un-noteworthy. Perhaps, if his condition was any indication, it was commonplace. Perhaps he was infested with the goddamned things.

"You did so well, my love. Look at what you've built. I think it's time, Aiden. Don't you?"

"For what," I demanded. "Time for what, Ali?"

"Watch," was all she said.

I didn't want to watch. I wanted to flee, but that wasn't an option, not unless I wanted to leave the hand she clasped behind. I stood there and did her bidding, because there was no other choice. There was only Ali and her lead resolve and lead grasp. There was only this moment she was forcing me to endure.

I watched.

I watched as Aidan fumbled with the buttons on his flannel shirt, slowly unearthing them from their soiled holes. I watched him reveal his heavily furred torso that had, not so long ago, been a study of fine angles and muscle; now it was unnaturally bloated. I watched him pull off his pants and strip to his boxer shorts, the front of them stained in ways I didn't like to think about. He didn't stop removing clothes until he was nude, his body weird and bulbous and flacid, which he didn't seem to mind, but I did. I tried keeping my eyes on his face, as much for his dignity as my own, but it was hard to do once I noticed the tiny moving shapes dancing across his body just below the surface. They were quarter-sized, no more, and they were frenzied under the too-taut skin, straining his dermis to the point I could clearly see their black carapaces.

They were *everywhere*.

"They're eager," Ali said, but I wasn't sure for whose ears, and I didn't care to know either. I wanted none of this, so much so that I jerked away from her, thrashing to free myself of her hold. I'd startled her enough she lost her grip, but it was far too late to escape the scene playing out before me.

Whatever thing she wanted me to watch had started, and it started with Aidan's pained, awful shrieking.

Birth was supposed to be a loud and bloody thing. I'd known that since we endured *The Miracle of Life* in sixth grade. Ali and I had absorbed it, horrified, later making a pact we would never in a million years let boys near us else we suffer that fate. Unnatural birth was worse. Aidan bellowed like a pained cow as the scuttling things inside tore their way through his thin skin to enter the world. It wasn't just one. It was dozens, all at once, an invisible signal traveling amongst the creatures to let them know they were ripe and ready.

Together, a hundred or more bore their way through their host with pointy, razor-like pinchers, until the once-fine man, once so beloved by my sister to the point she was willing to abandon her family for him, burst apart in an explosion of dark, brackish water and blood. It flooded the floor, the farthest reaching edges of the forming puddle kissing the white rubber of my Keds sneakers.

Aidan dropped, no longer a man, but a pile of withered, used flesh, the expression on his face as much ecstasy as it was pained terror.

The black crabs, shiny as polished onyx, scuttled their way to the pile in the corner, huddling inside their newly constructed nest.

It defied explanation, all of it. Ian said his son was sick, but this wasn't sick. This was an unnatural plague—an infestation—and he'd known it. Just as the men at the gas station had known it. No one had checked on Aidan because this had happened before. "They" had done it, those mysterious them, of whom my sister had become.

"Fucking women," that man had said.

Fucking women indeed. Looking back, I hadn't seen a single one on Three Sisters Island, and I think I knew why.

"You see now," Ali whispered, her words hot on my ear. "You understand."

My breath came in shallow pants. My body beneath the coat slathered in panic sweat. I swallowed past the lump in my throat, eyes following every movement of a single crab who'd so far defied joining its siblings.

"No, I don't, Ali. I don't see anything." My voice was ragged, my throat raw from screams I didn't remember escaping my mouth. "I don't understand anything at all."

Ali reached for my hair, stroking it, *tsk*ing quietly when she found a tangle. She gently unraveled it with her fingers, the gesture so at odds with the carnage that had played out before us. Her head dropped to my shoulder, her hand reached for mine and she laced our fingers together.

"It's okay, Sam," she said. "You will."

Arbor Day
by Kristi Petersen Schoonover

On Linden Island, kids are never told someone has died.

Instead, they're told, "So-and-so has gone to the family tree." As casually as "she's gone to chase her dream in Hollywood" or "he's run off to elope in Hawaii." As though Aunt Sylvie or Uncle Holt will be back once their temporary madness has passed.

I thought it was a quaint, provincial expression, something handed from the settling fishermen to our modern inhabitants who either work the businesses here or ferry to the mainland.

Then my wife Rowen was killed, and I learned it was anything but.

*   *   *

Less than an hour after Ro's car was crushed by a massive oak branch as she drove to her bakery, the bottom of the shower was still wet with the drops she'd shed while toweling off. Her panties were curled next to our bed, spilled coffee irrigated the kitchen counter, and her make-up dappled the vanity. It was as though she was going to show up any moment, castigate herself for leaving things out of order, and put them away.

After someone dies, I've often heard those left behind say, "I'd give *anything* to have them back."

I don't think that's what they really mean.

Saying you'd give *anything* is dangerous. Second, when a person that's left your life comes back, so do all of the problems between you.

No, I think what people really mean is, "I'd give anything to have a little more time."

I know I'm supposed to shred her personal papers, empty her handbag, donate her clothes, and move off this godforsaken island, which I never wanted to live on in the first place; it was for her, so she could be near her family and friends. But every time I start, I can't finish. I walk around with an emptiness so sharp it feels like my insides are full of broken glass. I wander about the house, see her scoop out a grapefruit, read a book, or tease me into bed.

I finally understand what it means to live in a haunted house, and it's been three weeks since I've seen a living soul.

Until there's a knock at the door.

I open it, expecting freezing salt air to saw through me; instead, I'm hugged by a warm, damp waft of mud and pine. The snow that'd blanketed my front steps has shrunk to filthy piles. The lawn's peppered with sopping patches of flattened grass.

In front of it all stands my wife's best friend, Dair—Adair is her real name—clad in three different shades of red: leggings, t-shirt, sherpa. She smiles widely. "A little February thaw, Tash, my friend?"

I think of Dair as more of a nuisance. She and Ro were tight—they grew up together here, and Dair was a kitchen fixture three nights a week—but I always got the sense that she was into *me*: if Ro weren't in the picture, she'd be in heavy pursuit.

She senses the hesitation. "I...wanted to give you space. But...I can help you clean out her things, or we can talk, or..." She buoys a basket. "I put this together. You know, it's not much, but I make these for everybody after someone...you know?"

I'm not quite sure what to say. I've never spent time with just Dair.

She bursts into tears. "I miss her, too!"

Ah, shit. "It's okay." I take the basket from her. "Come in."

I eye the bottle of white wine nestled between French bread and a hunk of Swiss. I haven't had a drink since the night before Ro's accident. "Is that...chilled?"

"Do ya think I'd bring anything to Ro's that wasn't?" She sniffs, laughs timidly, wipes her tears with her fingers. "Shit, the woman even put crackers in the fridge."

I laugh despite myself. I will miss that about Ro; she had a thing about consumables being out where bugs could get them. Right now, I'd drink cold anything weird from the refrigerator as long as she'd put it there. And Dair's not a bad person—sure, she's a little out there, and likes to tell creepy stories—but I'm sure that, in this small community where everyone knows everyone, she isn't going to make a classless move like jumping her dead best friend's husband less than a month after the funeral.

I'm also tired of being alone. "You up for a day drink?"

"Hell." Her voice still has that teary edge, but she sheds her sherpa and tosses it on the couch. "Absolutely."

I'm surprised at the easy conversation. She isn't shy about sharing stories, and when it begins to sleet, she's also not shy about sharing her cigarettes as long as we smoke inside, and I figure, *why the hell not?* It's been a long time, but I don't choke. We ash in a cereal bowl, fill it with butts, and drain the wine.

Four shots into the Grey Goose from my bar, I'm not shy either.

"Sometimes..." I pull one of her cigarettes from the pack and light up. "I could swear I see her. Like she's still walking the halls, doing what she does. I know she's at the cemetery, but I never feel like she's there."

She puts the lighter to the tip of another cigarette. "Well, of course. I understand that. You'll get used to it, though. Most of us do."

"What are you talking about?"

She furrows her brow. "You mean—Ro didn't tell you about the tree and everything?"

It's clear she's drunk. We both are. "Stop with the creepy stories."

"It's not...okay..." She appears to be steeling herself. She takes a long drag, exhales. "Um. Her body's not there. At the cemetery. Those stones are just for—for family members who don't live here to visit."

A pit forms in my stomach. "They thawed the ground." The menthol's starting to burn the back of my throat. "They put her in there. I saw them."

"They put the *casket* in there. *She's* not in there." She knocks back a shot of vodka and reaches for the bottle to pour more. "She's up at the Family Tree."

There's an uncomfortable silence.

"Ro...didn't let you in on *any* of it?"

I shook my head.

She pours us shot after shot as she fills in details. Finally, I cover the shot glasses with my palm. "We've had enough."

Her eyes bore into mine. "Fine. I'll show you."

Sleet pin-shots the kitchen windows.

*   *   *

Dair's Scout navigates the icy side wind that cuts up the island's only mountain. The temperature has dropped, and the sleet has mixed with snow and hail; it rushes at the windshield like angry stars.

The truck skids. I clutch the Jesus handle.

"Don't worry." Dair sets a hand on my thigh, making me uncomfortable. "This beast eats this crap for dinner."

It's gray, not quite night yet, and gloomy. I peer into the falling dark. The highway is so narrow I can see the waters below. And the rocks, black as obsidian, sharp and menacing.

I get dizzy and squeeze my eyes shut. "Oh, God."

"We're good, Tash," she says. "We're here."

The Scout fishtails to a stop at a chain link fence choked by brambles and gnarled, blackened vines that seem like things from other worlds shriveling in the throw of the headlights.

She kills the engine. "Welcome to the Family Tree Grove."

The door groans as she climbs out, and I follow suit. Hail stings my cheeks, and I'm immediately aware that the coat acceptable for being drunk in my toasty house won't keep me warm out here. The sleet has formed an icy crust on the melting pack beneath the fresh fall; when it collapses under my step, snow crushes into the tops of my hiking boots.

Dair passes me a Maglite. "Here."

She reaches her gloved hand into a break in the vines and tugs.

The gate doesn't budge. I reach in and root my bare fingers around a steel bar, my skin burning from the contact. We struggle, but manage to open it wide enough.

A lone sodium light at the far end of the grove casts an amber glow on the forlorn scene. Rows of massive oaks loom, hulking like monsters, their branches twisted in some kind of stricken rage. Many of the limbs are strewn with frayed ropes and pieces of what look like sheets. Others bear heavy burdens—hanging, long, lumpy canvas sacks—that swing listlessly in the wind.

I know what they are.

"Every family in town has a tree," Dair said back at the house. "When a loved one dies, we hang the body from it. As the body decomposes, the soul enters the trunk, the limbs, the leaves. All of our loved ones' souls are kept inside."

A bitter gust hits me. It is rife with the smell of snow and cold at first, and then heavy with rotten meat, cheap perfume, and fermented garbage. It is so sharp, so smothering, I can taste it.

"Dear. God."

"That's why it's up here," she says. "The stench blows right out to sea."

I lean over and throw up.

When I've finished, she helps me up and rubs my back, and it feels warm and wonderful—until I realize it's not Ro.

"You okay?" she asks.

I shrug her off.

"Everybody pukes. If not their first time, their second. I find if I'm drunk when I come here, I don't have a problem, so I kinda make a point of it."

I follow her. At the base of each tree a large stone bears a surname: BOYCE, KIEFER, CHASTAIN, OLMO.

We press on. My jeans are ice-wet and cling to me like restrictive bandages; the skin on my thighs burns. A blast of wind roars through the grove and sets the bodies swinging like pendulums. An ear-splitting crack rents the air.

A body-burdened limb above us shudders, gives way.

The next thing I know I'm on my back.

"Oh, shit!" Dair cries.

I open my eyes. Sleet stings them.

"Tash?"

I force myself to sit up. "I'm fine."

She grabs her flashlight, crawls forward and examines the limb's blackened, sickly core. "Oh my God. This tree is dying." She stands up, brushes herself off. She walks around the giant limb to get a look at the marker. "It's the Doubeks'."

"Mrs. D lives across the street from me." I rest my gaze on the fallen sack and my stomach somersaults. "Mr. D died last year. That's gotta be him."

She nods. "Her whole family's gone and it's just her. She probably can't get up here to tend it."

I struggle to my feet. I can't feel my toes.

"We have to tell her immediately, the second we get back," Dair says. "Come on. The Everly's tree is down here."

If I die on this island, where will they put me? With Ro's family?

Is there a tree for Outsiders?

EVERLY stands at the end of the row, and from the lowest limb swings a dingy canvas body bag.

I know damn well who's in it.

"You can talk to her if you'd like. She'll hear you." Dair faces me with a kind and knowing expression. She sets a hand on my shoulder. "Go ahead. It's okay. I'll—I'll go over there."

I nod, and she leaves me. Her boots crunch as she moves away.

I stare at the filthy bag as it twists in the wind, trying to envision my wife as a healthy person beneath, not rotting or disintegrating, but with her make-up as fresh as it was the day I last saw her. I imagine she looks like she's just sleeping, like she used to when I got up in the middle of the night, her hair tangled on the pillow, her small mouth slightly open.

"Ro," I whisper, and then I just sob.

*　*　*

The pain of Ro's absence throbs in my chest. Since she's been gone, I've slept little—my body wakes me every two hours from a shallow sleep plagued by lucid dreams.

After we get back from the grove, I lie in bed and stare at the ceiling. I can't shut out the image of the suspended bodies. I can't escape that

152

foul smell; it lingers even though I stripped, laundered the clothes, have showered, and have, after that, washed my hands, arms, and face countless times. I can't chase the chill of the winter winds; it's so deep in my bones that even a shower scalding enough to turn my skin lobster didn't exorcise it.

*   *   *

The night with Dair had ended badly.

We'd climbed back into the Scout and I was hoping we'd streak out of there, but she was preoccupied with the Doubeks' dead tree. "We have to tell her right away."

"Why?"

"If the tree dies, the souls are set free."

"Like—they go to heaven? Or hell?"

"No." She stared out the windshield. "They go back to the place they called home."

It sounded far-fetched. Believing the souls were in the trees was one thing. Proof of that, that it was *real*, well…that was another. "Come on."

She pressed her mouth into a sad smile. "It's happened before. I saw it…when I was a kid. In high school. Someone…brought people back."

I waited for her to elaborate. She didn't. Instead, she set her hand on mine. "I'm sorry. It was kind of intense."

I pulled my hand out from under hers. "How…did they do it?"

Her expression was haunted. She shifted toward me, reached over, and affectionately settled a hand on my neck. "It's better you don't know—"

I swatted her hand away. "Why, so you can have me all to yourself?"

I could tell I'd hurt her.

"How dare you!" Her eyes blazed. "Seriously?"

"You've been after me since the day I moved here."

"I have. Not." She whipped her keys from her pocket and started the truck. "Jesus. What would be the big deal if I had? Am I such a bad person?"

It was out of my mouth before I could stop it. "Ro should be here. Not you."

We said nothing more to each other on the trip home.

The roads were bad, so I offered Dair the couch, but she left in a hurry, her face tense like I've never seen it.

I watched as she descended my porch steps. I expected her to leap back in the Scout, but she didn't—she went across the street, to the Doubeks' house. She banged on the door. The porch light winked on, and rotund Mrs. Doubek let her in.

*   *   *

The day after we went to the grove, the sky is a perfect blue, and the ice-coated tree branches glimmer in the sun like crystals.

I decide it's time to go through Ro's closet. I call Dair.

She doesn't pick up. I leave an awkward message punctuated with *ums*.

I don't remember my wife's daily wear, but there are some standouts: our anniversary's emerald silk blouse; the New Year's Eve Go-Go dress; our Savannah vacation's orange pantsuit. All of it perfumed with a hint of her chocolate-scented body spray.

I can't do this alone.

I call Dair again.

Again, she doesn't pick up.

Did the last conversation really piss her off that much? I was only being honest.

I stop working with the clothes and move on to the shoes, not surprised to find Ro had several of the same pair in different colors, some with the tags still on.

For three days, I work late into the night, go to bed, get up, start again. Ro is everywhere: cooking in the kitchen, scrapbooking in the sunroom, humming in the shower, seducing me in the bedroom. Stacks of DVDs she'd purchased but never watched, brand new books she'd never read, tubs of body washes in every scent from almond blossom to midnight peony. An angry note when she said she needed space. Her coming home from work and taking all the frustrations of running her own business out on me, screaming at me for leaving a beer can on the living room coffee table. Her compulsive shopping and credit card debt.

I desperately miss all of it.

I call Dair. It goes to voicemail.

The silence is unbearable.

I need to get out of the house, shut my brain off, go somewhere.

Somewhere that doesn't remind me of Ro. On this island, that doesn't exist.

Work gave me a blank check: *Take all the time you need.* I'm certainly not ready to focus on balance sheets and budgets, but I take the car and ferry to the mainland.

I've made this journey five days a week for years, but everything—pulling onto the parking deck, the white-capped stretch of the gray sea, even the taste of the complimentary coffee—feels foreign.

The office is no different. Everyone makes nice. Women who barely spoke to me furrow their brows and ask me how I'm doing; men I buddied with make broken small talk and empty promises of future happy hours.

My dusty desk—a computer, a curled post-it that reads CALL BERGLUND, a framed photo of me and Ro, my favorite pen resting at a cock-eyed angle—looks like someone else's.

It's dark when I get back to the island, and the houses on the street are invitingly lit. I'm hit with the things Ro and I will never have, those family dramas playing out inside: people sitting down to dinner, watching TV, telling their kids to do their homework. I don't really know any of the neighbors, except for the Burches next door—but we're not friendly—and Mrs. Doubek. She is a soft, pudgy thing, always in her kitchen. Ro used to tell me Mrs. D could rob any bank and get away with it, because she handled the hot pans so much she had no fingerprints. She brought us Easter bread in April, apple cobbler in September, pumpkin pie for Thanksgiving, sugar cookies on Christmas Eve.

I try Dair one more time. Nothing changes.

Thinking, perhaps, that Mrs. D might have some leftover Valentine's Day tarts, I knock on her door.

There's no answer, which is odd. Every light in the house is on, even in the second floor windows, and through the sheers I see the bluish glow of the television. I wait several seconds and knock again.

No response.

I knock a third time, more forcefully. "Mrs. Doubek! It's Tash Ahlgren from across the street!"

A movement catches my eye—in the dining room to my left, the rustle of a drape, as though someone was just peering at me.

Feeling shunned, I trudge back to my house, which feels like a tomb.

*   *   *

In the night, I toss and turn, hyperaware of the empty half of the bed. I keep thinking, *I'd give anything to have her back.* What Dair said haunts me: *They go back to the place they called home.*

If the tree were dead, Ro would come back.

She'd *really* haunt the house.

Don't be stupid. Go get a few shots of whiskey and knock yourself out.

On the bar in the living room, there are the remnants of our last night together. Her favorite martini glass has the imprint of her lipstick on the rim.

If that tree were dead, I could be making her a martini right now.

Assuming, of course, that ghosts can drink.

If that tree were dead...

I'm into my fifth shot when an idea becomes a plan.

Nor'easters pound Linden Island with the force of category fives. Last fall, I battled Ro to get rid of the aged oak that overshadowed the roof of our house—I'd spent the previous winter terrified to sleep on the upper floors in the big winds.

She pushed back with a strangely haunted look. "We don't cut down trees unless they're dead."

I skeptically—and half-jokingly—Googled *how to make a tree die* and discovered that muriatic acid rots them from the inside out, and pretty quickly, too.

I did what I had to do, the tree died, nobody was the wiser, and it's gone now.

I still have plenty of muriatic acid—gallons of it—in the shed. I bought too much. So it's been sitting there, hidden under a tarp, behind tubs of random tools and cans of leftover paint.

I have a shovel and a pick. The ground is probably still frozen, but the earth up there seemed softer. I might be able to make it work.

I look at my watch. It's the armpit of the night.

No one will be up at the Grove now.

I down two more shots to bolster my courage, and then decide to just bring the bottle with me. Fortified, I layer up, grab my keys, and head to the shed.

*   *   *

The place isn't as creepy as it was the first time, but the smell still suffocates me. I bear it—maybe it's because I know, now, what this all means, for me, for Ro, for our future. I just have to get through this back-breaking chore, these few hours of torture: dig a trench around the gargantuan trunk to expose as much root as I can and dump gallon after gallon of acid into the pit. In a few days, the deed should be done.

The ground is much softer than I'd even dared hope.

I finish before dawn. I'm freezing but sweating, exhausted but elated. *Ro will be back soon!*

By the time I get home, I'm too wiped out to clean up. I lug the shovel and pick in the house—no sense leaving them in the car where it looks suspicious or leaning them against the stoop where my unfamiliar but nosy neighbors might question what the hell I was excavating in the middle of winter. I prop them against the wall in the foyer and flop on the couch, slipping into—for the first time since Ro's death—a peaceful slumber.

*   *   *

When I wake up, night has fallen. The living room walls are strobed with blue and red lights. There's a furious pounding at the door.

I wrest myself from the couch, muddy wet boots still on, head pounding, mouth dry as ash, shoulders, back, arms and legs on fire from my pre-dawn escapade.

"Tash! It's Dair!" *Bang bang bang.* "Tash! Open up!"

I haul myself to the door and pull it open.

Three police cars are camped across the street. Dair is out of breath. Mascara runs down her cheeks. Her hair's a mess. "Mrs. Doubek. She didn't have enough time to get off the island. She's dead."

Fear knots my insides. "What are you talking about?"

"The souls." She struggles to catch her breath. "The souls got her. The souls...if they're set free from the tree they...they're not who they used to be. They're angry."

She eyes the mud-caked tools against the wall behind me. Her face goes ashen.

"What did you *do*?"

The Stones of Grisbury
by Sidney Arcane

Lydie couldn't understand how *anyone* could accept it, let alone *everyone*.

Why do people go willingly once their headstone appears? Who carves the headstones? As she watched Mr. Banders settle into his coffin, she also thought, *What if they haven't actually passed?*

Lydie's gaze shifted to her best friend, Jeralda Banders. Wide-eyed and stoic for today, Jera'd had a week to reconcile with her father's Call to Quietus. The event would likely drive another wedge between them. Their friendship had been on increasingly unstable ground since Lydie had expressed doubts and curiosities around the ritual.

The town had its reasons, Lydie supposed.

For hundreds of years, no accidents or disease had come to Grisbury. Lydie and Jera had been taught their whole lives, and they'd seen: Everyone here passed from this life without pain or uncertainty, but with peace and intention instead.

"It's better this way," the adults professed, over and over, to convince children and maybe even themselves.

When someone was to pass, a grave marker appeared overnight in the Calling Garden, covered with velvet. Nobody knew how—adults and children alike adhered to a strict curfew. At noon, the whole town would gather to witness the unveiling. Attendance was required.

The honored Called had a week to prepare. On the seventh day, everyone gathered for the funeral. They celebrated the life of the to-be-passed, and said goodbye. The Called would change into burial robes and drink from the Fountain of Quietus. Then they'd climb into their coffin and *pass*.

Mr. Banders had done that just moments ago. The hooded Wardens of Burial leaned over and declared him passed. Not only did his eyes stay open, which often happened, they looked alive and alert—not vacant at all. As everyone paid their respects, this further fueled Lydie's concerns about the rite of passing. *Could nobody else see it?*

With farewells complete, a Warden provided Mrs. Banders the greenstones for her husband's eyes. The stones came from the Grisbury River and glowed like constellations at night. They reminded Lydie of *trapiche* emeralds—bright, translucent green stones, with six dark strips radiating from a pupil-like hexagon at the center. The green symbolized the natural order of passing and how the people of Grisbury chose to pass from life with eyes open. She'd learned about them in a book she'd found in the hidden room in the library basement, along with forbidden words like *die, dead,* and *death.*

As the Wardens carried Mr. Banders' coffin through the cemetery, Lydie thought about his eyes and decided to seek the truth. On one hand, Jera might never forgive her, but on the other, maybe she could win back her friendship—or even more.

The procession lifted their voices, but Lydie only moved her lips and hummed, faking her way through the unfathomable hymns for the graveward journey.

Ahh-AH-Ahh-AH- gris-ril-en-mah-yah-naaaaah.

Their song grew louder as the Wardens lowered the coffin into the ground. When the coffin reached the bottom right at sunset, all fell silent.

As twilight descended, the town returned to their homes. Lydie hid behind the headstone. Her parents were preoccupied with explaining *passing* to her younger brother, Brodwurd, and would assume she'd be with Jera. They wouldn't miss her anytime soon. Once the Wardens had ushered everyone out, Lydie sat at the edge of the open grave, preparing to slip in.

This close, she could see the walls weren't dirt but fabric instead, with soil and leaves fixed to it—like a prop from a school play. In the darkness of the hole, nobody would notice, even in broad daylight, especially with everyone's attention on the coffin.

About a foot down from grass level, she felt wooden beams behind the fabric. She used them for support as she climbed onto the coffin lid. From there, she lowered a foot to the bottom of the grave, and tapped. Wood and cloth covered with a layer of dirt.

Lydie was *right!*

*   *   *

Horatio Banders wanted to scream but couldn't. He didn't know what he'd expected, but *this* wasn't it.

A week ago, his headstone had appeared in the Calling Garden. As he spent those seven days with his family, he'd looked forward to reporting for his funeral. But now that he'd partaken of the Fountain of Quietus, he squirmed without moving in velvet burial robes inside his silk-lined coffin.

The Wardens of Burial declared him *passed* regardless, and he saw their eyes for the first time. Deep inside the hoods that kept their faces hidden, their eyes glowed green like the blessed stones of Grisbury's river. He might have thought them beautiful, if his passing weren't seemingly incomplete.

If he could speak, he would ask, but his voice was gone. His senses remained unaffected. As everyone bid their last farewells to him, he could still see and hear them. Only his family remained.

His daughter Jeralda stepped into view, placid and tearless—she'd done her crying through the week. She placed a sweetflower in his hand and looked at him for the last time as he stared back.

Jera left, and his beloved wife Doralee appeared. A tear rolled down her cheek, past her sad smile. She kissed his forehead and caressed his face. Her hand lingered, then closed his eyes for him.

In darkness, he felt the greenstones placed over his eyelids. The velvet hood rustled as Wardens draped it over his face.

Shouldn't I be passed by now? Did I not drink enough from the Fountain? His fear gave way to anger as he thought, *Uncertainty isn't part of passing here!*

Grisbury was different, evolved beyond and separate from the rest of the world. Here, the end of life never came as unexpected tragedy, incurable disease, or old age. It came without undue grief. They only knew of such suffering from scripture. Each townsperson went to their rest *in peace,* so long as they came when Called. Just three months ago, his friend Flynn had whispered as he lay down in his coffin, *"It's so peaceful!"*

But not for Horatio. He remained alive and living deeper into a nightmare of sensory perception:

The sound of the coffin's latches tormented him, then the movement as pallbearers carried his casket.

The chanting through the cemetery mocked him, as did the bump of his sealed box reaching the bottom of his grave.

The murmurs of the town scattering back into their lives left him alone amid the earthy scents surrounding him. Would the smell get stronger as they covered him with dirt?

Alone and trapped, no tears would come. Even that small act of despair stood beyond his reach.

Horatio pondered the enormity of what this could mean. *Have we been burying our brethren alive all this time? Or did something go wrong for me? Could this be some transitional state between life and the hereafter? If so, how long will it last?*

A light thump struck the coffin, interrupting his thoughts. The lid creaked as a weight shifted above him.

Someone—or someTHING—was out there!

*   *   *

Confronted by the reality of her suspicions, Lydie's heart pounded. Her discovery excited her, but she was afraid of being right. Given the enormous implications, she didn't want to investigate this alone. But she couldn't turn back. And nobody would come, anyway.

Their town's most sacred ritual had always given Lydie the heebie-jeebies, and her unease had only grown as she got older.

The hidden room of the library basement had fueled her suspicions in ways she'd never been able to share. To get to the room, she'd had to squeeze through a tiny window—its only access, found ajar after a storm. She'd searched for a door, but once inside, she had learned the futility of that—there simply was none. In those books, she'd learned of the outside world with its strange stories and forbidden words.

Lydie had been working up the courage to talk to the librarian, Mrs. Engrismann, about them. But Mrs. Engrismann's headstone had appeared a few weeks after Lydie had found the room. The new librarian, Mrs. Engrismann's wife Mrz. Engrismann, wasn't as approachable.

So Lydie fought her own curiosity. Whenever she brought it up to Jera, her only friend would scold her for it.

"Who carves the headstones?" Lydie had wondered, one sunny day.

"Why would you ask such things? Such deviant thoughts, Lydiana Watuska!"

"I'm just...just wondering how things came to be this way."

"There's nothing to wonder about. Our way is good and our way is law. Do you want your name on a red headstone? One that gets shattered so nobody remembers you? Do you want to get eaten by a bear?"

They'd seen that, once. Instead of going willingly when Called, Mr. Riley, the carpenter, had run away. It had astonished Lydie that someone so big and strong should be afraid of anything. She remembered his name specifically because they were all supposed to forget it.

He'd passed anyway. And badly. The Elders had found him in the woods, mauled and partly-eaten by a bear. He'd screamed for hours—that's how they'd found him—until they gave him water from the fountain to drink.

"He would have gone peacefully, if he'd gone when Called," all the adults had said.

Instead he was *shodden*. It was a cursed word rarely spoken, and only in place of a criminal's name. Some children secretly used it to scare each other: The *shodden* behind the outhouse would get you if you misbehaved. Jera never spoke it. Just using the word was inviting it to come get you.

Once Lydie had found the secret room, she had tried to bring the topics up several times, in vain. Jera had started acting like a teacher in church-school, pointing out and explaining things to Lydie, as if to a child. Even at Mr. Flynn's funeral three months ago, she'd said, "See how happy he his? Our way is a blessing."

Lydie had almost told Jera about the books, thinking proof might help. But if Jera told an adult, well... Lydie didn't want to think about that. So she'd shut up about it and let Jera treat her like a child, no matter how much it hurt. Lydie didn't have anyone else.

When Jera's own father joined the Called, Lydie had wanted to be supportive, but Jera had pulled away.

"Just because you haven't spewed your nonsense in a while doesn't mean I've forgotten it. You never apologized, nor admitted it was wrong. You just stopped. So that tells me you're still thinking deviant thoughts!"

Like everyone, Jera had accepted her father's Call. Rather than convincing Lydie to reconcile to it, it had only made her question the practice more. Which had brought her here, sitting on top of his casket in a false grave.

Now what?

In answer, the coffin lurched downward. The walls of the fake grave moved with it, so she stayed hidden. She peeked through where the fabric wasn't fully joined at the corners.

Ambient green illuminated a cavern below, part natural and part dug out, like a mine. Wooden supports, a giant basin, and many boulders provided possible hiding places. She spied a stone table, too. Given the coffin's current course, it would likely stop on the table. Stone stairs provided the likeliest way out—a better choice than the several visible tunnels. Water trickled from many places, streaming steadily down the stone stairway.

The walls sparkled with hundreds of greenstones.

As the coffin sank, dozens of hooded robed figures shuffled in from the tunnels. Three of them approached the descending coffin. The robes of the one in front absorbed all light, like a walking patch of night sky— an *Eldest*, like from a children's book! They looked up toward the coffin, each with glowing green eyes. The Eldest's sparkled impossibly bright. Lydie's heart skipped a beat, and she pulled back behind the fabric. Had they seen her? Maybe not, but soon they would. Perhaps she could slip under the table when the coffin got to it.

The coffin came to a halt. The fake walls fell with a clatter, leaving Lydie completely exposed. Hundreds of glowing eyes glared at her, and the eyes of the Eldest shone right through her.

Lydie leaped past the three and ran for the stairway. She didn't get very far. Two from the crowd grabbed her, fast.

"Let me go," she shouted. As she squirmed, she recognized a ring one of them wore. Ms. Alderness the arbitrator had worn it—the passed were allowed up to three pieces of jewelry—but she had passed *eight years ago.* Lydie's eyes shot up and glimpsed Ms. Alderness' face, just older, withered, and greenish from her glowing eyes.

Stunned, Lydie slowed her struggles and looked at the face of her other captor. Her stomach flipped as she recognized the red birthmark on Mr. Flynn's cheek, illuminated by his own green glowing eyes.

"Calm yourself, child," he said.

A large figure emerged from the gathering. The tall, hulking thing moved like a sack of rocks compelled to lethargic life. It had three dark features set into a mound of a head. Two lusterless obsidian stones filled its eye sockets, absorbing all light. The third was a greenstone on its forehead, bigger than a goose egg and ringed with woven riverweed to hold it there. The greenstone's black bands were so thick it showed hardly any green at all.

The creature had no other features or limbs. Foot-long, boneless tentacles with five-inch spikes at the end protruded directly from its chest and sides. They waggled at her as it moved. It didn't have feet, either. Whatever its means of locomotion, it stayed concealed beneath its rocky mass. It moved with slothful purpose toward Lydie.

Her captors marched her to meet the lumbering thing. Light revealed more detail—detail Lydie wished she didn't have to see. Large patches of yellow slymoss covered masses of burlap-like skin. Strings of dark green riverweed hung off in clumps. Lumps moved beneath its skin as it shuffled. It was as big as the *shodden* criminal whose name she wasn't supposed to remember.

The creature's appendages, brittle like dried twigs but absolutely unyielding, wrapped around her upper arms. Its scratchy skin and slimy growths pressed into her shoulders. It smelled *awful.*

Everyone's attention turned back toward Mr. Banders' coffin. The Eldest opened the lid and spoke with a deep, commanding voice. "Banders has survived the first test. Prepare the Ordeal..." Then they poured something into Mr. Banders' mouth.

"He's not passed, is he," Lydie couldn't help but ask.

"No, child," answered Mr. Flynn.

"W-what's wrong with him?"

"What's *right* is a better question. He has survived and may be worthy of the One Above."

A mechanical sound interrupted before Lydie could ask another question. A horizontal iron grate lowered onto Mr. Banders' coffin.

The creature held her arms wide, and Ms. Alderness and Mr. Flynn each grabbed a hand. Once the group had formed a circle around the coffin, everyone began chant and sway.

Ahh-AH-Ahh-AH- gris-RELril-en-mah-yah-rel-grisss-mah-naaaaah.

The ceiling above the casket now glowed. Lydie moved involuntarily with the circle's dance and song. It reminded her of the Burial chant, just *worse*. Lots worse.

She tried to keep her head and cling to her purpose here. She *had* to escape and warn everybody! But after two or three verses, Lydie felt her voice yearning to chant with them. From deep within her soul, she intoned the vowel sounds, until she had the pattern of it:

Ahh-AH-Ahh-AH- gris-RELril-en-mah-yah-rel-grisss-mah-naaaaah.Ahh-gah-ril-en-yah-mah-naaaaah.

The mouthless creature behind her grunted and moaned along, its fingers flexing around her arms.

Ahh-AH-Ahh-AH- gris-RELril-en-mah-yah-rel-grisss-mah-naaaaah.Ahh-gah-ril-en-yah-mah-naaaaah.

She closed her eyes and lost herself in the chant, hungering for that which she could neither fathom nor name.

*   *   *

Horatio still wanted to scream. And still could not.

The coffin sank downward, and in terror, he realized his town's ways weren't what they thought. A faint scraping might have been something shifting on the lid again. He hadn't heard much since the initial thump. Was it a Warden of Burial? Or someone else?

When the coffin halted, he heard a clattering followed by another thump, as if something jumped from the lid. It was followed by footsteps running and a shout. *"Let me go!"* It sounded like Lydiana, Jera's little friend. A quiet shuffling followed, with murmurs and sounds he could only guess at. The coffin lid opened, letting in cool, musty air. A hand pressed into his wrist.

"Banders has survived the first test," boomed a resounding, powerful voice. If it could be called a voice. It was *old*, like bellowing waves from the deepest ocean. "Prepare the Ordeal..." *What in all of Grisbury is happening? Into what have we been sending our townsfolk?*

The hood lifted from his face. Fingers pressed into his forehead and below his eyes, opening them without disturbing the greenstones that covered them. He could see now, but only what distortions the greenstones allowed.

Hands opened his mouth and fluid flowed into his belly. His heart leapt to life and his lungs gulped in air, but otherwise his body remained still and his voice silent. Would he ever get it back? With each moment, he wanted to scream even more.

The sounds of iron against iron came, and a grate lowered to rest just above his chest, interlocking with the walls of the coffin. Pinpoints of light appeared in the pitch black above him, dim at first and brightening fast. Chanting echoed with a more unearthly version of the Hymns of Burial. Mere carols above ground, the intonations grew into something forceful, like a *summoning*. His heart leapt with dread and anticipation.

The stars above swirled in a chaotic dance. A darkness formed in the center and stretched six bands, impossibly black and full of forever, to the edges of his view. Every tone in the universe resonated. Intolerably low through inaudibly shrill echoed in the chanters' song.

A sliver of the void snaked down, touched the stones on his eyes and flowed directly into his consciousness. The span between the whole of creation and complete nothingness poured into Horatio. Darkness, pure and divine, wriggled through to his wits' boundaries and far, far beyond. It reached into him through his eyes, past his mind, and gripped his soul.

No scream would ever be enough, ever again. That didn't stop him from trying through his muted throat. His voice did return, gradually. It started as a silent scream and grew into a body-wide shriek, bursting from every nerve cell. He sobbed great body-wracking sobs until he could take no more. After several deep breaths, he began to laugh even harder than he'd sobbed, with more joy than he ever imagined possible, at the Miracle of Grisbury.

Everything he'd ever known in life no longer mattered. He *understood* the chants' meaning and the town's purpose. Every hymn sung and every Call answered brought Grisbury closer to its destiny. In the face of eternity, he had witnessed the true power of the universe and the plan of the One Above.

Each townsperson would in turn be challenged, until all had joined or failed. Then they would bring their truth beyond their town. The outside world had forgotten Grisbury, but Grisbury would never forget them. The whole of humanity would bend to a new kingdom someday—with their town at its center.

They would wipe out the religions of superstition and speculation, and replace them with their vast, uncompromising certainty. Civilization would begin anew with unwavering observance of the wishes of the One Above.

When he could finally speak, Horatio had but one word worth saying:

"*Yes!*"

Dissonant chanting swelled to a crescendo as the paralysis lifted. Horatio joined their triumphant song. He would never look away from the abyss above. Now, he would never have to consider it. As the shape retreated back into the void above, the greenstones filled his eye sockets and fused to his eyes. His sight was permanently open to eternity.

The iron grate lifted, and Horatio sat up. The Eldest greeted him while others helped him climb out of his casket. He saw his enlightened townspeople who had *passed* and knew the eyes in the walls were those who had failed to survive or rejected their mission.

Horatio Banders couldn't understand how anyone could *fail*, let alone *reject* the One Above.

*   *   *

Lydie knelt among the townspeople whom everyone thought passed. The creature was gone and the chanting over.

How long had they chanted?

The coffin's importance loomed over the chamber until Jera's father climbed down.

"Mr. Banders!" Lydie shouted as the chanters stood, lifting her from the floor then letting her go. She didn't understand any of this, but Mr. Banders certainly had not passed, nor had anybody, as the town believed. They could go together and tell everybody what was really happening!

Mr. Banders turned to look at Lydie; his eyes glowed green like everyone else's. Her heart sank. The Eldest turned its brightest eyes on her.

"I know your questions, and you shall have your answers." A glowing fog puffed from its mouth and settled around her head as it spoke. Like a nightmare come to life, the fog took her hand and walked her through the cavern. She could not resist.

"The One Above chose the town of Grisbury. Its people will live forever and deliver sacred ways to humanity. Grisbury's water and Call to Quietus are blessing and test. Those who survive and accept their vocation become our blessed emissaries."

The people in robes with green eyes, Lydie thought.

"Those who survive but reject the sacred mission are soul-bound into greenstones. They must witness our triumphs for all eternity."

They approached the stairway, where the walls' greenstones were more concentrated—and set as pairs.

Like eyes. She recoiled at the thought. *All those souls!*

"Those who do not survive serve as nourishment for this underground community."

Ew.

"Those who commit crimes against the Rites of Passage..." The Eldest gestured to the creature and more of its kind shuffling around. "They become *shodden.* Whatever made them commit their crimes is taken from them, gnashed away by stone and weed, to make them worthy of the One Above."

Lydie's heart beat faster than it ever had. She looked at Mr. Banders and started to cry. Jera's father was one of *them* now. She'd never felt so alone.

"Once you enter this underworld, you cannot return." The Eldest's words bounced off every wall in the cave and then some. "But you cannot stay, either. Not as you are."

A flagon appeared from deep within its robes.

"It is your turn to drink."

"No!" Lydie's voice had no echo. "I don't belong here!"

"No, you don't," Mr. Flynn said. "Not yet."

"And yet you came," Ms. Alderness admonished. "Disobeyed."

Everyone stared at Lydie. She ran for the staircase, and nobody pursued. Three steps up, she slipped and fell, skinning her knees.

The walls sprung to life, shifting to trap her and staring with countless sets of greenstones. The stairs steepened and the wall protruded. Together they formed three walls of a chamber the size of an outhouse. The stream of water turned into a gush.

The crowd approached without hurry.

Water pooled at the bottom of the stairs, and Lydie's hopes sank as a giant greenstone, more than three inches thick but see-through, like rippled glass, rumbled up from the floor to form the fourth wall. She grabbed a loose rock and pounded at it, but it didn't even chip.

"The One Above will keep you," the deep voice rang clearly in her ears, even through the walls. "You came before you were Called, so your Call has now come."

Yellow slymoss sealed the cracks in the walls and floor. Lydie tried to climb the transformed staircase, but the slimy weed slickened every possible handhold. All she got was a hard fall and a face full of water. By then, the water was knee-deep.

"Do not fear. You have consumed the sacred liquid your whole life. Welcome our offered gift."

The water surged into a downpour. Lydie looked carefully at her surroundings. She didn't have much time, but panic wouldn't help. A pair of greenstones sat at eye level, embedded within the staircase-now-wall. They glowed bluer than the others, and Lydie recognized them.

The dark bands were the thinnest she'd ever seen in greenstones. These had been used for Mrs. Engrismann's Call. Lydie had commented about the bands to Jera, who didn't share Lydie's interest in such details.

The librarian had failed her Ordeal? Lydie didn't know how she felt about that. She had liked Mrs. Engrismann.

Hundreds of pairs sparkled from the walls. If Lydie could escape with some evidence, maybe she could get Jera to understand. The town could know the truth and put an end to the farce of *passing*.

"Drink, Lydiana," Ms. Alderness advised. Her sharp voice was distorted through the translucent greenstone wall. "Accept your passing. Redeem your soul." The crowd just stared. Several *shodden* lurked among them.

The water was at Lydie's waist by the time she pried the stones from the wall. But how would she carry them? Dresses didn't have pockets. Holding the greenstones would make swimming much more difficult. She had to keep them one way or another. The water poured down faster than ever.

A mechanical sound came from overhead, above the sound of rushing water. Another iron grate lowered, like the one for Mr. Banders' coffin. Any hope she had for treading water came to an end. The flooding increased ten-fold, and the water was at her chin. The grate hovered one foot above the waterline, and Lydie could hardly avoid taking in water with each breath.

Lydie cried, losing hope with every moment. The walls shook, and everything above became water.

Determined to hold her evidence no matter what, Lydie brought her hand to her mouth and swallowed the stones. A third gulp of water followed, the one that finally brought her down.

As the glow around her dimmed, the floor fell out and Lydie flushed away with the water.

*   *   *

The cold waters of Grisbury River pushed Lydie to its banks and continued on. She stared at the stars until dawn. Birds chirped for hours, and the sun rose high before the search party found her in the riverweed.

"She's here. Passed." The voice offered no surprise.

I'm not passed! Nor anyone! They're underground, all changed, and with monsters!

But her lips wouldn't move, and her voice wouldn't come.

"Of course she's passed." Jera's voice. "Her red headstone appeared this morning. That's what criminals get."

As they carted Lydie away, she wondered, *Who will close my eyes for me?*

When they got back to town, the Wardens propped her up like a scarecrow at the Calling Garden gates. Each member of the town came and dropped a plainstone at her feet. The larger the rock, the greater their disappointment. She remembered having to do this for Mr. Riley and how frightened she was at his mutilated body. They called them the plainstones of shame.

"May Grisbury's disappointment forever weigh you down," each person intoned in turn.

Lydie watched each stone fall, unable to lift her head to look her townsfolk in the eye. Her eyes stung and she wished she could cry, or just blink at the view.

An eternity of stones later, Lydie stared at the sky from a rough and narrow pine box behind the funeral home. A liaison of the Wardens spoke to her parents. The Wardens themselves didn't speak.

"Lydiana betrayed our ways. Her passing came early and unplanned. The river drowned her in a most unpeaceful way."

"Yes," her mother responded, absently. "The scrapes and bruises."

"We are ashamed at our daughter's glaring example of why we live this way." Her father's voice was harsher than she'd ever heard.

"Lydiana will atone in the world beyond," the liaison assured them, "and her crimes are not yours to bear."

"Good," said her mother, with disgust.

"She received the red headstone of a criminal and will be buried as such—at the grounds limits, in a standing coffin. She will never rest. Her headstone will be smashed to erase her name. She cannot wear the velvet robes of our honored passed."

"We will prepare wretch robes according to tradition."

"I will return when you are finished."

*   *   *

Lydie ached to scratch against the itchy burlap.

Wretch robes were more like a sack with the sleeves stitched to the front, holding her arms crossed over her chest.

The townspeople's plainstones had a purpose. Her parents used riverweed and dry slymoss to weave each rock into the layers of burlap. "May Grisbury's disappointment forever weigh you down," they repeated with each one. When they were done, the bulk took up more space within the wretchedness than she did. The itching was driving her so mad she could scarcely think.

The liaison returned and drew the bottom hem closed at her feet. "Tradition will not let the disobedient stray any further than they already have, even passed," he said.

Nor would tradition allow anyone to mourn them. Lydie did not get a wake. Only parents or elders could attend to a criminal. Her brother would not be allowed to say farewell, nor Jera, if either even wanted to. The plainstones were the only respects anyone would pay.

What would Jera say if she knew where her father was?

The Wardens appeared. Her mother tilted Lydie's head back, and a Warden poured from a flagon. She would've thought the ability to drink proof that she still lived. Would that even matter to them, anyway? Once the fluid had passed to her stomach, rocks and slymoss spilled into her mouth. A Warden pushed her lips closed and sealed them with slymoss.

Another Warden placed a large greenstone on her forehead and wove it into place with riverweed. It made her skull vibrate with its terrible power. Her father didn't close her eyes before covering them with two pieces of obsidian. Someone pulled the burlap hood over her face and knotted it at her neck.

They cursed her with the Rite of Transgression, which was a chant she had never heard before and didn't understand at all.

To distract from the itching, Lydie counted two hundred nails, one by one, as they hammered the coffin lid shut. They dragged her to the point furthest from the town and dropped it feet-first into a hole that she knew wasn't a grave.

And that was that. Lydie was passed to all who knew her, none of them knowing a shred of truth for her efforts.

Lydie wondered at what would happen next. *They* would be waiting for her, to present her to something horrible and strange and, as she recalled the chanting, faintly wonderful. Would she want to accept the One Above like Mr. Banders did, now that her time had come?

The coffin fell further into the earth, transporting her to her own Ordeal in the caves below. It landed with a splash and slowly began to sink.

A vicious chant shook the coffin walls. The greenstone on her forehead quaked and hummed. As it seared through her skin and into her skull, an unforgiving rift opened her mind. The possible outcomes paraded before her.

Which would she be, in the end? A blessed emissary? An imprisoned soul in the walls? Sustenance for the emissaries? Or, as one who had disobeyed…

Lydie remembered vividly the creature from last night. The three features on its head – *obsidian eyes* and a large greenstone *on its forehead*. Its form like *rocks in a sack*, covered in slymoss and riverweed.

Shodden!

Lydie's mind floundered to realize her fate. The rest of her stood motionless within rocks and vegetation. She'd already had her Ordeal at the staircase, and she'd resisted it.

The maddening chanting grew so loud it hurt her ears. The casket sank further into water. Mud breached its walls and seeped through the burlap. The stones and weeds inside convulsed, energized by the stone on her head. The rotten smell of fresh slymoss choked her as it clung to her wretch robes.

Under the burlap, her skin thickened and hardened until the itch bothered her no more. Bones cracked and fused. Muscles tore and reattached. Riverweed and slymoss pulled and pushed her joints into new alignments. The vegetation connected rock and mud as ligament and tendons.

Her hands twisted and fused to her upper arms. Claws sprung from her fingertips, ripping their way through burlap and stitches. Restructured fingers protruded bonelessly, spanning shoulder to elbow.

Lydie agonized as the rocks, vegetation, and coarse fabric became one with her body. Her mass all but filled what was left of the casket. The voice of the Eldest spoke through the rift in her mind, thunderous above the chanting.

See your self for the last time, before you are made worthy of the One Above.

Thick scales grew around her eye sockets and fused with the obsidian over her eyes. An image of herself as *shodden* appeared against the permanent black.

We must drown away that which made you commit your crimes.

Both in her mind and in her casket, waters rose. Lydie's mind fought, but it was like the water rising and the grate bearing down. Her *self* had no room to breathe.

Everything that is you will be destroyed.

Lydie's will began to melt into a dull and brute obeisance. *Good,* Lydie thought, letting go of hope. If she were gone, she wouldn't feel alone anymore. She let the waters take her. An opposite force welled up from her stomach, burning like she had eaten something undigestible.

The greenstones she swallowed while trying to escape! *Mrs. Engrismann's soul! I'm not alone!*

A fire grew in Lydie's belly. Her new skin grew thorns. Long spikes erupted from her elbows, knees, and spine. Her distorted fingers grew even longer, then multiplied to extend in every direction.

The waters rose higher and churned in her body and mind. Wave after wave crashed over the stowaway greenstones, eroding them first into pebbles, then sand, then nothing, all in a matter of seconds.

The librarian's fire went cold and fizzled out. The chanters ceased. The greenstone on Lydie's forehead went lifeless. The coffin burst around her in a shower of muck and splinters.

Lydie could move again, but she couldn't see. She shook her head but the obsidian over her eyes would not loosen. The rocks in her mouth stifled her scream.

Her new and numerous stone feet tumbled over each other, and she rolled forward, slow and wobbly. She lunged toward where she thought the Eldest stood, spinning her spikes and lashing with her fingers. But she hit nothing and crashed into what might have been a wall.

The Eldest spoke again, not into her ears, but like boiling water poured in through her forehead.

Your self *is still in there? Yes! The greenstone soul you swallowed! You thought the greenstones would help you. And they did. The Rite of Transgression destroys* one soul. *The other is gone, and yours intact.*

Something tapped the silent greenstone on her forehead.

As such, the One Above refuses you. You remain criminal. Even shodden *can receive the Great Will, and serve. But you cannot. We have no use for you. Go, wander the tunnels, shodden of all shodden.*

The voice in her mind went quiet, and she heard the quiet shuffling of everyone walking away.

Lydiana Watuska wanted to scream, but she couldn't.

The Hungry Heart
by Roxanne Dent

Ashley West stood under a ripped, grime-encrusted awning of a gated bodega on the Upper West Side of Manhattan. The building had more chains and locks than Fort Knox. Her black, spiky hair was wet, her jeans damp. She shivered underneath the quilted jacket and pulled her collar up.

Across the street, in a pay-by-the-hour hotel, Phil Lawson was doing the nasty with an underage prostitute. She yawned. It was after two a.m. Time to call it a night. But the steady drizzle and the sound of sudden laughter somewhere in the fog-shrouded streets took her back to Paris.

*   *   *

On her first night in the city of lovers, Ashley walked along the Seine. The lights were blurry in the mist. Couples appeared and disappeared out of the fog. Locked in a tight embrace, oblivious of their surroundings, they seemed like timeless actors on a 1950s, Gene Kelly movie set.

Instead of the romantic adventure Ashley had envisioned, she stumbled over the mangled, headless corpse of a woman in a sequined evening gown, velvet coat, and silver high heels. Blood stained her dress and pooled all around her. Something splashed in the water. Footsteps approached.

*   *   *

A jarring siren a couple of blocks away brought Ashley back to the present with a jolt. She glanced back across the street at the fleabag hotel, wondering if Phil had paid for the whole night. She doubted it. Phil was the cheap, cheating pervert his wife suspected. Ashley yawned again. She had enough damaging photographs. Divorce was in Phil's future. She headed to her small, parked blue Toyota Yaris.

Ashley's cases consisted of insurance fraud, computer hackers, and cheating spouses. It wasn't what she'd envisioned when she got her P.I.

license and opened her office. Murder cases never came her way. The time of the hard-boiled detective was over. The lone, private eye dodging bullets and murder had long since faded away —like a wisp of cigarette smoke the black-and-white hero inhaled as he unraveled the truth in a treacherous and unforgiving world.

*   *   *

Ashley's dream of being a detective had been born out of inconsolable grief. When she was ten, her mother was diagnosed with cancer. As the disease ravaged its way through her frail body, Ashley escaped by watching endless television. Bored with cartoons, soap operas, and sitcoms, and desperate for escape from the dread hanging over her, Ashley dug out her father's collection of film noir. The moody, black-and-white movies had instantly captivated her.

After school and all day and night on the weekends, she sat transfixed, lost in another era. Her favorite films starred men. Cynical Robert Mitchum and tough guy Humphrey Bogart. Women were cast as treacherous femme fatales. They wore dresses—unless they were really wicked.

Although the movies portrayed women as they saw them then, the flickering images allowed Ashley to forget, at least for a couple of hours, the pain and suffering taking place in the room down the hall.

When her mother died, her father retreated into work. Ashley graduated high school and went off to college. Eventually, she secured a writing job with the advertising giant, Norton, Griffin, and Bates. It was there she'd first met Emily Carew...

*   *   *

Ashley frowned. She hadn't thought about Emily in years. A hard worker, brilliant, with a quirky sense of humor, a sweet smile, and a ton of insecurity, she'd been Ashley's first female crush.

The clicking of heels on pavement caught Ashley's attention. A woman walked out of the fog. The lamppost's glow revealed she wore a red leather coat, belted at the waist, and walked with an easy, sensuous grace in six-inch, black leather, high-heeled boots. Her shiny, shoulder length, golden hair bounced as she walked. She halted a few steps away and gave a slow, sensuous smile.

"Ash, is that really you?" Her voice gave her away.

"Em—," Ashley stammered. "Emily Carew?"

She laughed. "Mya Bradly. I legally changed it three years ago."

"Why?"

"I hated who I was."

Ashley felt a stab of guilt.

Mya moved closer and touched her arm. "All that's in the past. Why don't we go for a drink and catch up on old times?"

Ashley wanted to reconnect with Mya, but old times held some dark memories. "There's not a lot open."

"What about your place?"

Ashley felt her heart skip a beat, even as she assessed the changes in Emily Carew. The green eyes were likely contacts and the rest must have been plastic surgery. This new, bold version oozed sex appeal, which Ashley felt was directed at her. It had been a while since Ashley had felt anything for anyone. Finally, she said, "No wine coolers. I have a bottle of twelve-year old Glenlivet."

Mya smiled and took her arm. "Scotch on the rocks is my drink now."

Mya was coming on strong. Ashley was flattered—and definitely interested—but uneasy. "I was just thinking about you," she said.

"Must be fate."

Ashley didn't want to spoil the mood, but felt she had to address the old wound. "The guys at Norton, Griffin, and Bates knew we were friends. They kept me out of the loop until it was too late. I phoned you at home a dozen times, but you never answered."

Mya's hand on Ashley's arm tightened. *She must be doing some serious weight-lifting,* Ashley thought. Her grip felt like iron.

"I'm a different person now, Ash." The pressure on her arm eased up.

Ashley wondered if Mya really had put the humiliating incident behind her. For a second or two when Mya took her arm, she thought her green eyes darkened and she saw a hint of the rage Mya must have felt. "I quit the firm not long after you did," Ashley said. What happened to Emily still pissed her off. She could have urged the Director to at least send the worst offenders for sensitivity training. Instead she quit.

*   *   *

Smart with a sense of humor, the overworked secretary lacked any sense of style or fashion. Emily was an easy target. Rolly, the office practical joker, had discovered Emily's profile at an on-line dating service and sought her out under a false name. He pretended to be interested. E-mails and texts went back and forth, revealing intimate details of Emily's life. He posted them all on the men's bathroom wall one Friday afternoon. Underneath, labeled as "Least Likely to Find Mr. or Ms. Right," was a photo of a slightly overweight Emily, wearing an unflattering tankini, her hair half covering a face bare of makeup.

When Emily discovered the humiliating betrayal, she quit in tears. Ashley thought the company was lucky she hadn't sued. All that had taken place ten years before the "Me Too" movement.

She *had* tried to call Emily but got nothing but hang-ups. She knew at the time the guilt she felt was irrational, but they'd been BFFs. Emily had trusted her. She should have pursued the whispering and snickers. Shortly after the incident, Ashley had quit the company and followed her heart. After getting her P.I. license, she apprenticed with a big company, and after three years, opened her own office.

*   *   *

Is that why I hardly recognize you now? Ashley thought as they waited for the green light to turn red. *Did that pain lead you to this drastic transformation?*

"I had a terrible crush on you, Ash." Mya gave her a sultry look out of the corner of her eye.

"I was attracted to you, too," Ashley admitted as the light turned red and they crossed the street to her car. She still was, even though she had mixed feelings about reasserting their friendship. There was something about Mya that was off.

"But not that way, Mya said. I was too ugly back then." She turned her face away.

"No, you weren't. I liked you the way you were. It was me being stupid. I didn't know who I was back then. The idea I could be attracted to a woman scared me."

Once they reached the car, Mya changed the subject "As you can see, I've had some work done."

"It's amazing, but you didn't need it," Ashley said as she opened the car door.

"You say that now." Mya walked over to the passenger side and waited for Ashley to unlock the door.

"Believe me, I wouldn't have made you happy," Ashley assured her as she opened the door. The car was new, and the smell of leather was comforting as she slid in. It was odd, but she did need comfort. When her old friend got in, and sat down she added, "I was bad news. Still am. I hurt those who get too close. You're lucky we were just friends."

"Oh, I don't know, Ash," Mya smoothed her coat over her lap as she settled in. "You still have that thin, athletic figure I always wished I had. And that sexy, black hair and violet eyes."

As Mya climbed in, Ashley said, "You look sensational, Em—I mean Mya. Are you happy now?"

Mya shut the door and faced Ashley. "I'm happy to see *you* again, Ash."

*　　*　　*

Ashley handed Mya the Glenlivet on the rocks and sat on the couch across from her, watching her check out the polished wood floors, expensively framed film noir posters, and fake Turkish carpets. Once inside, Mya had removed her coat, and Ashley had hung it up in the hall closet. She sat back and appreciated Mya's black, cashmere, cowl neck dress that hugged all her traffic-stopping curves.

Maya took a sip of her Scotch. "I'd heard you opened a detective agency."

"A dream of mine. I grew up on film noir, but a lot of things have changed since the forties." She twitched as Mya put a hand on her knee and squeezed.

"I remember going to the Angelica with you to watch a double feature with Humphrey Bogart." Mya smiled. "It was fun."

"It was," Ashley said as Mya removed her hand.

"You know, Ash, I called your office once last week, but you weren't in."

"I didn't get the message." Ashley wondered why Mya had called after all these years.

"I hung up before your answer machine went on."

Ashley smiled. "Not business, I hope."

Mya took a long swig of her drink. "Are you still in touch with the people we used to know?"

"Hell, no. Why?"

"They're missing," Maya said.

"Which ones?"

"All of them. Joe, the art director; Harry, the copy editor; Billy, the mail boy, and the writers, Scott, Nick. And that sadist, Rolly. None of their families has seen or heard from any of them. It's as if they just walked off into another dimension."

"Sounds like the beginning of a sci-fi movie." Ashley frowned as she absorbed this new information.

"I'm serious. It actually happened. What are the odds six former employees from the same company vanished?"

Ashley felt a chill. Mya's story was weird. Twilight Zone weird. Was she making it up? Why? It wasn't a turn-on. Did she think it would intrigue her, get her attention because of her interest in crime? Was she looking to get back together as friends. Or something closer? " How did you find out? They weren't your favorite people."

Mya downed the last of her Scotch. "I couldn't sleep one night. Curiosity led me to search for Harry Tompkins. You remember Harry."

"Sure." Ashley nodded for her to continue.

"I was under the illusion *he*, at least, respected me."

"He did. He liked you. Harry and I got rid of the crap on the wall and took your picture down."

"He didn't fire the bastards."

Ashley felt a wave of guilt. "We were under a deadline. And Alan did the firing. He was in Thailand." It sounded lame, and it was. "Harry could have done more. Is this what you want to reminisce about? I hope not."

"Water under the bridge," Mya shrugged.

Ashley didn't feel it was. She began to wonder if running into each other was not by chance. *What did she want? Sympathy? An apology?* Once they'd been close. She missed that closeness, but Mya was different now. *She* was different now.

The cowl slipped off Mya's right shoulder. She didn't seem to notice. Or did she? Ashley wondered what it would be like to run her tongue over that smooth, creamy flesh. She'd hoped for a night of catching up or a brief night of pleasure, but Mya's story was too weird. It made her uncomfortable. If true, had Mya killed them? Was she that unstable? Could she be a serial killer? It seemed unlikely, but she knew murderers could be as unlikely as a little old lady or a ten-year-old. She decided to let Mya continue to talk. See where it led.

"You must have spent a lot of time doing the research."

"We knew them, Ash. You're a private investigator. I thought you'd be interested."

"Okay, you got my attention," Ashley said. "I am interested. What did you learn?"

"Harry walked out of his house three months ago and vanished. His family posted a reward. I looked up the others out of curiosity. They're all MIA." Maya leaned forward. "What if they were murdered?"

"All of them? By who?"

Maya leaned back. "A disgruntled client with a grudge. The company fired more people than they hired. You know how ruthless the firm was. Alan had affairs with the wives of his clients."

"What do the police think?"

Maya sighed. "It's New York City, Ash. No bodies ever turned up. Without a sign of foul play, there's no crime. The cops have enough murders to solve."

Ashley sighed. All she had were divorce and computer fraud. On the other hand, as a woman P.I. back in the thirties or forties, she doubted she'd have people banging down her door to solve a murder.

"The cops file paperwork, and that's that." Mya flushed. "What do you think?"

She tried to picture Mya as a serial killer. She had never been violent. Quite the opposite. She would look the people up, and if Mya was right, she would investigate. "It's worth looking into but you must have hated them. Why does it bother you?"

Mya flashed her a look of irritation. "If they were murdered, we could be next. I'm terrified. Aren't you?"

Ashley smiled. "I stopped being afraid of things five years ago, but I'll check it out if it makes you feel better."

"Thanks." Mya put down her empty glass. "Do you mind if I take my boots off. My feet hurt."

Ashley waved a hand. "Mi casa, su casa."

Mya rose and sat next to Ashley on the couch. She removed her boots and massaged feet encased in black silk, stockings. "Don't you want to know what happened to me when I left Norton, Griffin, and Bates?"

"I heard you went to work for an international bank." She had to make an effort to look at Mya's face rather than her shapely thigh.

"I worked long hours and never complained. They sent me to Japan."

"Did you learn Japanese?"

She leaned over and whispered in Ashley's ear.

Ashley laughed to hide the shiver of pleasure that ran down her spine. "What does it mean?"

Mya was definitely flirting. "I'll tell you later," she teased.

Ashley's body felt hot sitting next to Maya, whose perfume was heady with jasmine and hints of fresh-cut grass. She told herself she needed to be careful. Something wasn't right, but she was aroused. It had been a long time since she'd had sex. Too long. Her hands trembled. She took a gulp of Scotch. "Meet anyone special over there?"

"All work and no play..." Mya gave a coquettish giggle. "But I did get a tattoo."

Ashley realized Mya's glass was empty. She got up and refilled her drink.

"Want to see it?" Maya asked.

Ashley swallowed. "Sure."

Mya stood. Turning her back to Ashley, she said, "Unzip me, Ash. It's a sight you'll never forget."

Ashley rose and slowly pulled down the zipper on Maya's black dress. Her blonde hair smelled like she'd just washed it, with hints of coconut and vanilla. Underneath, Mya wore a lacy bra and thong and an old-fashioned, satin, garter belt. Her body was as lovely and curvaceous as Ashley envisioned, but it was the idea of closeness with someone she once liked very much that added to the attraction. She hadn't allowed herself to get close to anyone in a long time.

The tattoo was a shock. Down Maya's spine, disappearing beneath one deliciously covered, black silk-stocking leg, coiled a snake with scales of vibrant green with stripes of gold and white lightning.

Ashley touched the snake's head. It moved. She withdrew her hand and stepped away. Ashley swore the yellow eyes followed her. *It's a trick of light. Or Mya moving her body.* "Wow. And I thought maybe a rose," she said. "That took a lot of work. It must have been painful."

Mya slowly turned to face Ashley. They were both tall. Her face was only a few inches away from Ashley's. "It did, but it was worth it. The Japanese call a snake tattoo Hebi. Legend says it possess both good and evil and is considered an Avatar and messenger for the dragon King, Ryujin. He's the sea god and master of serpents, rain, and storms. The artist was a genius. I love it. Don't you?"

Ashley didn't but wasn't stupid enough to say so.

Mya leaned in and kissed Ashley. Her lips were soft. Ashley parted her lips, and the kisses deepened. Mya pressed her body against Ashley, nipples inside her silky lace bra hard.

Years of loneliness melted away as Maya's lips moved against hers. Her pink tongue darted out; Ashley caught it between her teeth.

Ashley stepped away. Her body was on fire. She tore off her jeans and sweater as Maya undid her bra, which she tossed aside and stepped out of her thong. Ashely's body trembled with hunger for an intimacy long denied. She was starved for it. Nothing else mattered.

She ignored the little warnings going off in her head that something wasn't right and led Maya into the bedroom.

Black lacquered shutters covered the windows.

Mya made herself comfortable on the bed. Her green eyes sparkled, and she laughed as Ashley flipped on the soft light.

"Keep the shutters closed, Ash, and the light on. I've waited a long time to get you into the sack," she whispered in her ear as Ashley joined her.

The blood pounded in Ashley's veins. Her body awakened after a long denial. She hoped she could control herself and not hurt Maya.

Mya's body was smooth and cool to the touch. Her green eyes were dark and glittered as she reached for Ashley, who interpreted it as passion. As they kissed, and Ashley stroked her breasts, Mya's grip tightened until it was hard to breathe.

"Loosen up, bae," Ashley gasped.

A heave of convulsions nearly threw Ashley off Mya—but a powerful force held her in a vice-like grip. Her mind didn't get a chance to sort out the contradiction.

"You betrayed me, Ash," Mya hissed. Her eyes slowly moved toward the sides of her face as her body morphed into something that belonged on Creature Feature. What now wrapped its body around Ashley was twelve feet long, with scales of bright green, and a pattern of white lightning bolts. Gone were Mya's arms and golden hair. Her pointed face and flat head rose up to glare at Ashley. She hissed again, revealing dozens of tiny, sharp teeth pointed inward. Despite her struggles, the abomination squeezed the breath out of Ashley. She felt her bones crack and cried out.

Ashley just managed to dodge her head as the snake struck. The creature's teeth lacerated her shoulder. The giant snake began to rip and tear at Ashley's arm, swallowing the pieces as she squeezed her body even tighter.

Ashley surrendered to her own darkness. She closed her eyes. When she opened them again, they were black, soulless pits. She growled as her razor-sharp fangs dropped down. She sank them into Mya's neck and drank deep. It wasn't long before she felt the constriction on her body ease up, and she released Mya.

The snake slithered off the bed onto the floor. A few seconds later, a bald Mya stood. She was naked. A few drops of blood still dripped from the two bite marks on her slender neck.

Ashley's broken bones mended as she watched Mya hook on her bra and pull up her silk panties. Ashley's torn skin and bruises began to fade. By the time Mya slipped her dress over her head, her hair was back.

She looked at Ashley curiously before zipping up. "A vampire, Ash. Really?"

Ashley's fangs retracted. *Talk about a bizarre sexual experience.* She sat up. "Ditto to live snake tattoos." Whatever she'd suspected, it wasn't this.

"How did it happen?" Mya asked, pausing to study Ashley.

"You really want to know?" Ashley felt her ribs knit back together, and she stretched to work out the muscles.

"I do."

"I was bitten in Paris by someone who had a disagreement with a rival. He cut off her head and threw it in the river. I found the body, and he found me." She slid off the bed and began to gather her own clothes from where she'd tossed them on the way to the bed.

"What was he like?" Mya gathered her stockings and garter belt from a pile beside the bed.

"The vampire was terrifying. I thought I was going to die, but he let me live. If living includes never having a close relationship and never letting my lust for blood destroy me"

"In the Twenty-first Century. How bizarre." Mya sat on the edge of the bed, watching Ashley get dressed as she slid on her stockings.

"No stranger than morphing into a giant boa constrictor in the middle of sex."

Mya flushed, turning her attention to fastening the garters. "I'm sorry. I am. The humiliation I endured at the agency drove me over the edge. I couldn't sleep. I lost weight. I kept playing out the scene in my head until I thought I'd wind up in the loony bin. I considered suing the company..." She stood up, shrugged, and looked back at Ashley. "Instead, I got a new job, changed my name, and paid for one procedure after another, which helped. But what I really wanted was revenge. When I went to Japan, I met an exiled Shinto priest who, for a hell of a lot of money, gave me the power to shape-shift and take my revenge."

Ashley went over and grabbed Mya's wrist. "You crazy bitch. You killed those missing men."

Mya stared at her defiantly. "Yes, I did. I squeezed the breath out of the bastards before I swallowed them whole. The juices in my stomach dissolved them, hair, teeth, and all."

"Do you hear yourself?" Ashley said, as Maya twisted free. "It's sick."

"Don't sound so holier than thou, Ash. How many people have you drained of blood?" She demanded as she glared at Ashley.

"In the beginning, I couldn't control the hunger," Ashley said. "But now I pay top dollar for bags of blood on the black market. Now and again I take a sip from a neck or two. I've never turned anyone."

"You always did have a moral streak," Mya sneered.

"I wouldn't want to inflict my curse on anyone else."

They stared at each other for a few moments, before Mya said, "You hate me, but I'm glad I couldn't kill you." She gave a small smile. "I *was* really turned on, but then I started thinking you were in on the joke at work and laughing at me like the others, pretending to be my friend. To like me."

Ashley sighed, reached out and gently traced a finger along Mya's cheekbone. "I did like you. I still do. Not sure I can trust you, though."

Mya turned away and headed to the living room to retrieve her boots and coat. Ashley thought she saw tears in Mya's green eyes.

"I'll drive you home," Ashley said as she slipped her sweater over her head.

Mya smiled sadly. "Afraid I'll get mugged? Nothing scares me anymore, either, Ash. I'm the one who's scary now."

"Me too," Ashley said as she opened the door.

"It stopped raining. It's a nice night. I'd like to walk for a while," Mya said.

"I'll join you."

"Don't worry, I won't kill anyone else. It's over," Mya said as they walked toward Sixth Avenue."

"Are you glad it's over?" Ashley asked as she thought, *Mya turned out to be a serial killer, after all.*

"I guess. But I'm not happy. I feel depressed, empty inside, hollow like the tin man in the wizard of Oz, only not so nice. And I feel really bad about you."

"Is the tattoo permanent?" Ashley asked as they began to walk.

"As permanent as a vampire's curse. The priest said I could live for a thousand years."

"Can you make sure the snake never emerges again? *Will* you?"

"I killed for revenge. I have no reason to kill anymore unless someone is foolish enough to attack me."

The air smelled clean and fresh. A couple of stars even twinkled down in the night sky.

Ashley put an arm around Mya's shoulders. "Cheer up. We know each other's darkest secrets. Something tells me, this could be the beginning of a beautiful friendship."

Her Eyes Like Silver Dollars
by Gillian Daniels

When the television in the cabin finally broke, and when the days stretched long and hot with no yellow bus driving an hour and a half from town to cart Caleb and Sparky off to school, Daddy told them stories—like the one about the dark woman. It was a summer story. It was also a campfire story even if there wasn't any campfire.

"She has the back of a woman," Daddy said, scratching his chin through his shaggy, black and gray beard. "Knobby spine, long hair like a Rapunzel. From the front, though, she's a terror. Black nails, black teeth, white eyes. She sneaks out of the woods on all fours, her knuckles punching the earth as she lopes about. She was born to deer and raised up by old spirits, eating the hearts of men and chewing at their bones. If we didn't lock up the hutch at night, she'd probably make a snack out of our rabbits."

Sparky didn't like this story very much. She was a little, snub-nosed thing with a mop of unevenly cut hair and wild eyes like a spooked horse. "You're leaving something out, Daddy. Something important."

"What am I leaving out, precious?"

"The lady's got to have a husband. She's got to get married and have a baby."

Caleb thought the story was fine the way it was. Unlike his sister, he had a long nose. Recently, his legs and arms had grown lanky and thin to match. He didn't like looking in mirrors much anymore because he thought his head was too big and he reminded himself of a lollipop. "She probably eats kids."

Their father laughed. "I wouldn't tempt her."

"That's not fair," said Sparky. "You shouldn't tell tales on ladies."

"I said she was a woman," Daddy said. "Not a lady."

Caleb met her that autumn when he was looking through the graveyard between his house and the bus stop. Dad didn't like him going near it, preferred him taking the long way to the stop, but it was a good place to find starlings to shoot with his air rifle. It wasn't night, not yet, just dusk, pink creeping through the Rockies. He adjusted his hunting jacket as he squinted toward the sun, eyes watering.

The woman crouched in front of a tombstone, her back bent forward and her long hair running down to pool in her graying skirt. She was reading the inscription on the stone, which must have been awfully hard to do, seeing as how the words had smoothed over and away some time ago.

The notches of her spine stuck out, but they were covered with skin that was, as far as Caleb could tell, human.

"Ma'am?" he said softly. "You from town?"

A croak came from the back of her throat. She didn't turn. "No."

"You're not a hiker?"

"Does your pa treat you and the other one well?" the woman asked.

"What?"

"You and Samantha. Does he treat you well."

"Sure he does," said Caleb, shivering. "How do you know Sparky's real name?"

The woman skittered away on her hands and feet. She went fast into the darkness. He did not see her face, which, on later recollection, was all right with him.

When she was gone, good and properly terrified, he shot his gun in her direction.

Then he ran home.

That night, after seeing the thing that wasn't a lady, be brushed his teeth with an unsteady hand. Through a mouth thick with foam, he asked his father, "Is the dark woman really alive?"

"She's make-believe," he said.

"Yeah, but is she make-believe dead or make-believe alive?"

"Alive, I guess, for what it's worth."

Caleb nodded and spat in the sink. It was just a metal basin with green scum that sat like scales around the drain. "How old is she supposed to be?"

"Old as the Rockies. Her face never ages a day, though."

"So she's pretty?" Sparky had already changed into her pink pajamas with the chick on the front pocket. She stood in the doorway.

"No," said their father without looking at them.

Caleb checked the hutch twice before going to bed. He tried not to get too attached to the rabbits, as they, like the hens, would eventually end up on the dinner table. The chickens just happened to last a long time because they laid eggs for breakfast. Sometimes they gave blue eggs, and Caleb couldn't figure out why.

Much worse than killing the rabbits was going to school the day after with a brown bag lunch. He had to answer, "What's that?" when the other boys at his lunch table peered over to look at the fresh, rabbit meat set on white bread and carefully wrapped in tin foil or, if Daddy had the time, a thermos full of rabbit stew. They usually cringed when he told them. Because he didn't speak very much otherwise, he suspected the other kids didn't know him for much else beyond being a rabbit killer. That and his daddy, who went into the bank once a year to draw out enough money from an account that made all the tellers crowd around and stare.

After seeing the dark woman, Caleb started taking Sparky's way to the school bus stop in the mornings. That way added several minutes to their journey but meant he didn't walk through the graveyard. They stuck to the path that ran past open fields, yellow with tall, dry grass.

"I hate living out here," said Sparky when they reached the bus stop. She picked at her nails, which were coated in polish she had applied herself. Daddy hadn't been too happy when she brought it home, informing her he'd tell her off if she were to spill it. "Let's get Daddy to move us into town."

"I wouldn't mind that, I guess." Caleb heard the hedges near the side of the road rustle. He turned quickly, but all that came out were a couple of pheasants.

Sparky stooped to stare at Caleb's hands. "Your nails are all raggedy."

"Don't come near me with that polish," he said.

"Aw, you'd look good in it." She smiled like an adult smiled.

"Where did you even get it? Stole it?"

"Nah. Got it from a friend."

The bus pulled up in front of them, smoke pouring out of its exhaust pipe. The doors folded open and Caleb heard screams of laughter. One of the windows jumped as a tennis ball hit it.

Sparky was always the first to climb the steps into the school bus. Caleb usually lingered behind.

* * *

The lock for the hutch finally rusted shut. Daddy had to cut it off so they could feed the rabbits. He was worried they would eat their young if he didn't.

"Coyotes are going to get them this late in the season," he said. "We'll get a new lock in town."

"I can stay back and look after them," said Caleb. He knew exactly where his shotgun was and devised plans on when he would need it if the woman showed up.

"You're not staying out here by yourself."

"Why not? I'm old enough."

Daddy shook his head and locked the front door behind them while Sparky laced up her boots on the steps.

When they came back from the hardware store with the new lock, it was dark. A coyote lay in front of the door with its throat torn. Caleb always forgot how big they were, like German shepherds with matted fur.

Sparky thought it looked interesting. "Did a wolf get it?"

"One of the rabbits sure as hell didn't fight back," said Daddy.

"Oh," said Caleb. He stared down at it, surprised and curious. "Can I bury him?"

Daddy looked away, seeming cold and strange. "Do what you like."

Caleb wrapped the creature up in brown paper and dug a hole in the garden between the row of carrots and the fenced-in tomatoes. Wanting to see the open gash, Caleb pulled at the corners of that paper until it unraveled.

In the coyote's neck, he saw what looked like a black thorn poking out of the mess of fur and dried, brown blood. He ripped it out like a curved nail. It looked an awful lot like an incisor but was too small. The open cut already smelled of rot.

His father poked his head out back. "What are you doing!" It wasn't a question. He pushed the door open the rest of the way.

Caleb dropped the tooth. "Burying it!"

"No you aren't! Wrap it back up! We're going to town tomorrow." Daddy shut the door tight.

Caleb dug a deep grave, or as deep as he could dig for the creature, with its half-open eyes and pointed snout. "You could have just chased it away," he said aloud, though not to the coyote and certainly not loud enough for his father to hear. "We were all set to lose a rabbit or two. Next time you kill something, a pheasant will be fine, okay?"

He went to bed wondering what to do when a demon creature wants to show its affection. Kill it, probably. He chewed on his nails as he thought this over, nearly cutting his tongue on the edges.

He got up early the next morning for town. His father, it turned out, was going to sell the rabbits to the pet shop, an old, square building with a busted overhang and the lingering smell of gerbil turds.

"You and I and Sparky? We don't need rabbits anymore," Daddy said. "I'll just buy my meat from town, now, at least after we finish off the chickens."

"We'll need more money for that." Caleb used to think he just tolerated eating the chickens they raised. Now he already missed it.

"I have that." Daddy shrugged. "Guess I'll need a job, too."

Sparky gave a wide smile. "We could get a car, next."

To Caleb's horror, Daddy said, "Maybe."

When they got home, instead of a coyote, they found a pair of dead pheasants outside the front door.

Their father ordered them to get into the house so he could strip the birds. Why waste food?

"Think it's a mountain lion?" Sparky asked before bed.

Caleb frowned at her. "A what?"

"Leaving all the animals."

"Nothing. It's just the season," said Daddy, his face tired as he set the plucked pheasants on the kitchen table. "It happened a few times when you kids were little. Hey, you been chewing your nails?"

Caleb looked at his fingers. "No."

"Yeah you have. Stop it. They're getting all sharp."

*　*　*

The day Daddy got a job moving furniture in town, Caleb was sent home for biting another boy. He had had begun to have trouble sleeping. His eyes hurt all the time and staring directly at lights felt like lighting a fire in his skull.

The boy in question was Jaime Ronald, who was really just a know-nothing who hassled everyone, and he had started bothering Caleb before class. "Hey! Why're you squinting? Are you Chinese or something?" His friends started to laugh and, with no teacher to glare at them, the rest of the class did, too.

Caleb couldn't stand being hassled. Other people could, but he couldn't.

Jaime walked over, saying things like, "Ching chong, kung-fu," as the other students tittered around him.

Half of Caleb wanted to punch Jaime in the mouth while the other half, the half of him that loved waiting in the woods for an hour with his shotgun just to take aim at a buck making its way through, bared his teeth and bit.

Caleb was too ashamed to go home when the bus dropped him off. He kept rubbing his eyes as he went. The bushes grew taller beside him. He said to the wilderness, "I'm like this because I touched the tooth you left in the coyote."

A hedge rustled, but instead of starlings, a raspy voice croaked, "No." Her eyes, like silver dollars, reflected round and bright between the leaves.

Caleb didn't run because running might mean she would chase him. "Do you watch me a lot?"

The bush didn't answer.

"How long have you been doing it?" Caleb picked up a twisted stick from the path and drove it between the branches. He didn't hear scampering or hissing or anything. Pushing the leaves back with his hands, he found nothing but more branches.

He hurried back to the cabin, stick still in hand. His father met him in front of the house. Caleb figured he had already gotten the phone call from school because Daddy had just bought a cell phone.

"Are you trying to get kicked out?" Daddy asked. "Because we're moving. I know you don't want to, but we are."

His grip tightened on the stick. "You and Sparky move. I'll stay." Caleb wanted that. It seemed right to say it that way.

"Pack your things tonight." Dark circles were beneath his father's eyes. He probably hadn't been sleeping right, either. Probably not for days.

"We're not leaving that quick!"

"You bet we are. Now get inside and do it. Your sister's over at a friend's house tonight and she won't mind getting her stuff later. I'm going to town to see about buying a truck." He pointed toward the road and Caleb saw that his hand—all hairy knuckles—had a thumbnail that had turned black, as if he had held it over an open flame. It curled a bit, too, and was pointed like a claw.

When Daddy saw he was looking, he shoved his hand in his pocket. He looked embarrassed, like Caleb had accidentally seen him without clothes.

"Scoot right now or I'll pummel you." The threat sounded stiff coming from him.

Caleb didn't move. "Why move now?"

"Why not now?" His father stood tall as if ready to fight him.

"Is it the dark woman? Have you seen her, too?"

"She's made up. I made her up. Now get your things." His nostrils flared, like he was a bull fuming.

"No."

"No?" Daddy took in a deep breath, crouched down, and picked up one of the rocks next to the road he sometimes took to prop open the door. He threw it at Caleb's feet. "There's your no!"

Caleb jumped, shocked. He turned and ran into the woods.

He let branches crack beneath his feet. However hard he ran or fought, he realized, he was probably going to end up going back home and moving.

"You run slow," said the bright-eyed woman who fell into step beside him. When she pulled her lips back, all her teeth were black and more than a few were missing.

Caleb gasped and ran faster, but her pale face swam up beside him again.

She draped an arm behind his neck as they went, more spirit than solid, and planted a cold, wet kiss on his cheek. "You can go much more quickly than that."

He did. Fear ran up and down him, hot and cold. The trees were darker now, but Caleb wasn't sure if this was because it was getting dark or he was too deep in the woods to see the sun. It seemed too early.

"Caleb!" His father was behind him, all fury.

Caleb stopped and hid. The kiss on his cheek burned, a brand of shame.

Then he heard a hiss like a kettle on a stove. The woman had slipped away from him and was now with Daddy.

"Oh, you bitch." His father came out from between the trees and stood staring down at the creature as she crouched. In his hands was a rifle. "You're luring him, too."

"A gun?" The woman sat like a cat. "That's what you bring into the woods? Tell me. Are you hunting your son?"

Caleb stayed hidden. His heart beat fast.

"We could have lived in the cabin I built," said his father. He didn't put down his gun. "I just came to the mountains to hike and camp after college. I only wanted to stay once I met you."

"I was not made for cabins. I sleep underground, sometimes, or in a nest during spring. I told you this. I have only been waiting to see if the children would cast off their human skins. You once could have, though you aren't kin to me. This one is on his way."

In the dark, Caleb looked at his hands. How sharp his nails were. He stared up at his father and found he could see every detail in his sad, weakened face. When had he grown wrinkles?

"It would have been easier if you had ignored me when I came down from the mountains, Robert," she said. "Should I have left you alone?" She stood at her full height, bony spine straight as a wooden beam and the skirt shushing around her ankles. She touched the side of his face, resting her thumb on his closed mouth.

He let her, his grip on the rifle relaxing. His eyes shut and he cried. "I hate missing you."

"You shouldn't have stayed as long as you did."

"I looked every day."

"I saw. You said you didn't want to see me, so I stayed unseen."

Caleb could see them. It was dark, almost black as tar, and he could see every detail like an animal with night vision.

Daddy opened his eyes and the wind blew past, the leaves on the tree boughs rattling with it. He stared in Caleb's direction.

"I don't want to go with you and Sparky into town," Caleb announced. "I can't."

Daddy looked pained.

The woman leaned forward and whispered something into his father's ear.

Caleb, his hearing much sharper than he was used to, heard the woman say, "It's my turn to take care of him."

*   *   *

He could smell everything, now. Birds, water, fear, maple syrup when it was still in the trees, starlight, and spirits. The last was how he and Ma smelled, sometimes, when they slipped between shadow pockets where time passed strangely. She taught him to see the holes in the world.

The night his new teeth finished coming in and the old, blunt ones finished falling out, an itching burned across his skin. It was like ants and spiders running up his legs, arms, and torso, all biting him at once.

"Ma!" he sobbed. "I'm gonna die!"

She looked back at him and wrinkled her nose. "Oh, you're just fine."

He yelled and wanted to kill her. What about all times she had held him close, not like a human mother and child but like animals?

He felt his skin ripple. Shaking, he edged the tips of his claws beneath the loosest part on his shoulder and began to tear. It hurt for a pale moment. Then he pulled every last part of his old self away to reveal his new, shiny skin, too slick and baby soft for hair yet.

He laughed. She did, too. It really had been silly to be scared.

Daddy and Sparky bought a house in town, a new truck, and, once he changed jobs, a pool in the backyard. They seemed happy, more or less, though when he and Ma visited to look at the back of the house, where the dry, yellow grass in the yard met the trees, Sparky often stared out the window in their direction. When she did, she looked restless.

"She won't see us here in the shadow place until she questions her skin," Ma said.

"She must like it, I guess!"

With paper Ma kept in the trees, he left her letters on the back porch. He'd promised Daddy he would. That was part of the deal. He signed them "Caleb," though that was the name of someone else.

191

Getaway
by Lola J. Clemente

The Morning

The sun shone through the sheer curtains, bathing the white room in a golden glow. She had let him sleep while she had breakfast, but it didn't last long. His impatient wails echoed through the oblong room as she finished her last bite of pancake. She rushed over to the babe in the cradle.

"Don't cry, darling," she said, soothing his face with her hand. Her nails matched the red of his skin. "It's such a beautiful day. The sea is calm, my boy."

She walked to the window. Pushing back the curtain, her fingers caught the fragile lace. She frowned and hooked the curtain up to let in more light. She'd have to find time to mend the rip and wash the yellowing fabric.

The sun was harsh on the infant's face; it's warmth made him giggle. The water was calm and still against the rocks on the side of the cliff.

"Let's go for a walk, darling." She twirled back around to him. Her blue skirt billowed. She scooped the plump babe into her arm, feeling that rush of joy as she touched his soft skin. He always felt lighter than he looked.

She loved the lighthouse. It had belonged to her husband's late father, and though no longer in use, the structure stood tall, a beautiful home inside and out. It made a perfect little getaway for her and her boy.

The kitchen still smelled of bacon and syrup as she strapped him into his carriage. He reached up, touching a curl of her hair, and laughed. His happy gurgle was all that was light and good in the world. Her beacon of hope. Her joy. She pushed the carriage through the front door and down the dirt path along the rocks.

The Afternoon

After their walk, they sat under the big tree. She read *Emma* to him and whistled to the sea birds until the boy started getting fussy. Hungry, he cried. She picked him up from his blanket and brought him inside for a change and a feeding.

She sat on the rocker by the fireplace and pulled down her shirt. He always had trouble latching on, but he was gentle, which was nice. She barely ever felt anything, and he was quick; they were to the changing table in no time.

"Oh, my boy," she said, jumping up with her hand on her cheek. "It seems we're out of diapers."

She laid the baby back in his carriage and kissed him on the nose. They would need to go into town for more.

"Don't want you to get burned now, darling," she said, laying a dark veil over the carriage.

She strolled down the path, rolling the carriage to a stop beside the large lilac bush that marked the intersection with the main road. Lilacs were always her favorite. The smell reminded her of home, how her husband—how Nick would trim the flowers and bring them in a vase for her...

Town was rarely busy on Thursday afternoons. Town was rarely busy at all. Nevertheless, she was on a mission. She moved past the lilacs toward the center, stalking down the bricks with her head down.

The funny looks the townies gave her made her stomach swirl. Mrs. Newman stood outside her sewing shop, crinkling her crooked nose and scowling as they passed. A boy walking his dog saw her and scuttled across the street to avoid coming too near. She didn't like being around them. She didn't like them looking at her. Or her boy.

The young clerk at the register scanned her items and hastily shoved them in a bag, avoiding her eyes.

She had the sudden feeling that someone was staring at her, but she shook the silly thought away.

Hooking the grocery bag over her elbow, she pushed the stroller out of the store. Clouds had come on a string breeze, covering the sun. Distant thunder rumbled. They took the shortcut home, passing the lilacs without a second thought.

The Night

The glare of the car's headlights shined on the wet stones as he drove up the lane. He was angry at himself. Why hadn't he thought to look there sooner? Back when his father was still alive, they'd spent so many happy summer weekends at the lighthouse.

Having seen her at the store—pushing that old carriage—he wondered if he was too late. He'd been too afraid to confront her then, with all the people looking on. If that *had* been their son with her…

He'd driven aimlessly as the storm rolled in, waiting for her to return to the lighthouse, remembering better times when the sun shone and they lay on the rocks with the waves crashing far below.

He walked the path to the front door, past the abandoned carriage, rain soaking through his jacket, and looked up at his father's lighthouse. He thought about running away, about giving up. He was scared to go in, scared of what he would find.

Ten years of storms had battered the old structure until it was falling in on itself. The curved metal handle on the door snapped off in his hand. He put a shoulder to the wood and shoved. Something crashed inside as he forced the door open.

"Who's there?" *Her voice*, coarse and frantic, cried from inside. "Stay away!"

He took another step as the old door fell off its hinges. His wet boots slapped against the rotting floorboards. Wind blew sea water and rain through the cracked window panes. Transfixed, he took in the state of ruin.

The walls were stained with salt, paint peeling away. Barnacles and mold encrusted the drooping woodwork. In the corner, near the black hole of the fireplace, was his father's old rocking chair, decomposing like an abandoned artifact.

His heart ached. Had his wife been *living* here?

The sound of footsteps climbing the stairs jolted him back into the present. He bolted to the base of the narrow spiral stairs.

"Abigail? Gail! It's me, baby," he yelled. "Please, wait!"

"Stay away from us!" came her scream.

Us? He thought, *My God…*

"Gail!" he called, rushing the stairs two at a time. Ignoring the timber moaning beneath his feet, he ascended toward the old light that had guided past ships away from the sharp rocks of the shoreline.

A bolt of lightning lit up the dark. He looked up and saw her, frozen in the flash.

She stood on the parapet, caught in the thrash of the wind. Between them, the broken shell of the once proud lantern hung in space. Another bolt illuminated her silhouette. What was she holding?

A rotting step gave under his weight. Heart in his throat, he grabbed the rail, heaving himself up the last few steps.

He could barely see her; the last flash of light still etched across his retinas. Waves crashed far below, nearly as loud as the thunder from above. Rain pelted them.

In intermittent flashes he saw her, assaulted by wind, clutching the parapet's rusting rail with one slim hand. She cradled a bundle in the crook of her free arm.

The lamp was now just broken shards scattered around the multi-sided room of windows—most of which sported cracks of their own, if not completely broken.

Glass crunched beneath his heels as he stepped toward her. "Gail!"

He stopped at the open door leading to the platform of wood and metal and cried out, "Please, my love!" His voice sounded weak, as if it was swallowed by the storm.

Somehow she heard him and turned.

Lightning cracked and he gasped at the sight of her. Her clinging clothes were filthy and torn. Purple bruises and grey blotches marred her ghostly skin. Black crescents shadowed her haunted face. Once tall and fulsome, her body seemed shriveled and starved. Bloodshot and wild were her eyes.

A pale dead face peeked from the rags in her arms. *Him.* Their son, now only a shriveled carcass.

She backed against the railing.

"Honey—" He reached out to her.

"What—I don't know who you are." She squinted through the rain.

He stayed at the doorway so he wouldn't startle her. "It's me. It's Nick… Your *husband.*" He put his hand on his chest. "You ran from the hospital, you took our stillbor—"

"No, you're not…" She squeezed her eyes shut and shook her head, clutching the corpse to her. "No, my husband's—"

"Oh, God. Abigail, our baby is dead. He didn't make it—"

"Stop!" She squeezed her eyes shut. He could see her trying to grasp onto whatever terrible fantasy she had. She grabbed the railing, paint and rust chipping off.

"But you did make it! *You did! Put him down and let him go,* and we can heal and move on—*for* him!"

"No! I—no." She released a ragged wail of despair and anguish. The sound of her pain— the idea of clinging to her delusion curdled his blood. A hint of realization cracked over on her face as she slowly looked down at what she held in her arms. "No… I—He…"

"Gail, I'm here—I'm here to help," Nick said, trying to be calm and warm. He moved toward her, slowly. "I love you! We could… We could try again—"

"NO!"

The cold rain bit his face. Her gaze jerked from him—to the babe in her arms—to the sky. She gasped in each breath.

Her expression had been broken before. Now it was gone. She drifted outward, like a ghost behind her own eyes, decaying like the old lighthouse below her. She looked down at the shell that was once her baby boy.

Nick reached for her again. A bolt of lightning hit the water. The gold ring on his finger twinkled in the flash. The matching ring still glimmered on her finger. A crack of thunder boomed above them. He was almost close enough to reach her.

"*Get away!*" She jerked around and lost her grip on the bundle. She screamed as the corpse of her son tumbled over the rail. Frozen, they both watched as he fell, disappearing into the angry storm's abyss.

Abigail's body went rigid, and she wailed. She had lost her boy a second time.

Nick lunged for her as she threw herself toward the edge, catching her arm. Metal creaked and groaned under them. He pulled her toward the door, but she let out another scream, shoving him away with such desperate strength that he sprawled backward into the lantern room. Glass gouged his back and arms.

"I can help you!" He screamed, his voice hoarse as he pushed himself to his feet, blood mixing with the rain.

As she watched him, she began to sob. Her crying was somehow worse than the screaming.

He pulled himself back through the window, ripping the skin of his hands on the shards still in the frame. He rushed her once more.

His grip on her arm was stronger than before. He tried to reach around her, to secure her, but she was pushing hard against him, frantically shoving and kicking. Their struggle wedged up against the banister, rust flaking onto his bloody hands.

He pushed rain and tears from his eyes and her fighting slowed. Her expression returned to that emptiness.

"We'll just go to him," she breathed. The calmness of her voice scared him. "Together."

"Baby… please… I—" What could he say that would reach her? Was *she* even still in there?

With a sudden heave, she kicked a leg over the railing. The metal squealed and bent under their weight. Crumbling iron and splintered wood drifted down into the storm where their baby's corpse had fallen minutes before. Her grip pulled him closer as she looked greedily down at the waves.

"Abigail! No!"

She looked back at him with the sorrow-filled eyes of the woman who was once his wife. As if controlled by someone or something else, their grip on each other loosened.

He wished he could say she hit the water before he even saw. But he couldn't.

He watched. He watched her body flail. He watched until she hit the rocks below and angry black waves came, washing his wife away as they had their son.

Silently, lightning struck the water far out on the horizon.

Blood dripped from his stinging palms, washing down his limbs with the pelting rain. Aches radiated through his body. He wiped more rain and tears away from his face, eyes never leaving the spot where she disappeared.

He thought about jumping after her but he knew he never could. He had to let her go...let the woman she *had become* go—the woman that pregnancy and loss had changed her into—and clung to the memory of his wife. *His Abigail.* He thought back to those summer weekends they would spend together...

Nick hoped that his Abigail finally found the peace she had sought in their getaway.

The thunder finally followed.

Flesh Harvest
by Kameryn James

She propped the umbrella handle against her shoulder and peered at gathering crowds that strolled along brick walkways and narrow streets blocked off for festivities. The day's heavy mist saturated her to the bone. She did not mind the humidity and drizzle, for she was a woman of the South. She bundled herself in warm clothes and boots against the autumn chill.

The precipitation took its toll on Salem during its height of tourism, for less masses ventured out today for Halloween haunts and treats. No bother to her. Less crowded meant less annoying cell phone footage that would accidentally capture her current image.

She blended in well with people who shuffled in and out of bookstores, coffee shops, and stores specializing in natural products, charms, and curiosities. She smirked in recognition at trinkets such as hag stones with holes in them and little dolls.

Tokens and tiny idols believed to ward off evil, such as herself.

A handful of tourists circled around a young woman dressed in all black. She guided them on a walking tour that flocked around the old buildings. She told stories of hauntings, curses, and witch trials.

Curses and witches, indeed.

She fancied these travelers, guides, and entrepreneurs held no clue of true curses. Not even the slightest understanding of the cascading terror they cast. These walks and tours were for show, entertainment, and capital gain.

But she knew. And she had killed a few witches in her time, slowly and painfully.

This town was rumored to be cursed. Truthfully, when remaining still and calm, she could feel the moaning ghosts of innocents tortured and executed. She could feel them in the brick walkways and in the whispering autumn winds.

The tour guide narrated tales of enchantments and condemnations. The tales flowed from darkly painted lips shaped into a luscious pout.

She focused on those lips with a silver hoop pierced through one. In her prowls of Salem, she observed many people with hoops, studs, and spikes through noses, lips, eyebrows and possibly other places. People walked freely with tattoos and various bright and unnatural hair colors.

Two hundred years ago, along the Gullah corridor of the Southeastern states, women pierced and marked themselves to protect them from her.

At first, it had worked. She detested and cringed away from damaged skin. But currently, it was a way to express oneself on a human canvas. Or simply trendy. Yet, this trend posed a problem to her. Visible tattoos inked upon the skin were easily identifiable to law enforcement and the frightened public. The lone piercing, on the other hand, was easily removed.

She pondered if people grasped the value of their flesh. No, they did not. They would not.

Unless it was torn from their bones, as hers had been.

*   *   *

She was the daughter of a slave. It was not her fault the master of the estate found her dark eyes, high defined cheeks, graceful neck, and full lips far more desirable than his wife. Women could be jealous creatures of insatiable spite and vengeance. The wife had paid witches of her own fair-skinned ancestry that came from old woods. The wife had paid them well. As she stood in front of the large wooden spindle, their chants and motions had been sharper than knives. They stripped her supple, brown flesh, and in agony, she watched her skin peel away. She watched her youth and beauty flay. The three women wickedly strung her flesh through the spindle and wove it into a monstrous and grotesque mound. Her muscles and tendons were left exposed, vulnerable, and shining wet with blood. Her skull was stripped of its thick black hair. Her chocolate eyes no longer blinked but bulged in terror and melancholy.

A terrible red monster with a skeletal grin, she howled in anguish. Petrified and abandoned, she contemplated walking into the Atlantic and letting the oceans take her.

But not for long.

The wife's ancestry had its god, and the witches had their Earth-bound spirits. But they turned a blind eye to deities willing to grant judgment in the form of vengeance. Within time, she brutally took her revenge just as it had been given. She hunted throughout the land and first harvested the skin of the youngest witch. A few years later, she repaid the wife on the eve of her daughter's wedding day, leaving no bride to fill a lacy dress.

The curse made her too hideous and traumatic to be seen during the day, so she learned to travel at night and take what she needed to survive. Over the decades, she became legend in the Gullah corridor that stretched from the Carolinas to Florida. The descendants of her brothers and sisters still lived along the coastal regions. They told stories about her to scare children into behaving and to obey their parents. Tales of horror frightened girls away from vanity and ensured they would not stay out late in the night. Gruesome recounts steered young men away from savory woman and encouraged the choosing of appropriate wives and mothers.

Good night. Don't let the boo hag ride you, they said.

Hag, indeed. She vowed she would never be a wrinkled crone drawn in the illustrations of folklore and fairy tales. She would be young and beautiful throughout all her days. She would look like anyone she wanted.

She journeyed inland and dwelled in New Orleans for a long spell. She travelled the Mighty Mississippi, first by steamboat. The northern states were different. The air was not filled with aromas of spicy foods. It took some time to adjust to the cold. Quiet snowfalls and unrelenting blizzards had left her shivering and huddling in the shadows cast by fireplaces. So she sought a husband to warm her.

When she grew weak, she stole the breath from his lungs to revive her. He eventually withered, and she solemnly moved on.

*   *   *

She rather enjoyed lurking the streets of Salem during the Halloween season. It reminded her of bustling and festive New Orleans. Tourists beheld the historic buildings and were entertained by ghost stories that dwelt within. She was thankful for these aging structures. They held chimneys, large vintage keyholes, and even cracks in the foundation. While the residents felt these flaws caused drafts and needed repairs, they served as her entrances and gateways.

The tour guide she watched as a hawk targets a mouse lived in such a building. The huntress specter of blood and bone had followed her home a week ago. She had entered the girl's bedroom while she slept. She'd noticed the presence of old books, a lovely drawing of a pentacle with its five elements, and the metal witch's knot above her bed. Ah, this girl held some belief. Yet these charms had not stopped the crimson prowler from kneeling over her, patient and longing. Sweet breath had wheezed out of full lips, and she had sucked a bit in gratefully, causing the woman to slumber deeper.

The girl was lovely enough and had thick hair styled in a trendy faux hawk. But most importantly, she was covered in healthy, firm skin.

On this night, the haunt hung back as the candle-lit tour ended. The guide yawned wide, and her gothic-dressed co-workers offered to go out for coffee before settling in for the night. She declined and stated she needed rest.

Yes, rest.

The night huntress smiled when the girl departed for home. Only a slight smile could she afford, as her lips dried more and more each day. The rich lotions she purchased and spread over her skin no longer provided needed moisture. The breath she sucked from slumbering lovers did not enrich the pores and no longer gave her life or youth.

She turned away from the dispersing groups to retreat to her own sparsely-furnished dwelling. Under her knit hat, she felt the left ear slide downwards. She huffed and frowned, fumbling through the stitched yarn to straighten the wayward lobe. Taking a deep, relaxing breath, she reminded herself that this trifle would soon pass.

She waited patiently in the silence of her room and read until night blackened out the daylight. At a window, she watched and listened. Streetlamps illuminated two stories below her; the light danced like soft static in the misty rain. Excited voices of tourists faded. The drunk stumbled indoors. The occasional police and ambulance siren stopped wailing. Murmurs of televisions silenced.

She slid her knitted hat off. A lock of brittle auburn hair snapped free from the strained scalp. She had sighed a couple of nights ago when it had first happened, for this hair was quite lovely. She adored red hair ever since she'd first beheld it on some of the European immigrants with the charming accents. Whenever she chose to don red hair, she chose long and lustrous locks flowing like fire. But now, she paid no mind. New, strong hair would be hers soon.

She stripped off her sweater and flowing skirt and folded them neatly. She stood naked and listened briefly once more, confirming the lull and hush of the night as it rolled into early morning.

She rose a hand and snapped it open; her fingers flared out. The fingertips ruptured and nails split away. Talons of sharpened bone glinted in the room dimly lit by steady fire.

She bowed her head. With her dominant talon, she stabbed into the nape of her neck. The crunch sound of the initial pierce was no longer sickening, only familiar. It stirred her with thrill of the hunt and treasure she would possess before sunrise.

She dragged the talon forward and sliced it through the scalp. With learned grace, she rose her head when the bone blade reached her forehead. The eyelids shut when her hand crossed between them. The brows slipped apart lazily and shifted the eyelids sideways as the face severed. She cut the nose perfectly in half and sheared through pink lips, tilting her head back when the claw traveled over the chin. Carefully down the exposed neck it sliced.

Her face opened like a zipper, revealing a crimson and pink slit, yet she was far from done. She cut over the sternum and between plump breasts, stopping when her finger hooked the belly button.

Curling her fingers around the loosened flesh, she peeled it away from her scalp, unveiling a bald, blood red head with tissues stretched across the skull. She pulled the dry and cracking skin from the last harvest off her shoulders. Like a woman disrobing for her lover, she stripped the skin away from her breasts. The empty arms flapped loosely at her waist before she slithered the flesh down her thighs. Each foot gently stepped out.

She stood freely in her scarlet, macabre form created by the horrid anathema that stole her skin centuries ago.

She wadded up the hollow carcass like one folds clothes.

Chilly autumn air blustered into the room from the window, and she shuddered lightly. Upon hearing no people outside, she contorted her slender red body through the open window. She checked the area and saw no one moving. With the grace of a spider, she climbed up to the roof, avoiding the window on the third floor. She began her silent and acrobatic journey through the neighborhoods of Salem, hearing the occasional dog's bark followed by flustered commands to shush it.

If she were spotted or noticed, it was dismissed as a shadow or a trick of the mind, influenced by the Halloween season.

She reached the intended home: one of those houses that used to be mansions that now served as apartments or multi-family homes. So popular with denizens of New England, she noted. Circling the residence, she sought out the cracks and overlooked openings in old doors or windows. She summoned supernatural powers and reached back to the humidity of her southern home. Bones, muscles, and tendons morphed into a ruby mist. She squeezed herself through cracks, slithered between walls, and materialized in her prey's bedroom.

She called them prey. The media over the years called them victims.

The cozy, heated room turned unnaturally balmy and warm, marking her presence like the omen she was. This warning always came too late for the dormant.

She stood to her full height and paused. The calming smell of incense swirled around her.

Creeping along the smooth coolness of the hard wood floor, she took care not to make creaking sounds that would alert her prey.

One bare foot landed on sharp and burning crystalline grains. She winced and gasped with the pain she had not felt in years, not since before science and other logics had mostly wiped out superstition.

A lamp clicked, on and warm yellow light revealed the simple, ancient protection.

A thick line of salt circled the girl's bed. The creature snapped her gaze in all directions. Salt lined the floor of the doorway and was even sprinkled on the windowsill.

Her prey's sleepy voice asked, "What are you, devil?"

This devil was an expert at hiding in the shadows and avoiding detection. But this girl had detected her. This girl must have sensed her unholy and unnatural presence one week ago. She had not only put out her protective symbols of faith but laced the room in salt.

The boo hag doubted the modern witchy woman suspected anything like the form before her now.

The girl's mouth opened to scream. Her crimson devil leaped onto the bed and cupped a meaty hand over her mouth. Her bone claws tapped the cheek.

She must be careful not to harm the skin.

The woman grabbed a small silver container from the nightstand and jerked it toward her exposed face. More scorching shards rained. Although miniscule and light as snowflakes, salt to her bare and true form was nothing but pure pain. She hissed, and the girl struggled to escape her.

She must not harm the skin.

The specter rolled onto her back, forcing the girl on top of her. They both faced the ceiling, where on the other side, a neighbor slumbered unsuspectedly. She wrapped legs of bone and muscle around the woman to steady her and hooked one arm around her neck. She squeezed and trapped screams and breath in her throat. The young woman's flesh pressed against her. Black fingernails dug in desperation at her muscles and tendons before she fell limp.

The specter loosened the hold on her neck and listened. Had anyone heard the struggle? Would there be footsteps echoing from another apartment and a knock on the door? Would police sirens wail and send her running back to the faltering skin for another day or more?

None of those sounds disturbed the night.

The creature slithered out from under the unconscious girl and straddled her. She scanned her treasure, seeing no tears or cuts, but red discoloration on the neck from the hold. This was a trite setback. Bruises could be covered, especially in the autumn.

She waited while the girl's breathing eased from a gasping wheeze to a deep inhale. Leaning closer, she opened her skeletal grin wide. Her bare teeth hovered hungrily. She gratefully sucked and drank in the breath, savored it like smooth wine. It surged through her and rejuvenated her doddering body with life.

Satisfaction stirred when decompressing lungs sank beneath her hands. She swore she could feel the lungs sear under the ribs. She sucked until hearing the last wheeze of breath. The woman's face contorted in pain and loss. Her eyes fluttered.

The being of hag folklore stroked the thick hair, dyed black. With sensitive fingers, she caressed the lifeless face, hooking the hoop stuck in the lip. She plucked it out.

She knew anatomy better than the most educated and experienced of physicians. She could truly perform her ritual in the dark, yet what bliss lay in that?

She flashed her bone talons again, and then paused. Before devoting them to their precise craft, she carefully scraped the salt from her face, wincing and crying out softly. Such a terrible misjudgment she had made.

Her talons cut through the soft pajamas like razors and let rags flitter aside. The youthful body glowed scrumptious in the shadowy room. She exhaled a satisfied moan and caressed the torso. She thrust her dominant finger into the naked skin and opened the woman from pelvis to forehead with more exactitude than a skilled mortician. Blood spilled in streams and soaked the blankets.

She cupped the cheek, as if in tender affection, as her bone blades pared the face away from cheeks and temples. She relished the sensation of moist blood and newfangled skin as it sheared away from the head. Wriggling her tongue out, she clicked it against teeth at the whispers of skin peeling away. With sticky fingers, the hag lifted the skull out of its dissevered face, and the flesh folded down like a morbid collar.

Her own lidless, chocolate brown eyes stared down at bulging blue eyeballs.

The skin stealer tenderly, meticulously flayed her treasured pelt from its previous host. She pulled limbs out of dewy sleeves with the gentleness of a mother changing a baby's clothes.

For a moment, only a moment, the nightmarish huntress and her prey were nearly mirror images. Both without skin, both hellish, crimson sights to behold.

She glanced around, knowing millions of those burning salty crystals creased throughout the room. Standing on the bed, she held her newfound robe upside down to allow excess blood to drip on the floor and looked down at the body. The slightest twinge of empathy sparked. What a terrible vision it would be for whomever would discover this girl.

But what empowerment! Crime scene investigators would desperately search for nonexistent clues. Such glee it brought her to know that the keenest detective and most accurate technological instruments would never uncover a single fingerprint. If DNA were left, it would match no one among the living. What entertainment it was to watch modern day reporters pale at statements of a "completely skinned victim." The ensuing terror would rumble with the gasps and murmurs of citizens glued to the reports and whispers, asking if they'd heard about "that girl." It was electric to her.

She drew the pretty pelt closer to her and chanted.

Skin, skin, let me in.

She cautiously sat, eased each of her boney feet into the flesh, and pulled the skin over her legs. With a pause at the waist, she strategically laid the empty arms on the bed so they would not brush the salt. Not a single grain must sneak its way into the new flesh.

She had grown too confident and cocky in this stalk. She'd been wrong to think residents here would never suspect her presence.

She smoothed and tightened the body covering over her own calves, knees, and thighs. She wiggled her new toes. Standing close to the bed, she fixed skin over her hips. Sliding a red arm into a fleshy sleeve, she curved the skin around her elbow. She fit the fingers like a glove and straightened nails painted a glittery black shade. The other arm went through the same routine before she clenched and then stretched her fingers. Her ravenous body sealed the torso over her abdomen, ribs, and breast tissue. New flesh healed without stitching. She drew the face over her cranium like a delicate veil.

The newly clothed creature looked down at the salt barrier and smirked. She stepped over the line.

She headed into the bathroom, turned on the light, and looked in the mirror.

The new face sagged around the eyes, and the nose was slightly crooked, as were the lips. She pressed the lids over her oculus sockets until they fit comfortably, blinking a few times, making sure each lash was in place. She massaged the brows, groomed them into arches over her eyes, and molded the nose over her own cartilage and straightened the rose quartz lips. Smoothing the chin over her jaw, she opened her mouth wide to test elasticity. The tegument clung well to her muscles. Her jaws closed and lips puckered over teeth. She leaned closer and checked that the ears were level.

She gazed at the reflection of her firm face. Although she resembled the young woman she had just skinned, the new flesh forged differently over her cheekbones. The lips thinned slightly over her predominant teeth. The eyes held more of an almond shape, and they were brown instead of blue. Without gothic, witchy girl make-up, freckles sprinkled the cheeks. What ladies used to call a beauty mark dotted the corner of the left eye. Natural shading circled the eyelids.

Beautiful.

Lastly, she cupped supple cleavage and centered each sandy brown nipple over her breasts.

She then fished through an array of black, purple, and deep red clothing in the closet. The woman enjoyed flowing skirts just as she did. She chose such a skirt and pair of tights to protect her newly acquired flesh, along with a blouse, jacket, and scarf. She grabbed a pair of soft leather boots with thick soles. The woman even had some cozy hats, one of which she chose and popped on her head.

She slinked out of the apartment and down the stairs. Outside, approaching dawn blushed the pitch skies.

Over the next couple of days, shocked exclamations of the grisly scene rang though the town. Exhilaration bubbled inside her like champagne. Who could do such a thing? *What* could do such a thing?

What, indeed.

She strolled streets of Witch City and fused with other faces in the crowds. Yet she was not a killer that returned to the scene of the crime to gloat in the moment and secretly taunt investigators. She had evaded them for lifetimes.

This encounter, this girl, reminded her that perhaps one day she would not evade the humans.

Or perhaps over the next two hundred years, she would immortalize into legend here. Maybe her gory tale would be recounted to tourists for horrifying entertainment. Perhaps one night, parents and elders would warn Salem's daughters and sons of her terrible need.

Don't let the boo hag ride you.

The Monsters We Become
by Jennifer Williams

I was nine years old when I stopped being a little girl. It was a hot summer day and the cicadas were singing their songs, the ones you only hear when your clothes stick to your skin and your hair stays damp long after a bath. I was in our backyard, alone. I was always alone back then. I did not mind because I did not know any other way of being.

There were woods just beyond our backyard. When I would hold my hand out, the air was always cooler there, but that's not what drew me to the woods that day. A few feet away, just beyond the first row of trees and brush, there was a bird on the ground. It flopped helplessly, one wing sticking out awkwardly. Its plight tugged at me every time the bird flapped its useless wing.

I looked back at my house. The woods were forbidden. I didn't know why. I could guess though. I'd read enough books. A monster lived in the woods. Or maybe a witch. Or maybe the Devil himself. Whatever it was, it would get the bird if I didn't help it.

There was no movement behind me. I saw nothing out of the ordinary. The windows and back door were shut. Our grass was tall. Our grass was always tall. There was no laundry on the line that day. It was muggy, and that meant my mother would not need me for folding. Last I had seen, she was settling down in her chair in the living room to watch her stories.

I took a step toward the woods, watchful, scanning the tree line for movement other than the bird's. All was still and quiet apart from the small bird. I took another step. I asked God to keep me safe. Another, and my heart pounded as the sound of blood rushed through my ears. I was almost to the bird, and nothing had happened. It was a little brown thing. It eyed me warily before somersaulting itself into a new attempt at flight. I could see its little chest rising and falling rapidly with each breath after it landed.

I picked it up and it stilled. I imagined it knew I wanted to help it. I smiled as I patted its head with my finger. Everything would be alright. I would bring it inside. I would give it water. I would wrap its wing in tissue and feed it bread from my lunch. Mother would be proud of me.

The screen door banged shut, and I realized my error. Mother had spotted me. She marched across the back yard, and I rushed to the line of grass that marked the end of our property. When she reached me, her face was no longer the blank slate I had grown accustomed to. Her new face was twisted, and her eyes blazed, and I wondered if it was a trick of the hazy heat. I held out the bird so she could see why I risked breaking the rules. She looked at the bird cupped in my hands. It had begun to struggle. For a moment, I had hope in my heart that she would feel pity for it.

"Dirty things belong in the dirt," she said. Her nose crinkled as though she smelled something foul.

She snatched the bird and threw it deep back into the woods. I thought I heard it thud against a tree. She headed back inside without another word, wiping her hands on her apron as she went.

I stood there the whole rest of that day, staring into the woods beyond, waiting for whatever monster lived there to come and fetch the little bird corpse. It must have been a corpse, as I'd not heard a single flutter or twitch from it since. I was thirsty, and snot had dried on my upper lip from crying, and I had to pee, but I stood there, feeling the weight of responsibility like a heavy cloak. This was my fault. The monster would eat tonight because of me.

When I finally went back inside, it was long past supper time. My dinner sat, cold and congealed, on our wobbly kitchen table—Salisbury steak, mashed potatoes, peas and onions, and a cherry cobbler dessert. This was my favorite TV dinner, and I ate it gladly while mother stood watch over me. I knew if I didn't eat it now it would still be there for breakfast.

After, she threw the tray in the bin and dumped my utensils into the sink. I thought we were done, so I rose to go to bed but her hand on my shoulder stayed me. The TV was on in the living room, but I couldn't make out which show was playing.

Mother was behind me. She opened a kitchen drawer, and I heard the familiar sounds of her pulling a cigarette out of a pack and lighting it. She circled me as she smoked. This was a ritual I was familiar with. Punishment was coming, a reprimand for my disobedience, and I accepted whatever fate held in store. It wouldn't be my first, and at least this time I knew I did something wrong.

"I should have left you out there." She said this under her breath after an exhale, smoke pluming as she circled round and round. Part of me wished that she had. Maybe I could have saved the bird after all. Maybe I could have run very fast with it so that no monster at all could catch us. We would have come out the other side of the woods somewhere. Maybe in a new city. Maybe on the other side of the highway. Maybe to the very ocean itself. Then we could have lived there together, on the beach, and ate seaweed for lunch and counted the stars at night.

I pulled at strands of my hair as I lived out this fantasy in my head. My hair was long, and it curled and in the summer, when the sun shone through it, it glowed gold and orange. I loved my hair. I would braid it and put it in ponytails and pigtails and used paperclips as barrettes. When I felt shy, I would hide behind it, and if I was nervous, I would chew on it.

My mother stubbed out her cigarette and retreated to the bathroom. I sat obediently though fear tickled inside me. I squirmed, sitting on my hands to try and keep myself still. I wondered if she was getting the brush. I didn't like it when she brushed my hair. She was rough and pulled harder when it tangled.

Instead, she came back with a pair of scissors. School didn't start for another month. It wasn't time to trim my hair.

"Stay still." She stood behind me.

She gathered my hair in her hand and cut. It didn't register...what she was doing. My hair felt lighter, but I could not see it. Then the cool blade of the scissors was close to my scalp. She cut again, all around my head. I wanted to beg her to stop. Instead, my lips quivered as more tears threatened to come. By the time she was done, strands of my hair had fallen down my face to settle on my lashes and nose. My shoulders were dusted in fine bits, and larger locks had fallen into my lap. I looked down and saw a huge pile of it on the floor.

"Now clean this up." She dropped the scissors onto the table. They made a sharp sound in the vacuum of our small home.

I sat there staring at the amputated strands in my lap. I'd been punished before, but not like this. I did not notice her leave the room, but I knew she did because the TV went silent. Then I heard her bedroom door shut, and I was left in the milky florescent glow of the kitchen light with my hair all around me. Everything was quiet. I could hear the hum of the light, the chirping of the crickets outside, and the ticking of the clock on the wall. I sat for another ten minutes. My gaze drifted to the scissors.

I picked them up. They were heavy and all metal. I held the pointed end to the palm of my hand and pushed. Not enough to bleed, but enough that I could feel the first tender bite of pain. The wind picked up outside as I did this and a loose piece of siding stuttered against the side of our house, startling me. I thought about the bird. I thought about the monster in the woods.

I knew that monsters and devils liked sacrifices. Especially girl sacrifices. I'd read it in books, and I'd seen it on television. I stood up and hair fell from my lap. I stooped and picked up a long chunk of it. I ran my free hand over my head. It was choppy and stiff and uneven. I did not recognize myself reflected in the window above the sink. I had become someone new in her punishment.

I took the clump of hair that I held and shaped it into a bundle using a leftover twist tie from one of the kitchen drawers. I listened carefully for a moment. I knew I was taking yet another risk. If she caught me out there again, who knew what she would cut off next. But I heard nothing.

It was the first night that I made an offering to the monster in the woods.

*   *   *

I was fourteen when I learned that monsters are real. A man in my neighborhood shot his family and then himself. They were all dead. I did not know them well. I did not know anyone well. But my heart ached for the daughter the same way it did when I found the bird out back. She was my age, and we went to the same school. She even smiled at me once, before the others told her not to. I pulled my sweater tight around me and looked over at Mother.

She was sitting in her chair and I was on the couch. My mother always sat in that chair; I always sat on the couch. The couch was an old plaid thing, and the fabric scratched my skin.

Sometimes I wondered what my mother's skin felt like. Was it soft like mine? Or was it rough like our couch? I knew what she smelled like. I would know her scent anywhere. Cigarettes and sweat. I'd smelled it so many times in bed at night when she thought I was sleeping. She would lean over me and whisper in a sibilant hush, spittle flecking my face, but I could never make out her words. After she left, I would open my eyes. I always reached out a hand to touch the space she'd occupied beside me, but I could never feel anything. Just the air against my fingers.

I crawled into bed with her once. She shrank from my touch when I woke her. She didn't say no, but she didn't say yes either. She slept with her back to me the whole night.

As we watched the news, as we learned that death had visited just a few doors down, my mother smiled. It was a small, approving smile, and it made me shiver. That night I clipped my nails when I was getting ready for bed. I saved the clippings.

They were my second offering to the monster in the woods.

*   *   *

I was nineteen when I had sex for the first time. I liked to wander around the college campus and pretend I was a student. That is where I met him. Todd. His attention surprised me. I was not beautiful. Mother made sure to tell me this. But Todd didn't seem to mind.

He took me back to his dorm room. It was small, and he had a roommate who was tall and dark and seemed so at odds with the tiny space. It smelled like worn socks and the building was alive with noise. Todd handed me a warm beer after his roommate left, and we sat on his single-person bed with its messy cotton sheets.

Todd told me a girl died in this room back before we were even alive. He thought she slit her wrists or maybe hanged herself. He said he could hear her ghost sometimes late at night. I asked him her name but he didn't know. I think he meant to frighten me. He leaned in close and promised to keep me safe. When he kissed me, I let him. His breath tasted like beer. I laid on my back after he removed my clothes, and I stared at the ceiling when he entered me. He made noise while he rutted atop me, but I paid no mind. I was thinking about the dead girl.

When he finished, he got off me. He stood in the small room and pulled on his jeans, stumbling as he tried to get his second leg in. I thought maybe he'd had more beer than I knew. "Back in a sec', babe," he said before heading to the communal bathrooms. I didn't wait for him.

When I sat up, I could see that I'd bled a little. They say that you don't, but I did. I stared at the tiny spot of blood as I got dressed. I thought about the girl who died there. I thought about the girl I went to school with, whose father had shot her. I thought about the tiny bird in the backyard and the woods beyond. My chest ached.

I took the bloodied sheet with me when I left.

It was my third offering to the woods behind my house.

*   *   *

The next day Mother woke me.

"Get up," she said.

I was groggy from the beer and slow to wake.

"Get up," she said again, jostling me.

I squinted. The light from the open curtains hurt my eyes. My head ached and my mouth was dry.

"You want to be a whore?" She pulled my sheets back. "Then you can be one."

In my sleep addled state, it took me a second to realize what she was doing. She tugged at my pajama bottoms, pulling them down. Then she sat me up. My stomach protested and I thought I might vomit. When she tried to pull my top off, I resisted. I was cold and I didn't want to be naked in front of her.

She paused her assault and eyed me the same way she eyed the bird I'd tried to save. I shrunk back. Would she hurl me against a tree too? She retreated and I sighed in relief. I was gathering up my bottoms when she returned with the scissors.

Later, when I stood crying in the shower, watching my blood wash down the drain along with the water, I thought about the girl who'd hanged herself. I wondered if all mothers cut their girls the same way. I chided myself for being stupid. If I had been quieter, if I had been smarter, she would not have seen me, and she would not have known what I'd done. But I was not quiet and I was not smart and now I stood in the shower feeling my blood pulse painfully in my freshly made wounds.

Anger curled up around my edges, and I bit my lip to keep from crying out. I struck myself once, twice, three times, until my head spun and I felt dizzy. I picked at the skin of my lips until they turned plump and raw and tasted of copper.

I held the bits of peeled skin in the palm of my hand away from the water. They would make a fine offering.

* * *

I never met my father. Mother told me that I didn't have one, but I didn't think that was true. I liked to imagine that he was a spy and that's why he couldn't be home with us. He was off saving the world somewhere. He had better things to do than look after us. I told my teacher this once. She rapped me on my hands with a ruler and made me clean the graffiti off the bathroom stalls in the girls' restrooms. She said that lying was bad, and we shouldn't ever lie. But how is it a lie? It could have been true. It could have.

Once, when my mother had gone over to Mrs. Grant's place to collect some clothes that needed mending, I snuck into her room looking for clues. Mother didn't like to take me to see Mrs. Grant because Mrs. Grant always doted on me, giving me cake and ice-cold milk. Every time she called me "dear," my mother's hands would twitch.

"Look at the time," my mother would say.

But old Mrs. Grant, with her wrinkled face and blue gray hair, would just wave my mother off.

"Nonsense," she'd reply. "Let the poor dear finish her cake." She'd wink at me and smile. "'Sides," she'd continue, "she's nothing but skin and bones, that one."

Mother'd paced like a tiger as she'd watched me finish eating. After I was done, I'd asked for a second piece. She never brought me back to Mrs. Grant's place after that.

That was how I found the picture, while she was out. It was half faded, tucked behind her mirror. I'd only found it because her underwear drawer got stuck, and I had to slam it shut. I heard something flutter down to the floor behind the dresser. I knelt to pick it up.

A woman stared back at me—young and trim and pretty. It took me a moment to realize the woman was my mother. Not because they looked different, but rather, because this woman was smiling. The kind of smile you make when laughing and I'd never seen my mother laugh like that. She looked radiant.

I took a step back as I gaped at the picture. My legs hit the bed and I sat. My fingers traced her figure, round and round her smiling head as though I could capture that moment for myself and steal it away.

The other half of the photograph was the faded part. But I could see a man's legs and feet next to my mother's, and I could see his hand resting on her knee. She was turned toward him, that smiling face all for him, and I could just about see up her dress.

I wasn't allowed to wear dresses. I was thinking about this when I heard the car door slam shut. It always took two or three tries to really catch and close. I tucked the picture back behind the mirror, ran to the bathroom, and flushed the toilet. Her thin summer blanket was wrinkled where I'd sat.

There would be a new offering that night.

*   *   *

I was twenty six when I finally left home. I got a job calling people and asking them for money. We told the people we called that the money was for charity, but I didn't think that was true. My bosses weren't very nice about any of it. We worked long shifts in a mostly empty building at the end of a dead end street. Woods lined the back, and I wondered if all woods had monsters.

I took my dinner breaks outside no matter the weather. I would sit on a lopsided bench and stare at the woods while I picked at my peanut butter sandwich. The whole place was a pit. Weeds sprouted up in the cracked pavement, and most of the time, I could hear birds above me nesting in the crevices of the building.

The others didn't talk to me much. Except for one girl. She'd come outside to smoke and sometimes sit with me. She'd gabber on and on about this and that. Things I didn't really know about. Politics and men and whatever movies were playing downtown. I'd smile and nod, and she never seemed to mind if I didn't say anything at all.

On warm days, she smelled like my mother, and I was both repulsed by her and drawn to her. Beyond the cars baking in the sun, I could see the woods. I moved closer to her. I thought about the way my mother smiled in the photograph I found as a child. I wanted her to smile at me that way. I wanted to know what that felt like.

My hand lifted, slender and tremulous in the muggy breeze. It floated, just for a moment, a butterfly unsure of its wings, before coming to rest on her knee.

Silence.

I took this to mean acquiescence. My thumb brushed the bare skin of her knee. It was soft. I almost smiled. Almost. But then she stood, a row of expletives leaving her mouth. She towered over me, just like my mother. Her cigarette dropped to the ground, and I watched its smoke rise as she called my name, daring me to stand. She shoved me, hard, but I did not move. She hurled more insults at me, words I'd never heard before, posturing like some animal protecting its territory.

I sat. My fingers slid beneath my legs, locking me in place. She reared back and struck me. The impact from her fist nearly knocked me off the bench. My sight went black, and I tasted blood. When I opened my eyes, she had gone. I looked down. One pale tooth glistened in the sun.

It had been a while since I'd made an offering.

*   *   *

"I am a whore," I told him, when he asked.

I met a man in a bar, and I went home with him. Mother would be appalled. I think that's why I did it.

He had sandy hair that came down to his shoulders and a mustache that tickled my face when we kissed. He worked at the mill, like most men around here, and he didn't seem to mind that I wore my hair short. He put a record on and pulled me close to dance. His breath was hot on my neck, and I felt small in his bulky arms.

One of his large calloused hands slid down to cup my ass and he squeezed. Desire brewed within me, a hot and complicated storm that I summoned because I was weak. He guided me to his couch, and I sat while he knelt between my legs. He kissed my stomach, and already this felt different. He was going to love me, this one. I felt it the way some animals feel earthquakes before they hit. I wanted to run and seek higher ground, but his fingers were deft and quick and he unbuttoned my pants and pulled down the zipper before I could sprint away.

This stopped him. Of course it did.

Except it didn't. Not the way I thought it would. His fingers traced my scars. It felt strange to be touched there so tenderly. He did not make love to me on that night. Not in the way a man and a woman usually make love. Instead, he kissed me there—along my scars, between my legs. He kissed me until my whole body was itchy hot, and I was shaking, and then I cried like I did that summer day so long ago. He just held me and told me it was okay.

But it wasn't okay. I would have no offering for the monster in the woods.

*   *   *

I am sitting in my mother's chair and reading her newspaper. The ink stains my fingers, and I rub them together in a futile attempt to render them clean again. The house is quiet and stale around me. A murky cup of half-drunk coffee sits next to me, as does a crinkled pack of cigarettes. I take one out, setting aside the newspaper.

I am her in this moment: in her chair, reading her paper, drinking her coffee, lighting her cigarette. It burns my throat as I inhale, and I feel a momentary stab of guilt. I can still hear her sputum filled cough echoing around the house, like blood traveling through the chambers of a heart.

Her end was painful, and I cannot say I'm sorry.

I stand and stub out the cigarette. It is growing dark, and I have much to do. With her gone, I am free to explore.

Not much has changed since I was here last. The wallpaper is the same, pale white with tiny flowers. She made the curtains in every room. Wispy things, not the heavy kind. The rug is yellow and worn. There's no art on the walls. Never has been. But in her room, there's a cross above the bed with a withered palm frond stuck behind it.

I don't like the smell in here. Shit and piss and underneath, something sickly sweet. But this is where I must be. I am methodical in my search. I look behind the dresser mirror, but nothing is there, not even the photograph I'd seen when I was young. I pull out each drawer. The top one still sticks.

I never noticed until now how she always lacked color. Every item of clothing is muted in tone; mustard instead of yellow, coral instead of red, beige instead of brown. There's nothing vibrant. No verdant green. No cerulean blue. I look down at my own faded jeans and dirty sneakers and feel an urge to rip them from my body and run from this place. I take a deep breath and move on.

Her bedroom reveals nothing to me. There's some fabric in the small closet, along with her winter coat and a box of invoices from her seamstress days. Her sewing table sits dusty under the window. There's a small bookcase filled with brittle paperbacks I never saw her read. The emptiness of this space sucks me in, and I am released only when the wind picks up and the house creaks.

The rest of my search proves fruitless. My old room has been stripped bare. My bed is just a mattress on a frame. My table and lamp are gone, as are my drawings. She even took down the curtains she'd made for me. A pile of newspapers tied with twine sits in one corner. I think I see mouse droppings in the shadow next to it.

The kitchen is sparse. She never did like to cook. The cabinets are the same drab olive, and the fridge hums noisily. Inside is an open can of Dinty Moore Beef Stew. Her favorite. There's instant coffee, Olio, a carton of spoiled milk, and a loaf of bread. Tucked in the back of the bottom shelf is a coffee can. It looks old. Almost as old as I am.

My body is the space between breaths.

I am a skeleton reaching for life, reaching into the cold. I need to know what happened. I need to know who my father was. I need to understand why she never smiled at me the way she smiled at him.

Coffee can in hand, I shut the fridge door. I peel back the plastic lid. This is my future, I think. Divination in a rusting piece of metal. I peer inside.

Pennies. That's all.

I scatter them across the table. I shake the empty can upside down. I touch the coins with disbelieving hands. A few slide onto the floor and make a pinging sound as they bounce off the linoleum.

I am stone. I am sinking. Anger wells up inside me. Hot tears sting as I march back to her bedroom. I want to scream, but no sound comes out. Instead, I rage. I pull the sheets from her bed. I knock over her dresser mirror, shattering it. I want to destroy her sewing machine, but it's too heavy for me to lift. I yank on her flimsy closet door, hoping to tear it from its hinges. There's a cracking sound, but it stays put.

When I am spent, I sit on the floor. The world outside is dark now. I can hear a dog barking and crickets chirping. I can just about see one dull streetlamp from where I sit. I lie down on the floor. The mess around me is a comfort. It is my mess. I have made this my space.

Her ceiling is textured. It looks sharp, and there's a stain in one corner. It smells different down here. Mustier. I realize it's the books on the shelf next to me. Under her bed there's more dust. An empty pill bottle sits on its side, cap long gone. My breathing slows, and I place one hand low on my belly. Jake will wonder where I am.

I'm thinking of leaving when I notice the top drawer of her dresser. It's jutting out further than the rest. It never did shut right. I scooch over along the floor, too tired to sit upright, too weary to allow myself to really hope. I feel foolish for coming here. Like a child trying to catch the moon in a cup of water.

I pull the drawer out, steadying it with both hands as I lower it to my chest and then to the floor by my side. The stone of disappointment still weighs me down, so I continue to lie there, staring at the black space the drawer occupied moments ago. It is shadows and darkness. It is just a place that held a drawer, nothing more.

And yet. My hand rises.

I have to sit up to feel inside. I try not to think about spiders as my hand searches the darkness. At first, nothing. Rough wood. The sting of a splinter. The track the drawer is meant to slide along. Then, something. Paper. Stuffed in the back. Dread and hope wash over me in simultaneous waves. I am about to discover new lands, but I am afraid of what I might find.

It's an envelope. I grasp it, my fingers arching like the metal claws in those arcade games. Inside, there's something stiff. I forget to breathe. I withdraw slowly. The clock in the kitchen ticks. The envelope is pale, weathered by the years. The top flap can't quite fold over all the way. There are photographs inside. Time has stopped. The kitchen clock is silent. I have no need of breath. Not even my heart beats.

I open the already loose flap and pull out the first photograph. It's my mother, I think. She's so young I can barely tell. Her hair is dark and long, and she's standing on a beach. She's in a modest bikini, flashing that vibrant smile I've only ever seen in photographs.

Castle Beach, it says on the back. *1965.*

The next picture is her getting out of a taxi cab in the city. She's waving one gloved hand at the camera. Smiling. Always smiling in this other world. I shuffle through a few more. Her, lounging on a bed. Her, in the shower, just her head peeking out from behind the curtain. I grow frustrated and sloppy, shuffling them one after the other, faster and faster.

Then, finally.

He's dressed well. Dark slacks, shiny shoes, white button down shirt. He is sitting on the edge of a bed with his head of sandy hair turned away. He's trim, and though I can't see directly, handsome, I'm sure. I stare. He is water, and I have been in a desert my whole life. I cannot get enough. On the back it says *Hotel Carlton.*

I take in every detail. Not just of him but of the room as well. Floral bedspread, striped wallpaper, floor length curtains just visible in the corner. He is tall. I can see this from the way his legs bend even with his feet flat on the floor. There is an ease in the way he sits, and it's almost as if she's caught him laughing though I can't be sure. I linger a moment more. I find myself wondering what he smelled like.

The next photograph looks to be a match to the one I found when I was young. They are standing on a porch. My mother is wearing the same dress. This time he has a suit jacket casually flung over one shoulder, same pressed pants and white shirt. My mother stares longingly up at him. Her arm is wrapped tight around his waist. His eyes are for the camera. He *is* handsome. Thin face to match his thin frame. Long nose, sharp cheekbones. He's squinting because the sun is shining right on them. I don't recognize the house. It's pale colored, my guess is blue or gray. There's a trellis around the door with roses blooming between the whitewashed wood. *91* is on the door behind them.

It's not here, wherever they are. This house was my grandmother's before we moved in. I never met her. Like my father, I've only ever seen her in photographs. She is always stern, never smiling. Just like my mother, my real flesh and blood mother, not the one in these photographs. Just like me, too, I suppose. Three generations of women who forgot how to smile. Mother told me I was lucky. She said Grandma was worse to her than she had ever been to me. For a long time, I believed her.

I look at the next picture. This one is here. I recognize it immediately. He is in the backyard. I can see the woods beyond. The grass is trim and tidy. He is not. His pants are wrinkled. His skin glistens. The white button down is gone, replaced with a white undershirt with stained armpits. A lawnmower rests in front of him. He is smiling, but it doesn't reach his eyes. On the back it says, *D, June '69.*

The next photo is worse. He is outside again, smoking a cigarette. He is not smiling. He looks disappointed. The picture is grainy, as though it's been taken through a window with the screen down. I have to force myself to keep looking.

All the rest are of him. But they are different. Taken from far away. Him in front of another house. Him with his arms around another woman. Him coming out of an insurance agency. Until the last two.

One is in this very room. His coat and hat are still on. He is facing the window, and I can just see my mother's hand on his arm, beckoning him to turn toward her.

The last confuses me. I think it must be a mistake. It's just the woods out back, nothing more. It's a Polaroid, which is different from the others. Its colors are faded; I think it must be dusk, but I'm not sure. I turn it over. It's my mother's handwriting.

D's last sunset, October 16th

I turn it back over. I flip back and forth between the front and the back. I think about the way she smiled when that family got murdered in our neighborhood. I think about how callously she threw that injured bird against a tree. *I should have left you out there.* My stomach drops.

I get up. The pictures and envelope slide from my lap. All but the Polaroid. I carry it in my shaking hand. I walk to the kitchen and look out the window above the sink. The one that looks to our neglected back yard. Beyond are the same trees in the photograph. The same dark woods that never got sold off and developed. I feel a coldness deeper than any winter storm. I understand now why she never wanted me back there. I look down at the picture and drop it into the empty sink.

Outside, the air is crisp. The pokeweeds have dried, and the burdock has run rampant. Our old clothesline is rusted; the rope hangs down limply. A blue jay screams somewhere out of sight.

I rub my belly low, and it echoes pain back at me. If I go, there will be no turning back. I will walk into the woods to find my father. I will dig until my hands are stained black and they bleed. And then I will lie in the hole that I have made, curled against his bones. I will be the final offering to the woods.

And in spring I will rise. Beautiful, terrible, monstrous.

Just like my mother.

Tiger's Husband
by Jane Yolen

It was a wonderful battle
and her side won.
There would be food strewn
across the savannah.
She yowled at the moon,
stretched her back,
would have joined the feast.
But first she had to find his bones
and bury them.
She could not be married again
until that ritual was done.
She found his skull
where it had been tossed
by the intruders,
at the bottom of a cliff,
his backbone near the scratching tree.
The long leg bones were the last of them.
They filled the mourning mound.
She was wed again before dawn.

About the Cover Artist

Lynne Hansen is a horror artist who specializes in book covers. She loves creating art that tells a story and helps publishers and authors reach the audiences they deserve. Her clients include Cemetery Dance Publications, Thunderstorm Books, and Raw Dog Screaming Press. She has illustrated works by New York Times bestselling authors including Jonathan Maberry, George Romero, and Christopher Golden. Her art has been commissioned and collected throughout the United States and overseas. Art-Haus Gallery in Atlanta will be hosting her solo art show "Lyrical Nightmares: The Art of Lynne Hansen." For samples of her work and information on how to commission her, visit LynneHansenArt.com.

About the Authors

Sidney Arcane is an award-winning professional artist with an MFA in comics, a small herd of cats, inveterate geek tendencies and a great love for ska-punk. She's worked in children's books and comics as an illustrator and writer, and had a story, "Liars and Lies," included in the Horror Writers of Maine *Northern Frights* anthology. In addition to writing horror, she also creates and sells fine art.

E. A. Black has enjoyed telling scary stories to a captive audience since she was a child. She grew up in Baltimore, the home of Edgar Allan Poe who inspired her to write. Her short stories have appeared in *Zippered Flesh 2, Zippered Flesh 3, Teeming Terrors, Midnight Movie Creature Feature 2, Wicked Tales: The Journal of the New England Horror Writers Vol. 3, Heart of Farkness, The Horror Zine's Book of Ghost Stories, Horror For Hire: Second Shift,* and more. She won a Best Short Story mention on *The Solstice List@ 2017: The Best Of Horror* for "Invisible," which appeared in *Zippered Flesh 3*. She has written author interviews and fiction for *The Horror Zine.* Friend her on Facebook and follow her on Twitter, where she posts as Elizabeth Black. Check out her web site at eablack-writer.blogspot.com. Sign up for her newsletter: http://eepurl.com/b76GWD She lives on the Massachusetts coast in Lovecraft country. The beaches often call to her, but she has yet to run into Cthulhu.

Tracy L. Carbone lives in Southern California, after spending most of her life in cozy New England towns. She writes stories, novels, and the occasional screenplay. Her recent focus is on visual art, mosaics, and learning to play her mountain dulcimer. She is former Co-chair of the New England Horror Writers and edited their Bram Stoker Award nominated anthology, *Epitaphs*, a creepy collection of horror stories and poems by the group's authors including a handful of *NY Times* bestsellers. She also co-edited the *Cemetery Riots* anthology, which includes several legendary horror writers. To date, she has written six horror and mystery novels including a medical thriller, *The Proteus Cure*, co-written with F. Paul Wilson. She has published two short story collections, comprised of previously published and new stories. Her most recent publication is *Finding Zen in Rebound Dogs*, a collection of the first 100 entries of her real-life love story on which her blog www.Rebounddogs.com is based. Please visit her website for updates to her writing and life at www.tracylcarbone.com

Lola J. Clemente is a twenty-something college student studying Sociology at the University of New Hampshire and trying to figure out what comes next. Her aspirations involve moving abroad to Japan to teach English as a second language after she graduates. She makes art in many mediums from writing to drawing to music. Part of her life is dedicated to being in her father's band, the Ultrasonic Rock Orchestra. Creativity is a large part of her life and will always be something she uses to escape from the world.

Elaine Cunningham is a *New York Times* bestselling fantasy author, best known for her work in licensed settings such as the Forgotten Realms, Star Wars, Pathfinder Tales, and EverQuest. Her published works include twenty novels, over fifty short stories, and a graphic novel. For more information about her work, visit www.elainecunningham.com.

Victoria Dalpe is an artist and writer based out of Providence, RI. Her dark short fiction has appeared in over twenty-five anthologies and her first novel, *Parasite Life* came out in 2018 through ChiZne Publications and will be re-released in 2021 through Nightscape Press. She is a member of the HWA and the New England Horror Writers. Victoria co-edited the Necronomicon 2019 Memento Book with Justin Steele. Recently, she had a story in *Dim Shores Presents Volume 1* and a story in Flame Tree's *Strange Lands* out fall of 2020.

Gillian Daniels writes, works, and haunts the streets in Boston, MA. Since attending the 2011 Clarion Science Fiction and Fantasy Workshop, her poetry and short fiction have appeared in *Strange Horizons, Apex Magazine, Lady Churchill's Rosebud Wristlet,* and *Flash Fiction Online,* among others. She currently reviews for *The New England Theatre Geek.* She can be found at your house party, petting your cat.

Renee S. DeCamillis is the author of the psychological thriller/horror/supernatural novella *The Bone Cutters,* published through Eraserhead Press as part of their 2019 New Bizarro Authors Series, and she is currently writing the sequel. Renee is a member of the Horror Writers Association, the New England Horror Writers, and the Horror Writers of Maine. She is also an Editorial Intern for the 5-time Bram Stoker award-winning speculative and dark fiction publisher Crystal Lake Publishing, and a writer for Phi3 Comics. She has her BA in psychology from the University of Southern Maine, earned her MFA in Popular Fiction Writing from the Stonecoast Graduate Program, and attended Berklee College of Music as a music business major with guitar as her principal instrument. Her short fiction appears in *Deadman's Tome: The Conspiracy Issue, Siren's Call eZine Issue 37 the 6th Annual Women In Horror Month Edition, The Other Stories Podcast.* Her poetry appears in *The Horror Writers Association Poetry Showcase Volume IV.* Renee is a former model, school rock band teacher, creative writing teacher, private guitar instructor, A&R rep for an indie record label, therapeutic mentor, psychological technician, and preschool teacher. She is also a former gravedigger; she can get rid of a body fast without leaving a trace, and she is not afraid of getting her hands dirty. Renee lives in the woods of Maine with her husband, their son, and a house full of ghosts. You can visit her at reneesdecamillis.com.

Roxanne Dent is a full-time professional writer who lives in Massachusetts with her cat, Jockomo, and has sold nine novels to Avon Paperbacks, Signet, Jove, Manor as well as independent publishers and dozens of short stories in a variety of genres, including paranormal fantasy, Regency, mystery, horror, steampunk, drabbles, LGBT, middle grade, and YA. Roxanne has also co-authored short stories and plays with her sister, Karen Dent. *Young at Heart* and *Monkey Girl Blues* were put on at the Firehouse Theater in Newburyport. She wrote and directed her own three-minute thriller "Valentine's Day," which won the Audience Choice Awards in the Bare Bones International Film Festival. She is a member of New England Horror Writers, Essex Writers and Artists Guild, Fiction Writers Guild, and The Berlin Writers Group.

Currently in her second term as Poet Laureate of New Bedford, Massachusetts, **Patricia Gomes** is the former editor of *Adagio Verse*

Quarterly and has been published in numerous literary journals and anthologies. A 2018 and 2008 Pushcart Prize nominee, Gomes is the author of four chapbooks. Ms. Gomes recent publications include *Tidings, Star*Line, Muddy River Review, Rituals, Apex and Abyss,* and *Alien Buddha Press.* Ms. Gomes is the co-founder of the GNB Writers Block as well a member of the SciFi Poetry Association, New England Horror Writers, and the Massachusetts Poetry Society. She writes—she is writing now—she will continue to write.

Kameryn James writes various genres of horror and is devoted to challenging who deserves a "happy ever after." She is the author of the supernatural novel, *Doll House,* and later pieced her first short stories together in the anthology *A Book Full of Terrible Things.* When not riding her bike near Lowell, Massachusetts, Kameryn writes at a wooden, patina desk, where she is supervised by her cat overlord. Visit her on Facebook at www.facebook.com/kameryn.james.5. Or follow her on Instagram @alisonwrites_stuff.

Christine Lajewski was born and raised in Flint, Michigan and now lives in Cumberland, RI near her adult children. She is a writer, retired alternative high school teacher, a teacher naturalist at Mass Audubon and a haunt actor during the Halloween season. Her published works include the novels *Jhator* and *Bonebelly,* as well as a short story collection, *Erring on the Side of Calamity.*

After a mid-life crisis and failing out of college at the age of twenty, **Sara Marks** decided to live the life she wanted, not the one expected of her. Now a librarian with two master's degrees, she plans to never stop getting over educated. She started writing as part of the National Novel Writing Month program over fifteen years ago. She loves horror stories but is also an unlucky and hopeless romantic. She writes in the genres she enjoys: horror, fantasy, chick-lit, and romance. She has two horror story collections in the Lovecraftian tradition. *Kraulack* is a collection about a small town with a dark secret. *Bribre* is a collection that looks at the horrors of multi-level marketing companies. She is working on her first fantasy novel about hiring a new Devil and researching her next collection of horror stories about conspiracy theories.

Hillary Monahan is the *New York Times*-bestselling author of *Mary: The Summoning* through Disney Hyperion and the critically acclaimed *The Awesome* under Eva Darrows. An author of twelve titles, both young adult and adult, Hillary lives in Massachusetts with her family of some parts animals, some parts human. Fall 2021 sees her next title—about Miss

Havisham's formative years—dropping through Random House Delacorte.

Lindsay Moore is a Boston-based writer of prose and comics. In 2014, she co-founded Hellcat Press and has edited five of horror comics anthologies, which can be found at www.hellcatpress.com. Her prose has been featured on the *NoSleep* podcast. She enjoys knitting, cross stitch, and writing about terrible, terrible things. She lives with her husband, daughter, and two naughty cats.

Elaine Pascale has been writing her entire life. She took a break from fiction in order to give birth to two children and a doctoral dissertation. Her writing has been published in numerous magazines and anthologies. She is the author of *The Blood Lights; If Nothing Else, Eve, We've Enjoyed the Fruit;* and the nonfiction book: *Metamorphosis: Identity Outcomes in International Student Adaptation—A Grounded Theory Study.* After nearly three decades of life in New England, she recently relocated to the Everglades where she lives with a Skunk Ape and a congregation of friendly alligators. Find out more at elainepascale.com, www.amazon.com/Elaine-Pascale, www.facebook.com/elaine.pascale, and on Twitter and Instagram as @doclaney.

Kristi Petersen Schoonover has enjoyed visiting creepy forests since she was a kid, which isn't difficult when you live in New England. Her work has appeared in many magazines and anthologies, and she's the author of the collection *The Shadows Behind.* She was the recipient of three Norman Mailer Writers Colony Residencies and holds an MFA in Creative Writing from Goddard College. She serves as a co-host of the *Dark Discussions* podcast, as founding editor of the dark literary journal *34 Orchard*, and lives in the Connecticut woods with her husband, Nathan. Follow her adventures at kristipetersenschoonover.com.

Suzanne Reynolds-Alpert writes short fiction and poetry in the science fiction, horror, and dark fantasy genres. Her short stories have appeared in the anthologies *The Final Summons, Killing It Softly (Vol.1),* and *The Deep Dark Woods.* Read her poetry in the *HWA Poetry Showcase Vol. VI,* the anthologies *Beneath Strange Stars* and *Wicked Witches,* the websites Tales of the Zombie War, Eternal Haunted Summer, and Strong Verse; and in *The Wayfarer: A Journal of Contemplative Literature.* She published a short collection of poetry, *Interview with the Faerie (Part One) and Other Poems of Darkness and Light* in 2013. Suzanne is a freelance writer and editor, and also works as a technical services librarian. She writes in between painting (which she recently picked up), crocheting poorly, and meeting the incessant demands of her feline overlords. Find her online at suzannereynoldsalpert.com.

Mary Robles was born in El Paso, TX and earned a BFA in Creative Writing at Bowling Green State University. She was the recipient of a 2016 Creative Workforce Fellowship in Literature from the Community Partnership for Arts and Culture (CPAC) in Cleveland, OH. Her writing has been published in *Cactus Heart*, *Pinwheel*, *The Rio Grande Review*, *Paper and Ink Literary Zine*, and is forthcoming in *Salt Hill Journal*.

Morgan Sylvia is a metalhead, an Aquarius, a vodka snob, a coffee addict, and a work in progress. A former obituarist, she is now a full-time freelance writer. Her fiction and poetry have appeared in several places, including *Pseudopod*, *Wicked Witches*, *Wicked Haunted*, *Haunted House Short Stories, and Endless Apocalypse*. She is also the author of two poetry collections; a horror novel, *Abode*; and a fantasy novel, *Dawn*. She lives in Maine with her boyfriend, two spoiled tuxedo cats, and a chubby goldfish.

Jennifer Williams is an author and editor from Salem, Massachusetts. Prior to the pandemic she volunteered at a local queer youth center and spent her Sundays practicing Krav Maga. Now she mostly hangs out with her cat. She occasionally does editorial work for Circlet Press, and even organized a Circlet Press online writing group after the pandemic hit. Her work can be found in *Grim Magazine*, various small press anthologies, and on the Anatomy Of A Scream blog. Follow her online at @JenWilliams13

Jane Yolen's books and stories and poems have won the Caldecott Medal, two Nebula Awards, two Christopher Medals, three World Fantasy Awards, three Mythopoeic Fantasy Awards, two Golden Kite Awards, the Jewish Book Award and the Massachusetts Center for the Book award. She has also won the World Fantasy Association's Lifetime Achievement Award, the Science Fiction Writers of America's Grand Master Award, and the Science Fiction Poetry Associations Grand Master Award (the three together she calls the Trifecta). Plus she has won both the Association of Jewish Libraries Award and the Catholic Libraries Medal. Also the DuGrummond Medal and the Kerlan Award, and the Ann Izard story-telling award at least three times. Six colleges and universities have given her honorary doctorates for her body of work, so—she jokingly says—you could call her Dr. Dr. Dr. Dr. Dr. Dr. Yolen though she can't set a leg. However, she does warn about winning too many awards as one of them set her good coat on fire. If you meet her, you can ask about that!

About the Editors

Trisha J. Wooldridge writes novels, short fiction, non-fiction articles, and poetry that occasionally win awards—child-friendly ones are penned under T.J. Wooldridge. She's edited six anthologies and over a hundred novels for both publishers and independent authors. Find her in all the prior NEHW anthologies, the Shirley Jackson Award-winning *The Twisted Book of Shadows*, *HWA Poetry Showcase 5* and *6*, and *Don't Turn Out the Lights: A Tribute to Alvin Schwartz's Scary Stories to Tell in the Dark*. She spends rare moments of mystical "free time" with a very patient Husband-of-Awesome, a calico horse, and a bratty tabby cat. Join her adventures at www.anovelfriend.com.

Scott T. Goudsward: By day Scott is a slave to the cubicle world, by night to the voices in his head. He writes primarily horror but has branched out to sci-fi and fantasy. Scott is one of the coordinators of the New England Horror Writers. His short fiction has most recently appeared in *The Final Summons*. His latest novel *Fountain of the Dead* is out from Crossroad Press. The new co-edited non-fiction book *Horror Guide to Northern New England* is out from Post Mortem Press. Anthology projects include the forthcoming *Wicked* book from the New England Horror Writers. *Would But Time Await* from Haverhill Press and a Train Anthology co-edited with Tony Tremblay and Charles Rutledge also from Haverhill House. Scott is currently working on a YA novel and looking homes for new anthology possibilities.

The New England Horror Writers (NEHW) provides peer support and networking for authors of horror and dark fantasy in the New England Area. NEHW is primarily a writer's organization, focusing on authors of horror and dark fiction in all mediums (novels, short stories, screenplays, poetry, etc) in the New England area. We are also open to professional editors, artists & illustrators, agents and publishers of horror and dark fiction. NEHW activities include book signings, readings, panel discussions at conventions, and social gatherings. With members ranging from Maine to Connecticut, NEHW events take place in varying locations in an effort to provide support for our members throughout New England. Find us on Facebook or at www.newenglandhorror.org.

www.ingramcontent.com/pod-product-compliance
Lightning Source LLC
Chambersburg PA
CBHW050513260626
47157CB00004B/1301